Alice's Adventures in Wonderland
& Through the Looking-Glass

路易斯・卡洛爾——著
Lewis Carroll

約翰・坦尼爾——插圖
Sir John Tenniel

盛世教育——譯

─中英對照奇幻夢境版─

愛麗絲
夢遊仙境&鏡中奇遇

笛藤出版

目錄

愛麗絲夢遊仙境
Alice's Adventures in Wonderland

目錄

愛麗絲鏡中奇遇
Through the Looking-Glass,
and What Alice Found There

愛麗絲中英全文音檔下載連結：https://bit.ly/324Bguu

愛麗絲夢遊仙境

Alice's
Adventures
in Wonderland

第 1 章

掉進兔子洞

掉啊，掉啊，掉啊，沒有別的事情可以做了。

因此，過了一會兒愛麗絲又說話了：

「我敢肯定，黛娜今晚一定很想我。」（黛娜是一隻貓）

「我希望他們別忘了在下午茶時幫牠準備一碟牛奶。」

愛麗絲陪姊姊坐在岸邊，沒有事情可以做，她開始感到厭倦，不時偷瞄姊姊正在讀的那本書，可是書裡既沒有圖畫，也沒有對話，愛麗絲想：「一本沒有圖畫和對話的書有什麼意思呢？」

她的腦袋瓜認真地盤算著（盡她所能，天氣太熱了，讓她昏沉沉的）起來摘些雛菊，做個漂亮的花圈，應該更有趣吧？就在這時，一隻有著粉紅色眼睛的白兔，從她旁邊跑了過去。

愛麗絲不覺得奇怪，就連聽到兔子自言自語地說：「哦，天啊，哦，天啊，我要遲到了！」的時候，愛麗絲也沒有大驚小怪。（雖然事後她認為這非常奇怪，但當時的她的確覺得很自然。）等到兔子竟然從背心口袋裡掏出懷錶看了看，接著又匆匆忙忙跑走時，愛麗絲才跳了起來，驚覺自己從來沒有見過穿著背心的兔子，更沒見過兔子還能從口袋裡拿出錶來。她好奇地穿越田野，緊緊地追趕那隻兔子，看著牠跳進了樹籬下的一個巨大兔子洞。

愛麗絲也跟著跳下去，完全沒考慮到要怎麼出來。

兔子洞有如一條筆直的走廊，但瞬間突然往下降，愛麗絲還來不及停住，就掉進了一口深井裡。

也許是這口井太深了，也許她覺得自己下降得很慢，因為她竟然有充裕的時間東張西望，還能想像接著會發生什麼事。首先，她往下看，想知道會掉到什麼地方。但是下面太黑了，什麼也看不見，於是她往周圍看，只見井壁上排滿了碗櫥和書架，還掛了地圖和圖畫。她從一個架子上拿了罐頭，上面雖然寫著「橘子果醬」，裡面卻是空的。她很失望，但不敢把空罐頭往下扔，深怕會砸傷人。在持續下降的過程中，她就把空罐頭放到另一個碗櫥裡去了。

「好啊，」愛麗絲想，「經過了這次，我從樓梯上滾下來也不算什麼了。家裡的人都會說我多麼勇敢啊，嘿，就算從屋頂上掉下來也沒什麼了不起！」（這點倒很可能是真的）。

掉啊，掉啊，掉啊，難道會永無止境的墜落嗎？愛麗絲大聲說：「好想知道我這次跌了多少英里了，我一定快接近地心了！這麼說來應該有四千英里了吧，我想……（愛麗絲已經在學校裡學到了一點這類的東西，雖然現在不是炫耀知識的時候，因為沒有人在聽她說話，但這仍是個很好的練習機會。）……對，大概就是這個距離。那麼，現在的經度和緯度又是多少呢？」（愛麗絲不知道經度和緯度是什麼，但她覺得唸起來很厲害。）

才過了一會，她又開始說：「我想知道我會不會穿過地球，到那些頭朝下走路的人們那裡，這該多有趣呀！我想這叫做『對稱人』吧？」這次她很高興沒人聽她說話，因為「對稱人」這個名字似乎不太對。）「我應該問他們國家叫什麼名字，例如：『女士，請問這裡是紐西蘭還是澳洲？』」（她說這句話時，還試著行屈膝禮。你想想，從空中掉下來時怎麼行屈膝禮呢？你覺得你辦得到嗎？）如果我這樣問，人們一定會認為我是一個無知的小女孩。不，我絕對不能這樣問，或許會寫在某處吧！」

　　掉啊，掉啊，掉啊，沒有別的事情可以做了。因此，過了一會兒愛麗絲又說話了：「我敢肯定，黛娜今晚一定很想我。（黛娜是一隻貓）我希望他們別忘了在下午茶時幫牠準備一碟牛奶。親愛的黛娜，我多麼希望你也掉到這裡，和我在一起呀！我擔心空中沒有你要吃的小老鼠，但你可能會捉到蝙蝠，反正牠跟老鼠很像。不過，貓到底吃不吃蝙蝠呢？」這時，愛麗絲開始打瞌睡了，她睏得迷迷糊糊時還在說：「貓吃蝙蝠嗎？貓吃蝙蝠嗎？」有時又說成：「蝙蝠吃貓嗎？」這兩個問題她同樣都答不出來，所以說成哪個都無所謂。這時候她覺得自己已經睡著，還開始做起夢來。她夢見自己跟黛娜手牽著手走在一起，並且很認真地問：「黛娜，你老實說，你吃過蝙蝠嗎？」就在這時，突然「砰」地一聲，她掉到了一堆枯枝落葉上，總算到底了！

　　愛麗絲完全沒摔傷，她立刻站起來，上面看起來烏漆抹黑的。往前一看，是個很長的走廊，她又看見那隻白兔急急忙忙地往前跑。這次一定要把握時機，愛麗絲像一陣風似地追了過去。她聽到兔子在轉彎時說：「哎呀，我的耳朵和鬍子呀，現在太遲了！」這時愛麗絲已經離兔子很近了，但是當她趕到轉角時，兔子卻不見了。她發現自己在一個很長很低的大廳裡，天花板上亮著一排燈。

　　大廳四周都是門，愛麗絲從這邊走到那邊，推一推，拉一拉，試了每一扇門，但是全都鎖上了。她傷心地走到大廳中間，思索著該怎麼出去。

　　突然，她發現了一張只有三隻腳的小桌子，是用堅固的玻璃製成的。桌上什麼也沒有，除了一把很小的金鑰匙，愛麗絲立刻想到這把鑰匙可能是其中一扇門的。可是，哎呀，不是鎖太大，就是鑰匙太小，每扇門都開不了。不過，在她繞第二圈時，突然發現剛才沒注意到的低垂的門簾後面，有一扇約十五英寸高的小門。她把金色的鑰匙放進小門的鎖眼中，太棒了，剛剛好！

　　愛麗絲打開了門，門外是一條小走廊，比老鼠洞還小。她跪下來，順著走廊望出去，看到一座從沒見過的美麗花園。她渴望離開這個黑暗的大廳，到美麗的花圃和清涼的噴泉去玩，可是她連頭都過不去，可憐的愛麗絲想：「哎，就算頭能過去，肩膀過不去也沒用，我多麼希望縮小成望遠鏡裡的小人呀！只要知道方法，我想我可以變小的。」你看，一連串稀奇古怪的事，讓愛麗絲開始認為沒有什麼是不可能的。

　　看來，守在小門旁也沒什麼意思，於是她回到桌子旁邊，希望還能再找到一把鑰匙，或者至少找到一本書，教人怎麼變成望遠鏡裡的小人。這次，她發現桌上有個小瓶子。（愛麗絲說：「這個瓶子剛才真的不在這裡。」）瓶口上有一張小紙條，上面印著很漂亮的大字：「喝我吧」。

　　「喝我吧」這幾個字看起來不錯，可是聰明的小愛麗絲不急著喝。她說：「不行，我得先看看上面有沒有寫著『毒藥』。」因為她讀過一些故事，裡面講的是孩子們因為沒有記住朋友說過的教訓，結果被燒傷、被野獸吃掉，甚至是其他不幸的事。例如：握著火鉗太久會把手燙傷；用刀子割手指會流血。愛麗絲可沒有忘記，如果喝了寫著「毒藥」的藥水瓶，遲早會不舒服。

　　不過，這個瓶子上並沒有「毒藥」的標示，所以愛麗絲冒險地嚐了一下，覺得非常好喝（老實說，有點像櫻桃餡餅、奶油蛋糕、鳳梨、烤火雞、牛奶糖、熱奶油麵包混在一起的味道），她一口氣就喝光了。

　　「多麼奇怪的感覺呀！」愛麗絲說，「我一定會變成望遠鏡裡的小人。」

　　事實也的確如此，愛麗絲高興得眉飛色舞。現在她只有十英寸高，可以到那座可愛的花園裡去了。不過，她又等了幾分鐘，看看會不會繼續縮小下去。想到這點，她覺得有點不安。「究竟會如何呢？」愛麗絲對自己說，「或許會像蠟燭那樣，全部融在一起了。那麼我會怎麼樣呢？」她又努力試著想像蠟燭被吹熄之後的火焰會是什麼樣子，但是她想不起來有沒有見過那樣的東西。

　　過了一陣子，好像沒有再發生什麼事情了，她決定立刻到花園去。但是，哎喲！可憐的愛麗絲！她走到門口，發現自己忘記拿那把金色的小鑰匙了。當她又回到桌子前準備再拿的時候，發現自己碰不到鑰匙了，只能透過玻璃清楚地看著它。她使盡全力沿著桌腳向上爬，可是桌腳太滑了，她一次又一次地滑了下來，直到精疲力竭。於是，這個可憐的小東西坐在地上哭了起來。

　　「起來，哭有什麼用？」愛麗絲嚴厲地對自己說，「限你一分鐘內停止哭泣！」她經常對自己下命令（雖然她很少聽從這種命令），有時甚至把自己罵哭了。這個充滿好奇心的小孩喜歡一人分飾兩角，記得有一次她跟自己玩槌球，因為作弊還想打自己一巴掌。「但是現在假扮成兩個人也沒用啊！」可憐的小愛麗絲想，「唉！現在我小得連做一個像樣的人都不行了。」

　　她突然間看見桌子下面有個小玻璃盒。打開看到裡面有塊很小的蛋糕，上面用葡萄乾精緻地嵌著「吃我吧」三個字。「好，我就吃，」愛麗絲說，「如果能讓我變大，我就撈得著鑰匙；如果變小，我可以從門縫下面爬過去。反正不管怎樣，我都可以到那個花園，我不在乎會發生什麼事。」

　　她只吃了一小口，就焦急地問自己：「是哪一種？是哪一種？」她用手摸摸頭頂，想知道會變怎樣。可是她很驚訝地發現一點變化也沒有，說實話，這本來就是吃蛋糕的正常現象，可是愛麗絲已經習慣稀奇古怪的事了，生活中稀鬆平常的事反而顯得難以理解了。

　　於是，她開動了，很快就吃完蛋糕了。

第 2 章

涙之池

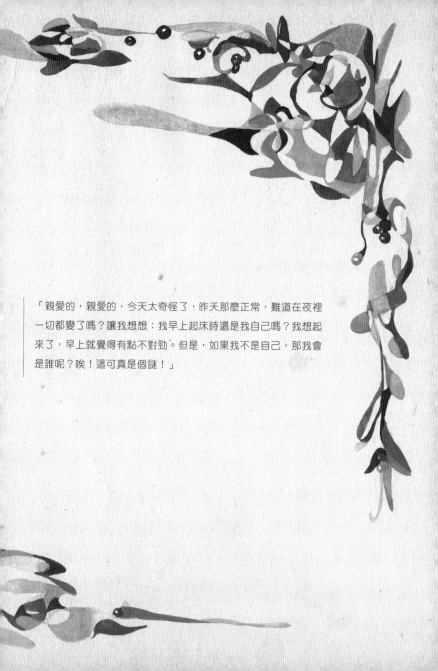

「親愛的，親愛的，今天太奇怪了，昨天那麼正常，難道在夜裡一切都變了嗎？讓我想想：我早上起床時還是我自己嗎？我想起來了，早上就覺得有點不對勁。但是，如果我不是自己，那我會是誰呢？唉！這可真是個謎！」

「奇怪啊奇怪！」愛麗絲喊道（她驚訝到語無倫次了），「現在我一定變成望遠鏡裡最巨大的人了！再見了，我的雙腳！」（她俯視自己的腳，兩條腿已經遠得快看不見了。）哦，我可憐的小腳，還有誰會幫你們穿鞋和綁鞋帶呢？親愛的，我辦不到了，你們太遠了，我無法照顧你們了，你們一定要照顧自己…但我還是要好好對待他們。」愛麗絲心想，「不然他們會可能不會走到我想去的地方，我想想，每年耶誕節我都要送他們新的靴子。」

她繼續盤算著該怎麼送禮：「我要把禮物用包裹寄給他們」。她想，「那會有多好玩，寄禮物給自己的腳！地址寫起來會有多奇怪：

壁爐邊
擱腳欄杆一處
愛麗絲的右腳收
（愛麗絲寄）

哦，親愛的，我在說什麼！」就在那一刻，她的頭撞到了大廳的屋頂。她現在至少有九英尺高，她急忙拿起金色小鑰匙跑向通往花園的門。

可憐的愛麗絲！現在她只能側身躺在地上，用一隻眼睛往花園裡望，更不可能進去了，於是她又哭了。

「你不害羞嗎？」愛麗絲對自己說，「像你這麼大的女孩子，還哭！（說得很對。）我命令你：馬上停止！」但她還是不停地哭，足足掉了一桶眼淚。她一直哭，直到身邊成了個大池塘，有四英尺深，半個大廳都變成池塘了。

過了一會兒，她聽到遠處傳來輕微的腳步聲。她急忙擦乾眼淚，看看誰來了。那隻小白兔又回來了，打扮得漂漂亮亮的，一手戴著白色羊皮手套，另一手拿著一把大扇子，正急急忙忙地小跑步過來。白兔邊跑邊喃喃自語地說：「哦，公爵夫人，公爵夫人！唉！假如我害她久等了，她可別生氣啊！」愛麗絲很希望有個人來幫助自己，因此見到小白兔很失望。但是當小白兔走近時，她還是怯生生地說：「勞駕，先生……」這可把兔子嚇了一跳，牠扔掉了白手套和扇子，拼命地往暗處跑。

愛麗絲撿起了扇子和手套。這時屋裡很熱，她一邊搧著扇子，一邊自言自語地說：「親愛的，親愛的，今天太奇怪了，昨天那麼正常，難道在夜裡一切都變了嗎？讓我想想：我早上起床時還是我自己嗎？我想起來了，早上就覺得有點不對勁。但是，如果我不是自己，那我會是誰呢？唉！這可真是個謎！」於是她一個個地去想和她同年齡的女孩們，看看自己是不是變成了其中一個人。

「我敢說，我不是艾達，」愛麗絲說，「因為她有長捲髮，而我的頭髮一點也不捲；我肯定也不是梅布爾，因為我知道各種事情，而她，哼！她什麼也不知道。再說，她是她，我是我，哎喲！我的天，這太令人想不通了！我試試看，還記不記得自己以前知道的事情。讓我想一想，四乘五是十二，四乘六是十三，四乘七……唉，這樣背下去永遠到不了二十。算了，乘法表不能代表什麼。讓我試試地理：倫敦是巴黎的首都，而巴黎是羅馬的首都，羅馬是……不，不，全錯了。我一定……一定已經變成梅布爾了。讓我再試試背誦《小鱷魚》吧。」

於是她把手交叉放在膝蓋上，就像背課文那樣，一本正經地背了起來。她的聲音嘶啞、古怪，咬字也和平常不一樣：

> 小鱷魚啊小鱷魚
> 保養著閃亮的尾巴，
> 把尼羅河水灌進，
> 每一片金色的鱗甲！

> 牠笑得多麼開朗，
> 張開爪子的姿勢多麼文雅，
> 歡迎著那些小魚
> 游進牠溫柔微笑著的嘴巴！

「我一定背錯了。」可憐的愛麗絲說著說著，又掉下了眼淚：「我真的變成梅布爾了，我得住在破房子裡，什麼玩具也沒有，還有那麼多課要上。不行！我決定了，如果我是梅布爾，我乾脆待在井裡，就算他們把頭伸到井口說：『上來吧！親愛的！』我也不要上去。我要抬頭向他們說：『先告訴我，我到底是誰，如果是我樂意變成的那個人，我就上去，否則我就一直待在這裡，直到我變成

其他人』……可是，哦，親愛的！」愛麗絲突然哭起來：「我真想
讓他們來叫我上去呀！我真的不想孤伶伶地待在這裡！」

她說這句話時看了她的雙手，驚訝地發現在她說話時，某隻手
上戴了小白兔的白色羊皮手套。「這是怎麼回事？」她想，「我一

定又變小了。」她起來走到桌子邊，量了量自己，正像她猜測的那
樣，她現在大約只有兩英尺高，而且還在迅速地縮下去。她很快發
現是拿著的那把扇子在作怪，於是她趕緊扔掉扇子，還好來得及，
要不然就要縮到消失了。

「好險呀！」愛麗絲說。她被突如其來的轉變給嚇壞了，又很
慶幸自己還在。「現在能去花園了！」她飛快地跑回小門那裡，但
是，天哪，小門又鎖上了，那把小小的金色鑰匙像從前一樣躺在玻
璃桌子上。「現在更糟了，」可憐的小愛麗絲想，「我從來沒有這
麼小過，從來沒有，我發誓，這真是糟透了！」

就在她說這些話的同時，她腳一滑，接著「砰」的一聲，鹽水淹到了她的下巴。她首先想到自己不知怎麼地掉進海裡了，「要是這樣的話，我可以坐火車回去，」她自言自語道（愛麗絲曾經去過海邊，得出的結論是，不管你在英格蘭海岸線上的哪個地方，海裡都有許多淋浴設施，還有些孩子拿著木鏟子在海灘上挖土，海灘上還有一排木屋，房子後面就是火車站。）但是，她很快就意識到自己是在當她還是九英尺高時所流下的眼淚池裡。

「真希望我剛才沒哭得那麼慘！」愛麗絲邊說話邊來回游著，想找條路游出去，「現在我受到懲罰了，我快被自己的眼淚淹死了！這真是一件奇怪的事！說真的，今天全是怪事！」

這時，她聽到不遠處有潑水聲。她想看看是什麼，於是游向了那個聲音。起初，她以為一定是一隻海象或河馬。不過，她想起自己現在有多麼渺小，立刻就明白那只不過是隻老鼠，和自己一樣掉進了水裡。

「跟一隻老鼠說話有什麼用處呢？」愛麗絲想，「這裡那麼奇怪，我想牠很有可能會說話，不管怎樣，試試也沒壞處。」於是愛麗絲說：「老鼠啊，你知道從池塘裡出去的路嗎？我已經游得很累了。老鼠啊！」（愛麗絲認為這是跟老鼠說話的方式，以前她沒有做過這種事，但是她記得哥哥的《拉丁語文法》中寫著：「一隻老鼠、一隻老鼠的、給一隻老鼠、老鼠啊！」）這隻老鼠疑惑地看著她，還向她眨了眨小眼睛，但什麼也沒說。

「也許牠不懂英語，」愛麗絲想，「牠大概是一隻法國老鼠，是跟征服者威廉一起來的。」（雖然愛麗絲知道一些歷史知識，可是她分不清這些事情已經多久了。）於是，她又用法語說：「我的小貓在哪裡？」這是她法文課本裡的第一句話。老鼠聽了突然跳出水面，嚇得渾身發抖。愛麗絲怕自己讓這個可憐的小動物難受，趕緊說：「請原諒我！我忘了你不喜歡貓。」

「不喜歡貓！」老鼠激動地尖聲喊著，「如果你是我，你會喜歡貓嗎？」

「這個嘛……也許不會，」愛麗絲用安慰的口氣說，「別生氣了。但我還是希望你能見見我的黛娜，只要你看到牠，就會喜歡貓了，牠是一個多麼可愛又安靜的小東西！」愛麗絲一面懶散地游著，一面自言自語地繼續說道，「她坐在火爐邊打起盹來真好玩，還不時舔舔爪子，洗洗臉，牠摸起來軟綿綿的真可愛。還有，她真會抓老鼠……哦，請原諒我。」這次她把老鼠氣壞了。愛麗絲又喊道：「如果你不高興的話，我們就不說牠了。」

「還說『我們』呢！」老鼠喊著，連尾巴末端都發抖了，「好像我願意說似的！我們家族都恨貓，這種可惡的、低下的、粗鄙的東西！別再讓我聽到這個名字了！」

「我不說了，真的！」愛麗絲說著，急忙改變了話題，「那你……你喜歡、喜歡……狗嗎？」老鼠沒回答。於是，愛麗絲急切地說了下去：「我家附近有一隻小狗，我應該讓你見見牠，一隻眼睛明亮的小獵腸狗，長著那麼長的棕色捲毛！牠還會接住你扔的東西，會坐起來討晚餐吃，還會玩各式各樣的把戲，有一半我都不記得了。牠的主人是一個農民，那個農民說牠很管用，要值一百英鎊！

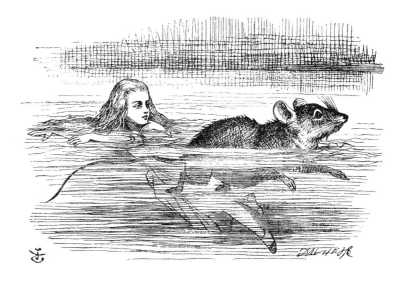

他說牠能殺掉所有的老鼠……哦，親愛的！」愛麗絲傷心地說，「我恐怕又惹你生氣了。」老鼠已經拼命游遠了，牠游開時，還把池塘弄得水花四濺。

愛麗絲跟在老鼠的後面輕聲細語地說：「老鼠啊，親愛的，你還是回來吧，你不喜歡的話，我們再也不談貓和狗了！」老鼠聽了，轉過身慢慢地向她游來。牠臉色蒼白（愛麗絲想，牠一定是被氣成這樣的），用顫抖的聲音低聲說：「讓我們上岸去吧，然後我會告訴你我的故事，這樣你就會明白我為什麼這麼恨貓和狗了。」

真的該走了，因為池子裡已經聚集了一大群鳥獸，有一隻鴨子、一隻渡渡鳥、一隻鸚鵡，一隻小鷹和一些稀奇古怪的動物。愛麗絲帶著路，和這群鳥獸一起往岸邊游去。

第 *3* 章

會議式賽跑和長篇故事

「我說的是，能讓我們把濕衣服弄乾最好的辦法，就是來場
會議式的賽跑。」渡渡鳥惱怒地說。

「什麼是會議式賽跑？」愛麗絲問。她本來不想多問，可是
渡渡鳥說到這裡停住了，似乎想等別人問，偏偏又沒人問牠。

「最好的解釋就是做一遍。」渡渡鳥說。

集合在岸上的這一大群，看起來確實稀奇古怪：羽毛濕了的鳥，汗毛緊貼在身上的小動物們，全都濕答答的，凌亂且狼狽。

目前，牠們的首要問題是如何把身體弄乾。

牠們商量了好一會兒，不到幾分鐘，愛麗絲就跟牠們混熟了，彷彿老朋友似的。你瞧，愛麗絲已經跟鸚鵡辯論了好長一段時間，最後鸚鵡生氣了，一個勁兒地說：「我年紀比你大，知道的也肯定比你多。」可是愛麗絲不同意這點，因為她根本不曉得鸚鵡的年齡，而牠又拒絕說出來，於是兩人就沒話可說了。

最後，那隻老鼠好像很有權威似地喊道：「你們全坐下，聽我說，我很快就會把你們弄乾的！」牠們立刻坐下了，圍成一大圈，老鼠在中間，愛麗絲焦急地盯著牠，她很清楚，如果濕衣服沒有快點弄乾的話，會得重感冒的。

「咳，咳！」老鼠煞有其事地說：「你們都準備好了嗎？接著我要說個最乾巴巴的故事了，請大家安靜點……征服者威廉的事業是教皇支持的，沒多久就攻克了英國。英國當時需要有人領導，而且已經習慣了篡位和被征服。莫西亞和諾森不里亞的伯爵愛德溫以及莫卡……」

「啊！」鸚鵡打了個哆嗦。

「嗯？」老鼠皺著眉頭，但仍然很禮貌地問：「你有什麼話想要說嗎？」

「沒有！」鸚鵡急忙答道。

「我還以為你有話想說，」老鼠說，「那我繼續講，這兩個地方的愛德溫伯爵以及莫卡伯爵都宣告支持威廉，甚至坎特伯里的愛國大主教斯蒂坎德也發現這是可行的……」

「發現什麼？」鴨子問。

「發現『這個』，」老鼠有點不耐煩地回答，「你當然不知道『這個』的意思。」

「我發現了什麼吃的東西時，當然知道『這個』是指什麼，通常是指青蛙或蚯蚓。現在的問題是，大主教發現了什麼？」鴨子說道。

老鼠完全不理會這個問題，只是急急忙忙地繼續講：「……他發現與愛德格‧亞瑟林一起去親自迎接威廉，並授予他皇冠是可行的，威廉的行動起初還有點節制，可他那諾曼人的傲慢……你感覺怎麼樣了，我親愛的？」牠突然轉向愛麗絲問道。

「跟原來一樣濕，」愛麗絲沮喪地說，「這些根本不能把我弄乾。」

「在這種情況下，我建議休會，並立即採取更加有效的措施……」渡渡鳥站起來嚴肅地說。

「講英語！」小鷹說，「你說的這些話，我連一半都聽不懂！更重要的是我不相信你自己懂。」小鷹說完後低下頭偷笑，某些鳥兒們也偷偷地笑出聲來。

「我說的是，能讓我們把濕衣服弄乾最好的辦法，就是來場會議式的賽跑。」渡渡鳥惱怒地說。

「什麼是會議式賽跑？」愛麗絲問。她本來不想多問，可是渡渡鳥說到這裡停住了，似乎想等別人問，偏偏又沒人問牠。

渡渡鳥說：「最好的解釋就是做一遍。」（你可能會想在冬天親自試試看，我會說明渡渡鳥是怎麼做的。）

首先，他畫出比賽路線，有點像個圓圈（「路線是什麼形狀都無所謂。」渡渡鳥說。）接著，這一大群傢伙就在圈子內散亂地站著，不用說「一，二，三，開始！」誰想開始就開始，誰想停就停，沒有誰知道這場比賽什麼時候結束。牠們跑了大約半個小時，衣服差不多都乾了，渡渡鳥突然喊：「比賽結束！」牠們一聽到，都喘著氣圍過來，不停地問：「誰贏了？」

這個問題，渡渡鳥得好好考慮一下才能回答。因此，牠坐下來，用一根指頭撐著前額想了好長一陣子（就像莎士比亞的畫像中的那種姿態），這段時間裡大家都安靜地等待著。最後，渡渡鳥說：「大家都贏了，大家都有獎品！」

「誰來發獎品給我們呢？」大家異口同聲的問。

「當然是她啦！」渡渡鳥用手指著愛麗絲說。於是，這一群動物立即圍住了愛麗絲，胡亂喊叫著：「獎品！獎品！」

愛麗絲不知道該怎麼辦，她無可奈何地把手伸進了衣服口袋，拿出了一盒糖果。（很幸運地鹽水沒滲進去，於是她把糖果作為獎品發給大家。正好每位分到一塊。）

「可是她自己應該也要有一份獎品啊！」老鼠說。

「當然啦，」渡渡鳥非常嚴肅地回答。「你的口袋裡還有別的東西嗎？」牠轉向愛麗絲問道。

「只剩一個頂針了。」愛麗絲傷心地說。

「拿過來。」渡渡鳥說。

這時，大家再一次圍住愛麗絲，渡渡鳥接過頂針後又嚴肅地遞給了她，並且說：「我們請求你接受這只精緻的頂針。」牠一結束這句簡短的演講，大家全都歡呼了起來。

愛麗絲認為這些事情全都非常荒謬，可是牠們卻十分認真，她也不敢笑，一時又想不出說什麼話，只好鞠了個躬，盡量裝得一本正經地接過了頂針。

接下來吃糖果時又引起一陣喧鬧。大鳥們抱怨嚐不出味道；小鳥們噎到了，還得幫牠們拍背。最後，糖果總算吃完了。這時牠們又圍成一個大圓坐下來，請求老鼠再講點故事。

「你答應過要告訴我你的過去的。」愛麗絲說，「你為什麼恨……喵和汪呀？」她壓低聲音有點怕說出「貓和狗」又會惹老鼠生氣。

「我的故事又漫長又悲傷。」老鼠嘆息著對愛麗絲說。

愛麗絲很疑惑地看著老鼠的尾巴：「牠的尾巴的確很長，可是為什麼尾巴是悲傷的呢？」

（註：英文 tale 和 tail 讀音相似）

老鼠講故事的過程中，愛麗絲一直納悶著，因此，她腦海裡把整個故事想像成這個樣子：

「獵狗對屋子裡的老鼠說：
『跟我上法庭，我要控告你，
我不會理睬你的辯解，
我要審判你。反正我
整個早上沒事做，有
很多時間跟你耗。』
老鼠對惡犬說：『這
種既沒有陪審員，
也沒有法官的
審判，只是浪
費時間。惡
犬說：『我既
是陪審員，
也是法官，
我要親自執
法審判，
判處你死
刑。』」

「你沒有注意聽！」老鼠嚴厲地對愛麗絲說，「你在想什麼呢？」

「請原諒我，」愛麗絲理虧地說，「我想你已經拐到第五個彎了吧？」

「我『沒有』！」老鼠非常生氣地說。

「打『結』了！」愛麗絲說，她總是希望自己能幫得上忙，因此焦急地四處尋找，「哦，讓我幫你解開。」

（註：英文 not 和 knot 讀音很相似）

「我不吃你這一套，你這些廢話侮辱了我！」老鼠說完起身就走。

「我沒有侮辱你的意思，可是你也太容易生氣了！」可憐的愛麗絲辯解著說。

老鼠咕嚕了一聲沒理她。

「請你回來講完你的故事！」愛麗絲喊著，其他動物也都齊聲說：「是啊！請回來吧！」但是，老鼠只是不耐煩地搖搖頭，走得更快了。

「牠走了，好可惜！」當老鼠走得看不見了時，鸚鵡嘆息著說。某隻老螃蟹趁這個機會對女兒說：「啊，我親愛的，這是一個教訓，告訴你以後不要亂發脾氣。」

「媽，別說了，你這樣就連牡蠣也忍耐不了。」小螃蟹沒好氣地說。

「我多麼希望我的黛娜在這裡呀！」愛麗絲大聲地自言自語道，「牠一定會馬上把牠抓回來的！」

「請允許我冒昧地問一下，黛娜是誰？」鸚鵡說。

愛麗絲隨時都樂意談論她的貓，她急切地回答：「黛娜是我的貓，牠抓老鼠的功力讓你難以想像。對了，我還希望你看到牠怎麼抓鳥，牠只要看見鳥！就會立刻吃進肚子裡！」

這話讓大家十分驚慌，有些鳥急急忙忙離開了。老喜鵲小心地把自己包得緊緊的，並解釋說：「我必須回家了，今晚的空氣對我的喉嚨不好！」金絲雀發抖對著孩子說：「走吧！我親愛的，你們早該睡覺了。」牠們全都在各種藉口下走掉了。不久，又只剩下愛麗絲一個人。

　　「要是我剛才沒有提到黛娜就好了！」愛麗絲傷心地自言自語：「這裡好像沒人喜歡牠，唉！只有我知道牠是世界上最好的貓！啊，我親愛的黛娜，真不知道什麼時候能再見到你！」說到這裡，可憐的愛麗絲又哭了，她感到非常孤獨和沮喪。過了一會，總算聽到不遠處傳來了腳步聲，她激動地抬頭，希望是老鼠改變主意，打算回來講完故事。

第 *4* 章

兔子派小比爾進屋

「……讀童話故事時我總認為那種事情永遠不會發生，
現在自己卻來到了童話世界，
等我長大一定要寫一本關於自己的童話故事……」

原來是那隻白兔慢慢地跑了回來。牠在剛才走過的路上焦急地到處尋找，好像丟了什麼東西似的。愛麗絲還聽到牠低聲嚷嚷著：「公爵夫人！公爵夫人，唉！我親愛的小爪子呀！我的小鬍子呀！她肯定會把我的頭砍掉，一定會的！就像雪貂是雪貂那樣千真萬確！我到底丟在哪？」愛麗絲馬上猜到牠在找那把扇子和那雙白手套。於是，她也好心地幫忙找，可是到處都找不到。自從她游進了池子，所有所有東西都變了，就連有著玻璃桌子和小門的大廳都消失了。

沒多久，當愛麗絲還在到處尋找的時候，兔子看見了她，生氣地向她喊道：「瑪麗安，你在外面做什麼？馬上回家拿一雙手套和一把扇子來。快點！」愛麗絲嚇得要命，顧不得解釋誤會，趕快照牠指的方向跑過去。

「牠把我當成女僕了，」她邊跑邊自言自語，「要是牠之後發現我是誰，會有多驚訝啊！可是，我最好還是幫牠把手套和扇子拿過去，要是我找得到的話。」說著她到了一棟整潔的小房子前，門上掛著一塊明亮的黃銅小牌，刻著「白兔先生」。她沒有敲門就進去了，急忙往樓上跑，深怕碰上真的瑪麗安。在找到手套和扇子之前被趕出去。

「這真奇怪！」愛麗絲對自己說，「幫一隻兔子跑腿，我看下一步就會輪到黛娜使喚我了。」於是她想像那種情景：「『愛麗絲小姐，快來我這，準備去散步囉！』『奶媽，我馬上就來！可是在黛娜回來之前，我還得看著老鼠洞，不能讓老鼠出來。』不過，假如黛娜這樣使喚人的話，他們不會讓她繼續待在家裡的。」這時，她已經走進了一間整潔的小房間，窗邊有張桌子，桌子上（如她所願）有一把扇子和兩三副很小的白色羊皮手套。她拿起扇子和一副手套，正要離開房間時，視線落在鏡子旁邊的一個小瓶子上。這一次瓶上沒有「喝我吧！」的標記，但她卻拔開瓶塞往嘴裡倒。她對自己說：「每次我吃或喝點東西，就會發生有趣的事。所以我要看看這一瓶能把我怎麼樣。我真希望它能讓我變大。說真的，像現在個子這麼小，真是煩死了。」

事情真的發生了，而且比她期望的還快，還喝不到一半，頭就已經碰到天花板了，她必須停下來，不要再喝了，以免脖子折斷。愛麗絲趕緊扔掉瓶子，對自己說：「真的夠了，我不想要再長了……現在這樣我就已經出不去了……剛剛別喝這麼多就好了！」

唉！現在已經太遲了！她繼續長啊，長啊！很快地就只能跪在地上，一分鐘後，她不得不躺下，一隻手肘撐在地上，一隻手抱著頭，可是還在長。這時她只能把一隻手臂伸出窗外，一隻腳伸進煙囪，然後對自己說：「要是繼續長的話該怎麼辦呢？我會變成怎樣呢？」

幸運的是，這罐小魔術瓶的作用已經發揮完了，她也沒有繼續變大，不過看來永遠不可能從這個房子裡出去了，還很不舒服，難怪她非常不開心。

「在家裡多舒服，」可憐的愛麗絲想，「在家裡不會一下變大，一下變小，而且不會被老鼠和兔子使喚。我真希望我從來沒有掉進這個兔子洞，可是……可是這種生活那麼奇怪，我還會變成什麼呢？讀童話故事時我總認為那種事情永遠不會發生，可是現在自

己卻來到了童話世界，等我長大了一定要寫一本關於自己的童話故事……可是我現在已經長大了。」她又傷心地加了一句：「至少這裡已經沒有空間讓我長得更大了。」

「不過，」愛麗絲想，「我的年紀應該不會再增加了吧？這倒是一個安慰，我永遠不會變成老太婆了。但是這樣就得一直上學了。噢，我不要！」

「啊，你這個傻愛麗絲！你這個笨蛋！」她又回答自己，「你在這裡怎麼上學？這間房子幾乎都裝不下你了，哪裡還有放書的地方呢？」

她就這樣繼續說著，先扮演這個人，然後扮演另一個，就這樣說了一大堆話。幾分鐘後，她聽到門外有聲音，才停下來仔細聽那個聲音。

「瑪麗安，瑪麗安！」那個聲音喊道，「趕快幫我拿手套來，」然後聽到細碎的腳步聲走上樓梯。愛麗絲知道這是兔子來找她了，她嚇得發抖，連屋子都跟著搖晃了。她完全忘記自己現在比兔子大一千倍，根本沒什麼好怕的。

兔子到了門外，想推開門，但是門是朝裡面開的，愛麗絲的手臂正好頂著門，兔子推也推不動。愛麗絲聽到牠自言自語地說：「我繞過去，從窗戶爬進去。」

「你休想，」愛麗絲想。她等了一會，直到聽見兔子走到窗下，她突然伸出手，在空中抓了一把，雖然沒有抓住任何東西，但是聽到摔倒了的尖叫聲和打碎玻璃的嘩啦聲，根據這些聲音，她斷定兔子掉進玻璃溫室之類的東西裡面了。

接著是兔子生氣的喊著：「派特！派特！你在哪？」然後，是一個陌生的聲音：「我在這裡挖蘋果樹，老爺！」

「還挖蘋果樹呢！」兔子氣憤地說，「到這裡來，把我拉出來！」（接著又是一陣弄碎玻璃的聲音。）

「派特，告訴我，窗戶裡是什麼？」

41

「是一隻手臂，老爺！」

「一隻手臂！你這個傻瓜，哪有這麼大的手臂！什麼？還塞滿整個窗戶？」

「沒錯，老爺，真的是一隻手臂。」

「好，別胡說八道了，把它拿走！」

接著安靜了一陣子，愛麗絲只能偶爾聽到竊竊私語的聲音，譬如：「我不想做，老爺，我真的不想！……照我說的做，你這個膽小鬼！」最後，她又張開手，在空中抓了一把，這次聽到了兩聲尖叫和更多打碎玻璃的聲音。「這裡一定有很多玻璃溫室！」愛麗絲想，「不知道他們下一步要幹什麼？是不是要把我從窗戶裡拉出去？我真希望他們這麼做，我不想繼續待在這裡了！」

她等了一下，什麼聲音都沒聽到，後來傳來了小車輪的滾動聲，以及許多說話的吵雜聲：「其他梯子呢？嗯，我只能搬一架，比爾正在搬另一架，比爾，拿過來，到這裡來，放到這個角落，不，先綁在一起，現在還沒一半高呢！對，夠了，你別挑剔啦！比爾，這裡，抓住這根繩子，屋頂承受得了嗎？小心那鬆動的瓦片，它要掉下來了，低頭！（一聲巨響）是誰做的？我認為是比爾，誰要從煙囪下去？不，我不做！你做！我不要！應該比爾下去，比爾！主人說讓你下煙囪！」

「啊，這麼說比爾就要從煙囪裡下來了？」愛麗絲對自己說，「他們好像把什麼事情都推到比爾身上，我才不要當比爾這個角色。說真的，這個壁爐很窄，不過我還是可以稍微踢一下。」

她把伸進煙囪裡的腳收了收，這時她聽到一個小動物（她猜不出是什麼動物）在煙囪裡連滾帶爬地接近了她的腳，她自言自語地說：「這就是比爾了。」說著她狠狠地踢了一腳，等著看接下來會發生什麼事。

首先，她聽到大家齊聲喊：「比爾飛出來啦！」然後是兔子的聲音：「喂，籬笆邊的人，快抓住牠！」安靜了一下子，又有一陣嚷嚷：「把他的頭抬起來，快，白蘭地，別嗆著牠！怎麼樣？老朋友，剛剛發生什麼事了？快告訴我們！」

最後傳來一個微弱尖細的聲音（愛麗絲認為這是比爾）「唉，我什麼也不知道，不喝了，謝謝，我現在好多了，我太緊張了，說不上來。我唯一知道的是，不知道是什麼東西，就像盒子裡的玩偶人一樣彈過來，於是，我就像火箭似的飛了出來！」

「你真的像火箭一樣，老朋友。」另外一個聲音說。

「我們必須把房子燒掉！」這是兔子的聲音。愛麗絲盡力喊道：「你們敢這樣，我就放黛娜來咬你們！」

43

接著一片死寂，愛麗絲想：「不知道他們接著想做什麼，如果他們有常識的話，就應該把屋頂拆掉。」過了一、兩分鐘，牠們又開始走動了，愛麗絲聽到兔子說：「先來一車就夠了。」

「先來一車什麼？」愛麗絲想了想，立刻就知道了。小石頭像暴雨似的從窗外扔了進來，有些還打到了她的臉上。「我要讓他們住手，」她對自己說，然後大聲喊道：「你們最好別再這樣了！」這一喊後，又是鴉雀無聲。

愛麗絲驚訝地注意到那些小石頭掉到地板上變成了小蛋糕，她腦子裡立刻閃過了一個念頭：「如果我吃一塊，也許會讓我變小，既然我已經不可能更大了，那麼它一定會把我變小的。」

於是，她吃了一塊蛋糕，很開心的發現自己馬上開始縮小。她在縮到能夠穿過門的大小時跑出了屋子，看到一群小動物和小鳥守在外面，那隻可憐的小蜥蜴比爾在中間，由兩隻天竺鼠扶著，牠們從瓶子裡倒些東西餵牠。牠們一看到愛麗絲出現就全部衝了過去。她拼了命地跑，不久後平安抵達一座茂密的樹林。

「我現在要做的第一件事，」愛麗絲在樹林中漫步時對自己說，「就是把我變成正常大小；第二件就是去尋找那條通往可愛小花園的路。這是我最好的計畫了。」

這聽起來真的是個絕佳的計畫，而且，毫無疑問的，安排得美妙又簡單，唯一困難的是她不知道怎樣才能達成。正當她在樹林中著急地到處張望時，頭頂上面傳來了尖細的狗叫聲，於是她急忙地抬頭往上看。

　　一隻巨大的狗正在用又大又圓的眼睛瞪著她，還伸出一隻爪子要抓她。「可憐的小東西！」愛麗絲用哄小孩的聲調說，一邊努力地向牠吹口哨。其實她心裡一直非常害怕，因為想到牠可能餓了，那麼不管怎麼哄牠，還是很有可能會被吃掉的。

　　她完全不知道該怎麼辦，撿了一根小樹枝，伸向那隻狗，那隻狗立即跳了起來，高興地汪汪叫著，並衝向樹枝假裝要咬。愛麗絲急忙躲進一排薊樹叢後面，免得被狗追到。她剛躲到另一邊，小狗就再次衝向樹枝，還因為衝得太快而跌一跤，愛麗絲覺得很像跟一匹馬玩耍，隨時都有被踩在腳下的危險，因此，她又圍著薊樹叢轉了起來，那隻狗又開始不斷衝向樹枝。每次都衝過頭，然後再後退得遠遠的，同時嘶聲狂吠著。最後牠在很遠的地方坐了下來，喘著氣，舌頭伸在外面，那雙大眼睛也半閉上了。

　　這是愛麗絲逃跑的好機會，她轉身就跑，跑得喘不過氣來，直到狗吠聲離她很遠了，她才停下來。

　　「可是，牠是隻多麼可愛的小狗啊！」愛麗絲說，一邊靠在一

45

棵毛茛上休息，一邊用一片葉子搧風，「要是我是正常的大小，真想教牠玩許多遊戲。啊，天哪，我都忘記我還想再變大！我想想，要怎麼做呢？我需要吃或喝點東西，但問題是，該吃或喝點什麼呢？」

的確，最大的問題是該吃或喝點什麼呢？愛麗絲看著周圍的花草，沒有可以吃或喝的東西。離她很近的地方長著一個大蘑菇，跟她差不多高。她打量了蘑菇的下方、邊緣、背面，還想到應該看看上面有什麼東西。

她踮起腳尖，沿著蘑菇的邊緣往上看，立即看到一隻藍色的大毛毛蟲，正環抱手臂坐在那裡，安靜地抽著一個很長的水煙管，根本沒有注意到她和其他任何事情。

第 *5* 章

毛毛蟲的忠告

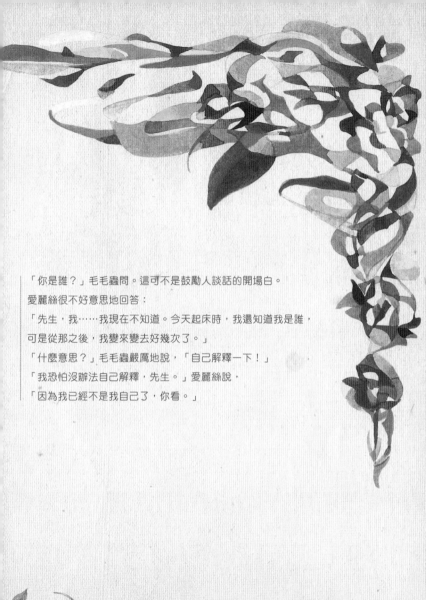

「你是誰?」毛毛蟲問。這可不是鼓勵人談話的開場白。

愛麗絲很不好意思地回答:

「先生,我……我現在不知道。今天起床時,我還知道我是誰,

可是從那之後,我變來變去好幾次了。」

「什麼意思?」毛毛蟲嚴厲地說,「自己解釋一下!」

「我恐怕沒辦法自己解釋,先生。」愛麗絲說,

「因為我已經不是我自己了,你看。」

毛毛蟲和愛麗絲沉默地注視了彼此一陣子，最後，毛毛蟲將水煙管從嘴裡拿了出來，懶洋洋、有氣無力地對愛麗絲說話。

「妳是誰？」毛毛蟲問，這可不是鼓勵人談話的開場白。愛麗絲很不好意思地回答：「先生，我……我現在不知道。今天起床時，我還知道我是誰，可是從那之後，我變來變去好幾次了。」

「什麼意思？」毛毛蟲嚴厲地說，「自己解釋一下！」

「我恐怕沒辦法自己解釋，先生。」愛麗絲說，「因為我已經不是我自己了，你看。」

「我看不出來。」毛毛蟲說。

「我沒辦法解釋得更清楚了，」愛麗絲非常有禮貌地回答，「因為我不知道是怎麼開始的，再說，一天內忽大忽小好幾次是很不舒服的。」

「唉，也許你還沒有體會，」愛麗絲說，「當你必須變成蝶蛹的時候，你知道自己總有一天會這樣的，才能變成蝴蝶，不過我想你還是會覺得有點奇怪，是不是？」

「一點也不。」毛毛蟲說。

「哦！可能你的感覺和我不一樣，」愛麗絲說，「我就是覺得這對我來說非常奇怪。」

「妳！」毛毛蟲輕蔑地說，「妳是誰？」

這句話又把他們帶回了對話的原點，對於毛毛蟲那些非常簡短的回答，愛麗絲有點不高興，她挺直了身子，一本正經地說：「我想還是你先告訴我，你是誰？」

「為什麼？」毛毛蟲說。

又多了一個難題。愛麗絲想不出任何好理由來回答，而且，毛毛蟲好像很不高興，因此愛麗絲轉身離開。

「回來！」毛毛蟲在她身後叫道，「我有幾句重要的話要說！」

這話聽起來蠻有希望的，於是愛麗絲又轉身回來。

「別亂發脾氣嘛。」毛毛蟲說。

「這就是你要說的？」愛麗絲盡可能忍住了怒氣問道。

「不。」毛毛蟲說。

愛麗絲想，反正沒什麼事，不如在這裡等等，也許最後他會說點值得聽的話。有好幾分鐘，他只是噴著煙霧不說話。最後，他鬆開手臂，把水煙管從嘴裡拿出來，說：「你認為你已經變了，是嗎？」

「我想是的，先生。」愛麗絲說，「我記不得平常知道的事，而且沒辦法維持同樣的身高超過十分鐘！」

「不記得什麼事？」毛毛蟲問。

「我試著背《忙碌的小蜜蜂》，可是背出來的完全變了樣！」愛麗絲憂鬱地回答。

「那就背誦《你老了，威廉爸爸》吧！」毛毛蟲說。

愛麗絲把雙手交叉放好，開始背－

　　年輕人說：「威廉爸爸，你老啦，
　　你頭上長滿了白髮，
　　可你老是頭朝下倒立著，
　　像你這把年紀，適合嗎？」
　　威廉爸爸回答兒子：「我年輕的時候，

我怕這樣會損壞腦子，
現在我很確定我沒有腦，
所以就玩個不停。」
年輕人說：「像我剛才說的一樣，你老啦，
而且你變得很胖，
可是你一個前空翻就翻進門來，
請告訴我訣竅是什麼？」
老哲人搖晃著灰白的捲髮說道：
「我年輕的時候，我總是讓關節保持柔軟靈巧，
我用的是這種一先令一盒的藥膏，
容許我向你推銷幾盒嗎？」

年輕人說：「你老啦，下巴應該衰弱得只能喝湯，
可是你把一整隻鵝，連皮帶骨全都吃光，

53

請問你怎麼能做到這樣？」
爸爸說：「我年輕的時候， 研究的是法律條文。
每個案子都拿來跟妻子辯論，
因此我下巴肌肉很發達，
讓我終身受用。」

年輕人說：「你老啦，很難想像，
你的眼睛像從前一樣閃閃發光。
可是你居然能把一條鰻魚豎在鼻尖上。
你怎麼會如此聰明？」

他的爸爸說：「夠啦， 我已經回答三個問題了。
不要太超過啦，
我不會整天聽你胡言亂語。
快滾，不然我一腳把你踢下樓。」

「背錯了。」毛毛蟲說。

「我想也是，」愛麗絲害羞地說，「很多字都背錯了。」

「從頭到尾都錯了。」毛毛蟲乾脆地說。然後他們又沉默了幾分鐘。

毛毛蟲先開了口：「你想變多大？」

「唉！我不是在乎大小。」愛麗絲急忙回答，「可是，你知道的，一個人不會喜歡常常變來變去。」

「我不知道。」毛毛蟲說。

愛麗絲不說話了，她從來沒有被反駁成這樣，她覺得快要發脾氣了。

55

「你滿意現在的樣子嗎？」毛毛蟲說。

「哦，如果你不介意的話，先生，我想再大一點，」愛麗絲說，「像這樣三英寸高，實在太可憐了！」

「三英寸是非常恰當的身高。」毛毛蟲生氣地說，說話時還使勁挺直了身子，剛好三英寸。

「可是我不習慣這個高度！」愛麗絲可憐兮兮地說，心裡想：「我希望這種生物不會那麼容易被激怒！」

「你很快就會習慣的！」毛毛蟲說著又把水煙管放進嘴裡抽了起來。

這次，愛麗絲耐心地等牠開口，一、兩分鐘之後，毛毛蟲從嘴裡拿出了水煙管，打了個哈欠，搖了搖身子，然後從蘑菇上下來，向草地爬去，爬的時候順口說：「一邊會讓你長高，另一邊會讓你變矮。」「什麼東西的一邊，什麼東西的另一邊？」愛麗絲想。

「蘑菇啊！」毛毛蟲說，好像愛麗絲有開口問過似的，說完話立刻就不見了。

愛麗絲盯著蘑菇看了好一陣子，試著找出哪裡是它的兩邊。由於蘑菇形狀圓潤，愛麗絲發現這個問題很困難。最後，她雙手環抱蘑菇，儘量伸到最遠，然後兩隻手分別剝下了一小塊蘑菇。

「現在哪邊是哪邊呢？」她問自己，然後嚐了一小口右手那塊，下一秒她覺得下巴猛烈地撞了一下，竟然碰到腳背了！這突如其來的變化使她害怕，縮小得這麼快，再不抓緊時間就完了！於是，她立刻吃了另一塊。雖然下巴跟腳頂得太緊，嘴巴幾乎張不開，但總算吃到了一點左手上的蘑菇，「啊，我的頭自由了！」愛麗絲高興地說，可是轉眼間高興就變成了恐懼，她發現看不到自己的肩膀了。她往下看的時候，只看到自己有很長的脖子，就像豎立在綠葉叢中的一根竹竿。

「那些綠色的東西是什麼？」愛麗絲說，「我的肩膀呢？噢！我可憐的雙手，怎麼看不到你們了？」她說話時揮動著雙手，可是除了遠處那叢綠葉輕微的搖晃了之外，什麼也沒有了。

看樣子，她的手無法舉到頭上來了。於是，她試著把頭彎下去靠近手。她高興地發現自己的脖子像蛇一樣，可以任意扭動。她把脖子朝下，變成一個「之」字形，伸進了那叢綠葉中，發現這些正是剛才曾在下面漫遊的樹林的樹梢。就在這時，一陣激烈的撲打聲使得她急忙縮回了頭。一隻大鴿子朝她臉上飛來，揮舞著翅膀瘋狂地拍打她。

「蛇！」鴿子尖叫著。

「我不是蛇！」愛麗絲生氣地說，「你走開！」

「我再說一遍，蛇！」鴿子重複著，語氣緩和了點，然後啜泣著說：「我各種方法都試過了，還是躲不開牠們！」

「你的話我完全聽不懂！」愛麗絲說道。

「我試過樹根邊，試過河畔，試過籬笆，」鴿子沒有理會她，繼續說著，「可是那些蛇！那些可惡的蛇！」

愛麗絲覺得越來越奇怪了，但是她知道，鴿子不說完自己的話，是不會讓別人說話的。

「光是孵蛋就夠麻煩了，」鴿子說，「我還得日夜防著蛇。天哪！我有三個星期沒有閉上眼了！」

「我很同情你被擾亂得不得安寧。」愛麗絲開始有點明白牠的意思了。

「我才剛把家搬到樹林裡最高的樹上，」鴿子繼續說，把嗓門提高成了尖叫聲，「我以為終於擺脫牠們了，結果牠們還要彎彎曲曲地從天上掉下來。唉！蛇呀！」

「我告訴你，我不是蛇！」愛麗絲說，「我是一個…我是一個…」

「嗯，你是什麼呢？」鴿子說，「我看得出來你想要撒謊！」

「我……我是一個小女孩。」愛麗絲相當懷疑地說，因為她想起了一天之中經歷的那麼多變化。「說得倒挺像回事的！」鴿子十分輕蔑地說，「我這輩子看見過許多小女孩，從來沒有一個像你有這樣子的脖子！沒有，絕對沒有！你是一條蛇，否認也沒用。我猜你還要告訴我，你從來沒有吃過蛋！」

「我確實吃過許多蛋，」愛麗絲說，她是非常誠實的孩子，「小女孩和蛇一樣會吃很多蛋。」

「我不相信，」鴿子說，「假如她們吃蛋的話，我只能說她們也是一種蛇。」

愛麗絲第一次聽到這種說法，所以愣了幾分鐘，鴿子趁機補了一句：「反正你是在找蛋，因此，你是女孩子還是蛇，對我來說都一樣。」

「對我而言很不一樣，」愛麗絲急忙地說，「而且我不是在找蛋，就算我是，我才不要你的蛋呢！我是不吃生蛋的。」

「哼，那就滾開！」鴿子生氣地說，同時飛回牠的巢裡。愛麗絲費勁地往樹林裡蹲，因為她的脖子常常會被樹枝卡住，隨時要停下來解開。過了一會兒，她想起了手裡的兩塊蘑菇，於是她小心地咬咬這塊，又咬一口那塊，她一會兒長高，一會兒縮小，最後終於讓自己變回了原本的身高。

由於她身高不正常已經有段時間了，一開始她覺得有點奇怪，不過幾分鐘後就習慣了。然後她又像平常那樣跟自己說話了，「好啊，現在我的計畫完成一半了。這些變化真奇怪，我永遠無法知道下一分鐘自己會是什麼模樣。不管怎樣！現在我總算回到原來的大小了，下一件事情就是去那座美麗的花園。可是我要如何到那裡呢？」說著說著她來到了一片開闊的空間，那裡有一間四英尺高的小房子。「不管是誰住在這裡，」愛麗絲想，「我現在這樣的大小進去，會把他們嚇死的。」她咬了一小口右手上的蘑菇，直到自己變成九英寸高，才敢走向那間房子。

第 6 章

小豬與胡椒

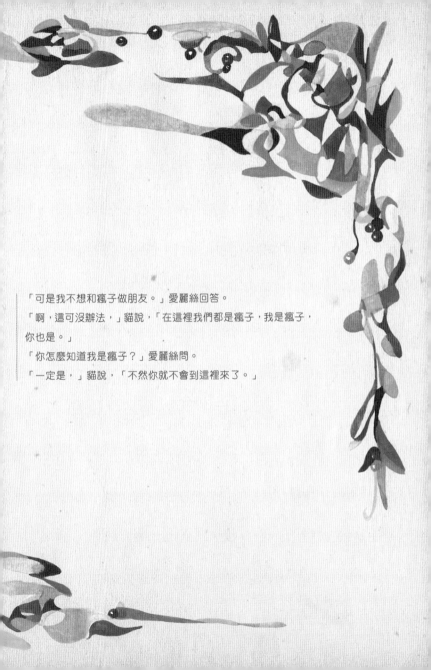

「可是我不想和瘋子做朋友。」愛麗絲回答。

「啊，這可沒辦法，」貓說，「在這裡我們都是瘋子，我是瘋子，你也是。」

「你怎麼知道我是瘋子？」愛麗絲問。

「一定是，」貓說，「不然你就不會到這裡來了。」

她站在小房子前看了一兩分鐘，想著接下來該怎麼做。突然間，一個穿著制服的僕人從樹林跑來，使勁地用腳踢著門（她根據他的穿著判斷這是僕人，如果只看臉，看上去像一條魚）；另一個穿著制服，有著圓圓的臉龐，大大的眼睛，長的像青蛙的僕人來應門，愛麗絲注意到這兩個僕人都戴著撲了粉的假捲髮。她非常想知道這到底是怎麼回事，於是就從樹林裡探出頭來聽。

魚僕人從手臂下拿出一封幾乎跟他一樣大的信封，遞給另一個僕人，同時用嚴肅的語氣說：「這是皇后給公爵夫人的信，皇后邀請她去玩槌球。」那位青蛙僕人只不過把順序變了一下，用同樣嚴肅的語氣重複著說：「皇后的邀請：請公爵夫人去玩槌球。」這情景讓愛麗絲笑了，她不得不跑回樹林裡，深怕被他們聽見。等她再出來偷看時，魚僕人已經走了，另一位坐在門口的地上，呆呆地凝視著天空。

愛麗絲怯生生地走到門口，敲了敲門。

「敲門沒用。」那位僕人說，「原因有兩個：第一，我跟你一樣都在門外；第二，他們在裡面吵吵鬧鬧，根本聽不到敲門聲。」裡面的確傳來了很奇特的吵鬧聲：接連不斷的咆哮和噴嚏聲，以及不時傳來類似打破盤子或瓷壺的聲音。

「那麼，請問，」愛麗絲說，「要怎麼進去呢？」

「如果這扇門在我們之間，你敲門可能還有意義，」那個僕人沒有理會愛麗絲，繼續說，「假如你在裡面敲門，我就能讓你出來。」他說話時，一直盯著天空，愛麗絲覺得很沒禮貌。「或許牠沒辦法控制吧，」她對自己說，「牠的兩隻眼睛幾乎長到頭頂上了。但至少還會回答問題，」她大聲地重複了一次「我該如何進去呢？」

「我坐在這裡，」那僕人繼續說，「直到明天……」

就在此時，房子的門打開了，一個大盤子朝僕人的頭飛來，掃過牠的鼻子，在牠身後的一棵樹上撞碎了。

「或者後天，」僕人繼續用同樣的口吻說著，好像什麼都沒發生過似的。

「我該如何進去呢？」愛麗絲更大聲地再問了一次。

「你到底要不要進去呢？應該先決定這件事。」僕人說。

　　這點毋庸置疑，不過愛麗絲不喜歡被這樣說。「真討厭，」她喃喃自語地說道，「這些生物討論問題的方式要把人逼瘋了。」

　　那個僕人似乎認為這是重複自己發言的好機會，牠稍微改變了說法：「我會從早到晚坐在這，一天又一天地坐下去。」

　　「可是我該做什麼呢？」愛麗絲說。

　　「你想做什麼就做什麼。」僕人說完就吹起口哨來了。

　　「唉，和牠說話真是沒用！」愛麗絲失望地說，「牠完全是個傻瓜！」接著她推開門走了進去。

　　這扇門直通一間滿是煙霧的大廚房，公爵夫人坐在房子中間的一張三腳凳上照顧著一個嬰兒。廚師倚身在爐火旁，攪拌著好像裝滿了湯的大鍋子。

「那鍋湯一定加太多胡椒了！」愛麗絲對自己說，一面用力地打著噴嚏。

空氣裡的胡椒味的確很濃，連公爵夫人也不時地打噴嚏。至於那個嬰兒，不是打噴嚏就是哭鬧，一刻都停不下來。這間廚房裡只有兩個生物不打噴嚏，就是廚師和一隻大貓，那隻貓正趴在爐子旁咧嘴笑著。

「請告訴我，」愛麗絲有點羞怯地問，因為她不太清楚自己先開口合不合規矩，「為什麼你的貓會笑呢？」

「他是隻柴郡貓，」公爵夫人說，「這就是為什麼他會笑。豬！」

公爵夫人兇狠說出的最後一個字，嚇了愛麗絲一大跳。但是愛麗絲馬上發覺她不是對自己，而是在跟嬰兒說話，於是她又鼓起了勇氣繼續說：

「我不知道柴郡貓會笑，實際上，我根本不知道貓會笑。」

「他們都會的，」公爵夫人說，「大部分的貓都會笑。」

「我不知道牠們會。」愛麗絲彬彬有禮地說，很高興能開始談話。

「你知道的太少了，」公爵夫人說，「這是事實。」

愛麗絲不喜歡這種口氣，覺得最好換個話題。她正在想話題的時候，廚師把湯鍋從爐火上移開，然後隨即把她隨手能拿到的東西扔向公爵夫人和嬰兒。首先是火鉤子，接著是燉鍋、碟子、餐盤像暴風雨似地飛過來。公爵夫人根本不理會，就連被打到了都沒有反應；而那個嬰兒一直都在哭鬧，無從得知這些東西有沒有傷到他。

「噢，請小心點！」愛麗絲喊著，嚇得直跳腳，「噢，他的小鼻子完了。」一個特大的燉鍋緊掠過嬰兒的鼻子，差點就把鼻子削掉了。

「如果每個人都能少管閒事，」公爵夫人低啞著嗓子嘟嚷著說，「地球會轉得比現在快很多。」

「這沒什麼好處，」愛麗絲說，她很高興有機會炫耀自己的知識，「你想想這會給白天和黑夜帶來什麼呢？你知道，地球繞著地軸自轉一周需要二十四個小時……」

「說到斧頭，」公爵夫人說，「砍掉她的頭！」

愛麗絲十分不安地看了廚師一眼，想知道她會不會執行命令，但是女廚師正忙著攪湯，好像沒在聽。於是愛麗絲繼續說：「我想是二十四個小時，或許是十二個小時？我……」

「唉，別煩我！」公爵夫人說，「我受不了數字！」說完又照顧起了孩子。她哄嬰兒時唱著某種搖籃曲，每唱完一句，就大力地搖幾下孩子。

> 對小孩說話別客氣，
> 他打噴嚏就揍他，

他只是想惹人生氣，
明知這樣會讓人不開心。

合唱（廚師和嬰兒跟著唱）

哇！哇！哇！

公爵夫人唱第二段時，不停把嬰兒用力地扔上扔下，可憐的小東西拚命大哭，所以愛麗絲幾乎聽不清楚歌詞：

對小孩說話要嚴厲，
他打噴嚏我就揍他，
只要他滿心歡喜，
明明可以品嚐胡椒的香氣。

合唱

哇！哇！哇！

「來！如果妳願意的話，妳來照顧他一下！」公爵夫人邊說邊把小孩扔給她，「我要去跟皇后玩槌球，得準備一下。」說著就急忙地走出了房間。她往外走時，廚師把煎鍋扔向她，但是沒打中。

愛麗絲費了好大的功夫才抓住那個小嬰兒，因為他的樣子很奇特，手臂和腿往各個方向伸展，「真像海星，」愛麗絲想。她抓著他時，這可憐的小東西像蒸汽機一樣悶哼著，身體一下子蜷曲起來，一下子伸展開來，就這樣不停地折騰，讓愛麗絲一開始只能勉強地抓住他。

當她找到能制住他的辦法（像打結般地抓緊他的右耳和左腳，他就伸展不開了），就把他帶到了屋子外面。「如果我不把嬰兒帶走，」愛麗絲想，「不用一、兩天他就會被殺死。把他扔在這裡不就害了他嗎？」最後一句話她說出聲來了，那小東西咕嚕了一聲作為回答（他已經不打噴嚏了）。「別咕嚕，」愛麗絲說，「你這樣太不成體統了。」

那嬰孩又咕嚕了一聲，愛麗絲很緊張地看了看他的臉，想知道是怎麼回事。

只見他鼻子朝天，根本不像個一般人的鼻子，倒像個豬鼻子，而且眼睛也小到不像個嬰兒。愛麗絲不喜歡這副模樣。「也許他在哭吧，」愛麗絲想，於是看了他的眼睛，想知道有沒有眼淚。

沒有，一點眼淚也沒有。「親愛的，如果你變成了一隻豬，」愛麗絲嚴肅地說，「我就不要理你了，聽到了嗎！」那可憐的小東西又抽泣了一聲（或者說又咕嚕了一聲，很難說到底是哪種），接著他們默默地走了一陣子。

愛麗絲正在想：「我帶他回家後要怎麼照顧他呢？」這時，

他又猛然地咕嚕了一聲，愛麗絲警戒地看他的臉。這次不會錯了，他完全是隻豬，她覺得如果再帶著他就太可笑了。

於是她把小生物放下，看著他快速跑進樹林，並且對此感到十分輕鬆。「他長大的話，」愛麗絲對自己說，「要嘛是個可怕的醜孩子，要嘛是隻漂亮的豬。」然後，她開始回想她認識的孩子有誰適合變成豬，她自言自語道：「只要有人告訴他們如何變來變去……」，此時，那隻柴郡貓正坐在幾碼遠的樹枝上，嚇了她一跳。

貓咪只是對著愛麗絲咧嘴笑。愛麗絲認為牠脾氣看起來不錯，不過畢竟牠有很長的爪子和許多牙齒，覺得還是應該對牠尊敬點。

「柴郡貓，」她膽怯地說。她還不知道牠喜歡不喜歡這個名字，可是，牠的嘴笑得咧開了。「哦，牠很高興，」愛麗絲想，就繼續說了：「請你告訴我，要離開這裡應該走哪條路？」

「這就要看你想去哪裡了。」貓說。

「我不在乎去哪裡……」愛麗絲說。

「那妳走哪條路都可以。」貓說。

「……只要能走到某個地方。」愛麗絲又補充了一句。

「噢，那是一定的，」貓說，「只要走得夠遠的話。」

愛麗絲無法反駁，所以她試著提了另一個問題：「這附近住了些什麼人？」

「那個方向，」貓揮了揮爪子說：「住著一位帽匠，至於那個方向。」牠揮了揮另一支爪子，「住了一隻三月兔。你想拜訪誰都可以，他們都是瘋子。」

「可是我不想和瘋子做朋友。」愛麗絲回答。

「啊，這可沒辦法，」貓說，「在這裡我們都是瘋子，我是瘋子，你也是。」

「你怎麼知道我是瘋子？」愛麗絲問。

「一定是，」貓說，「不然妳就不會到這裡來了。」

愛麗絲認為這沒有道理，不過她還是繼續問：「你怎麼知道你是瘋子呢？」

「首先」貓說，「狗不瘋，你同意嗎？」

「我想是吧！」愛麗絲說。

「好，那麼，」貓接著說，

「你知道，狗生氣時就叫，高興時就搖尾巴。可是我，卻是高興時就叫，生氣時就搖尾巴。所以我是瘋子。」

「我把這說成是打呼嚕，不是叫。」愛麗絲說。

「你怎麼說都行，」貓說，「你今天和皇后玩槌球嗎？」

「我應該會喜歡的，」愛麗絲說，「但是我還沒被邀請呢。」

「你會在那裡看到我。」貓說完突然就消失了。

愛麗絲並不驚訝，她已經習慣這些不斷發生的怪事了。她看著貓坐過的地方，這時，貓又突然出現了。

「對了，那個嬰兒變成什麼了？」貓說，「我差一點忘了問。」

「他變成一隻豬了。」愛麗絲平靜地回答，好像貓再次出現是正常的。

「我就知道。」貓說完又消失了。

愛麗絲等了一下子，希望能再見到牠，可是貓沒有再出現。於是她朝著三月兔住的方向走去。「我看過帽匠，」她對自己說，「三月兔一定非常有趣，而且現在是五月，也許牠還不會太瘋狂，至少不會像三月時那麼瘋吧。」就在說這些話時，她抬頭又看見那隻貓坐在樹枝上。

「妳剛才說的是『豬』，還是『無花果』？」貓問。

　　「我說的是『豬』，」愛麗絲回答，「我希望你不要一直突然地出現或消失，我的頭都暈了。」

　　「好吧。」貓回答。這次牠消失得非常慢，從尾巴尖開始消失，直到最後看不見牠的笑臉。那個笑臉在身體消失後，還停留了好一陣子。

　　「嗯，我常常看見沒有笑臉的貓，」愛麗絲想，「可是只剩下笑臉，貓卻不見了，這是我這輩子見過最奇怪的事了！」

　　沒走多遠，她就看到了一間房子，她想那一定是三月兔的房子，因為煙囪長得像兔子耳朵，屋頂鋪著兔毛。房子很大，她沒有馬上走近。她咬了一口左手的蘑菇，讓自己長到二英尺高，才提心吊膽地走過去，邊走邊對自己說：「要是牠很瘋狂怎麼辦？真希望我是去拜訪帽匠！」

第 7 章

瘋狂茶會

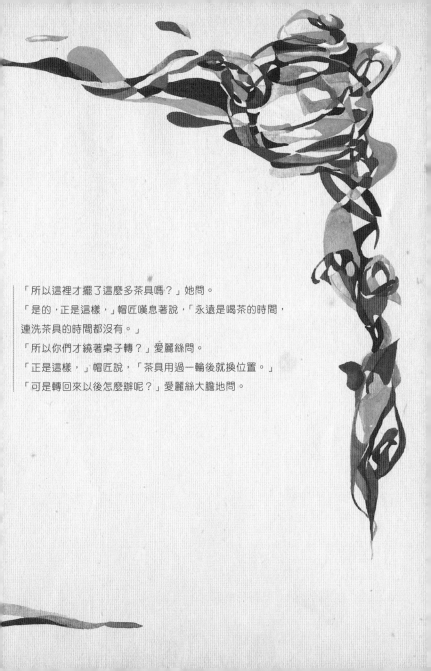

「所以這裡才擺了這麼多茶具嗎？」她問。

「是的，正是這樣，」帽匠嘆息著說，「永遠是喝茶的時間，連洗茶具的時間都沒有。」

「所以你們才繞著桌子轉？」愛麗絲問。

「正是這樣，」帽匠說，「茶具用過一輪後就換位置。」

「可是轉回來以後怎麼辦呢？」愛麗絲大膽地問。

房子前的大樹下有一張桌子，三月兔和帽匠正坐著喝茶，一隻睡鼠在他們中間睡著了。那兩位把牠當靠墊，將手臂枕在牠身上，又越過牠的頭頂談話。「這隻睡鼠應該很難受，」愛麗絲想，「不過，既然牠睡著了，我想牠也不在乎。」

　　桌子很大，他們三個卻擠在桌子的一角，「沒位子了！沒位子了！」他們看見愛麗絲走過來時大聲嚷嚷著。

　　「明明還有很多空位！」愛麗絲生氣地說，然後在桌子旁一大張有扶手的椅子上坐了下來。

　　「喝點酒吧。」三月兔熱情地問。

愛麗絲掃視了一下桌上，除了茶之外，什麼也沒有。「我沒看到酒啊！」她回答。

「是沒有酒。」三月兔說。

「那你還說要請我喝酒，真沒禮貌。」愛麗絲氣憤地說。

「你沒有被邀請就坐下來，也很沒禮貌。」三月兔說。

「我不知道這是『你』的桌子，」愛麗絲說，「這張桌子又不是為了你們三個擺在這裡的。」

「你的頭髮該剪了。」帽匠說。他早就好奇地盯著愛麗絲看了好一下子，這是他第一次開口。

「你應該學習不要隨便評論別人，」愛麗絲板著臉說，「很沒禮貌。」

帽匠睜大眼睛聽著，可是最後說了句：「為什麼烏鴉會像書桌？」

「好了，讓我們來做點有趣的事！」愛麗絲想，「真高興他們開始出謎語了，我一定猜得出來。」她大聲地說了出來。

「你的意思是你能猜出答案嗎？」三月兔說。

「沒錯。」愛麗絲說。

「那你應該想到什麼就說什麼。」三月兔繼續說。

「我是啊，」愛麗絲急忙回答，「至少⋯至少我說的就是我想的，那是一樣的。」

「完全不一樣！」帽匠說，「你不如說『我吃我看到的東西』和『我看到我吃的東西』，是一樣的！」

三月兔又加了句：「你不如說『我的東西我都喜歡』和『我喜歡的都是我的東西』，也是一樣的囉？」

睡鼠也像在說夢話般說道：「你不如說『我睡覺時呼吸』和『我呼吸時睡覺』也是一樣的！」

「這在你身上倒是沒錯。」帽匠對睡鼠說，談到這裡話題中斷了，大家沉默了一會。這時候愛麗絲努力地想著有關烏鴉和書桌的事，可是她知道的不多。

帽匠首先打破沉默，「今天是這個月的幾號？」他問愛麗絲，一面從口袋裡掏出懷錶，不安地看著，時不時搖一搖，還拿到耳朵旁邊聽。

愛麗絲想了想說：「四號。」

「差了兩天！」帽匠嘆氣著說。「我告訴過你奶油跟懷錶不能放在一起。」他生氣地看著三月兔又說了一句。

「那是最好的奶油了。」三月兔畏畏縮縮地回答。

「沒錯，但一定也有不少麵包屑掉進去了。」帽匠嚷嚷著，「你不應該用麵包刀抹奶油的。」

三月兔拿起懷錶洩氣地看了看，然後把它放到茶杯裡泡了泡，又拿起來看一看，但他除了說「那是**最好**的奶油了」，再也想不到要說什麼了。

愛麗絲好奇地越過他的肩膀看了看。「好奇怪的錶！」她說，「有顯示月份和日期，卻沒有幾點幾分。」

「為什麼要顯示呢？」帽匠嘀咕著，「你的錶能告訴你現在是哪一年嗎？」

「當然不能，」愛麗絲不假思索地回答，「那是因為有很長一段時間都會停在同一年。」

「所以**我**的錶才不報時。」帽匠說。

愛麗絲完全搞糊塗了。帽匠的話讓人摸不著頭緒，但他說的確實是道地的英語。「我不太懂你的話。」她盡可能以很禮貌的口吻說。

「睡鼠又睡著了。」帽匠說，還在睡鼠的鼻子上倒了一點熱茶。

睡鼠不耐煩地搖搖頭，閉著眼睛說：「當然，當然，我自己正要這麼說呢。」

「你猜到那個謎語了嗎？」帽匠轉向愛麗絲問道。

「沒有，我放棄了，」愛麗絲回答，「謎底是什麼呢？」

「我也不知道。」帽匠說。

「我也不知道。」三月兔說。

愛麗絲輕輕嘆了口氣：「我認為你應該珍惜時間，像這樣出個沒有謎底的謎語，簡直是浪費時間。」

「如果你也像我一樣認識時間，」帽匠說，「你就不會說浪費『它』，應該說浪費『他』。」

「我不懂你的意思。」愛麗絲說。

「你當然不懂，」帽匠輕蔑地搖搖頭說，「我敢說你從來沒有跟時間說過話！」

「也許沒有，」愛麗絲謹慎地回答，「但是我學音樂的時候要打拍子。」

「啊，這就是問題所在了！」帽匠說，「他經不住打的。如果你跟他交情好，他就會讓鐘錶照著你的意思做。舉例來說，現在是早上九點，正是上課的時間，你只要悄悄地給時間一點暗示，鐘錶就會立刻快轉走到一點半，變成午餐時間了。」

（「我真希望這樣！」三月兔小聲地自言自語。）

「那真是太棒了，」愛麗絲想了想又說，「可是如果我那時還不餓怎麼辦呢？」

「就算一開始不餓，」帽匠說，「但是你能讓時間停在一點半，想停多久就停多久。」

「你就是這樣掌控時間的嗎？」愛麗絲問。

帽匠傷心地搖搖頭說：「我沒辦法了，」他回答，「三月時我和時間吵了一架，就在牠發瘋前（他用茶匙指著三月兔）。在紅心皇后舉辦的一場盛大的演奏會上，我唱了：

> 一閃一閃小蝙蝠，
> 我很好奇你在哪！

「這首歌你應該聽過吧？」

「我聽過類似的。」愛麗絲說。

帽匠繼續說，「後面是這樣唱的」：

> 高高在上把翅展，
> 好似空中一茶盤。
> 一閃，一閃……

唱到這兒，睡鼠一邊搖著身子，一邊在睡夢中開始唱道：「一閃，一閃，一閃，一閃……」沒完沒了，他們不得不捏他一下，好讓牠停下來。

「我還沒唱完第一段，」帽匠說，「皇后就跳起來大聲咆哮『他在謀殺時間！砍掉他的頭！』」

「好殘忍！」愛麗絲嚷道。

帽匠傷心地繼續說：「他再也不照我的要求做了！現在總是停在六點鐘。」

愛麗絲的腦子裡突然閃過一個念頭，她問：「所以這裡才擺了這麼多茶具嗎？」

「是的，正是這樣，」帽匠嘆息著說，「永遠是喝茶的時間，連洗茶具的時間都沒有。」

「所以你們才繞著桌子轉？」愛麗絲問。

「正是這樣，」帽匠說，「茶具用過一輪後就換位置。」

「可是轉回來以後怎麼辦呢？」愛麗絲大膽地問。

「我們換個話題吧！」三月兔打著呵欠中斷了他們的談話，「這件事我聽膩了，我提議讓這位小女孩講個故事。」

「可是我什麼故事都不會講。」愛麗絲說。這個提議讓她緊張了起來。

「那就讓睡鼠講！」三月兔和帽匠齊聲喊道，「睡鼠，醒醒啊！」他們同時從兩邊一起捏牠。

睡鼠慢慢地睜開眼，用嘶啞微弱的嗓音說：「我沒睡著，你們說的每一個字我都聽著呢。」

「講個故事給我們聽吧！」三月兔說。

「請講一個吧！」愛麗絲懇求著。

「而且要講快一點，要不然你還沒講完又睡著了。」帽匠補了一句。

睡鼠急急忙忙地開始講：「從前有三個小姊妹，她們的名字是：愛絲、萊絲、緹麗，她們住在一個井底……」

「她們吃什麼維生呢？」愛麗絲總是最關心飲食的問題。

「靠吃糖漿。」睡鼠想了一下，然後說。

「這樣不行，她們會生病的。」愛麗絲輕聲說。

「所以她們都病得很嚴重。」睡鼠說。

愛麗絲試著想像那會是怎樣的生活，但實在想不通，於是她又繼續問：「她們為什麼要住在井底呢？」

「再多喝一點茶吧！」三月兔誠懇地對愛麗絲說。

「我一點都還沒喝，」愛麗絲不高興地回答，「所以我沒辦法再多喝一點。」

「你是說你不能再少喝一點，」帽匠說，「多喝一點比一點都沒喝容易多了。」

「沒人問你的意見。」愛麗絲說。

「現在是誰失禮了？」帽匠得意地問。

愛麗絲不知道該回什麼，於是自己倒了點茶喝，又吃了塗了奶油的麵包，然後轉頭向睡鼠重複她的問題：「她們為什麼要住在井底呢？」

睡鼠想了一下，然後說：「那是一口糖漿井。」

「沒有這樣的井！」愛麗絲開始生起氣來。帽匠和三月兔發出「噓、噓……」的聲音，睡鼠不高興地說：「如果你不懂禮貌的話，最好你自己來講完故事。」

「不，請繼續講吧！」愛麗絲懇求道，「我再也不打岔了，也許有那樣的井。」

「當然有！」睡鼠憤憤地說。不過牠還是繼續往下講：「這三個小姊妹正在學著汲取……。」

「她們要汲取什麼呢？」愛麗絲又開口了，完全忘了自己的承諾。

「糖漿。」睡鼠這次毫不猶豫地回答。

「我想要一個乾淨的茶杯，」帽匠插嘴說，「讓我們換一下位子吧。」

他說著就挪到了下一個位子上，睡鼠跟著挪了，三月兔換到了睡鼠的位子上，愛麗絲很不情願地坐到了三月兔的位子上。這次挪動唯一得到好處的是帽匠，愛麗絲的位子比以前差多了，因為三月兔打翻了牛奶罐，牛奶都流到盤子裡了。

愛麗絲不願意再惹睡鼠生氣，於是小心地開口問道：「可是我不懂，她們從哪裡舀出糖漿呢？」

「水井能取水，」帽匠說，「糖漿井當然能夠取糖漿，是吧？傻瓜。」

「但是她們在井裡啊。」愛麗絲對睡鼠說，並不打算在意帽匠最後那句話。

「她們當然在井裡，」睡鼠說，「還在很裡面呢。」

這個回答讓可憐的愛麗絲很疑惑，她沒打斷睡鼠，讓牠一直講下去。

「她們在學習汲取，」睡鼠繼續說，又打哈欠又揉揉眼睛，牠開始睏了，「她們汲取各種各樣的東西……所有『M』開頭的東西。」

「為什麼是『M』開頭的東西呢？」愛麗絲問。

「為什麼不能呢？」三月兔說。

愛麗絲不說話了。

這時候的睡鼠已經閉上眼睛，打起瞌睡來了，但是被帽匠捏了一下，牠尖叫了一聲，繼續講，「『M』開頭的東西，例如捕鼠器、月亮、記憶、還有大同小異…你會說某些東西『大同小異』，可是你有看過汲取『大同小異』這樣的事嗎？」

「說真的，既然你問我，」愛麗絲很困惑地說，「我覺得沒有……」

「那麼你就不應該說話！」帽匠說。

愛麗絲再也無法忍受這樣無禮的對待了。她憤而起身離開。睡鼠立刻睡著了，另外兩位完全沒注意到她的離去，愛麗絲還是回頭

看了一、兩次，有點希望他們能留住她。但是當她最後一次回頭時，他們正要把睡鼠塞進茶壺裡。

「無論如何我再也不要去那裡了，」愛麗絲穿越樹林時說，「這是我這輩子參加過最愚蠢的茶會。」

她在說這些話時，發現了其中某棵樹上開了一扇門。「真奇怪！」她想，「不過今天的每件事都很奇怪，我還是馬上進去看看吧。」於是她就走進去了。

她再次來到那個很長的大廳，而且離那張玻璃小桌子很近。「嗯，這次我可要表現得好一點！」她自言自語著，拿起那把金色小鑰匙，打開了通往花園的門，然後輕輕地咬了一口蘑菇（她還留了一小塊在口袋裡），直到縮成大約一英尺高，她走過了那條小通道，發現自己終於到了美麗的花園裡，周圍都是漂亮的花壇和清涼的噴泉。

第 8 章

皇后的槌球場

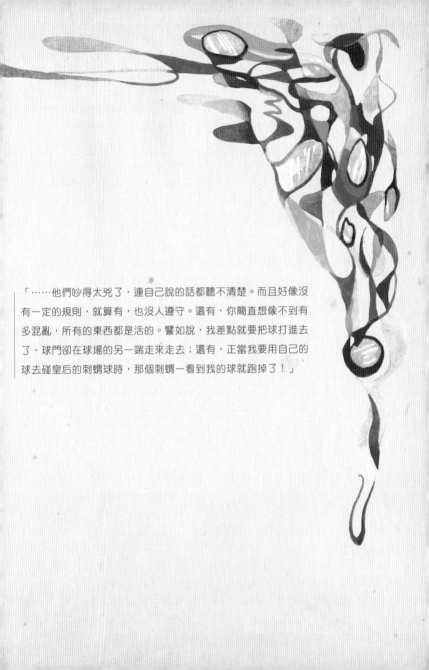

「……他們吵得太兇了，連自己說的話都聽不清楚。而且好像沒有一定的規則，就算有，也沒人遵守。還有，你簡直想像不到有多混亂，所有的東西都是活的。譬如說，我差點就要把球打進去了，球門卻在球場的另一端走來走去；還有，正當我要用自己的球去碰皇后的刺蝟球時，那個刺蝟一看到我的球就跑掉了！」

靠近花園入口有一棵大玫瑰樹，開著白色的花。三個園丁正忙著把白花染紅。愛麗絲覺得很奇怪，於是走過去看看。當她朝那裡走過去時，聽見其中一個人說：「小心點，老五！別老是把顏料潑到我身上。」

「沒辦法啊，」老五生氣地說，「老七撞了我的手臂。」

這時老七抬起頭說：「很好！老五，你總是把責任推給別人。」

「你最好別說話！」老五說，「我昨天才聽皇后說，你應該被砍頭！」

「為什麼？」第一個說話的人問。

「不關你的事，老二！」老七說。

「不，與他有關！」老五說，「我正要告訴他，都是他沒拿洋蔥，而是拿了鬱金香球根給廚師。」

老七扔掉了手上的刷子說：「哦，說起不公平的事……」他的眼光碰巧落到了愛麗絲身上，愛麗絲正站在那兒注視著他們。他隨即停下來，另外兩個人也回過頭來看，然後三人都深深地鞠了躬。

「請你們告訴我，」愛麗絲小心翼翼地說，「你們為什麼要把玫瑰花染色呢？」

老五和老七都不吭聲，看著老二。老二低聲說：「小姐，你知道，這裡應該種紅玫瑰的，我們弄錯了，種成白玫瑰。如果皇后發現，我們全都得被砍頭。你看，我們正在盡最大的努力，要在皇后來以前把……」就在這時，一直不安地注視花園另一邊的老五突然喊道：「皇后！皇后！」這三個園丁立即臉朝下趴在地上。這時傳來了許多腳步聲。愛麗絲好奇地四處張望著，急切地想看看皇后。

走在最前面的是十個手拿棍棒的士兵，他們全都和三個園丁一樣長長扁扁的，手和腳長在四個角上；接著是十個大臣，這些人全都用方塊裝飾著，像那些士兵一樣兩個兩個並排走；大臣後面是王室的孩子們，一共十個。這些可愛的小孩，一對對手拉著手，愉快地蹦蹦跳跳，全都用紅心裝飾著。後面是賓客，大部份是國王和皇后。在那些賓客中，愛麗絲認出了那隻白兔，牠急促不安地說著話，別人講什麼牠都點頭微笑，沒注意到愛麗絲就走過去了。接著是紅心傑克，雙手捧著放在紫紅色絲絨墊子上的王冠。這支龐大隊伍的最後是紅心國王與紅心皇后。

愛麗絲不知道該不該像三個園丁那樣臉朝地面趴下，她根本不記得王室經過時有這樣的規矩。「而且，人們臉朝下趴著，誰也看不到他們，又有什麼用呢？」她這樣想著，所以站在原地不動。

隊伍走到愛麗絲對面時，全都停下來看著她。皇后嚴厲地問紅心傑克：「這是誰呀？」紅心傑克只是用鞠躬和微笑作為回答。

「傻瓜！」皇后不耐煩地搖搖頭說，然後轉向愛麗絲問道：「小朋友，你叫什麼名字？」

「陛下，我叫愛麗絲。」她很有禮貌地回答，說完卻自言自語道：「說來說去，他們只不過是一堆紙牌，不需要怕他們！」

「這些又是誰？」皇后指著三個園丁問。那三個園丁圍著剛才那株玫瑰樹趴著，他們背上的圖案跟其他人一樣，所以皇后看不出他們是園丁、士兵還是大臣，又或者是她自己的三個孩子。

「我怎麼會知道？這與我無關！」愛麗絲回答，她對自己的勇氣感到驚訝。

　　皇后氣得漲紅了臉，兩眼像野獸般瞪了愛麗絲一會兒，然後尖聲喊道：「砍下她的頭，砍下……」

　　「別亂說！」愛麗絲非常堅定地大聲說。皇后沉默了。

　　國王把手放在皇后的手臂上，小心地說：「冷靜點，親愛的，她只是個孩子！」

　　皇后生氣地從國王身邊走開了，並對傑克說：「把他們翻過來。」

　　傑克照辦了，用一隻腳小心地把三個園丁翻了過來。

　　「站起來！」皇后用又尖又高的嗓音叫道，三個園丁立刻從地上跳起來，向國王、皇后、王室的孩子們以及其他人鞠躬。

　　「停下來！」皇后尖叫著，「我頭都暈了！」她轉身看著那株玫瑰樹繼續問：「你們剛才在這做什麼？」

　　「陛下，願您開恩，」老二單腳下跪，低聲下氣地說，「我們正想……」

　　「我知道了。」皇后說，她剛才問話時就在旁邊看了看玫瑰花。「砍掉他們的頭！」隊伍繼續前進，留下三個士兵來處死這三個不幸的園丁，園丁急忙跑向愛麗絲，想得到她的保護。

　　「你們不會被砍頭的！」愛麗絲說著就把他們藏進旁邊的一個大花盆裡。三個士兵找了一陣子沒找到，就悄悄地跟在隊伍後面離開了。

「把他們的頭砍掉了沒？」皇后怒吼道。

「陛下，他們的頭已經不見了！」三個士兵大聲回答。

「好極了！」皇后說，「你會玩槌球嗎？」

三個士兵都不出聲，看著愛麗絲，這個問題顯然是問她的。

「會！」愛麗絲大聲回答。

「那就過來！」皇后吼道。於是愛麗絲就加入了這個隊伍。好奇著之後會發生什麼事。

「今天……今天天氣真好啊！」愛麗絲身旁一個膽怯的聲音說。原來愛麗絲恰巧走在白兔旁邊，白兔正焦慮地偷偷看著她的臉。

「嗯，」愛麗絲說，「公爵夫人在哪裡呢？」

「噓！噓！」兔子急忙低聲制止她，同時還擔心地轉過頭看看皇后，然後踮起腳尖，把嘴湊到愛麗絲的耳朵旁，悄悄地說：「她被判處了死刑。」

「為什麼？」愛麗絲問。

「你是要說『真遺憾！』嗎？」兔子問。

「不，我沒說。」愛麗絲回答，「我一點都不覺得遺憾，我是說『為什麼？』」

「她打了皇后耳光……」兔子說。愛麗絲聽了笑了出來。

「噓！」兔子害怕地低聲說，「皇后會聽到的！你知道，公爵夫人來晚了，皇后說過……」

「各就各位！」皇后雷鳴般地喊了一聲，人們就朝各個方向跑開了，撞來撞去的，但總算很快地站好位子，於是遊戲開始了。

愛麗絲想，這輩子還沒見過這麼奇怪的槌球場：到處都崎嶇不平，球是活生生的刺蝟，槌球棒是活生生的紅鶴，士兵們彎下腰，手腳著地當球門。

起初，愛麗絲遇到最大的難題是應付她的紅鶴，後來總算成功地把紅鶴的身體夾在手臂下，並讓紅鶴的腿往下垂。可是每當她好不容易把紅鶴的脖子弄直，準備用牠的頭去打刺蝟時，紅鶴就會把脖子往上扭，一臉疑惑地看著愛麗絲，惹得她大笑起來。當她把紅鶴的頭按下去，準備再打一次的時候，卻又生氣地發現刺蝟已經伸直身子爬走了。此外，每當愛麗絲把刺蝟球打出去，路上總有一些溝渠或隆起，而弓腰充當球門的士兵們常常站起來走到其他地方。很快地，愛麗絲就得出了結論：這確實是一個非常難玩的遊戲。

打球的人都不等輪到自己，就玩了起來。他們不停地爭吵，還為了刺蝟打架。沒多久，皇后就大發雷霆，跺著腳走來走去，幾乎每分鐘就喊一次：「砍掉他的頭！」或「砍掉她的頭！」

愛麗絲感到非常不安，當然，她還沒有跟皇后吵架，可是她知道隨時都可能發生。「如果吵架的話，」她想，「我會怎麼樣呢？這裡的人太喜歡砍別人頭了，可是很奇怪，大家都還活著。」

愛麗絲到處尋找可以逃走的路，思索著自己能不能逃跑而不被發現。這時，她注意到空中出現了一個怪東西，起初她覺得很困惑，看了一兩分鐘後，她認出這是一個咧嘴的笑容，她自言自語道：「是柴郡貓，現在有人和我說話了。」

「妳好嗎？」當嘴巴完全出現後，柴郡貓跟愛麗絲打招呼。

愛麗絲等到牠的眼睛也出現了，才點點頭。「現在跟牠說話沒有用，」她想，「應該等兩個耳朵也出來了，或者至少出來一個，我再說話。」又過了幾分鐘，整個頭都出現了，愛麗絲這才放下紅鶴，跟牠敘述打槌球的情況。對於有人聽她說話，她感到非常高興。至於那隻貓似乎認為出現的部分已經夠了，就沒有露出身體來了。

「我覺得他們的比賽很不公平，」愛麗絲抱怨了起來，「他們吵得太兇了，連自己說的話都聽不清楚。而且好像沒有一定的規則，就算有，也沒人遵守。還有，你簡直想像不到有多混亂，所有的東西都是活的。譬如說，我差點就要把球打進去了，球門卻在球場的另一端走來走去；還有，正當我要用自己的球去碰皇后的刺蝟球時，那個刺蝟一看到我的球就跑掉了！」

「你喜歡皇后嗎？」貓低聲說。

「一點都不喜歡，」愛麗絲說，「她簡直⋯⋯」說到這裡，她發現皇后就在她身後聽著，於是她馬上接著說：「就快贏了，根本不用等到比賽結束。」

皇后微笑著走開了。

「你在跟誰說話？」國王走來問愛麗絲，非常好奇地看著那個貓頭。

「請允許我介紹，這是我的朋友，柴郡貓。」愛麗絲說。

「我一點也不喜歡牠的樣子。不過，如果牠想的話，可以吻我的手。」國王說。

「我可不想。」貓表示說。

「不得無禮！」國王說，「另外，不准那樣看我！」他邊說邊走到愛麗絲的身後。

「貓是可以看國王的，我在某本書上看過這句話，不過不記得是哪一本了。」愛麗絲說。

「把這隻貓弄走！」國王堅決地說，接著就向剛走過來的皇后喊道：「親愛的，我希望你把這隻貓弄走！」

不管問題大小，皇后的解決辦法就只有一種：「砍掉牠的頭！」她看也不看，就立刻這樣說。

「我親自去找劊子手。」國王迫不及待地說著，匆匆忙忙走了。

　　愛麗絲聽到皇后在遠處尖聲吼叫，想起該回去看看遊戲進行得怎樣了。愛麗絲已經聽到皇后又宣判了三個人死刑，原因是輪到他們打球，但他們沒有跟上。愛麗絲很不喜歡這種場面，整個遊戲亂七八糟的，根本不知道什麼時候輪到她，她索性離開去找她的刺蝟。

　　愛麗絲的刺蝟正在和一隻刺蝟打架，這對她來說可真是打中球的好機會，唯一困難的是她的紅鶴跑到花園的另一邊了，愛麗絲看到牠正徒勞地想飛到一棵樹上。

　　等她捉住紅鶴把牠帶回來以後，兩隻刺蝟已經打完架，跑得無影無蹤了。愛麗絲想：「這也沒什麼關係，反正這邊的球門都不見了。」為了不讓紅鶴再次逃跑，愛麗絲把牠夾在手臂下，又跑回去想跟她的朋友多聊一陣子。

　　愛麗絲走回柴郡貓那裡時，驚訝地看到一大群人圍著牠：劊子手、國王、皇后正在激烈地辯論。他們說話的同時，旁邊的人都靜悄悄地，顯得十分不安。

　　愛麗絲一出現，這三個人立刻要她評評理。他們爭先恐後地向她重複各自的論述，愛麗絲根本聽不清楚他們在說什麼。

　　劊子手的理由是：一定要有身體，才能把頭從身上砍掉，光有一顆頭是沒辦法砍頭的。他說他從來沒做過這種事，這輩子也不打算做這樣的事。

　　國王的觀點是：任何有頭的東西就能被砍頭，劊子手執行就是了，少說廢話。

　　皇后的說法是：如果有任何事情沒有立即執行的話，她就要把每個人的頭都砍掉，一個也不留。（正是她最後這句話，讓大家既沉重又擔憂。）

　　愛麗絲想不到要說什麼，只好說：「這隻貓是公爵夫人的，你們最好去問她。」

　　「她在監獄裡，」皇后對劊子手說，「把她帶來！」劊子手像箭一般地跑去了。

　　劊子手一離開，貓的頭開始消失，等劊子手帶著公爵夫人抵達時，已經完全看不見貓頭了。於是，國王和劊子手發瘋似地跑來跑去，到處找那隻貓，而其他人又回去接著玩槌球了。

第 9 章

假海龜的故事

「……而這裡面的格言是：『你看著像什麼就是什麼』，簡單來說就是『永遠不要把自己想像成和別人心目中的你不一樣，因為你曾經或可能曾經在別人心中是另外一個樣子。』」

「你都不知道能再見到你，我有多高興，親愛的老朋友！」公爵夫人說，很親切地挽著愛麗絲的手臂一起離開了。

愛麗絲對公爵夫人脾氣這麼好感到非常高興，想起之前在廚房裡見到公爵夫人的情景，她的蠻橫可能都是胡椒造成的。

「要是我當了公爵夫人，」愛麗絲自言自語（並不是滿懷希望的口氣），「我的廚房裡不要有任何胡椒，沒有胡椒的湯也能煮得好喝……也許正是胡椒讓人們脾氣暴躁。」她對這個新發現感到非常高興，繼續自言自語：「醋使人們酸溜溜的……甘菊讓人們苦澀……麥芽糖則是讓孩子脾氣溫和。我只希望大家都懂得這些，這樣他們就不會吝嗇給孩子糖吃了。你知道……」

愛麗絲完全忘了公爵夫人，所以聽到公爵夫人在她耳邊說話時，她吃了一驚。「親愛的，你在想什麼吧，想到都忘了要說話！有句格言可以表達現在的情形，不過我需要想想。」

「或許根本沒有格言。」愛麗絲大膽地發表自己的意見。

「嘖，嘖，小孩子，」公爵夫人說，「每件事都有隱含的格言，只是看妳找不找得到。」她一面說著，一面緊緊地靠近愛麗絲。

愛麗絲不太喜歡她靠得那麼近，首先，公爵夫人長得很醜，再來，她的高度正好會把下巴頂在愛麗絲的肩膀上，偏偏又是讓人不舒服的尖下巴。但是愛麗絲不想失禮，只好盡量忍耐。

「現在遊戲進行得好多了。」愛麗絲沒話找話地說。

「是啊，」公爵夫人
說，「這件事裡的格言是……
『噢，是愛，是愛，讓世界
運轉！』」

愛麗絲小聲說：「有人
說過，少管閒事才會讓世界
運轉。」

「啊，是的！意思是一
樣的。」公爵夫人說，使勁地
把尖下巴往愛麗絲的肩上壓
了壓，又加了句：「這裡的格
言是『只要核心思想一致，不
同的表達一樣合乎情理。』」

「她還真喜歡尋找事情中的格言！」愛麗絲想。

「我猜你一定在想，為什麼我不摟妳的腰，」停頓了一會兒後，
公爵夫人繼續說，「因為我不知道妳的紅鶴脾氣好不好。我可以做
個實驗嗎？」

「牠可能會咬妳。」愛麗絲小心地回答，完全不想讓她做實驗。

「非常正確，」公爵夫人說，「紅鶴和芥末都會咬人，這裡的
格言是：『物以類聚』。」

「芥末又不是鳥。」愛麗絲說。

「對，像往常一樣，」公爵夫人說：「你把事情分得非常清楚！」

「我想它是一種礦物。」愛麗絲說。

「當然是啦！」公爵夫人好像準備同意愛麗絲說的每句話。「這附近有個大芥末礦，這裡有句格言是：『我的越多，你的就越少』。」

「噢，我知道！」愛麗絲沒注意她後面一句，大聲說道，「芥末是一種蔬菜，雖然看起來不像，不過就是蔬菜。」

「我十分同意你所說的，」公爵夫人說，「而這裡面的格言是：『你看著像什麼就是什麼』，簡單來說就是『永遠不要把自己想像成和別人心目中的你不一樣，因為你曾經或可能曾經在別人心中是另外一個樣子。』」

「要是我有把您的話記在紙上，也許我會更清楚一點，」愛麗絲很有禮貌地說，「可是我完全跟不上妳說的。」

「這不算什麼，要是我願意，我還能說更多呢。」公爵夫人愉快地說。

「請不必費心說得更長了。」愛麗絲說道。

「說不上費心，」公爵夫人說，「我剛才說的每句話，都是送給妳的禮物。」

「真便宜的禮物！」愛麗絲心想，「幸好其他人不是這樣送生日禮物的。」

「又在想事情了嗎？」公爵夫人問，又用她那小小的尖下巴頂了一下。

「我有想事情的權利。」愛麗絲尖銳地回答，她有點不耐煩了。

「是的，」公爵夫人說道，「就像小豬也想飛。這裡的格……」

說到這公爵夫人的聲音突然消失了，連她最愛說的「格言」也沒說完，就連挽著愛麗絲的那隻手臂也顫抖了起來，這讓愛麗絲很驚訝，於是她抬起頭，發現皇后站在她們面前，交叉著雙臂，臉色陰沉得像雷雨前的天色一樣。

「天氣真好啊，陛下。」公爵夫人用低沉而微弱的聲音說。

「現在我清楚地警告你！」皇后跺著腳嚷道，「不是人不見，就是頭不見！馬上決定！」

公爵夫人做出了選擇，馬上消失了。

「我們再去玩槌球吧。」皇后對愛麗絲說。愛麗絲嚇得不敢吭聲，只能慢慢地跟著她回到槌球場。其他客人趁皇后不在時跑到樹蔭下乘涼。他們一看到皇后，立刻又跳起來玩槌球。因為皇后說過，誰要是敢耽擱，就要誰沒命。

玩槌球的時候，皇后不斷跟人吵架，嚷著「砍掉他的頭！」或「砍掉她的頭*！」。被判刑的人一個個被帶走，士兵們為了執行命令而不能做球門了。大約半小時之後，球場上已經一個球門也沒有了。除了國王、皇后和愛麗絲，所有參加槌球遊戲的人都因為被判了砍頭而被關起來了。

累得喘不過氣的皇后停了下來，對愛麗絲說：「你還沒有見過假海龜吧？」

「還沒有，」愛麗絲說，「我連假海龜是什麼都不知道。」

「就是用來做假海龜湯的東西。」皇后說。

「我從沒看過也沒聽說過。」愛麗絲說。

「那麼，快點跟我來，」皇后說，「牠會和你講牠的故事。」

她們一起離開的時候，愛麗絲聽到國王小聲地對客人們說「你們都被赦免了。」「那真是件好事！」愛麗絲心想。因為皇后要砍那麼多人的頭，讓她很不開心。

她們很快就碰見了一隻鷹頭獅，正在太陽下睡覺。（要是你不知道什麼是鷹頭獅，可以看看插圖。）

「快起來，懶東西！」皇后說道，「帶這位年輕小姐去看假海龜，聽牠的故事。我必須回去看看我的命令執行得怎樣了。」她說完就走了，把愛麗絲留在鷹頭獅那裡。愛麗絲不太喜歡這個動物的長相，但是她想，與其跟那個野蠻的皇后在一起，還不如跟牠在一起比較安全，所以她留下來等候著。

鷹頭獅坐起來揉揉眼睛，看看皇后，直到她走得看不見了，才咯咯笑了起來。「真好笑！」鷹頭獅一邊對自己，一邊對愛麗絲說。

「有什麼好笑的？」愛麗絲問。

「噢，她呀，」鷹頭獅說，「都是她的想像，他們從沒有砍掉任何人的頭。跟我來。」

愛麗絲慢慢地跟在後面走，心裡想道：「這裡每個人都對我說『跟我來』，我從來沒有被人這麼呼來喚去的，從來沒有！」

他們走了沒多遠，就看見了遠方的假海龜孤獨又悲傷地坐在岩石上。再走近一點時，愛麗絲聽見牠在嘆息，好像心都要碎了，她發自內心同情牠。

「牠為什麼那麼傷心？」她問鷹頭獅。鷹頭獅還是用了跟剛才差不多的話回答：「都是牠的想像，牠根本沒有什麼傷心事。跟我來。」

他們走近了假海龜，牠用充滿淚水的大眼睛望著他們，一句話也沒說。

「這位年輕小姐想聽聽你的故事。」鷹頭獅對假海龜說，「她真的想。」

「我很樂意告訴她。」假海龜用深沉的聲音說，「你們都坐下，在我講完之前別說話。」

於是他們都坐了下來，有好一陣子誰都不說話。愛麗絲想：「要是他不開始，又要如何結束呢？」但是她仍然耐心地等著。

「從前，」假海龜終於開口了，牠深深地嘆了口氣說，「我曾經是一隻真海龜。」

說完這句話之後，又是一陣很長的沉默，只有鷹頭獅偶爾發出「嘿喀！」聲，以及假海龜連續的啜泣聲。愛麗絲幾乎要站起來說：「謝謝你，先生，謝謝你那麼有趣的故事。」但是，她覺得應該還有下文，所以她仍然靜靜地坐著，什麼話也不說。

「小時候，」假海龜終於繼續說下去，平靜多了，只不過仍然不時地啜泣。「我們都到海裡的學校去上學。我們的老師是一隻老海龜，我們都習慣叫牠陸龜。」

「既然牠不是陸龜，為什麼要那樣叫牠呢？」愛麗絲問。

「我們叫牠陸龜，因為牠教我們呀。」假海龜生氣地說，「真笨！」

「這麼簡單的問題都要問！」鷹頭獅說。於是牠們就靜靜地坐在那裡看著可憐的愛麗絲，讓她真想鑽到地底下去。最後，鷹頭獅對假海龜說：「別介意了，老朋友，繼續說吧。」假海龜繼續說了這些話：「是的，我們到海裡上學，雖然你可能不相信……」

「我沒說過我不相信。」愛麗絲插嘴說。

「你說了！」假海龜說。

「別說話！」愛麗絲還沒來得及接話，就被鷹頭獅就制止了。然後假海龜又講了下去：「我們受的是最好的教育，事實上，我們每天都上學。」

「我也是每天都上學，」愛麗絲說，「你不用這麼得意。」

「你們有額外的課程嗎？」假海龜有點不安地問。

「當然啦，」愛麗絲說，「我們學法語和音樂。」

「有洗衣課嗎？」假海龜問。

「當然沒有！」愛麗絲生氣地說。

「啊！那你們的學校就算不上真正的好學校，」假海龜鬆了口氣說，「我們學校繳費單的最後一項就是額外課程：法語、音樂，還有洗衣服。」

「你們住在海底，根本不太需要洗衣服。」愛麗絲說。

「不過我負擔不起額外課程，」假海龜長嘆了一聲說，「我只上正課。」

「正課是什麼呢？」愛麗絲問。

「開始當然先學旋轉和翻滾，」假海龜回答，「然後學習各種算術——抱負、消遣、醜化和嘲笑。」

「我從來沒聽說過什麼醜化，」愛麗絲大膽地說，「那是什麼？」

鷹頭獅驚訝到舉起了牠的一對爪子大叫：「什麼！你從沒聽過醜化！你知道什麼叫美化吧？」

愛麗絲不太確定地說：「是……讓什麼……東西……變得更好看。」

「那麼，」鷹頭獅繼續說，「如果你還不知道什麼是醜化，就是個傻瓜了。」

愛麗絲不敢再針對這個問題

繼續發問，她轉向假海龜問道：「你們還學些什麼呢？」

「我們還學秘史，」假海龜拍打著他的闊鰭逐一數著科目，「秘史，古代的和現代的，還有海洋學，接下來是拉長聲。我們的拉長聲老師是一條老海鰻，一個星期來一次，教我們拉長聲、伸展和捲成一團昏倒。」

「那是什麼樣子呢？」愛麗絲問道。

「我沒辦法做給你看，我身體太僵硬了，偏偏鷹頭獅又沒學過。」假海龜說。

「我沒時間啊！」鷹頭獅說，「不過我上過古典文學老師的課，牠是一隻老螃蟹，我是說真的。」

「我沒上過牠的課，」假海龜嘆息著說，「牠們說牠教大笑和悲傷。」

「沒錯，沒錯。」這下子鷹頭獅也嘆息了，牠們兩個都用爪子遮住了臉。

「你們每天上幾小時的課呢？」愛麗絲想換個話題，急忙地問。假海龜回答：「第一天十小時，第二天九小時，依此類推。」

「好奇怪的教學安排！」愛麗絲說。

「這就是人們把這叫『課程』的原因，」鷹頭獅說，「因為他們一天一天『減少』。」這對愛麗絲可真是個新鮮事，她想了一下才接著說：「那麼第十一天一定是假日了？」

「當然是。」假海龜說。

「那麼你們第十二天做什麼呢？」愛麗絲急切地問。

「上課的問題談夠了，」鷹頭獅用堅定的口氣打了岔，「現在告訴她一點遊戲的事吧。」

第 *10* 章

龍蝦方塊舞

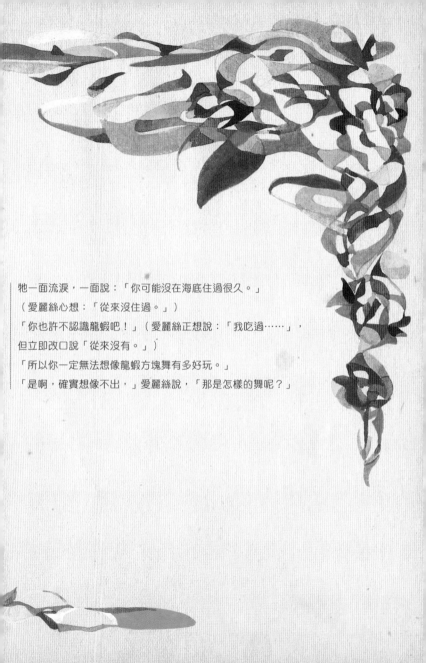

牠一面流淚，一面說：「你可能沒在海底住過很久。」

（愛麗絲心想：「從來沒住過。」）

「你也許不認識龍蝦吧！」（愛麗絲正想說：「我吃過……」，但立即改口說「從來沒有。」）

「所以你一定無法想像龍蝦方塊舞有多好玩。」

「是啊，確實想像不出，」愛麗絲說，「那是怎樣的舞呢？」

假海龜深深地嘆了一口氣，舉起一隻闊鰭，用鰭背摸摸眼睛。牠看著愛麗絲想說話，可是有好一陣子泣不成聲。「牠嗓子裡好像卡了根骨頭。」鷹頭獅說著就動手搖了搖牠，還拍了拍牠的背，假海龜終於能開口說話了。牠一面流淚，一面說：「你可能沒在海底住過很久。（愛麗絲心想：「從來沒住過。」）你也許不認識龍蝦吧！（愛麗絲正想說：「我吃過……」，但立即改口說「從來沒有。」），所以你一定無法想像龍蝦方塊舞有多好玩。」

「是啊，確實想像不出來，」愛麗絲說，「那是怎樣的舞呢？」

鷹頭獅說：「先在岸邊站成一排……」

「兩排！」假海龜喊道，「海豹、海龜和鮭魚都排排站好。然後，把所有的水母都清掉……」

「通常得花好一陣子呢！」鷹頭獅插嘴說。

「前進兩步……」

「每位都有一個龍蝦舞伴！」鷹頭獅叫道。

「當然啦，」假海龜說道，「前進兩步，組好舞伴……」

「…交換龍蝦，後退兩步回到原位。」鷹頭獅接著說。

假海龜說：「然後把龍蝦……」

「扔出去！」鷹頭獅跳起來大聲說。

「…盡可能把龍蝦遠遠地扔到海裡去…」

「再游過去追牠們。」鷹頭獅尖聲叫道。

「在海裡翻一個跟斗！」假海龜叫道，發狂似地跳來跳去。

「再交換龍蝦！」鷹頭獅用牠最尖的嗓門大叫。

「再回到陸地上，再……這就是第一小節。」假海龜說。牠的聲音突然低了下來。這兩個剛才像瘋子似跳來跳去的傢伙，又坐了下來不說話，悲傷地看著愛麗絲。

「一定是很美的舞。」愛麗絲膽怯地說。

「你想看一小段嗎？」假海龜問。

「我很想看。」愛麗絲說。

「我們來跳第一節吧！」假海龜對鷹頭獅說道，「你知道我們沒有龍蝦也行的。不過誰來唱呢？」

「你唱，」鷹頭獅說，「我忘記歌詞了。」

於是牠們莊嚴地圍著愛麗絲跳起舞來。當牠們跳得太近的時候，常常會踩到愛麗絲的腳。當假海龜緩慢而悲傷地唱到下面這一段時，牠舞動著前爪和前鰭打著拍子：

> 「鱈魚對蝸牛說：『你不能走快一點嗎？
> 海豚緊跟著我們，牠常踩到我的尾巴。

　　　　你瞧龍蝦和海龜走得多急切，
　　　　牠們在鵝卵石上等著，你願意來跳舞嗎？
　　　　願意，不願意，願意，不願意，願意跳舞嗎？
　　　　願意，不願意，願意，不願意，你不願意跳舞嗎？

　　　　你一定不知道那會有多麼有趣，
　　　　和龍蝦一起被扔到海裡。
　　　　『太遠了，太遠了。』蝸牛斜眼回答。
　　　　牠說謝謝鱈魚的好意，但牠不願意參加舞會。
　　　　牠不願，牠不能，牠不願，牠不能，他不願參加舞會。
　　　　牠不願，牠不能，牠不願，牠不能，他不能參加舞會。

　　　　牠那些有鱗片的朋友回答：『扔得遠有什麼關係？』
　　　　你要知道，在大海那邊，還有另一個海岸。
　　　　離英格蘭越遠，就越接近法蘭西。
　　　　親愛的蝸牛別害怕，
　　　　趕快去跳舞。
　　　　你願意，不願意，你願意，不願意，你願意跳舞嗎？
　　　　你願意，不願意，你願意，你不願意，你不願意跳舞嗎？」

　「謝謝，這支舞真有趣，」愛麗絲說，她很高興終於結束了，「我很喜歡那首有關鱈魚的好玩歌。」

　　假海龜說：「哦，說到鱈魚，牠們……你肯定見過牠們啦？」

　「是的，」愛麗絲回答，「我常常在飯……」，她想說在飯桌上，但是急忙停住了。

「我不知道『飯』是什麼地方，」假海龜說，「不過，如果你常常看見牠們，你當然知道牠們的樣子了。」

「我想我知道，」愛麗絲思索著說，「牠們把尾巴彎到嘴裡，身上鋪滿了麵包屑。

「麵包屑？你錯了。」假海龜說，「海水會把麵包屑沖掉的。不過牠們的尾巴倒真的是彎到嘴裡的。這是因為……」說到這裡，假海龜打個呵欠，闔上了眼。「告訴她這是什麼原因。」他對鷹頭獅說。

鷹頭獅說：「因為牠們跟龍蝦一起參加舞會。所以牠們扔進海裡。所以，牠們被丟得老遠。所以牠們把尾巴塞到嘴裡，所以牠們沒辦法把尾巴弄出來了。就是這樣。」

「謝謝你，」愛麗絲說，「真有意思，我從來都不知道這麼多有關鱈魚的故事。」

「如果你願意，我還可以告訴你更多。」鷹頭獅說，「你知道鱈魚的名字是怎麼來的嗎？」

「我沒想過，」愛麗絲說，「是怎麼來的？」

「牠是擦靴子和鞋子的。」鷹頭獅嚴肅地說。

愛麗絲感到很困惑。「擦靴子和鞋子？」她懷疑地重複道。

「你的鞋是用什麼擦的？」鷹頭獅說，「我的意思是，你用什麼把鞋子擦得那麼亮？」

愛麗絲看了看自己的鞋子，想了一下說：「我想是用黑鞋油。」

「在海裡，」鷹頭獅說，「靴子和鞋子是用鱈魚擦亮的，現在你明白了吧。」

「海裡的靴子和鞋子是由什麼做成的呢？」愛麗絲好奇地問。

「當然是比目魚和鰻魚啦！」鷹頭獅很不耐煩地回答，「就算是蝦子也會這樣告訴你的。」

「如果我是鱈魚，」愛麗絲說，腦子裡還想著那首歌，「我會對海豚說『離我們遠一點，我們不要你跟我們在一起！』」

「牠們不得不讓海豚跟牠們一起，」假海龜說，「沒有一種聰明的魚外出旅行時，不帶上海豚的。」

「這不是真的吧？」愛麗絲驚訝地說。

「當然是真的，」假海龜說，「如果一條魚來找我，告訴我牠要外出旅行，我就會說『帶哪隻海豚去？』」

「你想說的是『目的』吧？」 愛麗絲說。

「我剛才說過了。」假海龜不高興地回答。

鷹頭獅加了句：「好了！讓我們聽聽你的冒險吧。」

「我可以告訴你們我的故事……從今天早上開始，」愛麗絲有點膽怯地說，「從昨天開始也沒用，因為我已經變成另一個人了。」

「解釋一下這是怎麼回事。」假海龜說。

「不，不！先講故事。」鷹頭獅不耐煩地說，「解釋太浪費時間了。」

於是愛麗絲開始講她的故事，從看見白兔講起。剛開始她還有點緊張，那兩隻動物坐得離她那麼近，一邊一個，眼睛和嘴巴睜得那麼大。但是她講著講著膽子逐漸大了起來，她的聽眾安靜地聽著，直到她講到給毛毛蟲背《你老了，威廉爸爸》，背出來的字完全不對，假海龜深深地吸了一口氣說道：「好奇怪。」

「怪得不能更怪啦。」鷹頭獅說。

「整首詩全背錯了，」假海龜沉思著重複說，「我想再聽聽她背點別的東西，讓她開始吧。」牠看看鷹頭獅，好像鷹頭獅對愛麗絲有某種權威似的。

「站起來背《那是懶惰蟲的聲音》。」鷹頭獅說。

「這些動物老愛命令人，總是叫人背書，」愛麗絲想，「我還不如馬上回學校去。」她還是站起來背了。可是她腦子裡塞滿了龍蝦方塊舞，根本不知道自己在說什麼，背出來的東西確實非常古怪：

　　「那是龍蝦的聲音，我聽見牠在講話，
　　『你們把我烤得太焦，我頭髮裡還得加點糖。』
　　就像鴨子用自己的眼瞼一樣，牠用自己的鼻子，

121

整理腰帶和鈕扣，還把腳趾翻成外八字。

當沙灘全變乾的時候，牠像雲雀一樣高興。

談起鯊魚，牠用輕蔑的語氣，

但潮水上漲，鯊魚將他包圍時，

牠的聲音就變得膽小又恐懼！」

「這跟我小時候背的完全不一樣。」鷹頭獅說。

「我也從來沒聽過，」假海龜說，「聽起來還真不是普通的奇怪。」愛麗絲什麼話也沒說，她坐了下來，雙手遮住臉，不知道一切能不能恢復正常。

「我希望她解釋一下。」假海龜說。

「她解釋不了，」鷹頭獅急忙說，「背下一段吧。」

「但是腳趾是怎麼回事？」假海龜堅持說，「怎麼能用自己的鼻子把腳趾翻成外八字呢？」

「那是跳舞的第一個姿勢。」愛麗絲說。可是她也覺得莫名其妙，所以非常希望換個話題。

「接著背下一段，」鷹頭獅不耐煩地說，「開頭是『我經過牠的花園』。」

愛麗絲不敢違背，雖然她明知道全部都會背錯。她用發抖的聲音背道：

「我經過牠的花園，並且用一隻眼睛看見，
花豹和貓頭鷹正分食一個餡餅。
花豹吃掉了派皮、肉汁和肉餡，
貓頭鷹只分到一個空盤。
在餡餅吃完以後，花豹仁慈地答應貓頭鷹，
把湯匙放進衣袋裡作為禮品。
可花豹發出一聲怒吼，
把刀子和叉子通通拿走。
並且宣佈，宴會就此結束……」

這時假海龜打斷說：「要是你不能一邊背一邊解釋，那麼背這些胡說八道的東西有什麼用？這是我聽過最亂七八糟的東西了。」

「你最好停下來。」鷹頭獅說。愛麗絲十分高興。

「我們再跳一段龍蝦方塊舞好嗎？」鷹頭獅繼續說，「還是你要聽假海龜唱首歌？」

「啊，請來一首歌吧，要是假海龜願意的話。」愛麗絲說得那麼熱情，使得鷹頭獅用不高興的口氣說：「哼，人各有所好！給她唱首『海龜湯』怎麼樣，老朋友？」

假海龜深深地嘆了口氣，時不時哽咽地唱道：

> 「美味的湯，綠色的濃湯，
> 在熱氣騰騰的蓋碗裡裝。
> 誰不願意嚐一嚐，
> 這樣的好湯？
> 晚餐用的湯，美味的湯，
> 晚餐用的湯，美味的湯，
> 美……味的湯……湯！
> 美……味的湯……湯！
> 晚……晚……晚餐用的……湯，
> 美味的……美味的湯！
> 美味的湯！誰還會把魚想，把野味和別道菜來嚐？
> 誰不想嚐一嚐，
> 兩便士一碗的好湯？
> 兩便士一碗的好湯？
> 美……味的湯……湯！
> 美……味的湯……湯！
> 晚……晚……晚餐的湯……湯，
> 美味的，美……味的湯！」

「再唱一遍！」鷹頭獅說道。假海龜剛要開口，就聽到遠處傳來一聲「審判開始啦！」

「走吧！」鷹頭獅大喊，拉住愛麗絲的手，也不等那首歌唱完就急忙跑走了。

　　「什麼審判呀？」愛麗絲邊跑邊喘氣發問，但是鷹頭獅只是說「快點！」，而且跑得更快了。只聽到微風傳來越來越微弱的憂鬱的歌聲：

　　　　「晚……晚……晚餐的湯……湯，
　　　　美味的……美味的湯！」

第 *11* 章

誰偷了餡餅？

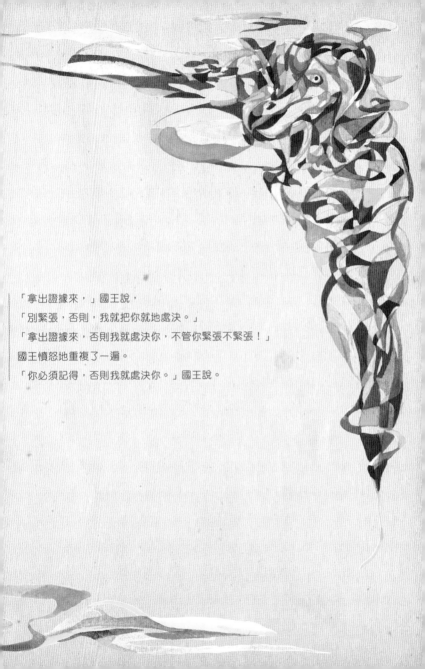

「拿出證據來，」國王說，

「別緊張，否則，我就把你就地處決。」

「拿出證據來，否則我就處決你，不管你緊張不緊張！」

國王憤怒地重複了一遍。

「你必須記得，否則我就處決。」國王說。

當他們抵達時，紅心國王和紅心皇后正坐在王座上，他們身旁圍繞著一大群各式各樣的小鳥、野獸以及整副撲克牌。紅心傑克站在他們面前，被上了鐐銬，兩側各有一名士兵看守著。白兔站在國王旁邊，一手拿著喇叭，一手拿著一卷羊皮紙。法庭正中央有張桌子，上面放著一大盤餡餅。餡餅看起來很可口，愛麗絲看得都餓了。愛麗絲想：「希望審判已經結束，然後讓大家吃點心。」但是看來不太可能，於是她開始東張西望來打發時間。

愛麗絲從沒上過法庭，只在書上讀到過。她高興自己幾乎喊得出每樣東西的名稱。「那是法官，」她對自己說，「因為他戴著假髮。」

　　順道一提，那位法官就是國王。他的假髮上還戴著王冠，所以他看起來很不舒服。

　　「那是陪審員席，」愛麗絲心想，「那十二隻動物」（她不得不稱之為「動物」，因為有的是獸類，有的是鳥類），「我想是陪審員。」最後這一句，她對自己說了兩三遍，覺得蠻自豪的。因為她覺得和她這樣同年齡的女孩，幾乎沒有人懂得這麼多。不過其實也可以叫他們「陪審團」。

　　十二位陪審員都忙著在石板上寫東西。「牠們在做什麼？」愛麗絲低聲問鷹頭獅。「在審判開始前，沒什麼需要記錄的事。」

　　鷹頭獅低聲回答：「牠們在寫自己的姓名，免得在審判結束前就忘記。」

　　「蠢東西！」愛麗絲不耐煩地高聲說，但她立刻就不說話了，因為白兔喊著：「法庭上請肅靜！」而國王戴上了眼鏡，迅速地掃視了四周，想找出誰在說話。

　　愛麗絲看得很清楚，就像靠在陪審員肩膀上似的，她看到所有的陪審員都在石板上寫下了「蠢東西」。甚至還看到有個陪審員不會寫「蠢」字，要求鄰座的告訴牠。「審判還沒結束，牠們的石板都寫得一塌糊塗了！」愛麗絲想。

　　其中有名陪審員的鉛筆在書寫時發出刺耳的聲音。愛麗絲當然受不了，她在法庭裡轉了一圈，走到牠的背後，找機會搶走了那枝鉛筆。她做得乾淨俐落，以至於那個可憐的小陪審（就是壁虎比爾）根本不知道發生了什麼事。他到處都找不到自己的鉛筆，只能用手指頭來寫了，這當然毫無用處，因為手指無法在石板上留下任何痕跡。

「傳令官，宣讀起訴書。」國王宣佈。

白兔吹響了三次喇叭，然後攤開羊皮紙宣讀道：

> 「紅心皇后做了餡餅，
> 夏日白晝竟發生這種事情：
> 紅心傑克偷走了餡餅，
> 全都帶走匆忙離境！」

「請量刑。」國王對陪審員說。

「不行，還不行！」兔子趕緊插話說，「在這之前還有好多事情要做呢！」

於是國王說：「傳第一個證人。」白兔又吹響了三次喇叭，喊道：「傳第一個證人！」

第一個證人就是帽匠。他進來時，一手拿著茶杯，一手拿著奶油麵包。他說：「陛下，請原諒我帶這些進來，因為我還沒吃完茶點就被傳喚來了。」

「你早就該吃完了。你什麼時

候開始吃的？」國王問。

帽匠看了看三月兔，三月兔是和睡鼠手拉著手跟來的。帽匠說：
「我想是三月十四日。」

「是十五日。」三月兔說。

「十六日。」睡鼠說。

「記下來！」國王對陪審員說，陪審員急忙在石板上寫下了這
三個日期，然後把它們加起來，再把結果換算成先令和便士。

「脫掉你的帽子！」國王對帽匠說。

「不是我的。」帽匠說。

「偷來的！」國王叫了起來，並看了看陪審員。陪審員立即記
下，作為事實備忘錄。

「我是個帽匠，賣帽子的，所以沒有一頂帽子是我的。」帽匠
解釋道。

這時，皇后戴上眼鏡盯著帽匠，帽匠臉色蒼白，侷促不安。

「拿出證據來，」國王說，「別緊張，否則我就把你就地處決。」

這些話對證人根本沒有鼓勵作用。他不時把身體重心從這隻
腳換到那隻腳，不自在地看著皇后，慌亂中還把茶杯錯當成奶油麵
包，咬了一大口。

　　就在此時，愛麗絲出現了奇怪的感覺，讓她迷惑了好一陣子，後來才慢慢地搞清楚，原來她又長大了。起初，她想站起來走出法庭，但下一秒又決定只要這裡還有空間，她就要留下來。

　　「我希望你不要一直擠，我快窒息了。」坐在愛麗絲旁邊的睡鼠說。

　　「我無法控制啊，我還在長大！」愛麗絲非常溫和地說。

　　「你沒有權利在這裡長大！」睡鼠說。

　　「別說廢話了，你自己也在長呀！」愛麗絲稍微大著膽子說。

　　「但是我是以合理的速度生長，才不像你這麼可笑！」睡鼠說著，不高興地站了起來，走到法庭的另一邊。

　　在愛麗絲和睡鼠說話的時候，皇后的眼睛始終盯著帽匠。就在睡鼠走到法庭另一邊時，她對一位官員說：「把上次音樂會上唱歌的人的名單給我。」聽到這話，這個可憐的帽匠嚇得發抖，連鞋子都掉了。

　　「拿出證據來，否則我就處決你，不管你緊張不緊張！」國王憤怒地重複了一遍。

　　「我是個可憐的人，陛下，」帽匠顫抖著說，「我才剛開始吃茶點⋯⋯沒有超過一星期⋯⋯再說為什麼奶油麵包變得這麼薄呢⋯⋯還有茶在閃閃發光⋯⋯」

「什麼閃閃發光？」國王問。

「是從茶開始的。」帽匠回答。

「閃閃發光這個字當然是 T 開頭的！」國王尖銳地指出，「你當我是笨蛋嗎？接著說！」

「我是個可憐人，」帽匠繼續說，「從那以後，大部分東西都發光了……只有三月兔說……」

三月兔急忙地插嘴：「我沒說過。」

「你說了！」帽匠說。

「我否認！」三月兔說。

「既然牠不承認，就說點別的吧！」國王說。

「好，無論如何，睡鼠說過……」說到這，帽匠不安地瞧瞧睡鼠，看牠會不會也否認。然而睡鼠什麼也沒說，牠已經睡著了。

「然後，我又切了點奶油麵包……」帽匠繼續說。

「但是睡鼠說了什麼？」一位陪審員問。

「我記不得了。」帽匠說。

「你必須記得，否則我就處決你。」國王說。

可憐的帽匠嚇得把茶杯和奶油麵包都弄掉了，單膝跪下來說：

133

「我是個可憐人，陛下。」

「你是很不會說話的人。」國王說。

這時，一隻天竺鼠突然歡呼了起來，但立刻被法庭上的官員制止了。（所謂制止，實在很難說明，我只能試著解釋是怎麼回事。他們用大帆布袋把天竺鼠的頭塞進去，再用繩子把袋口綁起來，然後坐在袋子上。）

愛麗絲心想：「我很高興親眼目睹這件事。我常在報紙上看到，審判結束時，『有人鼓掌歡呼，當場被法庭上的官員制止。』現在我才明白是怎麼回事。」

「如果沒有別的要補充，你可以退下了。」國王宣佈說。

「我無法再退得更下了，我已經站在地板上了。」帽匠說。

「那你可以坐下。」國王說。

這時，又一隻天竺鼠歡呼了起來，又被制止了。

愛麗絲心裡想：「唉，天竺鼠都被收拾完了，現在應該會好一點。」

「我想喝完這杯茶。」帽匠說著，不安地看著皇后，而皇后正在看歌手清單。

「你可以走了。」國王一說，帽匠立即跑出法庭，鞋子都來不及穿好就走了。

　　這時，皇后吩咐一位官員：「在庭外砍掉他的頭。」可是當官員追到大門口時，帽匠已經無影無蹤了。

　　「傳下一個證人！」國王吩咐。

　　下一個證人是公爵夫人的廚師。她手裡帶著胡椒盒。她還沒上法庭，愛麗絲就猜出是誰了。因為她看到站在法庭門口的人開始打噴嚏。

　　「說說你的證詞。」國王對她說。

　　「不要。」廚師回答。

　　國王著急地看了看白兔，白兔低聲說：「陛下必須盤問這個證人。」

「好，如果非得這樣，我會質問犯人的。」國王面帶憂鬱地說。然後他交叉雙臂，對廚師皺眉，直到視野模糊了，才用低沉的聲音說：「餡餅是用什麼做的？」

「大部分是胡椒。」廚師說。

「糖漿。」一個充滿睡意的聲音從廚師後面傳來。

「把睡鼠揪出來，」皇后尖叫起來，「砍了牠的頭！把牠趕出法庭！制止牠！捏牠！拔掉牠的鬍鬚！」在把睡鼠趕出去的時候，整個法庭混亂了好幾分鐘。等大家重新安頓下來，廚師已經消失了。

「沒關係！傳下一個證人。」國王坦然地說，一副鬆了一口氣的神情。然後他對皇后耳語說：「親愛的，真的必須由妳來盤問下一個證人了，我的頭已經痛得無法忍受了。」

愛麗絲看到白兔翻著名單，非常好奇，想看看下一個證人是誰。她想：「他們恐怕還沒有收集到足夠的證據。」所以當白兔用細小尖銳的嗓音高聲唱名「愛麗絲！」時，你可以想像她有多吃驚。

第 *12* 章

愛麗絲的證詞

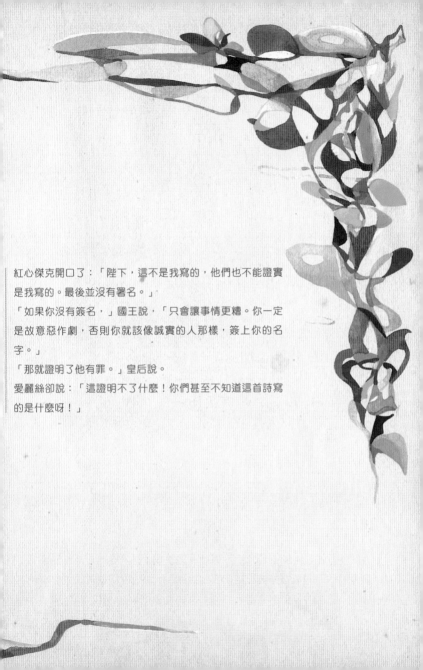

紅心傑克開口了:「陛下,這不是我寫的,他們也不能證實是我寫的。最後並沒有署名。」

「如果你沒有簽名,」國王說,「只會讓事情更糟。你一定是故意惡作劇,否則你就該像誠實的人那樣,簽上你的名字。」

「那就證明了他有罪。」皇后說。

愛麗絲卻說:「這證明不了什麼!你們甚至不知道這首詩寫的是什麼呀!」

「在這！」愛麗絲大聲說，完全忘了剛才在混亂中，她已經長得很大了。她急著跳起來，裙角掃到了陪審團席，把陪審員們翻倒在台下聽眾的頭頂上，然後全員跌成一團，這讓愛麗絲想起一個星期前不小心打翻了魚缸。

「啊，請大家原諒！」愛麗絲尷尬地說，儘快地把陪審員們扶回原位。因為魚缸事件的回憶還在她腦海裡，使她隱約地意識到，如果不立即把陪審員放回座位上，牠們會像當時的金魚一樣死掉的。

這時，國王莊重地宣稱：「審訊暫停，直到全體陪審員返回原位，全體！」他加重語氣重複這兩個字，並且嚴厲地盯著愛麗絲。

愛麗絲看了一眼陪審員席，發現由於自己的疏忽，竟然讓壁虎頭朝下坐著了。那個可憐的小東西無力動彈，只能憂傷地搖著尾巴，愛麗絲馬上把牠擺正。愛麗絲想，「這也沒有多大的意義，無論牠頭朝哪，在審判中都起不了什麼作用。」

等到陪審員們稍微從剛才的騷動中鎮定下來，也都找到了紙板和鉛筆之後，他們馬上勤奮地記錄剛才的事件，除了壁虎，牠已經筋疲力盡，不能做任何事情了，牠張著嘴坐著，兩眼無神地望著法庭的屋頂。

國王開口了：「關於這個案子你知道些什麼？」

「不知道。」愛麗絲回答。

「什麼也不知道？」國王再問。

「什麼也不知道。」愛麗絲答。

「這點很重要。」國王對陪審員們說。

陪審員們正在把這些問答記在石板上，白兔忽然插嘴說：「不重要，陛下的意思當然是不重要。」他的口氣十分尊敬，對著國王擠眉弄眼。

國王趕緊快接話：「當然，我的意思是不重要。」接著又喃喃自語道，「重要……不重要……不重要……重要」，好像在反覆推敲到底哪個詞最好。

有些陪審員記下了「重要」，有些寫了「不重要」。愛麗絲離陪審員們很近，牠們在石板上記的字她都看得一清二楚。她心想：「反正怎麼寫都沒關係。」

國王一直忙著在記事本上寫什麼，這時他高聲喊道：「保持肅靜！」接著他看著本子宣讀：「第四十二條，所有身高超過一英里者退出法庭。」大家都望著愛麗絲。

「我不到一英里高。」愛麗絲說。

「你有。」國王說。

「將近兩英里了。」皇后加了一句。

「不管怎麼說，反正我不走，」愛麗絲說，「再說，那根本不是正式規定，你剛才才規定的。」

「這是書裡最古老的一條規定。」國王說。

「那麼它應該是第一條呀！」愛麗絲說。

國王臉色蒼白，急忙蓋上了本子，以發抖的聲調低聲對陪審團說：「請考慮你們的裁決。」

「陛下，又發現新的證據了。」白兔急忙跳起來說，「這是剛才撿到的一張紙。」

「上面寫了什麼？」皇后問。

白兔回答：「我還沒打開來呢！但是看來是一封信，是那個罪犯寫給……給一個什麼人的。」

「肯定是這樣，」國王說，「除非它是寫給沒有人的，但這就不合理了。」

「信是寫給誰的？」一個陪審員問。

「看不出來，事實上，信封外面什麼也沒寫，」白兔邊說邊打開折疊的信紙，「不是信，是一首詩。」

「那是罪犯的筆跡嗎？」另一個陪審員問。「不是的，這真奇怪。」白兔說。（陪審員看起來糊里糊塗的。）

「他一定模仿了別人的筆跡。」國王說。（這時陪審員全都恍然大悟。）

紅心傑克開口了：「陛下，這不是我寫的，他們也不能證實是我寫的。最後並沒有署名。」

「如果你沒有簽名，」國王說，「只會讓事情更糟。你一定是故意惡作劇，否則你就該像誠實的人那樣，簽上你的名字。」

對此出現了一片掌聲，這是國王到目前為止所講的第一句聰明話。

「那就證明了他有罪。」皇后說。

愛麗絲卻說：「這證明不了什麼！你們甚至不知道這首詩寫的是什麼呀！」

「快讀！」國王命令道。

白兔戴上了眼鏡，問道「我該從哪裡開始呢？陛下。」

「從最前面開始吧，一直讀到最後，然後停下來。」國王鄭重地說。

以下是白兔所讀的詩句：

> 「他們告訴我你去找過她，
> 又跟他提起了我。
> 她給我良好的評價，
> 卻說我不會游泳。
>
> 他帶話給他們說我沒有走，
> （我們知道這並非撒謊。）
> 假如她讓事情推進，
> 你又當處於何種景況？

我給她一個，他們給他一雙，
你給我們三個或更多，
它們都從他那裡歸於你方，
雖然這些從前都是屬於我。

假如我或她掉進是非漩渦，
他相信你會將他們釋放，
正如我們曾被釋放那樣。

我的想法就是你已經成為，
（在她對此大發雷霆之前），
一個障礙橫在，
他、我們和它之間。

切勿告訴他：她最喜歡他們，
這必須永遠是個秘密。
切勿告訴其他人，
只有你知我知。」

「這是我們聽到的最重要的證據了，」國王搓著雙手說，「現在請陪審員……」

「如果有誰能解釋這些詩，我願意給他六便士，我不相信這些詩有任何意義。」愛麗絲這麼說。（她已經長得很大了，所以一點也不怕打斷國王的話。）

陪審員們都在石板上寫下：「她不相信這些詩有任何意義。」但是他們當中沒有一個試著解釋這些詩句。

「如果詩沒有任何意義，」國王說，「那就省了許多麻煩。你知道，我們並不是要找出意義，而且目前我也不懂。」國王說著，把這些詩攤開在膝上，用一隻眼睛看著說：「啊！我好像看出其中的端倪了，『說我不會游泳』，你不會游泳，是嗎？」國王對著紅心傑克說。

傑克傷心地搖搖頭說：「我像是會游泳嗎？」（他不可能會游泳，因為他是厚紙片做成的。）

「好，現在，」國王說，一面繼續嘟嚷著這些詩句：「『我們知道這並非撒謊』，這當然是指陪審員，『我給她一個，他們給他一雙』，看，這肯定是指偷的餡餅了，是嗎……」

「但後面說『它們都從他那裡歸於你方。』」愛麗絲說。

「是啊，它們都在，沒有比這更清楚的了。」國王手指著桌上的餡餅，得意地說。「那麼再看『在她對此大發雷霆之前，』親愛的，我想你沒有大發雷霆吧？」他對皇后說。

「從來沒有！」皇后怒吼著，把桌上的墨水瓶扔到了壁虎比爾身上。那個不幸的比爾已經不再用手指在紙板上寫字了，因為牠發現這樣是寫不出東西來的。不過現在牠又急忙沾著臉上的墨水開始寫字。

「說這句話與你的身分可不相符。」國王笑著環視著法庭說。但是法庭上一片寂靜。

「這句話一語雙關！」國王發怒了，而大家卻笑了起來。「讓陪審員做出裁決！」這大約是國王今天第二十次說出這句話了。

「不，不，」皇后說，「應該先處決再審判。」

「胡說八道，竟然先處決！」愛麗絲大聲說。

「閉嘴！」皇后氣得臉色都發紫了。

「我不要！」愛麗絲毫不示弱地回答。

「砍掉她的頭！」皇后聲嘶力竭地喊道。但是沒有人動作。

「誰理你！」愛麗絲說，這時她已經恢復到原來的身高了，「你們只不過是一副紙牌！」

這時，整副紙牌上升到空中，然後散落在她身上。她輕聲尖叫，又驚又怒。當她踢開紙牌的瞬間，發現自己躺在河岸邊，頭還枕在姊姊的腿上，而姊姊正輕輕地拿起落在她臉上的枯葉。

「醒醒吧，親愛的愛麗絲，」她姊姊說，「看看你睡了多久！」

「噢，我做了一個好奇怪的夢！」愛麗絲把自己記得的那些奇怪經歷告訴了姊姊，也就是你剛才讀過的那些。當她說完後，姊姊親了她，然後說：「真奇怪的夢，親愛的，現在快去喝茶吧，已經不早了。」於是愛麗絲站起來跑走了，一面跑，一面想著她做了

個很奇妙的夢！愛麗絲跑走後，她姊姊仍然坐在那裡，一隻手托著頭，望著夕陽，想著小愛麗絲和她夢中可能出現的奇幻經歷，然後自己進入了夢鄉。下面是她的夢：

起初，她夢見了小愛麗絲又一次用雙手抱住膝蓋，明亮而熱切地仰視著她。她聽到小愛麗絲的聲音，看到了她的頭微微一擺，把蓬亂的頭髮撩整齊了些，這是她常常見到的情景。當她聽著愛麗絲說話時，周圍的環境隨著妹妹夢中的那些奇異動物的出現而活躍了起來。

那隻白兔從她身邊匆匆經過，弄得腳下的草沙沙作響。那隻受到驚嚇的老鼠穿過鄰近的水池，濺起水花。她還能聽到三月兔跟朋友們享用著無止盡的佳餚時，碰擊茶杯的聲音，以及皇后嘶吼著下令要處決那些不幸的客人。還有伴隨著碗盤摔碎，豬寶寶在公爵夫人腿上打噴嚏的聲音。甚至還聽到鷹頭獅的尖叫，壁虎寫字時的沙沙聲，被制裁的天竺鼠的哽咽聲等等。這種種聲音彌漫在空中，還混雜著遠處傳來的假海龜那悲哀的啜泣聲。

於是她將身子坐正，閉上雙眼，想像自己真的來到了奇幻仙境。儘管她知道只要她再睜開眼睛，一切都仍會變回乏味的現實：草只是迎風作響，蘆葦的擺動使池水泛起漣漪。茶杯的碰擊聲實際是羊頸上的鈴鐺聲，皇后的尖叫起源于牧童的吆喝，豬寶寶的噴嚏聲、鷹頭獅的尖叫聲和各種奇怪聲音，原來只是農村中繁忙季節的各種喧鬧聲。而遠處耕牛的低吟，在夢中則變成了假海龜的哀泣聲。

最後，她描繪了這樣一幅場景：她的妹妹在往後的日子裡，將慢慢成長為一位淑女。而在她逐漸成熟的時期，也會保持她童年時的純潔珍愛之心。她會把她的小孩子們聚在身邊，講述許多奇異的故事，或許就是許久以前的這個夢遊奇境，使他們眼睛發亮而急切地要聽故事。她將能感受孩子們天真的憂愁，也會從他們的天真快樂中找到樂趣，而這一切會讓她回憶起自己的童年，以及那愉快的夏日。

Chapter *1*

Down the Rabbit-Hole

Down, down, down. Would the fall never come to an end! "I wonder how many miles I've fallen by this time?"
she said aloud. "I must be getting somewhere near the centre of the earth.

Alice was beginning to get very tired of sitting by her sister on the bank, and of having nothing to do: once or twice she had peeped into the book her sister was reading, but it had no pictures or conversations in it, "and what is the use of a book," thought Alice, "without pictures or conversations?"

So she was considering in her own mind (as well as she could, for the hot day made her feel very sleepy and stupid), whether the pleasure of making a daisy-chain would be worth the trouble of getting up and picking the daisies, when suddenly a white rabbit with pink eyes ran close by her.

There was nothing so *very* remarkable in that; nor did Alice think it so *very* much out of the way to hear the Rabbit say to itself, "Oh dear! Oh dear! I shall be late!" (When she thought it over afterwards, it occurred to her that she ought to have wondered at this, but at the time it all seemed quite natural.) But when the Rabbit actually *took a watch out of its waistcoat-pocket,* and

looked at it, and then hurried on, Alice started to her feet, for it flashed across her mind that she had never before seen a rabbit with either a waistcoat-pocket, or a watch to take out of it, and burning with curiosity, she ran across the field after it, and fortunately was just in time to see it pop down a large rabbit-hole under the hedge.

In another moment down went Alice after it, never once considering how in the world she was to get out again.

The rabbit-hole went straight on like a tunnel for some way, and then dipped suddenly down, so suddenly that Alice had not a moment to think about stopping herself before she found herself falling down a very deep well.

Either the well was very deep, or she fell very slowly, for she had plenty of time as she went down to look about her and to wonder what was going to happen next. First, she tried to look down and make out what she was coming to, but it was too dark to see anything; then she looked at the sides of the well, and noticed that they were filled with cupboards and book-shelves; here and there she saw maps and pictures hung upon pegs. She took down a jar from one of the shelves as she passed; it was labeled "ORANGE MARMALADE", but to her great disappointment it was empty: she did not like to drop the jar for fear of killing somebody, so managed to put it into one of the cupboards as she fell past it.

"Well!" thought Alice to herself, "after such a fall as this, I shall think nothing of tumbling down stairs! How brave they'll all think me at home! Why, I wouldn't say anything about it, even if I fell off the top of the house!" (Which was very likely true.)

Down, down, down. Would the fall *never* come to an end! "I wonder how many miles I've fallen by this time?" she said aloud. "I must be getting somewhere near the centre of the earth. Let me see: that would be four thousand miles down, I think –" (for, you see, Alice had learnt several things of this sort in her lessons in the schoolroom, and though this was not a *very* good opportunity for showing off her knowledge, as there was no one to listen to her, still it was good practice to say it over) " – yes, that's about the right distance – but then I wonder what Latitude or Longitude I've got to?" (Alice had no idea what Latitude was, or Longitude either, but thought they were nice grand words to say.)

Presently she began again. "I wonder if I shall fall right *through* the earth! How funny it'll seem to come out among the people that walk with their heads downward! The Antipathies, I think – " (she was rather glad there was no one listening, this time, as it didn't sound at all the right word) " – but I shall have to ask them what the name of the country is, you know. Please, Ma'am, is this New Zealand or Australia?" (And she tried to curtsey as she spoke – fancy *curtseying* as you're falling through the air! Do you think you could manage it?) "And what an ignorant little girl she'll think me for asking! No, it'll never do to ask: perhaps I shall see it written up somewhere."

Down, down, down. There was nothing else to do, so Alice soon began talking again. "Dinah'll miss me very much to-night, I should think!" (Dinah was the cat.) "I hope they'll remember her saucer of milk at tea-time. Dinah, my dear! I wish you were down here with me! There are no mice in the air, I'm afraid, but you might catch a bat, and that's very like a mouse, you know. But do cats eat bats, I wonder?" And here Alice began to get rather sleepy, and went on saying to herself, in a dreamy sort of way, "Do cats eat bats? Do cats eat bats?" and sometimes, "Do bats eat cats?" for, you see, as she couldn't answer either question, it didn't much matter which way she put it. She felt that she was dozing off, and had just begun to dream that she was walking hand in hand with Dinah, and saying to her very earnestly, "Now, Dinah, tell me the truth: did you ever eat a bat?" when suddenly, thump! thump! down she came upon a heap of sticks and dry leaves, and the fall was over.

Alice was not a bit hurt, and she jumped up on to her feet in a moment: she looked up, but it was all dark overhead; before her was another long passage, and the White Rabbit was still in sight, hurrying down it. There was not a moment to be lost: away went Alice like the wind, and was just in time to hear it say, as it turned a corner, "Oh my ears and whiskers, how late it's getting!" She was close behind it when she turned the corner, but the Rabbit was no longer to be seen: she found herself in a long, low hall, which was lit up by a row of lamps hanging from the roof.

There were doors all round the hall, but they were all locked; and when Alice had been all the way down one side and up the other, trying every door, she walked sadly down the middle, wondering how she was ever to get out again.

Suddenly she came upon a little three-legged table, all made of solid glass; there was nothing on it except a tiny golden key, and Alice's first thought was that it might belong to one of the doors of the hall; but, alas! either the locks were too large, or the key was too small, but at any rate it would not open any of them. However, on the second time round, she came upon a low curtain she had not noticed before, and behind it was a little door about fifteen inches high: she tried the little golden key in the lock, and to her great delight it fitted!

Alice opened the door and found that it led into a small passage, not much larger than a rat-hole: she knelt down and looked along the passage into the loveliest garden you ever saw. How she longed to get out of that dark hall, and wander about among those beds of bright flowers and those cool fountains, but she could not even

get her head through the doorway; "and even if my head *would* go through," thought poor Alice, "it would be of very little use without my shoulders. Oh, how I wish I could shut up like a telescope! I think I could, if only I knew how to begin." For, you see, so many out-of-the-way things had happened lately, that Alice had begun to think that very few things indeed were really impossible.

There seemed to be no use in waiting by the little door, so she went back to the table, half hoping she might find another key on it, or at any rate a book of rules for shutting people up like telescopes: this time she found a little bottle on it, ("which certainly was not here before," said Alice), and round the neck of the bottle was a paper label, with the words "DRINK ME" beautifully printed on it in large letters.

It was all very well to say "Drink me," but the wise little Alice was not going to do that in a hurry. "No, I'll look first," she said, "and see whether it's marked *'poison'* or not": for she had read several nice little histories about children who had got burnt, and eaten up by wild beasts and other unpleasant things, all because they *would* not remember the simple rules their friends had taught them: such as, that a red-hot poker will burn you if you hold it too long; and that if you cut your finger *very* deeply with a knife, it usually bleeds; and she had never forgotten that, if you drink much from a bottle marked "poison," it is almost certain to disagree with you, sooner or later.

However, this bottle was *not* marked "*poison*," so Alice ventured to taste it, and finding it very nice (it had, in fact, a sort of mixed flavour of cherry-tart, custard, pine-apple, roast turkey, toffee, and hot buttered toast) , she very soon finished it off.

"What a curious feeling!" said Alice, "I must be shutting up like a telescope."

And so it was indeed: she was now only ten inches high, and her face brightened up at the thought that she was now the right size for going through the little door into that lovely garden. First, however, she waited for a few minutes to see if she was going to shrink any further: she felt a little nervous about this, "for it might end, you know," said Alice to herself, "in my going out altogether, like a candle. I wonder what I should be like then?" And she tried to fancy what the flame of a candle is like after the candle is blown out, for she could not remember ever having seen such a thing.

After a while, finding that nothing more happened, she decided on going into the garden at once; but, alas for poor Alice! when she got to the door, she found she had forgotten the little golden key, and when she went back to the table for it, she found she could not possibly reach it: she could see it quite plainly through the glass, and she tried her best to climb up one of the legs of the table, but it was too slippery; and when she had tired herself out with trying, the poor little thing sat down and cried.

"Come, there's no use in crying like that!" said Alice to herself, rather sharply, "I advise you to leave off this minute!" She generally gave herself very good advice (though she very seldom followed it), and sometimes she scolded herself so severely as to bring tears into her eyes; and once she remembered trying to box her own ears for having cheated herself in a game of croquet she was playing against herself, for this curious child was very fond of pretending to be two people. "But it's no use now," thought poor Alice, "to pretend to be two people! Why, there's hardly enough of me left to make *one* respectable person!"

Soon her eye fell on a little glass box that was lying under the table: she opened it, and found in it a very small cake, on which the words "EAT ME" were beautifully marked in currants. "Well, I'll eat it," said Alice, "and if it makes me grow larger, I can reach the key; and if it makes me grow smaller, I can creep under the door; so either way I'll get into the garden, and I don't care which happens!"

She ate a little bit, and said anxiously to herself, "Which way? Which way?" holding her hand on the top of her head to feel which way it was growing, and she was quite surprised to find that she remained the same size. To be sure, this is what generally happens when one eats cake, but Alice had got so much into the way of expecting nothing but out-of-the-way things to happen, that it seemed quite dull and stupid for life to go on in the common way.

So she set to work, and very soon finished off the cake.

Chapter 2

The Pool of Tears

"Dear, dear! How queer everything is to-day! And yesterday things went on just as usual. I wonder if I've been changed in the night? Let me think: was I the same when I got up this morning? I almost think I can remember feeling a little different. But if I'm not the same, the next question is, Who in the world am I? Ah, that's the great puzzle!"

"Curiouser and curiouser!" cried Alice (she was so much surprised, that for the moment she quite forgot how to speak good English). "Now I'm opening out like the largest telescope that ever was! Good-bye feet!" (for when she looked down at her feet, they seemed to be almost out of sight, they were getting so far off). "Oh, my poor little feet, I wonder who will put on your shoes and stockings for you now, dears? I'm sure *I* shan't be able! I shall be a great deal too far off to trouble myself about you: you must manage the best way you can – but I must be kind to them," thought Alice, "or perhaps they won't walk the way I want to go! Let me see: I'll give them a new pair of boots every Christmas."

And she went on planning to herself how she would manage it. "They must go by the carrier," she thought; "and how funny it'll seem, sending presents to one's own feet! And how odd the directions will look!

Alice's Right Foot, Esq.,

Hearthrug,
near the Fender,
(with Alice's love.)

Oh dear, what nonsense I'm talking!"

Just then her head struck against the roof of the hall: in fact she was now more than nine feet high, and she at once took up the little golden key and hurried off to the garden door.

Poor Alice! It was as much as she could do, lying down on one side, to look through into the garden with one eye; but to get through was more hopeless than ever: she sat down and began to cry again.

"You ought to be ashamed of yourself," said Alice, "a great girl like you." (she might well say this), "to go on crying in this way! Stop this moment, I tell you!" But she went on all the same, shedding gallons of tears, until there was a large pool all round her, about four inches deep and reaching half down the hall.

After a time she heard a little pattering of feet in the distance, and she hastily dried her eyes to see what was coming. It was the White Rabbit returning, splendidly dressed, with a pair of white kid gloves in one hand and a large fan in the other: he came trotting along in a great hurry, muttering to himself as he came, "Oh! the Duchess, the Duchess! Oh! won't she be savage if I've kept her waiting!" Alice felt so desperate that she was ready to ask help of any one; so, when the Rabbit came near her, she began, in a low, timid voice, "If you please, sir – " The Rabbit started violently, dropped the white kid gloves and the fan, and skurried away into the darkness as hard as he could go.

Alice took up the fan and gloves, and, as the hall was very hot, she kept fanning herself all the time she went on talking. "Dear, dear! How queer everything is to-day! And yesterday things went on just as usual. I wonder if I've been changed in the night? Let me think: *was* I the same when I got up this morning? I almost think I can remember feeling a little different. But if I'm not the same, the next question is, Who in the world am I? Ah, *that's* the great puzzle!" And she began thinking over all the children she knew that were of the same age as herself, to see if she could have been changed for any of them.

"I'm sure I'm not Ada," she said, "for her hair goes in such long ringlets, and mine doesn't go in ringlets at all; and I'm sure I can't be Mabel, for I know all sorts of things, and she, oh! she knows such a very little! Besides, *she's* she, and *I'm* I, and – oh dear, how puzzling it all is! I'll try if I know all the things I used to know. Let me see: four times five is twelve, and four times six is thirteen, and four times seven is – oh dear! I shall never get to twenty at that rate! However, the Multiplication Table doesn't signify: let's try Geography. London is the capital of Paris, and Paris is the capital of Rome, and Rome – no, *that's* all wrong, I'm certain! I must have been changed for Mabel! I'll try and say *'How doth the little* – ' " and she crossed her hands on her lap as if she were saying lessons, and began to repeat it, but her voice sounded hoarse and strange, and the words did not come the same as they used to do: –

"How doth the little crocodile

Improve his shining tail,
And pour the waters of the Nile
On every golden scale!

How cheerfully he seems to grin,
How neatly spread his claws,
And welcome little fishes in
With gently smiling jaws!"

"I'm sure those are not the right words," said poor Alice, and her eyes filled with tears again as she went on, "I must be Mabel after all, and I shall have to go and live in that poky little house, and have next to no toys to play with, and oh! ever so many lessons to learn! No, I've made up my mind about it; if I'm Mabel, I'll stay down here! It'll be no use their putting their heads down and saying "Come up again, dear!" I shall only look up and say "Who am I then? Tell me that first, and then, if I like being that person, I'll come up: if not, I'll stay down here till I'm somebody else" – but, oh dear!" cried Alice, with a sudden burst of tears, "I do wish they *would* put their heads down! I am so *very* tired of being all alone here!"

As she said this she looked down at her hands, and was surprised to see that she had put on one of the Rabbit's little white kid gloves while she was talking. "How *can* I have done that?" she thought. "I must be growing small again." She got up and went to the table to measure herself by it, and found that, as nearly as she could guess, she was now about two feet high, and was going on shrinking rapidly: she soon found out that the cause of this was the fan she was holding, and she dropped it hastily, just in time to avoid shrinking away altogether.

"That *was* a narrow escape!" said Alice, a good deal frightened at the sudden change, but very glad to find herself still in existence. "And now for the garden!" and she ran with all speed back to the little door: but, alas! the little door was shut again, and the little golden key was lying on the glass table as before, "and things are worse than ever," thought the poor child, "for I never was so small as this before, never! And I declare it's too bad, that it is!"

As she said these words her foot slipped, and in another moment, splash! she was up to her chin in salt water. Her first idea was that she had somehow fallen into the sea, "and in that case I can go back by railway," she said to herself (Alice had been to the seaside once in her life, and had come to the general conclusion, that wherever you go to on the English coast you find a number of bathing machines in the sea, some children digging in the sand with wooden spades, then a row of lodging houses, and behind them a railway station.) However, she soon made out that she was in the pool of tears which she had wept when she was nine feet high.

"I wish I hadn't cried so much!" said Alice, as she swam about, trying to find her way out. "I shall be punished for it now, I suppose, by being drowned in my own tears! That *will* be a queer thing, to be sure! However, everything is queer to-day."

Just then she heard something splashing about in the pool a

little way off, and she swam nearer to make out what it was: at first she thought it must be a walrus or hippopotamus, but then she remembered how small she was now, and she soon made out that it was only a mouse that had slipped in like herself.

"Would it be of any use, now," thought Alice, "to speak to this mouse? Everything is so out-of-the-way down here, that I should think very likely it can talk: at any rate, there's no harm in trying." So she began: "O Mouse, do you know the way out of this pool? I am very tired of swimming about here, O Mouse!" (Alice thought this must be the right way of speaking to a mouse: she had never done such a thing before, but she remembered having seen in her brother's Latin Grammar, "A mouse – of a mouse – to a mouse – a mouse – O mouse!") The Mouse looked at her rather inquisitively, and seemed to her to wink with one of its little eyes, but it said nothing.

"Perhaps it doesn't understand English," thought Alice; "I daresay it's a French mouse, come over with William the Conqueror." (For, with all her knowledge of history, Alice had no very clear notion how long ago anything had happened.) So she began again: "Où est ma chatte?" which was the first sentence in her French lesson-book. The Mouse gave a sudden leap out of the water, and seemed to quiver all over with fright. "Oh, I beg your pardon!" cried Alice hastily, afraid that she had hurt the poor animal's feelings. "I quite forgot you didn't like cats."

"Not like cats!" cried the Mouse, in a shrill, passionate voice. "Would *you* like cats if you were me?"

"Well, perhaps not," said Alice in a soothing tone: "don't be angry about it. And yet I wish I could show you our cat Dinah: I think you'd take a fancy to cats if you could only see her. She is such a dear quiet thing," Alice went on, half to herself, as she swam lazily about in the pool, "and she sits purring so nicely by the fire, licking her paws and washing her face – and she is such a nice soft thing to nurse – and she's such a capital one for catching mice – oh, I beg your pardon!" cried Alice again, for this time the Mouse was bristling all over, and she felt certain it must be really offended. "We won't talk about her any more if you'd rather not."

"We indeed!" cried the Mouse, who was trembling down to the

end of his tail. "As if *I* would talk on such a subject! Our family always hated cats: nasty, low, vulgar things! Don't let me hear the name again!"

"I won't indeed!" said Alice, in a great hurry to change the subject of conversation. "Are you – are you fond – of – of dogs?" The Mouse did not answer, so Alice went on eagerly: "There is such a nice little dog near our house I should like to show you! A little bright-eyed terrier, you know, with oh, such long curly brown hair! And it'll fetch things when you throw them, and it'll sit up and beg for its dinner, and all sorts of things – I can't remember half of them – and it belongs to a farmer, you know, and he says it's so useful, it's worth a hundred pounds! He says it kills all the rats and – oh dear!" cried Alice in a sorrowful tone, "I'm afraid I've offended it again!" For the Mouse was swimming away from her as hard as it could go, and making quite a commotion in the pool as it went.

So she called softly after it, "Mouse dear! Do come back again, and we won't talk about cats or dogs either, if you don't like them!" When the Mouse heard this, it turned round and swam slowly back to her: its face was quite pale (with passion, Alice thought), and it said in a low trembling voice, "Let us get to the shore, and then I'll tell you my history, and you'll understand why it is I hate cats and dogs."

It was high time to go, for the pool was getting quite crowded with the birds and animals that had fallen into it: there were a Duck and a Dodo, a Lory and an Eaglet, and several other curious creatures. Alice led the way, and the whole party swam to the shore.

Chapter 3

*A Caucus-Race
and
a Long Tale*

"What I was going to say," said the Dodo in an offended tone, "was, that the best thing to get us dry would be a Caucus-race."

"What is a Caucus-race?" said Alice; not that she wanted much to know, but the Dodo had paused as if it thought that somebody ought to speak, and no one else seemed inclined to say anything.

"Why," said the Dodo, "the best way to explain it is to do it."

They were indeed a queer-looking party that assembled on the bank – the birds with draggled feathers, the animals with their fur clinging close to them, and all dripping wet, cross, and uncomfortable.

The first question of course was, how to get dry again: they had a consultation about this, and after a few minutes it seemed quite natural to Alice to find herself talking familiarly with them, as if she had known them all her life. Indeed, she had quite a long argument with the Lory, who at last turned sulky, and would only say, "I am older than you, and must know better"; and this Alice would not allow without knowing how old it was, and, as the Lory positively refused to tell its age, there was no more to be said.

At last the Mouse, who seemed to be a person of authority among them, called out, "Sit down, all of you, and listen to me! I'll soon make you dry enough!" They all sat down at once, in a large ring, with the Mouse in the middle. Alice kept her eyes anxiously fixed on it, for she felt sure she would catch a bad cold if she did not get dry very soon.

"Ahem!" said the Mouse with an important air, "are you all ready? This is the driest thing I know. Silence all round, if you please! 'William the Conqueror, whose cause was favoured by the pope, was soon submitted to by the English, who wanted leaders, and had been of late much accustomed to usurpation and conquest. Edwin and Morcar, the earls of Mercia and Northumbria – '"

"Ugh!" said the Lory, with a shiver.

"I beg your pardon?" said the Mouse, frowning, but very politely.

"Did you speak?"

"Not I!" said the Lory hastily.

"I thought you did," said the Mouse. "I proceed. 'Edwin and Morcar, the earls of Mercia and Northumbria, declared for him; and even Stigand, the patriotic archbishop of Canterbury, found it advisable – '"

"Found *what*?" said the Duck.

"Found *it*," the Mouse replied rather crossly; "of course you know what 'it' means."

"I know what 'it' means well enough, when I find a thing," said the Duck: "it's generally a frog or a worm. The question is, what did the archbishop find?"

The Mouse did not notice this question, but hurriedly went on, "' – found it advisable to go with Edgar Atheling to meet William and offer him the crown. William's conduct at first was moderate. But the insolence of his Normans – ' How are you getting on now, my dear?"

it continued, turning to Alice as it spoke.

"As wet as ever," said Alice in a melancholy tone: "it doesn't seem to dry me at all."

"In that case," said the Dodo solemnly, rising to its feet, "I move that the meeting adjourn, for the immediate adoption of more energetic remedies – "

"Speak English!" said the Eaglet. "I don't know the meaning of half those long words, and, what's more, I don't believe you do either!" And the Eaglet bent down its head to hide a smile: some of the other birds tittered audibly.

"What I was going to say," said the Dodo in an offended tone, "was, that the best thing to get us dry would be a Caucus-race."

"What *is* a Caucus-race?" said Alice; not that she wanted much to know, but the Dodo had paused as if it thought that *somebody* ought to speak, and no one else seemed inclined to say anything.

"Why," said the Dodo, "the best way to explain it is to do it." (And as you might like to try the thing yourself, some winter day, I will tell you how the Dodo managed it.)

First it marked out a race-course, in a sort of circle ("the exact shape doesn't matter," it said), and then all the party were placed along the course, here and there. There was no "One, two, three, and away," but they began running when they liked, and left off when they liked, so that it was not easy to know when the race was over. However, when they had been running half an hour or so, and were quite dry again, the Dodo suddenly called out "The race is over!" and they all crowded round it, panting, and asking, "But who has won?"

This question the Dodo could not answer without a great deal of thought, and it sat for a long time with one finger pressed upon its forehead (the position in which you usually see Shakespeare, in the pictures of him), while the rest waited in silence. At last the Dodo said, "*everybody* has won, and all must have prizes."

"But who is to give the prizes?" quite a chorus of voices asked.

"Why, *she*, of course," said the Dodo, pointing to Alice with one finger; and the whole party at once crowded round her, calling out in a confused way:

"Prizes! Prizes!"

Alice had no idea what to do, and in despair she put her hand in her pocket, and pulled out a box of comfits (luckily the salt water had not got into it), and handed them round as prizes. There was exactly one a-piece all round.

"But she must have a prize herself, you know," said the Mouse.

"Of course," the Dodo replied very gravely. "What else have you got in your pocket?" he went on, turning to Alice.

"Only a thimble," said Alice sadly.

179

"Hand it over here," said the Dodo.

Then they all crowded round her once more, while the Dodo solemnly presented the thimble, saying "We beg your acceptance of this elegant thimble"; and, when it had finished this short speech, they all cheered.

Alice thought the whole thing very absurd, but they all looked so grave that she did not dare to laugh; and, as she could not think of anything to say, she simply bowed, and took the thimble, looking as solemn as she could.

The next thing was to eat the comfits: this caused some noise and confusion, as the large birds complained that they could not taste theirs, and the small ones choked and had to be patted on the back. However, it was over at last, and they sat down again in a ring, and begged the Mouse to tell them something more.

"You promised to tell me your history, you know," said Alice, "and why it is you hate – C and D," she added in a whisper, half afraid that it would be offended again.

"Mine is a long and sad tale!" said the Mouse, turning to Alice, and sighing.

"It *is* a long tail, certainly," said Alice, looking down with wonder at the Mouse's tail; "but why do you call it sad?" And she kept on puzzling about it while the Mouse was speaking, so that her idea of the tale was something like this: –

"Fury said to a mouse, that he
met in the house,'Let us both
go to law: I will prose-cute
you. – Come, I'll take no
de-nial; We must have
a trial: For really
this morning I've
nothing to do.'
Said the mouse
to the cur, 'Such
a trial, dear
sir,With no jury
or judge, would
be wasting our
breath.''I'll
be judge, I'll
be jury,' said
cunning old
Fury:'I'll
try the whole
cause, and
condemn
you to
death.' "

"You are not attending!" said the Mouse to Alice severely. "What are you thinking of?"

"I beg your pardon," said Alice very humbly: "you had got to the fifth bend, I think?"

"I had *not*!" cried the Mouse, sharply and very angrily.

"A knot!" said Alice, always ready to make herself useful, and looking anxiously about her. "Oh, do let me help to undo it!"

"I shall do nothing of the sort," said the Mouse, getting up and walking away. "You insult me by talking such nonsense!"

"I didn't mean it!" pleaded poor Alice. "But you're so easily offended, you know!"

The Mouse only growled in reply.

"Please come back and finish your story!" Alice called after it; and the others all joined in chorus, "Yes, please do!" but the Mouse only shook its head impatiently, and walked a little quicker.

"What a pity it wouldn't stay!" sighed the Lory, as soon as it was quite out of sight; and an old Crab took the opportunity of saying to her daughter "Ah, my dear! Let this be a lesson to you never to lose *your* temper!"

"Hold your tongue, Ma!" said the young Crab, a little snappishly. "You're enough to try the patience of an oyster!"

"I wish I had our Dinah here, I know I do!" said Alice aloud, addressing nobody in particular. "*She'd* soon fetch it back!"

"And who is Dinah, if I might venture to ask the question?" said the Lory.

Alice replied eagerly, for she was always ready to talk about her pet: "Dinah's our cat. And she's such a capital one for catching mice you can't think! And oh, I wish you could see her after the birds! Why, she'll eat a little bird as soon as look at it!"

This speech caused a remarkable sensation among the party. Some of the birds hurried off at once. One old Magpie began wrapping itself up very carefully, remarking, "I really must be getting home; the night-air doesn't suit my throat!" and a Canary called out in a trembling voice to its children, "Come away, my dears! It's high time you were all in bed!" On various pretexts they all moved off, and Alice was soon left alone.

"I wish I hadn't mentioned Dinah!" she said to herself in a melancholy tone. "Nobody seems to like her, down here, and I'm sure she's the best cat in the world! Oh, my dear Dinah! I wonder if I shall ever see you any more!" And here poor Alice began to cry again, for she felt very lonely and low-spirited. In a little while, however, she again heard a little pattering of footsteps in the distance, and she looked up eagerly, half hoping that the Mouse had changed his mind, and was coming back to finish his story.

Chapter 4

The Rabbit
Sends in a Little Bill

"…When I used to read fairy-tales, I fancied that kind of thing never happened, and now here I am in the middle of one! There ought to be a book written about me, that there ought! And when I grow up, I'll write one —"

It was the White Rabbit, trotting slowly back again, and looking anxiously about as it went, as if it had lost something; and she heard it muttering to itself "The Duchess! The Duchess! Oh my dear paws! Oh my fur and whiskers! She'll get me executed, as sure as ferrets are ferrets! Where *can* I have dropped them, I wonder?" Alice guessed in a moment that it was looking for the fan and the pair of white kid gloves, and she very good-naturedly began hunting about for them, but they were nowhere to be seen – everything seemed to have changed since her swim in the pool, and the great hall, with the glass table and the little door, had vanished completely.

Very soon the Rabbit noticed Alice, as she went hunting about, and called out to her in an angry tone, "Why, Mary Ann, what *are* you doing out here? Run home this moment, and fetch me a pair of gloves and a fan! Quick, now!" And Alice was so much frightened that she ran off at once in the direction it pointed to, without trying to explain the mistake it had made.

"He took me for his housemaid," she said to herself as she ran. "How surprised he'll be when he finds out who I am! But I'd better take him his fan and gloves – that is, if I can find them." As she said this, she came upon a neat little house, on the door of which was a bright brass plate with the name "W. RABBIT" engraved upon it. She went in without knocking, and hurried upstairs, in great fear lest she should meet the real Mary Ann, and be turned out of the house before she had found the fan and gloves.

"How queer it seems," Alice said to herself, "to be going messages for a rabbit! I suppose Dinah'll be sending me on messages next!" And she began fancying the sort of thing that would happen: "Miss Alice! Come here directly, and get ready for your walk!" "Coming in a minute, nurse! But I've got to see that the mouse doesn't get out." "Only I don't think," Alice went on, "that they'd let Dinah stop in the house if it began ordering people about like that!"

By this time she had found her way into a tidy little room with a table in the window, and on it (as she had hoped) a fan and two or three pairs of tiny white kid gloves: she took up the fan and a pair of the gloves, and was just going to leave the room, when her eye fell upon a little bottle that stood near the looking-glass. There was no label this time with the words "DRINK ME," but nevertheless she uncorked it and put it to her lips. "I know *something* interesting is sure to happen," she said to herself, "whenever I eat or drink anything; so

187

I'll just see what this bottle does. I do hope it'll make me grow large again, for really I'm quite tired of being such a tiny little thing!"

It did so indeed, and much sooner than she had expected: before she had drunk half the bottle, she found her head pressing against the ceiling, and had to stoop to save her neck from being broken. She hastily put down the bottle, saying to herself "That's quite enough – I hope I shan't grow any more – As it is, I can't get out at the door – I do wish I hadn't drunk quite so much!"

Alas! It was too late to wish that! She went on growing, and growing, and very soon had to kneel down on the floor: in another minute there was not even room for this, and she tried the effect of lying down with one elbow against the door, and the other arm curled round her head. Still she went on growing, and, as a last resource, she put one arm out of the window, and one foot up the chimney, and said to herself "Now I can do no more, whatever happens. What *will* become of me?"

Luckily for Alice, the little magic bottle had now had its full effect, and she grew no larger: still it was very uncomfortable, and, as there seemed to be no sort of chance of her ever getting out of the room again, no wonder she felt unhappy.

"It was much pleasanter at home," thought poor Alice, "when one wasn't always growing larger and smaller, and being ordered about by mice and rabbits. I almost wish I hadn't gone down that rabbit-hole – and yet – and yet – it's rather curious, you know, this sort of life! I do wonder what *can* have happened to me! When I used to read fairy-tales, I fancied that kind of thing never happened, and now here I am in the middle of one! There ought to be a book written about me, that there ought! And when I grow up, I'll write one – but I'm grown up now," she added in a sorrowful tone; "at least there's no room to grow up any more *here.*"

"But then," thought Alice, "shall I *never* get any older than I am now? That'll be a comfort, one way – never to be an old woman – but then – always to have lessons to learn! Oh, I shouldn't like *that*!"

"Oh, you foolish Alice!" she answered herself. "How can you learn lessons in here? Why, there's hardly room for you, and no room at all for any lesson-books!"

And so she went on, taking first one side and then the other, and making quite a conversation of it altogether; but after a few minutes she heard a voice outside, and stopped to listen.

"Mary Ann! Mary Ann!" said the voice. "Fetch me my gloves this moment!" Then came a little pattering of feet on the stairs. Alice knew it was the Rabbit coming to look for her, and she trembled till she shook the house, quite forgetting that she was now about a thousand times as large as the Rabbit, and had no reason to be afraid of it.

Presently the Rabbit came up to the door, and tried to open it; but, as the door opened inwards, and Alice's elbow was pressed hard against it, that attempt proved a failure. Alice heard it say to itself "Then I'll go round and get in at the window."

"*That* you won't" thought Alice, and, after waiting till she fancied she heard the Rabbit just under the window, she suddenly spread out her hand, and made a snatch in the air. She did not get hold of anything, but she heard a little shriek and a fall, and a crash of broken glass, from which she concluded that it was just possible it had fallen into a cucumber-frame, or something of the sort.

Next came an angry voice – the Rabbit's – "Pat! Pat! Where are you?" And then a voice she had never heard before, "Sure then I'm here! Digging for apples, yer honour!"

"Digging for apples, indeed!" said the Rabbit angrily. "Here! Come and help me out of *this!*" (Sounds of more broken glass.)

"Now tell me, Pat, what's that in the window?"

"Sure, it's an arm, yer honour!" (He pronounced it "arrum.")

"An arm, you goose! Who ever saw one that size? Why, it fills the whole window!"

"Sure, it does, yer honour: but it's an arm for all that."

"Well, it's got no business there, at any rate: go and take it away!"

There was a long silence after this, and Alice could only hear whispers now and then; such as, "Sure, I don't like it, yer honour, at all, at all!" "Do as I tell you, you coward!" and at last she spread out her hand again, and made another snatch in the air. This time there were *two* little shrieks, and more sounds of broken glass. "What a number of cucumber-frames there must be!" thought Alice. "I wonder what they'll do next! As for pulling me out of the window, I only wish they *could*! I'm sure I don't want to stay in here any longer!"

She waited for some time without hearing anything more: at last came a rumbling of little cartwheels, and the sound of a good many voices all talking together: she made out the words: "Where's the other ladder? – Why, I hadn't to bring but one; Bill's got the other – Bill! fetch it here, lad! – Here, put 'em up at this corner – No, tie 'em together first – they don't reach half high enough yet – Oh! they'll do well enough; don't be particular – Here, Bill! catch hold of this rope – Will the roof bear? – Mind that loose slate – Oh, it's coming down! Heads below!" (a loud crash) – "Now, who did that? – It was Bill, I fancy – Who's to go down the chimney? – Nay, *I* shan't! *You* do it! – That I won't then! – Bill's to go down – Here, Bill! the master says you're to go down the chimney!"

"Oh! So Bill's got to come down the chimney, has he?" said Alice to herself. "Shy, they seem to put everything upon Bill! I wouldn't be in Bill's place for a good deal: this fireplace is narrow, to be sure; but I think I can kick a little!"

She drew her foot as far down the chimney as she could, and waited till she heard a little animal (she couldn't guess of what sort it was) scratching and scrambling about in the chimney close above her: then, saying to herself "This is Bill," she gave one sharp kick, and waited to see what would happen next. The first thing she heard was a general chorus of "There goes Bill!" then the Rabbit's voice along: "Catch him, you by the hedge!" – then silence, and then another confusion of voices – "Hold up his head – Brandy now – Don't choke him – How was it, old fellow? What happened to you? Tell us all about it!"

Last came a little feeble, squeaking voice. ("That's Bill," thought Alice.) "*Well*, I hardly know – No more, thank ye; I'm better now – but I'm a deal too flustered to tell you – all I know is, something comes at me like a Jack-in-the-box, and up I goes like a sky-rocket!"

"So you did, old fellow!" said the others.

"We must burn the house down!" said the Rabbit's voice; and Alice called out as loud as she could:

"If you do. I'll set Dinah at you!"

There was a dead silence instantly, and Alice thought to herself, "I wonder what they will do next! If they had any sense, they'd take the roof off." After a minute or two, they began moving about again, and Alice heard the Rabbit say, "A barrowful will do, to begin with."

"A barrowful of *what*?" thought Alice; but she had not long to doubt, for the next moment a shower of little pebbles came rattling in

at the window, and some of them hit her in the face. "I'll put a stop to this," she said to herself, and shouted out: "You'd better not do that again!" which produced another dead silence.

Alice noticed with some surprise that the pebbles were all turning into little cakes as they lay on the floor, and a bright idea came into her head.

"If I eat one of these cakes," she thought, "it's sure to make some change in my size; and as it can't possibly make me larger, it must make me smaller, I suppose."

So she swallowed one of the cakes, and was delighted to find that she began shrinking directly. As soon as she was small enough to get through the door, she ran out of the house, and found quite a crowd of little animals and birds waiting outside. The poor little Lizard, Bill, was in the middle, being held up by two guinea-pigs, who were giving it something out of a bottle. They all made a rush at Alice the moment she appeared; but she ran off as hard as she could, and soon found herself safe in a thick wood.

"The first thing I've got to do," said Alice to herself, as she wandered about in the wood, "is to grow to my right size again; and the second thing is to find my way into that lovely garden. I think that

193

will be the best plan."

It sounded an excellent plan, no doubt, and very neatly and simply arranged; the only difficulty was, that she had not the smallest idea how to set about it; and while she was peering about anxiously among the trees, a little sharp bark just over her head made her look up in a great hurry.

An enormous puppy was looking down at her with large round eyes, and feebly stretching out one paw, trying to touch her. "Poor little thing!" said Alice, in a coaxing tone, and she tried hard to whistle to it; but she was terribly frightened all the time at the thought that it might be hungry, in which case it would be very likely to eat her up in spite of all her coaxing.

Hardly knowing what she did, she picked up a little bit of stick, and held it out to the puppy; whereupon the puppy jumped into the air off all its feet at once, with a yelp of delight, and rushed at the stick, and made believe to worry it; then Alice dodged behind a great thistle, to keep herself from being run over; and the moment she appeared on the other side, the puppy made another rush at the stick, and tumbled head over heels in its hurry to get hold of it; then Alice, thinking it was very like having a game of play with a cart-horse, and expecting every moment to be trampled under its feet, ran round the thistle again; then the puppy began a series of short charges at the stick, running a very little way forwards each time and a long way back, and barking hoarsely all the while, till at last it sat down a good way off, panting, with its tongue hanging out of its mouth, and its great eyes half shut.

This seemed to Alice a good opportunity for making her escape; so she set off at once, and ran till she was quite tired and out of breath, and till the puppy's bark sounded quite faint in the distance. "And yet what a dear little puppy it was!" said Alice, as she leant against a buttercup to rest herself, and fanned herself with one of the leaves: "I should have liked teaching it tricks very much, if – if I'd only been the right size to do it! Oh dear! I'd nearly forgotten that I've got to grow up again! Let me see – how *is* it to be managed? I suppose I ought to eat or drink something or other; but the great question is, what?"

The great question certainly was, what? Alice looked all round her at the flowers and the blades of grass, but she did not see anything that looked like the right thing to eat or drink under the circumstances. There was a large mushroom growing near her, about the same height as herself; and when she had looked under it, and on both sides of it, and behind it, it occurred to her that she might as well look and see what was on the top of it.

She stretched herself up on tiptoe, and peeped over the edge of the mushroom, and her eyes immediately met those of a large caterpillar, that was sitting on the top with its arms folded, quietly smoking a long hookah, and taking not the smallest notice of her or of anything else.

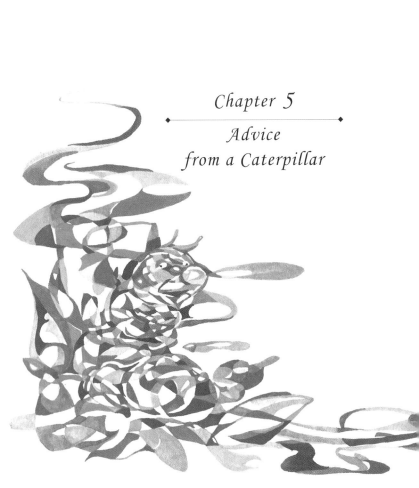

Chapter 5

Advice
from a Caterpillar

"Who are you?" said the Caterpillar.
This was not an encouraging opening for a
conversation. Alice replied, rather shyly, "I – I
hardly know, sir, just at present – at least I know
who I was when I got up this morning, but I think
I must have been changed several times since then."
"What do you mean by that?" said the Caterpillar
sternly. "Explain yourself!"
"I can't explain myself, I'm afraid, sir" said Alice,
"because I'm not myself, you see."

The caterpillar and Alice looked at each other for some time in silence: at last the Caterpillar took the hookah out of its mouth, and addressed her in a languid, sleepy voice.

"Who are you?" said the Caterpillar.

This was not an encouraging opening for a conversation. Alice replied, rather shyly, "I – I hardly know, sir, just at present – at least I know who I *was* when I got up this morning, but I think I must have been changed several times since then."

"What do you mean by that?" said the Caterpillar sternly. "Explain yourself!"

"I can't explain *myself*, I'm afraid, sir" said Alice, "because I'm not myself, you see."

"I don't see," said the Caterpillar.

"I'm afraid I can't put it more clearly," Alice replied very politely, "for I can't understand it myself to begin with; and being so many different sizes in a day is very confusing."

"It isn't," said the Caterpillar.

"Well, perhaps you haven't found it so yet," said Alice; "but when you have to turn into a chrysalis – you will some day, you know – and then after that into a butterfly, I should think you'll feel it a little queer, won't you?"

"Not a bit," said the Caterpillar.

"Well, perhaps your feelings may be different," said Alice; "all I know is, it would feel very queer to *me*."

"*You!*" said the Caterpillar contemptuously. "Who are you?"

Which brought them back again to the beginning of the conversation. Alice felt a little irritated at the Caterpillar's making such *very* short remarks, and she drew herself up and said, very gravely, "I think, you ought to tell me who *you* are, first."

"Why?" said the Caterpillar.

Here was another puzzling question; and as Alice could not think of any good reason, and as the Caterpillar seemed to be in a *very* unpleasant state of mind, she turned away.

"Come back!" The Caterpillar called after her. "I've something important to say!"

This sounded promising, certainly: Alice turned and came back again.

"Keep your temper," said the Caterpillar.

"Is that all?" said Alice, swallowing down her anger as well as she could.

"No," said the Caterpillar.

Alice thought she might as well wait, as she had nothing else to do, and perhaps after all it might tell her something worth hearing. For some minutes it puffed away without speaking, but at last it unfolded its arms, took the hookah out of its mouth again, and said:

"So you think you're changed, do you?"

"I'm afraid I am, sir," said Alice; "I can't remember things as I used – and I don't keep the same size for ten minutes together!"

"Can't remember *what* things?" said the Caterpillar.

"Well, I've tried to say '*How doth the little busy bee*', but it all came different!" Alice replied in a very melancholy voice.

"Repeat, '*You are old, father William,*' " said the Caterpillar.

Alice folded her hands, and began: –

"You are old, Father William," the young man said,
"And your hair has become very white;
And yet you incessantly stand on your head –
Do you think, at your age, it is right?"

"In my youth," Father William replied to his son,
"I feared it might injure the brain;
But, now that I'm perfectly sure I have none,
Why, I do it again and again."

"You are old," said the youth, "as I mentioned before,
And have grown most uncommonly fat;
Yet you turned a back-somersault in at the door –
Pray, what is the reason of that?"

"In my youth," said the sage, as he shook his grey locks,
"I kept all my limbs very supple
By the use of this ointment – one shilling the box –
Allow me to sell you a couple."

"You are old," said the youth, "and your jaws are too weak
For anything tougher than suet;
Yet you finished the goose, with the bones and the beak –

203

Pray, how did you manage to do it?"

"In my youth," said his father, "I took to the law,
And argued each case with my wife;
And the muscular strength, which it gave to my jaw,
Has lasted the rest of my life."

"You are old," said the youth, "one would hardly suppose
That your eye was as steady as ever;
Yet you balanced an eel on the end of your nose –
What made you so awfully clever?"

"I have answered three questions, and that is enough,"
Said his father; "don't give yourself airs!
Do you think I can listen all day to such stuff?
Be off, or I'll kick you down stairs!"

"That is not said right," said the Caterpillar.

"Not *quite* right, I'm afraid," said Alice, timidly; "some of the words have got altered."

"It is wrong from beginning to end," said the Caterpillar decidedly, and there was silence for some minutes.

The Caterpillar was the first to speak.

"What size do you want to be?" it asked.

"Oh, I'm not particular as to size," Alice hastily replied; "only one doesn't like changing so often, you know."

"I *don*'t know," said the Caterpillar.

Alice said nothing: she had never been so much contradicted in her life before, and she felt that she was losing her temper.

"Are you content now?" said the Caterpillar.

"Well, I should like to be a *little* larger, sir, if you wouldn't mind," said Alice: "three inches is such a wretched height to be."

"It is a very good height indeed!" said the Caterpillar angrily, rearing itself upright as it spoke (it was exactly three inches high).

"But I'm not used to it!" pleaded poor Alice in a piteous tone. And she thought of herself, "I wish the creatures wouldn't be so easily offended!"

"You'll get used to it in time," said the Caterpillar; and it put the hookah into its mouth and began smoking again.

This time Alice waited patiently until it chose to speak again. In a minute or two the Caterpillar took the hookah out of its mouth and yawned once or twice, and shook itself. Then it got down off the mushroom, and crawled away in the grass, merely remarking as it went, "One side will make you grow taller, and the other side will make you grow shorter."

"One side of *what*? The other side of *what*?" thought Alice to herself.

"Of the mushroom," said the Caterpillar, just as if she had asked it aloud; and in another moment it was out of sight.

Alice remained looking thoughtfully at the mushroom for a minute, trying to make out which were the two sides of it; and as it was perfectly round, she found this a very difficult question. However, at last she stretched her arms round it as far as they would go, and broke off a bit of the edge with each hand.

"And now which is which?" she said to herself, and nibbled a little of the right-hand bit to try the effect: the next moment she felt a violent blow underneath her chin: it had struck her foot!

She was a good deal frightened by this very sudden change, but she felt that there was no time to be lost, as she was shrinking rapidly; so she set to work at once to eat some of the other bit. Her chin was pressed so closely against her foot, that there was hardly room to open her mouth; but she did it at last, and managed to swallow a morsel of the left-hand bit.

"Come, my head's free at last!" said Alice in a tone of delight, which changed into alarm in another moment, when she found that her shoulders were nowhere to be found: all she could see, when she looked down, was an immense length of neck, which seemed to rise like a stalk out of a sea of green leaves that lay far below her.

"What *can* all that green stuff be?" said Alice. "And where *have* my shoulders got to? And oh, my poor hands, how is it I can't see you?" She was moving them about as she spoke, but no result seemed to follow, except a little shaking among the distant green leaves.

As there seemed to be no chance of getting her hands up to her head, she tried to get her head down to them, and was delighted to find that her neck would bend about easily in any direction, like a serpent. She had just succeeded in curving it down into a graceful zigzag, and was going to dive in among the leaves, which she found to be nothing but the tops of the trees under which she had been wandering, when a sharp hiss made her draw back in a hurry: a large pigeon had flown into her face, and was beating her violently with its wings.

"Serpent!" screamed the Pigeon.

"I'm *not* a serpent!" said Alice indignantly. "leave me alone!"

"Serpent, I say again!" repeated the Pigeon, but in a more subdued tone, and added with a kind of sob, "I've tried every way, and nothing seems to suit them!"

"I haven't the least idea what you're talking about," said Alice.

"I've tried the roots of trees, and I've tried banks, and I've tried hedges," the Pigeon went on, without attending to her; "but those serpents! There's no pleasing them!"

Alice was more and more puzzled, but she thought there was no use in saying anything more till the Pigeon had finished.

"As if it wasn't trouble enough hatching the eggs," said the Pigeon; "but I must be on the look-out for serpents night and day! Why, I haven't had a wink of sleep these three weeks!"

"I'm very sorry you've been annoyed," said Alice, who was beginning to see its meaning.

"And just as I'd taken the highest tree in the wood," continued the Pigeon, raising its voice to a shriek, "and just as I was thinking I should be free of them at last, they must needs come wriggling down from the sky! Ugh! Serpent!"

"But I'm not a serpent, I tell you!" said Alice. "I'm a – I'm a – "

"Well! *What* are you?" said the Pigeon. "I can see you're trying to invent something!"

"I – I'm a little girl," said Alice, rather doubtfully, as she remembered the number of changes she had gone through that day.

"A likely story indeed!" said the Pigeon in a tone of the deepest contempt. "I've seen a good many little girls in my time, but never one with such a neck as that! No, no! You're a serpent; and there's no use denying it. I suppose you'll be telling me next that you never tasted an egg!"

"I *have* tasted eggs, certainly," said Alice, who was a very truthful child; "but little girls eat eggs quite as much as serpents do, you know."

"I don't believe it," said the Pigeon; "but if they do, why then they're a kind of serpent, that's all I can say."

This was such a new idea to Alice, that she was quite silent for a minute or two, which gave the Pigeon the opportunity of adding, "You're looking for eggs, I know *that* well enough; and what does it matter to me whether you're a little girl or a serpent?"

"It matters a good deal to *me*," said Alice hastily; "but I'm not looking for eggs, as it happens; and if I was, I shouldn't want yours: I don't like them raw."

"Well, be off, then!" said the Pigeon in a sulky tone, as it settled down again into its nest. Alice crouched down among the trees as well as she could, for her neck kept getting entangled among the branches, and every now and then she had to stop and untwist it. After a while she remembered that she still held the pieces of mushroom in her hands, and she set to work very carefully, nibbling first at one and then at the other, and growing sometimes taller and sometimes shorter, until she had succeeded in bringing herself down to her usual height.

It was so long since she had been anything near the right size, that it felt quite strange at first; but she got used to it in a few minutes, and began talking to herself, as usual. "Come, there's half my plan done now! How puzzling all these changes are! I'm never sure what I'm going to be, from one minute to another! However, I've got back to my right size: the next thing is, to get into that beautiful garden – how *is* that to be done, I wonder?" As she said this, she came suddenly upon an open place, with a little house in it about four feet high. "Whoever lives there," thought Alice, "it'll never do to come upon them this size: why, I should frighten them out of their wits!" So she began nibbling at the right hand bit again, and did not venture to go near the house till she had brought herself down to nine inches high.

Chapter **6**

Pig and Pepper

"But I don't want to go among mad people," Alice remarked.

"Oh, you can't help that," said the Cat: "we're all mad here. I'm mad. You're mad."

"How do you know I'm mad?" said Alice.

"You must be," said the Cat, "or you wouldn't have come here."

For a minute or two she stood looking at the house, and wondering what to do next, when suddenly a footman in livery came running out of the wood – (she considered him to be a footman because he was in livery: otherwise, judging by his face only, she would have called him a fish) – and rapped loudly at the door with his knuckles. It was opened by another footman in livery, with a round face, and large eyes like a frog; and both footmen, Alice noticed, had powdered hair that curled all over their heads. She felt very curious to know what it was all about, and crept a little way out of the wood to listen.

The Fish-Footman began by producing from under his arm a great letter, nearly as large as himself, and this he handed over to the other, saying, in a solemn tone, "For the Duchess. An invitation from the Queen to play croquet." The Frog-Footman repeated, in the same solemn tone, only changing the order of the words a little, "From the Queen. An invitation for the Duchess to play croquet." Then they both bowed low, and their curls got entangled together.

Alice laughed so much at this, that she had to run back into the wood for fear of their hearing her; and when she next peeped out the Fish-Footman was gone, and the other was sitting on the ground near the door, staring stupidly up into the sky.

Alice went timidly up to the door, and knocked.

"There's no sort of use in knocking," said the Footman, "and that for two reasons. First, because I'm on the same side of the door as you are; secondly, because they're making such a noise inside, no one could possibly hear you." And certainly there was a most extraordinary noise going on within – a constant howling and sneezing, and every now and then a great crash, as if a dish or kettle had been broken to pieces.

"Please, then," said Alice, "how am I to get in?"

"There might be some sense in your knocking," the Footman went on without attending to her, "if we had the door between us. For instance, if you were *inside*, you might knock, and I could let you out, you know." He was looking up into the sky all the time he was speaking, and this Alice thought decidedly uncivil. "But perhaps he can't help it," she said to herself; "his eyes are so *very* nearly at the top of his head. But at any rate he might answer questions. – How am

I to get in?" she repeated, aloud.

"I shall sit here," the Footman remarked, "till tomorrow – "

At this moment the door of the house opened, and a large plate came skimming out, straight at the Footman's head: it just grazed his nose, and broke to pieces against one of the trees behind him.

" – or next day, maybe," the Footman continued in the same tone, exactly as if nothing had happened.

"How am I to get in?" asked Alice again, in a louder tone.

"*Are* you to get in at all?" said the Footman. "That's the first question, you know."

It was, no doubt: only Alice did not like to be told so. "It's really dreadful," she muttered to herself, "the way all the creatures argue. It's enough to drive one crazy!"

The Footman seemed to think this a good opportunity for repeating his remark, with variations. "I shall sit here," he said, "on and off, for days and days."

"But what am *I* to do?" said Alice.

"Anything you like," said the Footman, and began whistling.

"Oh, there's no use in talking to him," said Alice desperately: "he's perfectly idiotic!" And she opened the door and went in.

The door led right into a large kitchen, which was full of smoke from one end to the other: the Duchess was sitting on a three-legged stool in the middle, nursing a baby; the cook was leaning over the fire, stirring a large cauldron which seemed to be full of soup.

"There's certainly too much pepper in that soup!" Alice said to herself, as well as she could for sneezing.

There was certainly too much of it in the air. Even the Duchess sneezed occasionally; and as for the baby, it was sneezing and howling alternately without a moment's pause. The only things in the kitchen that did *not* sneeze, were the cook, and a large cat which was sitting on the hearth and grinning from ear to ear.

"Please would you tell me," said Alice, a little timidly, for she was not quite sure whether it was good manners for her to speak first, "why your cat grins like that?"

"It's a Cheshire cat," said the Duchess, "and that's why. Pig!"

She said the last word with such sudden violence that Alice quite jumped; but she saw in another moment that it was addressed to the baby, and not to her, so she took courage, and went on again: –

"I didn't know that Cheshire cats always grinned; in fact, I didn't know that cats *could* grin."

"They all can," said the Duchess; "and most of em do."

"I don't know of any that do," Alice said very politely, feeling quite pleased to have got into a conversation.

"You don't know much," said the Duchess; "and that's a fact."

Alice did not at all like the tone of this remark, and thought it would be as well to introduce some other subject of conversation. While she was trying to fix on one, the cook took the cauldron of soup off the fire, and at once set to work throwing everything within her reach at the Duchess and the baby – the fire-irons came first; then followed a shower of saucepans, plates, and dishes. The Duchess took no notice of them even when they hit her; and the baby was howling so much already, that it was quite impossible to say whether the blows hurt it or not.

"Oh, *please* mind what you're doing!" cried Alice, jumping up and down in an agony of terror. "Oh, there goes his *precious* nose"; as an unusually large saucepan flew close by it, and very nearly carried it off.

"If everybody minded their own business," the Duchess said in a hoarse growl, "the world would go round a deal faster than it does."

"Which would *not* be an advantage," said Alice, who felt very glad to get an opportunity of showing off a little of her knowledge. "Just think of what work it would make with the day and night! You see the earth takes twenty-four hours to turn round on its axis – "

"Talking of axes," said the Duchess, "chop off her head!"

Alice glanced rather anxiously at the cook, to see if she meant to take the hint; but the cook was busily stirring the soup, and seemed not to be listening, so she went on again: "Twenty-four hours, I *think*; or is it twelve? I – "

"Oh, don't bother *me*," said the Duchess; "I never could abide figures!" And with that she began nursing her child again, singing a sort of lullaby to it as she did so, and giving it a violent shake at the end of every line:–

> *"Speak roughly to your little boy,*
> *And beat him when he sneezes;*
> *He only does it to annoy,*
> *Because he knows it teases."*

CHORUS
(In which the cook and the baby joined)

"Wow! wow! wow!"

While the Duchess sang the second verse of the song, she kept tossing the baby violently up and down, and the poor little thing howled so, that Alice could hardly hear the words: –

"I speak severely to my boy,
I beat him when he sneezes;
For he can thoroughly enjoy
The pepper when he pleases!"

CHORUS
"Wow! wow! wow!"

"Here! you may nurse it a bit, if you like!" the Duchess said to Alice, flinging the baby at her as she spoke. "I must go and get ready to play croquet with the Queen," and she hurried out of the room. The cook threw a frying-pan after her as she went out, but it just missed her.

Alice caught the baby with some difficulty, as it was a queer-shaped little creature, and held out its arms and legs in all directions, "just like a star-fish," thought Alice. The poor little thing was snorting like a steam-engine when she caught it, and kept doubling itself up and straightening itself out again, so that altogether, for the first minute or two, it was as much as she could do to hold it.

As soon as she had made out the proper way of nursing it (which was to twist it up into a sort of knot, and then keep tight hold of its right ear and left foot, so as to prevent its undoing itself) she carried it out into the open air. "IF I don't take this child away with me," thought Alice, "they're sure to kill it in a day or two: wouldn't it be murder to leave it behind?" She said the last words out loud, and the little thing grunted in reply (it had left off sneezing by this time). "Don't grunt," said Alice; "that's not at all a proper way of expressing yourself."

The baby grunted again, and Alice looked very anxiously into its face to see what was the matter with it.

There could be no doubt that it had a *very* turn-up nose, much more like a snout than a real nose; also its eyes were getting extremely small for a baby: altogether Alice did not like the look of the thing at all. "But perhaps it was only sobbing," she thought, and looked into its eyes again, to see if there were any tears.

No, there were *no* tears. "If you're going to turn into a pig, my dear," said Alice, seriously, "I'll have nothing more to do with you. Mind now!" The poor little thing sobbed again (or grunted, it was impossible to say which), and they went on for some while in silence.

Alice was just beginning to think to herself, "Now, what am I to do with this creature when I get it home?" when it grunted again, so

violently, that she looked down into its face in some alarm. This time there could be no mistake about it: it was neither more nor less than a pig, and she felt that it would be quite absurd for her to carry it further.

So she set the little creature down, and felt quite relieved to see it trot away quietly into the wood. "If it had grown up," she said to herself, "it would have made a dreadfully ugly child: but it makes rather a handsome pig, I think." And she began thinking over other children she knew, who might do very well as pigs, and was just saying to herself, "if one only knew the right way to change them – " when she was a little startled by seeing the Cheshire Cat sitting on a bough of a tree a few yards off.

The Cat only grinned when it saw Alice. It looked good- natured, she thought: still it had *very* long claws and a great many teeth, so she felt that it ought to be treated with respect.

"Cheshire Puss," she began, rather timidly, as she did not at all know whether it would like the name: however, it only grinned a little wider. "Come, it's pleased so far," thought Alice, and she went on. "Would you tell me, please, which way I ought to go from here?"

"That depends a good deal on where you want to get to," said the Cat.

"I don't much care where – " said Alice.

"Then it doesn't matter which way you go," said the Cat.

" – so long as I get *somewhere*," Alice added as an explanation.

"Oh, you're sure to do that," said the Cat, "if you only walk long enough."

Alice felt that this could not be denied, so she tried another question. "What sort of people live about here?"

"In *that* direction," the Cat said, waving its right paw round, "lives a Hatter: and in *that* direction," waving the other paw, "lives a March Hare. Visit either you like: they're both mad."

"But I don't want to go among mad people," Alice remarked.

"Oh, you can't help that," said the Cat: "we're all mad here. I'm mad. You're mad."

"How do you know I'm mad?" said Alice.

"You must be," said the Cat, "or you wouldn't have come here."

Alice didn't think that proved it at all; however, she went on "And how do you know that you're mad?"

"To begin with," said the Cat, "a dog's not mad. You grant that?"

"I suppose so," said Alice.

"Well, then," the Cat went on, "you see a dog growls when it's angry, and wags its tail when it's pleased. Now I growl when I'm pleased, and wag my tail when I'm angry. Therefore I'm mad."

"I call it purring, not growling," said Alice.

"Call it what you like," said the Cat. "Do you play croquet with the Queen to-day?"

"I should like it very much," said Alice, "but I haven't been invited yet."

"You'll see me there," said the Cat, and vanished.

Alice was not much surprised at this: she was getting so used to queer things happening. While she was looking at the place where it had been, it suddenly appeared again.

"By-the-bye, what became of the baby?" said the Cat. "I'd nearly forgotten to ask."

"It turned into a pig," Alice quietly said, just as if it had come back in a natural way.

"I thought it would," said the Cat, and vanished again.

Alice waited a little, half expecting to see it again, but it did not appear, and after a minute or two she walked on in the direction in which the March Hare was said to live. "I've seen hatters before," she said to herself; "the March Hare will be much the most interesting, and perhaps as this is May it won't be raving mad – at least not so mad as it was in March." As she said this, she looked up, and there was the Cat again, sitting on a branch of a tree.

"Did you say 'pig,' or 'fig'?" said the Cat.

"I said 'pig'," replied Alice; "and I wish you wouldn't keep appearing and vanishing so suddenly: you make one quite giddy."

"All right," said the Cat; and this time it vanished quite slowly, beginning with the end of the tail, and ending with the grin, which remained some time after the rest of it had gone.

"Well! I've often seen a cat without a grin," thought Alice; "but a grin without a cat! It's the most curious thing I ever saw in my life!"

She had not gone much farther before she came in sight of the house of the March Hare: she thought it must be the right house, because the chimneys were shaped like ears and the roof was thatched with fur. It was so large a house, that she did not like to go nearer till she had nibbled some more of the left hand bit of mushroom, and raised herself to about two feet high: even then she walked up towards it rather timidly, saying to herself "Suppose it should be raving mad after all! I almost wish I'd gone to see the Hatter instead!"

Chapter 7

A Mad Tea-Party

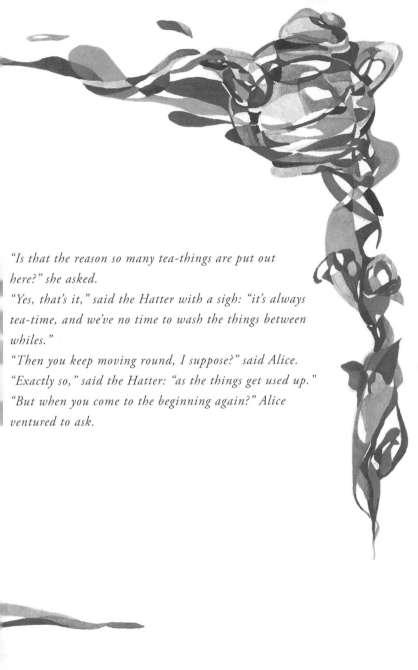

"Is that the reason so many tea-things are put out here?" she asked.

"Yes, that's it," said the Hatter with a sigh: "it's always tea-time, and we've no time to wash the things between whiles."

"Then you keep moving round, I suppose?" said Alice.

"Exactly so," said the Hatter: "as the things get used up."

"But when you come to the beginning again?" Alice ventured to ask.

There was a table set out under a tree in front of the house, and the March Hare and the Hatter were having tea at it: a Dormouse was sitting between them, fast asleep, and the other two were using it as a cushion, resting their elbows on it, and talking over its head. "Very uncomfortable for the Dormouse," thought Alice; "only, as it's asleep, I suppose it doesn't mind."

The table was a large one, but the three were all crowded together at one corner of it: "No room! No room!" they cried out when they saw Alice coming. "There's *plenty* of room!" said Alice indignantly, and she sat down in a large arm-chair at one end of the table.

"Have some wine," the March Hare said in an encouraging tone.

Alice looked all round the table, but there was nothing on it but tea. "I don't see any wine," she remarked.

"There isn't any," said the March Hare.

"Then it wasn't very civil of you to offer it," said Alice angrily.

"It wasn't very civil of you to sit down without being invited," said the March Hare.

"I didn't know it was *your* table," said Alice; "it's laid for a great many more than three."

"Your hair wants cutting," said the Hatter. He had been looking at Alice for some time with great curiosity, and this was his first speech.

"You should learn not to make personal remarks," Alice said with some severity: "it's very rude."

The Hatter opened his eyes very wide on hearing this; but all he said was, "Why is a raven like a writing-desk?"

"Come, we shall have some fun now!" thought Alice. "I'm glad they've begun asking riddles. – I believe I can guess that," she added aloud.

"Do you mean that you think you can find out the answer to it?" said the March Hare.

"Exactly so," said Alice.

"Then you should say what you mean," the March Hare went on.

"I do," Alice hastily replied; "at least – at least I mean what I say – that's the same thing, you know."

"Not the same thing a bit!" said the Hatter. "Why, you might just as well say that 'I see what I eat' is the same thing as 'I eat what I see'!"

"You might just as well say," added the March Hare, "that 'I like what I get' is the same thing as 'I get what I like'!"

"You might just as well say," added the Dormouse, who seemed to be talking in his sleep, "that 'I breathe when I sleep' is the same thing as 'I sleep when I breathe'!"

"It *is* the same thing with you," said the Hatter, and here the conversation dropped, and the party sat silent for a minute, while Alice thought over all she could remember about ravens and writing-desks, which wasn't much.

The Hatter was the first to break the silence. "What day of the month is it?" he said, turning to Alice: he had taken his watch out of his pocket, and was looking at it uneasily, shaking it every now and then, and holding it to his ear.

Alice considered a little, and then said "The fourth."

"Two days wrong!" sighed the Hatter. "I told you butter wouldn't suit the works!" he added looking angrily at the March Hare.

"It was the *best* butter," the March Hare meekly replied.

"Yes, but some crumbs must have got in as well," the Hatter grumbled: "you shouldn't have put it in with the bread-knife."

The March Hare took the watch and looked at it gloomily: then he dipped it into his cup of tea, and looked at it again: but he could think of nothing better to say than his first remark, "It was the *best* butter, you know."

Alice had been looking over his shoulder with some curiosity. "What a funny watch!" she remarked. "It tells the day of the month, and doesn't tell what o'clock it is!"

"Why should it?" muttered the Hatter. "Does *your* watch tell you what year it is?"

"Of course not," Alice replied very readily; "but that's because it stays the same year for such a long time together."

"Which is just the case with *mine*," said the Hatter.

Alice felt dreadfully puzzled. The Hatter's remark seemed to have no sort of meaning in it, and yet it was certainly English. "I don't quite understand you," she said, as politely as she could.

"The Dormouse is asleep again," said the Hatter, and he poured a little hot tea upon its nose.

The Dormouse shook its head impatiently, and said, without opening its eyes, "Of course, of course: just what I was going to remark myself."

"Have you guessed the riddle yet?" the Hatter said, turning to Alice again.

"No, I give up," Alice replied; "what's the answer?"

"I haven't the slightest idea," said the Hatter. "Nor I," said the March Hare.

Alice sighed wearily. "I think you might do something better with the time," she said, "than waste it in asking riddles that have no answers."

"If you knew Time as well as I do," said the Hatter, "you wouldn't talk about wasting it. It's *him*."

"I don't know what you mean," said Alice.

"Of course you don't!" the Hatter said, tossing his head contemptuously. "I dare say you never even spoke to Time!"

"Perhaps not," Alice cautiously replied: "but I know I have to beat time when I learn music."

"Ah! that accounts for it," said the Hatter. "He won't stand beating. Now, if you only kept on good terms with him, he'd do almost anything you liked with the clock. For instance, suppose it were nine o'clock in the morning, just time to begin lessons: you'd only have to whisper a hint to Time, and round goes the clock in a twinkling! Half-past one, time for dinner!"

("I only wish it was," the March Hare said to itself in a whisper.)

"That would be grand, certainly," said Alice thoughtfully: "but then – I shouldn't be hungry for it, you know."

"Not at first, perhaps," said the Hatter: "but you could keep it to half-past one as long as you liked."

"Is that the way *you* manage?" Alice asked.

The Hatter shook his head mournfully. "Not I!" he replied. "We quarrelled last March – just before *he* went mad, you know – " (pointing with his tea spoon at the March Hare) " – it was at the great concert given by the Queen of Hearts, and I had to sing

"Twinkle, twinkle, little bat!
How I wonder what you're at!"

You know the song, perhaps?"

"I've heard something like it," said Alice.

"It goes on, you know," the Hatter continued, in this way: –

"*Up above the world you fly,*
Like a tea-tray in the sky
Twinkle, twinkle –"

Here the Dormouse shook itself, and began singing in its sleep *"Twinkle, twinkle, twinkle, twinkle –* " and went on so long that they had to pinch it to make it stop.

"Well, I'd hardly finished the first verse," said the Hatter, "when the Queen jumped up and bawled out, "He's murdering the time! Off with his head!"

"How dreadfully savage!" exclaimed Alice.

"And ever since that," the Hatter went on in a mournful tone, "he won't do a thing I ask! It's always six o'clock now."

A bright idea came into Alice's head. "Is that the reason so many tea-things are put out here?" she asked.

"Yes, that's it," said the Hatter with a sigh: "it's always tea-time, and we've no time to wash the things between whiles."

"Then you keep moving round, I suppose?" said Alice.

"Exactly so," said the Hatter: "as the things get used up."

"But when you come to the beginning again?" Alice ventured to ask.

"Suppose we change the subject," the March Hare interrupted, yawning. "I'm getting tired of this. I vote the young lady tells us a story."

"I'm afraid I don't know one," said Alice, rather alarmed at the proposal.

"Then the Dormouse shall!" they both cried. "Wake up, Dormouse!" And they pinched it on both sides at once.

The Dormouse slowly opened his eyes. "I wasn't asleep," he said in a hoarse, feeble voice: "I heard every word you fellows were saying."

"Tell us a story!" said the March Hare.

"Yes, please do!" pleaded Alice.

"And be quick about it," added the Hatter, "or you'll be asleep again before it's done."

"Once upon a time there were three little sisters," the Dormouse began in a great hurry; "and their names were Elsie, Lacie, and Tillie; and they lived at the bottom of a well – "

"What did they live on?" said Alice, who always took a great interest in questions of eating and drinking.

"They lived on treacle," said the Dormouse, after thinking a minute or two.

"They couldn't have done that, you know," Alice gently remarked. "they'd have been ill."

"So they were," said the Dormouse; "*very* ill."

Alice tried to fancy to herself what such an extraordinary ways of living would be like, but it puzzled her too much, so she went on: "But why did they live at the bottom of a well?"

"Take some more tea," the March Hare said to Alice, very earnestly.

"I've had nothing yet," Alice replied in an offended tone, "so I can't take more."

"You mean you can't take *less*," said the Hatter: "it's very easy to take *more* than nothing."

"Nobody asked *your* opinion," said Alice.

"Who's making personal remarks now?" the Hatter asked triumphantly.

Alice did not quite know what to say to this: so she helped herself to some tea and bread-and-butter, and then turned to the Dormouse, and repeated her question.

"Why did they live at the bottom of a well?"

The Dormouse again took a minute or two to think about it, and then said, "It was a treacle-well."

"There's no such thing!" Alice was beginning very angrily, but the Hatter and the March Hare went "Sh! sh!" and the Dormouse sulkily remarked, "If you can't be civil, you'd better finish the story for yourself."

"No, please go on!" Alice said very humbly: "I won't interrupt again. I dare say there may be *one.*"

"One, indeed!" said the Dormouse indignantly. However, he consented to go on. "And so these three little sisters – they were learning to draw, you know – "

"What did they draw?" said Alice, quite forgetting her promise.

"Treacle," said the Dormouse, without considering at all this time.

"I want a clean cup," interrupted the Hatter: "let's all move one place on."

He moved on as he spoke, and the Dormouse followed him: the March Hare moved into the Dormouse's place, and Alice rather unwillingly took the place of the March Hare. The Hatter was the only one who got any advantage from the change: and Alice was a good deal worse off than before, as the March Hare had just upset the milk-jug into his plate.

Alice did not wish to offend the Dormouse again, so she began very cautiously: "But I don't understand. Where did they draw the treacle from?"

"You can draw water out of a water-well," said the Hatter; "so I should think you could draw treacle out of a treacle-well – eh, stupid?"

"But they were IN the well," Alice said to the Dormouse, not choosing to notice this last remark.

"Of course they were", said the Dormouse; " – well in." This answer so confused poor Alice, that she let the Dormouse go on for some time without interrupting it.

"They were learning to draw," the Dormouse went on, yawning and rubbing its eyes, for it was getting very sleepy; "and they drew all manner of things – everything that begins with an M – "

"Why with an M?" said Alice.

"Why not?" said the March Hare.

Alice was silent.

The Dormouse had closed its eyes by this time, and was going off into a doze; but, on being pinched by the Hatter, it woke up again with a little shriek, and went on: " – that begins with an M, such as mouse-traps, and the moon, and memory, and muchness – you know you say things are 'much of a muchness' – did you ever see such a thing as a drawing of a muchness?"

"Really, now you ask me," said Alice, very much confused, "I don't think – "

"Then you shouldn't talk," said the Hatter.

This piece of rudeness was more than Alice could bear: she got up in great disgust, and walked off; the Dormouse fell asleep instantly, and neither of the others took the least notice of her going, though she looked back once or twice, half hoping that they would call after her: the last time she saw them, they were trying to put the Dormouse into the teapot.

"At any rate I'll never go *there* again!" said Alice as she picked her way through the wood. "It's the stupidest tea-party I ever was at in all my life!"

Just as she said this, she noticed that one of the trees had a door leading right into it. "That's very curious!" she thought. "But everything's curious today. I think I may as well go in at once." And in she went.

Once more she found herself in the long hall, and close to the little glass table. "Now, I'll manage better this time," she said to herself, and began by taking the little golden key, and unlocking the door that led into the garden. Then she went to work nibbling at the mushroom (she had kept a piece of it in her pocket) till she was about a foot high: then she walked down the little passage: and *then* – she found herself at last in the beautiful garden, among the bright flower-beds and the cool fountains.

Chapter 8

◆ ─────────────────── ◆

The Queen's
Croquet-Ground

"……and they all quarrel so dreadfully one can't hear oneself speak – and they don't seem to have any rules in particular; at least, if there are, nobody attends to them – and you've no idea how confusing it is all the things being alive; for instance, there's the arch I've got to go through next walking about at the other end of the ground – and I should have croqueted the Queen's hedgehog just now, only it ran away when it saw mine coming!"

A large rose-tree stood near the entrance of the garden: the roses growing on it were white, but there were three gardeners at it, busily painting them red. Alice thought this a very curious thing, and she went nearer to watch them, and just as she came up to them she heard one of them say, "Look out now, Five! Don't go splashing paint over me like that!"

"I couldn't help it," said Five, in a sulky tone; "Seven jogged my elbow."

On which Seven looked up and said, "That's right, Five! Always lay the blame on others!"

"*you'd* better not talk!" said Five. "I heard the Queen say only yesterday you deserved to be beheaded!"

"What for?" said the one who had spoken first.

"That's none of *your* business, Two!" said Seven.

"Yes, it *is* his business!" said Five, "and I'll tell him – it was for bringing the cook tulip-roots instead of onions."

Seven flung down his brush, and had just begun "Well, of all the unjust things – " when his eye chanced to fall upon Alice, as she stood watching them, and he checked himself suddenly: the others looked round also, and all of them bowed low.

"Would you tell me," said Alice, a little timidly, "why you are painting those roses?"

Five and Seven said nothing, but looked at Two. Two began in a low voice, "Why the fact is, you see, Miss, this here ought to have been a *red* rose-tree, and we put a white one in by mistake; and if the Queen was to find it out, we should all have our heads cut off, you know. So you see, Miss, we're doing our best, afore she comes, to – " At this moment Five, who had been anxiously looking across the garden, called out "The Queen! The Queen!" and the three gardeners instantly threw themselves flat upon their faces. There was a sound of many footsteps, and Alice looked round, eager to see the Queen.

First came ten soldiers carrying clubs; these were all shaped like the three gardeners, oblong and flat, with their hands and feet at the corners: next the ten courtiers; these were ornamented all over with diamonds, and walked two and two, as the soldiers did. After these came the royal children; there were ten of them, and the little dears came jumping merrily along hand in hand, in couples: they were all ornamented with hearts. Next came the guests, mostly Kings and Queens, and among them Alice recognised the White Rabbit: it was talking in a hurried nervous manner, smiling at everything that was said, and went by without noticing her. Then followed the Knave of Hearts, carrying the King's crown on a crimson velvet cushion; and, last of all this grand procession, came THE KING AND QUEEN OF HEARTS.

Alice was rather doubtful whether she ought not to lie down on her face like the three gardeners, but she could not remember ever having heard of such a rule at processions: "and besides, what would be the use of a procession," thought she, "if people had all to lie down upon their faces, so that they couldn't see it?" So she stood still where she was, and waited.

When the procession came opposite to Alice, they all stopped and looked at her, and the Queen said severely "Who is this?" She said it to the Knave of Hearts, who only bowed and smiled in reply.

"Idiot!" said the Queen, tossing her head impatiently; and, turning to Alice, she went on, "What's your name, child?"

"My name is Alice, so please your Majesty," said Alice very politely; but she added, to herself, "Why, they're only a pack of cards, after all. I needn't be afraid of them!"

"And who are *these*?" said the Queen, pointing to the three gardeners who were lying round the rosetree; for, you see, as they were lying on their faces, and the pattern on their backs was the same as

the rest of the pack, she could not tell whether they were gardeners, or soldiers, or courtiers, or three of her own children.

"How should *I* know?" said Alice, surprised at her own courage. "It's no business of *mine*." The Queen turned crimson with fury, and, after glaring at her for a moment like a wild beast, screamed "Off with her head! Off – "

"Nonsense!" said Alice, very loudly and decidedly, and the Queen was silent.

The King laid his hand upon her arm, and timidly said "Consider, my dear: she is only a child!"

The Queen turned angrily away from him, and said to the Knave "Turn them over!"

The Knave did so, very carefully, with one foot.

"Get up!" said the Queen, in a shrill, loud voice, and the three gardeners instantly jumped up, and began bowing to the King, the Queen, the royal children, and everybody else.

"Leave off that!" screamed the Queen. "You make me giddy." And then, turning to the rose-tree, she went on, "What *have* you been doing here?"

"May it please your Majesty," said Two, in a very humble tone, going down on one knee as he spoke, "we were trying – "

"*I* see!" said the Queen, who had meanwhile been examining the roses. "Off with their heads!" and the procession moved on, three of the soldiers remaining behind to execute the unfortunate gardeners, who ran to Alice for protection.

"You shan't be beheaded!" said Alice, and she put them into a large flower-pot that stood near. The three soldiers wandered about for a minute or two, looking for them, and then quietly marched off after the others.

"Are their heads off?" shouted the Queen.

"Their heads are gone, if it please your Majesty!" the soldiers shouted in reply.

"That's right!" shouted the Queen. "Can you play croquet?"

The soldiers were silent, and looked at Alice, as the question was evidently meant for her.

"Yes!" shouted Alice.

"Come on, then!" roared the Queen, and Alice joined the procession, wondering very much what would happen next.

"It's – it's a very fine day!" said a timid voice at her side. She was walking by the White Rabbit, who was peeping anxiously into her face.

"Very," said Alice: " – where's the Duchess?"

"Hush! Hush!" said the Rabbit in a low, hurried tone. He looked anxiously over his shoulder as he spoke, and then raised himself upon tiptoe, put his mouth close to her ear, and whispered "She's under sentence of execution."

"What for?" said Alice.

"Did you say 'What a pity!'?" the Rabbit asked.

"No, I didn't," said Alice: "I don't think it's at all a pity. I said 'What for?'"

"She boxed the Queen's ears – " the Rabbit began. Alice gave a little scream of laughter. "Oh, hush!" the Rabbit whispered in a frightened tone. "The Queen will hear you! You see, she came rather late, and the Queen said – "

"Get to your places!" shouted the Queen in a voice of thunder, and people began running about in all directions, tumbling up against each other; however, they got settled down in a minute or two, and the game began.

Alice thought she had never seen such a curious croquet-ground in her life; it was all ridges and furrows; the balls were live hedgehogs, the mallets live flamingoes, and the soldiers had to double themselves up and to stand on their hands and feet, to make the arches.

The chief difficulty Alice found at first was in managing her flamingo: she succeeded in getting its body tucked away, comfortably enough, under her arm, with its legs hanging down, but generally, just as she had got its neck nicely straightened out, and was going to give the hedgehog a blow with its head, it *would* twist itself round and look up in her face, with such a puzzled expression that she could not help bursting out laughing: and when she had got its head down, and was going to begin again, it was very provoking to find that the hedgehog had unrolled itself, and was in the act of crawling away: besides all this, there was generally a ridge or furrow in the way wherever she wanted to send the hedgehog to, and, as the doubled-up soldiers were always getting up and walking off to other parts of the ground, Alice soon came to the conclusion that it was a very difficult game indeed.

The players all played at once without waiting for turns, quarrelling all the while, and fighting for the hedgehogs; and in a very short time the Queen was in a furious passion, and went stamping about, and shouting "Off with his head!" or "Off with her head!" about once in a minute.

Alice began to feel very uneasy: to be sure, she had not as yet had any dispute with the Queen, but she knew that it might happen any minute, "and then," thought she, "what would become of me? They're dreadfully fond of beheading people here; the great wonder is, that there's any one left alive!"

She was looking about for some way of escape, and wondering whether she could get away without being seen, when she noticed a curious appearance in the air: it puzzled her very much at first, but, after watching it a minute or two, she made it out to be a grin, and she said to herself "It's the Cheshire Cat: now I shall have somebody to talk to."

"How are you getting on?" said the Cat, as soon as there was mouth enough for it to speak with.

Alice waited till the eyes appeared, and then nodded. "It's no use speaking to it," she thought, "till its ears have come, or at least one of them." In another minute the whole head appeared, and then Alice put down her flamingo, and began an account of the game, feeling very glad she had someone to listen to her. The Cat seemed to think that there was enough of it now in sight, and no more of it appeared.

"I don't think they play at all fairly," Alice began, in rather a complaining tone, "and they all quarrel so dreadfully one can't hear oneself speak – and they don't seem to have any rules in particular; at least, if there are, nobody attends to them – and you've no idea how confusing it is all the things being alive; for instance, there's the arch I've got to go through next walking about at the other end of the ground – and I should have croqueted the Queen's hedgehog just now, only it ran away when it saw mine coming!"

"How do you like the Queen?" said the Cat in a low voice.

"Not at all," said Alice: "she's so extremely – " Just then she noticed that the Queen was close behind her, listening: so she went on, " – likely to win, that it's hardly worth while finishing the game."

The Queen smiled and passed on.

"Who *are* you talking to?" said the King, going up to Alice, and looking at the Cat's head with great curiosity.

"It's a friend of mine – a Cheshire Cat," said Alice: "allow me to introduce it."

"I don't like the look of it at all," said the King: "however, it may kiss my hand if it likes."

"I'd rather not," the Cat remarked.

"Don't be impertinent," said the King, "and don't look at me like that!" He got behind Alice as he spoke.

"A cat may look at a king," said Alice. "I've read that in some book, but I don't remember where."

"Well, it must be removed," said the King very decidedly, and he called the Queen, who was passing at the moment, "My dear! I wish you would have this cat removed!"

The Queen had only one way of settling all difficulties, great or small. "Off with his head!" she said, without even looking round.

"I'll fetch the executioner myself," said the King eagerly, and he hurried off.

Alice thought she might as well go back, and see how the game was going on, as she heard the Queen's voice in the distance, screaming with passion. She had already heard her sentence three of the players to be executed for having missed their turns, and she did not like the look of things at all, as the game was in such confusion that she never knew whether it was her turn or not. So she went in search of her hedgehog.

The hedgehog was engaged in a fight with another hedgehog, which seemed to Alice an excellent opportunity for croqueting one of them with the other: the only difficulty was, that her flamingo was gone across to the other side of the garden, where Alice could see it trying in a helpless sort of way to fly up into a tree.

By the time she had caught the flamingo and brought it back, the fight was over, and both the hedgehogs were out of sight: "but it doesn't matter much," thought Alice, "as all the arches are gone from this side of the ground." So she tucked it away under her arm, that it might not escape again, and went back for a little more conversation with her friend.

When she got back to the Cheshire Cat, she was surprised to find quite a large crowd collected round it: there was a dispute going on between the executioner, the King, and the Queen, who were all talking at once, while all the rest were quite silent, and looked very uncomfortable.

The moment Alice appeared, she was appealed to by all three to settle the question, and they repeated their arguments to her, though, as they all spoke at once, she found it very hard indeed to make out exactly what they said.

The executioner's argument was, that you couldn't cut off a head unless there was a body to cut it off from: that he had never had to do such a thing before, and he wasn't going to begin at *his* time of life.

The King's argument was, that anything that had a head could be beheaded, and that you weren't to talk nonsense.

The Queen's argument was, that if something wasn't done about it in less than no time she'd have everybody executed, all round. (It was this last remark that had made the whole party look so grave and anxious.)

Alice could think of nothing else to say but "It belongs to the Duchess: you'd better ask *her* about it."

"She's in prison," the Queen said to the executioner: "fetch her here." And the executioner went off like an arrow.

The Cat's head began fading away the moment he was gone, and, by the time he had come back with the Duchess, it had entirely disappeared; so the King and the executioner ran wildly up and down looking for it, while the rest of the party went back to the game.

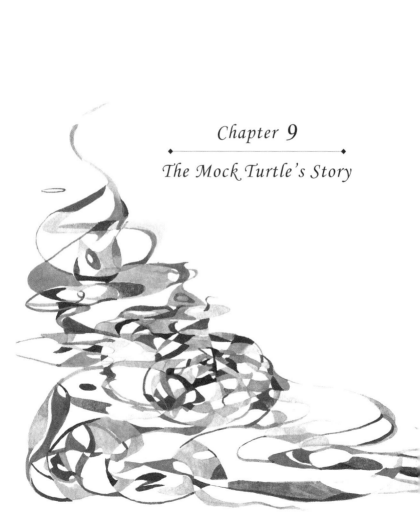

Chapter 9

The Mock Turtle's Story

... "and the moral of that is – 'Be what you would seem to be' – or if you'd like it put more simply – 'Never imagine yourself not to be otherwise than what it might appear to others that what you were or might have been was not otherwise than what you had been would have appeared to them to be otherwise.' "

"You can't think how glad I am to see you again, you dear old thing!" said the Duchess, as she tucked her arm affectionately into Alice's, and they walked off together.

Alice was very glad to find her in such a pleasant temper, and thought to herself that perhaps it was only the pepper that had made her so savage when they met in the kitchen.

"When *I'm* a Duchess," she said to herself, (not in a very hopeful tone though), "I won't have any pepper in my kitchen at all. Soup does very well without – Maybe it's always pepper that makes people hot-tempered," she went on, very much pleased at having found out a new kind of rule, "and vinegar that makes them sour – and camomile that makes them bitter – and – and barley-sugar and such things that make children sweet-tempered. I only wish people knew *that:* then they wouldn't be so stingy about it, you know – "

She had quite forgotten the Duchess by this time, and was a little startled when she heard her voice close to her ear. "You're thinking about something, my dear, and that makes you forget to talk. I can't tell you just now what the moral of that is, but I shall remember it in a bit."

"Perhaps it hasn't one," Alice ventured to remark.

"Tut, tut, child!" said the Duchess. "Everything's got a moral, if only you can find it." And she squeezed herself up closer to Alice's side as she spoke.

Alice did not much like keeping so close to her: first, because the Duchess was *very* ugly; and secondly, because she was exactly the right height to rest her chin upon Alice's shoulder, and it was an uncomfortably sharp chin. However, she did not like to be rude, so she bore it as well as she could.

"The game's going on rather better now," she said, by way of keeping up the conversation a little.

"'Tis so," said the Duchess: "and the moral of that is – 'Oh, 'tis love, 'tis love, that makes the world go round!' "

"Somebody said," Alice whispered, "that it's done by everybody minding their own business!"

"Ah, well! It means much the same thing," said the Duchess, digging her sharp little chin into Alice's shoulder as she added, "and the moral of *that is* – 'Take care of the sense, and the sounds will take care of themselves.' "

"How fond she is of finding morals in things!" Alice thought to herself.

"I dare say you're wondering why I don't put my arm round your waist," the Duchess said after a pause: "the reason is, that I'm doubtful about the temper of your flamingo. Shall I try the experiment?"

"*He* might bite," Alice cautiously replied, not feeling at all anxious to have the experiment tried.

"Very true," said the Duchess: "flamingoes and mustard both bite. And the moral of that is – 'Birds of a feather flock together.' "

"Only mustard isn't a bird," Alice remarked.

"Right, as usual," said the Duchess: "what a clear way you have of putting things!"

"It's a mineral, I *think,*" said Alice.

"Of course it is," said the Duchess, who seemed ready to agree to everything that Alice said; "there's a large mustard-mine near here. And the moral of that is – 'the more there is of mine, the less there is of yours.' "

"Oh, I know!" exclaimed Alice, who had not attended to this last remark, "it's a vegetable. It doesn't look like one, but it is."

"I quite agree with you," said the Duchess; "and the moral of that is – 'Be what you would seem to be' – or if you'd like it put more simply – 'Never imagine yourself not to be otherwise than what it might appear to others that what you were or might have been was not otherwise than what you had been would have appeared to them to be otherwise.' "

"I think I should understand that better," Alice said very politely, "if I had it written down: but I can't quite follow it as you say it."

"That's nothing to what I could say if I chose," the Duchess replied, in a pleased tone.

"Pray don't trouble yourself to say it any longer than that," said Alice.

"Oh, don't talk about trouble!" said the Duchess. "I make you a present of everything I've said as yet."

"A cheap sort of present!" thought Alice. "I'm glad they don't give birthday presents like that!" But she did not venture to say it out loud.

"Thinking again?" the Duchess asked, with another dig of her sharp little chin.

"I've a right to think," said Alice sharply, for she was beginning to feel a little worried.

"Just about as much right," said the Duchess, "as pigs have to fly; and the m – "

But here, to Alice's great surprise, the Duchess's voice died away, even in the middle of her favourite word "moral," and the arm that was linked into hers began to tremble. Alice looked up, and there stood the Queen in front of them, with her arms folded, frowning like a thunderstorm.

"A fine day, your Majesty!" the Duchess began in a low, weak voice.

"Now, I give you fair warning," shouted the Queen, stamping on the ground as she spoke; "either you or your head must be off, and that in about half no time! Take your choice!"

The Duchess took her choice, and was gone in a moment.

"Let's go on with the game," the Queen said to Alice; and Alice was too much frightened to say a word, but slowly followed her back to the croquet-ground. The other guests had taken advantage of the Queen's absence, and were resting in the shade: however, the moment they saw her, they hurried back to the game, the Queen merely remarking that a moment's delay would cost them their lives.

All the time they were playing the Queen never left off quarrelling with the other players, and shouting "Off with his head!" or "Off with her head!" Those whom she sentenced were taken into custody by the soldiers, who of course had to leave off being arches to do this, so that by the end of half an hour or so there were no arches left, and all the players, except the King, the Queen, and Alice, were in custody and under sentence of execution. Then the Queen left off, quite out of breath, and said to Alice, "Have you seen the Mock Turtle yet?"

"No," said Alice. "I don't even know what a Mock Turtle is."

"It's the thing mock turtle soup is made from," said the Queen.

"I never saw one, or heard of one," said Alice.

"Come on, then," said the Queen, "and he shall tell you his history,"

As they walked off together, Alice heard the King say in a low voice, to the company generally, "You are all pardoned." "Come, *that's* a good thing!" she said to herself, for she had felt quite unhappy at the number of executions the Queen had ordered.

They very soon came upon a Gryphon, lying fast asleep in the sun. (*If* you don't know what a Gryphon is, look at the picture.) "Up, lazy thing!" said the Queen, "and take this young lady to see the Mock Turtle, and to hear his history. I must go back and see after some executions I have ordered"; and she walked off, leaving Alice alone with the Gryphon. Alice did not quite like the look of the creature, but on the whole she thought it would be quite as safe to stay with it as to go after that savage Queen: so she waited.

The Gryphon sat up and rubbed its eyes: then it watched the Queen till she was out of sight: then it chuckled. "What fun!" said the Gryphon, half to itself, half to Alice.

"What *is* the fun?" said Alice.

"Why, *she,*" said the Gryphon. "It's all her fancy, they never executes nobody, you know. Come on!"

"Everybody says 'come on!' here," thought Alice, as she went

265

slowly after it: "I never was so ordered about in all my life, never!"

They had not gone far before they saw the Mock Turtle in the distance, sitting sad and lonely on a little ledge of rock, and, as they came nearer, Alice could hear him sighing as if his heart would break. She pitied him deeply.

"What is his sorrow?" she asked the Gryphon, and the Gryphon answered, very nearly in the same words as before, "It's all his fancy, that: he hasn't got no sorrow, you know. Come on!"

So they went up to the Mock Turtle, who looked at them with large eyes full of tears, but said nothing.

"This here young lady," said the Gryphon, "she wants for to know your history, she do."

"I'll tell it her," said the Mock Turtle in a deep, hollow tone. "Sit down, both of you, and don't speak a word till I've finished."

So they sat down, and nobody spoke for some minutes. Alice thought to herself, "I don't see how he can even finish, if he doesn't begin." But she waited patiently.

"Once," said the Mock Turtle at last, with a deep sigh, "I was a real Turtle."

These words were followed by a very long silence, broken only by an occasional exclamation of "Hjckrrh!" from the Gryphon, and the constant heavy sobbing of the Mock Turtle. Alice was very nearly getting up and saying, "Thank you, sir, for your interesting story," but she could not help thinking there *must* be more to come, so she sat still and said nothing.

"When we were little," the Mock Turtle went on at last, more calmly, though still sobbing a little now and then, "we went to school in the sea. The master was an old Turtle – we used to call him Tortoise – "

"Why did you call him Tortoise, if he wasn't one?" Alice asked.

"We called him Tortoise because he taught us," said the Mock Turtle angrily: "really you are very dull!"

"You ought to be ashamed of yourself for asking such a simple question," added the Gryphon; and then they both sat silent and looked at poor Alice, who felt ready to sink into the earth. At last the Gryphon said to the Mock Turtle, "Drive on, old fellow! Don't be all day about it!" and he went on in these words:

"Yes, we went to school in the sea, though you mayn't believe it – "

"I never said I didn't!" interrupted Alice.

"You did," said the Mock Turtle.

"Hold your tongue!" added the Gryphon, before Alice could speak again. The Mock Turtle went on.

"We had the best of educations – in fact, we went to school every day – "

"*I've* been to a day-school, too," said Alice; "you needn't be so proud as all that."

"With extras?" asked the Mock Turtle a little anxiously.

"Yes," said Alice, "we learned French and music."

"And washing?" said the Mock Turtle.

"Certainly not!" said Alice indignantly.

"Ah! then yours wasn't a really good school," said the Mock Turtle in a tone of great relief. "Now at *ours* they had at the end of the bill,

'French, music, *and washing* – extra.' "

"You couldn't have wanted it much," said Alice; "living at the bottom of the sea."

"I couldn't afford to learn it." said the Mock Turtle with a sigh. "I only took the regular course."

"What was that?" inquired Alice.

"Reeling and Writhing, of course, to begin with," the Mock Turtle replied: "and then the different branches of Arithmetic – Ambition, Distraction, Uglification, and Derision."

"I never heard of "Uglification," Alice ventured to say. "What is it?"

The Gryphon lifted up both its paws in surprise. "What! Never heard of uglifying!" it exclaimed. "You know what to beautify is, I suppose?"

"Yes," said Alice doubtfully: "it means – to – make – anything – prettier."

"Well, then," the Gryphon went on, "if you don't know what to uglify is, you *are* a simpleton."

Alice did not feel encouraged to ask any more questions about it, so she turned to the Mock Turtle, and said "What else had you to learn?"

"Well, there was Mystery," the Mock Turtle replied, counting off the subjects on his flappers, " – Mystery, ancient and modern, with Seaography – then Drawling – the Drawling-master was an old conger-eel, that used to come once a week: *he* taught us Drawling, Stretching, and Fainting in Coils."

"What was that like?" said Alice.

"Well, I can't show it you myself," the Mock Turtle said: "I'm too stiff. And the Gryphon never learnt it."

"Hadn't time," said the Gryphon: "I went to the Classics master, though. He was an old crab, *he* was."

"I never went to him," the Mock Turtle said with a sigh: "he taught Laughing and Grief, they used to say."

"So he did, so he did," said the Gryphon, sighing in his turn, and both creatures hid their faces in their paws.

"And how many hours a day did you do lessons?" said Alice, in a hurry to change the subject.

"Ten hours the first day," said the Mock Turtle: "nine the next, and so on."

"What a curious plan!" exclaimed Alice.

"That's the reason they're called lessons," the Gryphon remarked: "because they lessen from day to day." This was quite a new idea to Alice, and she thought it over a little before she made her next remark. "Then the eleventh day must have been a holiday?"

"Of course it was," said the Mock Turtle.

"And how did you manage on the twelfth?" Alice went on eagerly.

"That's enough about lessons," the Gryphon interrupted in a very decided tone. "Tell her something about the games now."

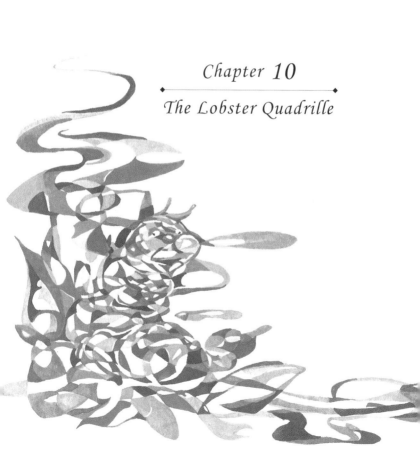

Chapter 10

The Lobster Quadrille

"You may not have lived much under the sea – "
("I haven't," said Alice) – "and perhaps you were
never even introduced to a lobster – " (Alice began to
say "I once tasted – " but checked herself hastily, and
said "No, never") –"so you can have no idea what a
delightful thing a Lobster Quadrille is!"
"No, indeed," said Alice. "What sort of a dance is it?"

The mock Turtle sighed deeply, and drew the back of one flapper across his eyes. He looked at Alice, and tried to speak, but for a minute or two sobs choked his voice. "Same as if he had a bone in his throat," said the Gryphon, and it set to work shaking him and punching him in the back. At last the Mock Turtle recovered his voice, and, with tears running down his cheeks, he went on again:

"You may not have lived much under the sea – " ("I haven't," said Alice) –"and perhaps you were never even introduced to a lobster –" (Alice began to say "I once tasted – but checked herself hastily, and said "No, never") –"so you can have no idea what a delightful thing a Lobster Quadrille is!"

"No, indeed," said Alice. "What sort of a dance is it?"

"Why," said the Gryphon, "you first form into a line along the seashore – "

"Two lines!" cried the Mock Turtle. "Seals, turtles, salmon, and so on; then, when you've cleared all the jelly-fish out of the way – "

"That generally takes some time," interrupted the Gryphon.

" – you advance twice – "

"Each with a lobster as a partner!" cried the Gryphon.

"Of course," the Mock Turtle said: "advance twice, set to partners – "

" – change lobsters, and retire in same order," continued the

Gryphon.

"Then, you know,"the Mock Turtle went on,"you throw the – "

"The lobsters!"shouted the Gryphon, with a bound into the air.

" – as far out to sea as you can – "

"Swim after them!"screamed the Gryphon.

"Turn a somersault in the sea!"cried the Mock Turtle, capering wildly about.

"Change lobsters again!"yelled the Gryphon at the top of its voice.

"Back to land again, and – that's all the first figure,"said the Mock Turtle, suddenly dropping his voice; and the two creatures, who had been jumping about like mad things all this time, sat down again very sadly and quietly, and looked at Alice.

"It must be a very pretty dance,"said Alice timidly.

"Would you like to see a little of it?"said the Mock Turtle.

"Very much indeed,"said Alice.

"Come, let's try the first figure!"said the Mock Turtle to the Gryphon."We can do without lobsters, you know. Which shall sing?"

"Oh, *you* sing," said the Gryphon. "I've forgotten the words." So they began solemnly dancing round and round Alice, every now and then treading on her toes when they passed too close, and waving their forepaws to mark the time, while the Mock Turtle sang this, very slowly and sadly: –

"Will you walk a little faster?" said a whiting to a snail,
"There's a porpoise close behind us, and he's treading on my tail.
See how eagerly the lobsters and the turtles all advance!
They are waiting on the shingle – will you come and join the dance?
Will you, won't you, will you, won't you, will you join the dance?
Will you, won't you, will you, won't you, won't you join the dance?"

"You can really have no notion how delightful it will be
When they take us up and throw us, with the lobsters, out to sea!"
But the snail replied "Too far, too far!" and gave a look askance –
Said he thanked the whiting kindly, but he would not join the dance.
Would not, could not, would not, could not, would not join the dance.
Would not, could not, would not, could not, could not join the dance.

"What matters it how far we go?" his scaly friend replied,
"There is another shore, you know, upon the other side.
The further off from England the nearer is to France –
Then turn not pale, beloved snail, but come and join the dance.
Will you, won't you, will you, won't you, will you join the dance?
Will you, won't you, will you, won't you, won't you join the dance?"

"Thank you, it's a very interesting dance to watch," said Alice, feeling very glad that it was over at last; "and I do so like that curious song about the whiting!"

"Oh, as to the whiting," said the Mock Turtle, "they – you've seen them, of course?"

"Yes," said Alice, "I've often seen them at dinn – " she checked herself hastily.

"I don't know where dinn may be,"said the Mock Turtle, "but if you've seen them so often, of course you know what they're like."

"I believe so,"Alice replied thoughtfully."They have their tails in their mouths – and they're all over crumbs."

"You're wrong about the crumbs,"said the Mock Turtle: "crumbs would all wash off in the sea. But they *have* their tails in their mouths; and the reason is – "here the Mock Turtle yawned and shut his eyes. "Tell her about the reason and all that,"he said to the Gryphon.

"The reason is,"said the Gryphon,"that they *would* go with the lobsters to the dance. So they got thrown out to sea. So they had to fall a long way. So they got their tails fast in their mouths. So they couldn't get them out again. That's all."

"Thank you,"said Alice,"it's very interesting. I never knew so much about a whiting before."

"I can tell you more than that, if you like,"said the Gryphon. "Do you know why it's called a whiting?"

277

"I never thought about it," said Alice. "Why?"

"*It does the boots and shoes*." the Gryphon replied very solemnly.

Alice was thoroughly puzzled. "Does the boots and shoes!" she repeated in a wondering tone.

"Why, what are *your* shoes done with?" said the Gryphon. "I mean, what makes them so shiny?"

Alice looked down at them, and considered a little before she gave her answer. "They're done with blacking, I believe."

"Boots and shoes under the sea," the Gryphon went on in a deep voice, "are done with a whiting. Now you know."

"And what are they made of?" Alice asked in a tone of great curiosity.

"Soles and eels, of course," the Gryphon replied rather impatiently: "any shrimp could have told you that."

"If I'd been the whiting," said Alice, whose thoughts were still running on the song, "I'd have said to the porpoise,'Keep back, please: we don't want *you* with us!'"

"They were obliged to have him with them," the Mock Turtle said.

"No wise fish would go anywhere without a porpoise."

"Wouldn't it really?" said Alice in a tone of great surprise.

"Of course not," said the Mock Turtle. "Why, if a fish came to me, and told me he was going a journey, I should say 'With what porpoise?'"

"Don't you mean 'purpose'?" said Alice.

"I mean what I say," the Mock Turtle replied in an offended tone. And the Gryphon added "Come, let's hear some of *your* adventures."

"I could tell you my adventures – beginning from this morning," said Alice a little timidly: "but it's no use going back to yesterday, because I was a different person then."

"Explain all that," said the Mock Turtle.

"No, no! The adventures first," said the Gryphon in an impatient tone: "explanations take such a dreadful time."

So Alice began telling them her adventures from the time when she first saw the White Rabbit. She was a little nervous about it just at first, the two creatures got so close to her, one on each side, and opened their eyes and mouths so *very* wide; but she gained courage as she went on. Her listeners were perfectly quiet till she got to the part about her repeating "*you are old, father William,*" to the Caterpillar, and the words all coming different, and then the Mock Turtle drew a long breath, and said "That's very curious."

"It's all about as curious as it can be," said the Gryphon.

"It all came different!" the Mock Turtle repeated thoughtfully. "I should like to hear her try and repeat something now. Tell her to begin." He looked at the Gryphon as if he thought it had some kind of authority over Alice.

"Stand up and repeat *'tis the voice of the sluggard*,' " said the Gryphon.

"How the creatures order one about, and make one repeat lessons!" thought Alice; "I might as well be at school at once." However, she got up, and began to repeat it, but her head was so full of the Lobster Quadrille, that she hardly knew what she was saying, and the words came very queer indeed: –

> *"Tis the voice of the Lobster; I heard him declare,*
> *'You have baked me too brown, I must sugar my hair.'*
> *As a duck with its eyelids, so he with his nose*
> *Trims his belt and his buttons, and turns out his toes.*
> *When the sands are all dry, he is gay as a lark,*
> *And will talk in contemptuous tones of the Shark:*
> *But, when the tide rises and sharks are around,*
> *His voice has a timid and tremulous sound."*

"That's different from what I used to say when I was a child," said the Gryphon.

"Well, *I* never heard it before," said the Mock Turtle; "but it sounds uncommon nonsense."

Alice said nothing; she had sat down with her face in her hands, wondering if anything would *ever* happen in a natural way again.

"I should like to have it explained," said the Mock Turtle.

"She can't explain it," said the Gryphon hastily. "Go on with the next verse."

"But about his toes?" the Mock Turtle persisted. "How *could* he turn them out with his nose, you know?"

"It's the first position in dancing." Alice said; but she was dreadfully puzzled by the whole thing, and longed to change the subject.

"Go on with the next verse," the Gryphon repeated impatiently: "it begins *'I passed by his garden.'*"

Alice did not dare to disobey, though she felt sure it would all come wrong, and she went on in a trembling voice: –

"I passed by his garden, and marked, with one eye,
How the Owl and the Panther were sharing a pie –
The Panther took pie-crust, and gravy, and meat,
While the Owl had the dish as its share of the treat.
When the pie was all finished, the Owl, as a boon,
Was kindly permitted to pocket the spoon:
While the Panther received knife and fork with a growl,
And concluded the banquet by – "

"What is the use of repeating all that stuff," the Mock Turtle interrupted, "if you don't explain it as you go on? It's by far the most confusing thing I ever heard!"

"Yes, I think you'd better leave off," said the Gryphon: and Alice was only too glad to do so.

"Shall we try another figure of the Lobster Quadrille?" the Gryphon went on."Or would you like the Mock Turtle to sing you a song?"

"Oh, a song, please, if the Mock Turtle would be so kind," Alice replied, so eagerly that the Gryphon said, in a rather offended tone,"Hm! No accounting for tastes! Sing her'*Turtle Soup,*'will you, old fellow?"

The Mock Turtle sighed deeply, and began, in a voice sometimes choked with sobs, to sing this: –

> *"Beautiful Soup! Who cares for fish,*
> *Game, or any other dish?*
> *Who would not give all else for two*
> *Pennyworth only of beautiful Soup?*
> *Pennyworth only of beautiful Soup?*
> *Beau – ootiful Soo – oop!*
> *Beau – ootiful Soo – oop!*
> *Soo – oop of the e – e – evening,*
> *Beautiful, beauti – FUL SOUP!"*

> *"Beautiful Soup, so rich and green,*

Waiting in a hot tureen!
Who for such dainties would not stoop?
Soup of the evening, beautiful Soup!
Soup of the evening, beautiful Soup!
Beau – ootiful Soo – oop!
Beau – ootiful Soo – oop!
Soo – oop of the e – e – evening,
Beautiful, beautiful Soup!

"Chorus again!" cried the Gryphon, and the Mock Turtle had just begun to repeat it, when a cry of "The trial's beginning!" was heard in the distance.

"Come on!" cried the Gryphon, and, taking Alice by the hand, it hurried off, without waiting for the end of the song.

"What trial is it?" Alice panted as she ran; but the Gryphon only answered "Come on!" and ran the faster, while more and more faintly came, carried on the breeze that followed them, the melancholy words:

"Soo – oop of the e – e – evening,
Beautiful, beautiful Soup!"

Chapter 11

Who Stole the Tarts?

"Give your evidence," said the King; "and don't be nervous, or I'll have you executed on the spot."

"Give your evidence," the King repeated angrily, "or I'll have you executed, whether you're nervous or not."

"You must remember," remarked the King, "or I'll have you executed."

The king and queen of hearts were seated on their throne when they arrived, with a great crowd assembled about them – all sorts of little birds and beasts, as well as the whole pack of cards: the Knave was standing before them, in chains, with a soldier on each side to guard him; and near the King was the White Rabbit, with a trumpet in one hand, and a scroll of parchment in the other. In the very middle of the court was a table, with a large dish of tarts upon it: they looked so good, that it made Alice quite hungry to look at them – "I wish they'd get the trial done," she thought, "and hand round the refreshments!" But there seemed to be no chance of this, so she began looking at everything about her, to pass away the time.

Alice had never been in a court of justice before, but she had read about them in books, and she was quite pleased to find that she knew the name of nearly everything there. "That's the judge," she said to herself, "because of his great wig."

The judge, by the way, was the King; and as he wore his crown over the wig (look at the frontispiece if you want to see how he did it) he did not look at all comfortable, and it was certainly not becoming.

"And that's the jury-box," thought Alice, "and those twelve creatures" (she was obliged to say "creatures," you see, because some of them were animals, and some were birds) "I suppose they are the jurors." She said this last word two or three times over to herself, being rather proud of it: for she thought, and rightly too, that very few little girls of her age knew the meaning of it at all. However, "jury-men" would have done just as well.

The twelve jurors were all writing very busily on slates. "What are they doing?" Alice whispered to the Gryphon. "They can't have anything to put down yet, before the trial's begun."

"They're putting down their names," the Gryphon whispered in reply, "for fear they should forget them before the end of the trial."

"Stupid things!" Alice began in a loud, indignant voice, but she stopped hastily, for the White Rabbit cried out, "Silence in the court!" and the King put on his spectacles and looked anxiously round, to make out who was talking.

287

Alice could see, as well as if she were looking over their shoulders, that all the jurors were writing down "Stupid things!" on their slates, and she could even make out that one of them didn't know how to spell "stupid," and that he had to ask his neighbour to tell him. "A nice muddle their slates'll be in before the trial's over!" thought Alice.

One of the jurors had a pencil that squeaked. This of course, Alice could *not* stand, and she went round the court and got behind him, and very soon found an opportunity of taking it away. She did it so quickly that the poor little juror (it was Bill, the Lizard) could not make out at all what had become of it; so, after hunting all about for it, he was obliged to write with one finger for the rest of the day; and this was of very little use, as it left no mark on the slate.

"Herald, read the accusation!" said the King.

On this the White Rabbit blew three blasts on the trumpet, and then unrolled the parchment scroll, and read as follows: –

"The Queen of Hearts, she made some tarts,
All on a summer day:
The Knave of Hearts, he stole those tarts,
And took them quite away!"

"Consider your verdict," the King said to the jury.

"Not yet, not yet!" the Rabbit hastily interrupted. "There's a great deal to come before that!"

"Call the first witness," said the King; and the White Rabbit blew three blasts on the trumpet, and called out, "First witness!"

The first witness was the Hatter. He came in with a teacup in one hand and a piece of bread-and-butter in the other. "I beg pardon, your Majesty," he began, "for bringing these in: but I hadn't quite finished my tea when I was sent for."

"You ought to have finished," said the King. "When did you begin?"

The Hatter looked at the March Hare, who had followed him into the court, arm-in-arm with the Dormouse.

"Fourteenth of March, I *think* it was," he said.

"Fifteenth," said the March Hare.

289

"Sixteenth," added the Dormouse.

"Write that down," the King said to the jury, and the jury eagerly wrote down all three dates on their slates, and then added them up, and reduced the answer to shillings and pence.

"Take off your hat," the King said to the Hatter.

"It isn't mine," said the Hatter.

"Stolen!" the King exclaimed, turning to the jury, who instantly made a memorandum of the fact.

"I keep them to sell," the Hatter added as an explanation; "I've none of my own. I'm a hatter."

Here the Queen put on her spectacles, and began staring at the Hatter, who turned pale and fidgeted.

"Give your evidence," said the King; "and don't be nervous, or I'll have you executed on the spot."

This did not seem to encourage the witness at all: he kept shifting from one foot to the other, looking uneasily at the Queen, and in his confusion he bit a large piece out of his teacup instead of the bread-and-butter.

Just at this moment Alice felt a very curious sensation, which puzzled her a good deal until she made out what it was: she was beginning to grow larger again, and she thought at first she would get up and leave the court; but on second thoughts she decided to remain where she was as long as there was room for her.

"I wish you wouldn't squeeze so." said the Dormouse, who was sitting next to her. "I can hardly breathe."

"I can't help it," said Alice very meekly: "I'm growing."

"You've no right to grow *here*," said the Dormouse.

"Don't talk nonsense," said Alice more boldly: "you know you're growing too."

"Yes, but I grow at a reasonable pace," said the Dormouse: "not in that ridiculous fashion." And he got up very sulkily and crossed over to the other side of the court.

All this time the Queen had never left off staring at the Hatter, and, just as the Dormouse crossed the court, she said to one of the officers of the court, "Bring me the list of the singers in the last concert!" on which the wretched Hatter trembled so, that he shook both his shoes off.

"Give your evidence," the King repeated angrily, "or I'll have you executed, whether you're nervous or not."

"I'm a poor man, your Majesty," the Hatter began, in a trembling voice, "and I hadn't but just begun my tea – not above a week or so – and what with the bread-and-butter getting so thin – and the twinkling of the tea – "

"The twinkling of the *what*?" said the King.

"It *began* with the tea," the Hatter replied.

"Of course twinkling begins with a T!" said the King sharply. "Do you take me for a dunce? Go on!"

"I'm a poor man," the Hatter went on, "and most things twinkled after that – only the March Hare said – "

"I didn't!" the March Hare interrupted in a great hurry.

"You did!" said the Hatter.

"I deny it!" said the March Hare.

"He denies it," said the King: "leave out that part."

"Well, at any rate, the Dormouse said – " the Hatter went on, looking anxiously round to see if he would deny it too: but the Dormouse denied nothing, being fast asleep.

"After that," continued the Hatter, "I cut some more bread-and-butter – "

"But what did the Dormouse say?" one of the jury asked.

"That I can't remember," said the Hatter.

"You *must* remember," remarked the King, "or I'll have you executed."

The miserable Hatter dropped his teacup and bread-and-butter, and went down on one knee. "I'm a poor man, your Majesty," he began.

"You're a *very* poor *speaker,*" said the King.

Here one of the guinea-pigs cheered, and was immediately suppressed by the officers of the court.

(As that is rather a hard word, I will just explain to you how it was done. They had a large canvas bag, which tied up at the mouth with strings: into this they slipped the guinea-pig, head first, and then sat upon it.)

"I'm glad I've seen that done," thought Alice. "I've so often read in the newspapers, at the end of trials, 'There was some attempts at applause, which was immediately suppressed by the officers of the court,' and I never understood what it meant till now."

"If that's all you know about it, you may stand down," continued the King.

"I can't go no lower," said the Hatter: "I'm on the floor, as it is."

"Then you may *sit* down," the King replied.

Here the other guinea-pig cheered, and was suppressed.

"Come, that finished the guinea-pigs!" thought Alice. "Now we shall get on better."

"I'd rather finish my tea," said the Hatter, with an anxious look at the Queen, who was reading the list of singers.

"You may go," said the King, and the Hatter hurriedly left the court, without even waiting to put his shoes on.

" – and just take his head off outside," the Queen added to one of the officers; but the Hatter was out of sight before the officer could get to the door.

"Call the next witness!" said the King.

The next witness was the Duchess's cook. She carried the pepper-box in her hand, and Alice guessed who it was, even before she got into the court, by the way the people near the door began sneezing all at once.

"Give your evidence," said the King.

"Shan't," said the cook.

The King looked anxiously at the White Rabbit, who said in a low voice, "Your Majesty must cross-examine *this* witness."

"Well, if I must, I must," the King said, with a melancholy air, and, after folding his arms and frowning at the cook till his eyes were nearly out of sight, he said in a deep voice, "What are tarts made of?"

"Pepper, mostly," said the cook.

"Treacle," said a sleepy voice behind her.

"Collar that Dormouse!" the Queen shrieked out. "Behead that Dormouse! Turn that Dormouse out of court! Suppress him! Pinch him! Off with his whiskers!"

For some minutes the whole court was in confusion, getting the Dormouse turned out, and, by the time they had settled down again, the cook had disappeared.

"Never mind!" said the King, with an air of great relief. "Call the next witness." And he added in an undertone to the Queen, "Really, my dear, *you* must cross-examine the next witness. It quite makes my forehead ache!"

Alice watched the White Rabbit as he fumbled over the list, feeling very curious to see what the next witness would be like, " – for they haven't got much evidence *yet*," she said to herself. Imagine her surprise, when the White Rabbit read out, at the top of his shrill little voice, the name "Alice!"

Chapter 12

Alice's Evidence

"Please your Majesty," said the Knave: "I didn't write it, and they can't prove I did: there's no name signed at the end."

"If you didn't sign it," said the King, "that only makes the matter worse. You must have meant some mischief, or else you'd have signed your name like an honest man."

"That proves his guilt," said the Queen.

"It proves nothing of the sort!" said Alice. "Why, you don't even know what they're about!"

"Here!" cried Alice, quite forgetting in the flurry of the moment how large she had grown in the last few minutes, and she jumped up in such a hurry that she tipped over the jury-box with the edge of her skirt, upsetting all the jurymen on to the heads of the crowd below, and there they lay sprawling about, reminding her very much of a globe of goldfish she had accidentally upset the week before.

"Oh, I *beg* your pardon!" she exclaimed in a tone of great dismay, and began picking them up again as quickly as she could, for the accident of the goldfish kept running in her head, and she had a vague sort of idea that they must be collected at once and put back into the jury-box, or they would die.

"The trial cannot proceed," said the King in a very grave voice, "until all the jurymen are back in their proper places – *all*," he repeated with great emphasis, looking hard at Alice as he said so.

Alice looked at the jury-box, and saw that, in her haste, she had put the Lizard in head downwards, and the poor little thing was waving its tail about in a melancholy way, being quite unable to move. She soon got it out again, and put it right; "not that it signifies much," she said to herself; "I should think it would be *quite* as much use in the trial one way up as the other."

As soon as the jury had a little recovered from the shock of being upset, and their slates and pencils had been found and handed back to them, they set to work very diligently to write out a history of the accident, all except the Lizard, who seemed too much overcome to do anything but sit with its mouth open, gazing up into the roof of the court.

"What do you know about this business?" the King said to Alice.

"Nothing," said Alice.

"Nothing *whatever*?" persisted the King.

"Nothing whatever," said Alice.

"That's very important," the King said, turning to the jury. They were just beginning to write this down on their slates, when the White Rabbit interrupted: *"un*important, your Majesty means, of course," he said in a very respectful tone, but frowning and making faces at him as he spoke.

*"Un*important, of course, I meant," the King hastily said, and went on to himself in an undertone, "important – unimportant – unimportant – important – " as if he were trying which word sounded best.

Some of the jury wrote it down "important," and some "unimportant." Alice could see this, as she was near enough to look over their slates; "but it doesn't matter a bit," she thought to herself.

At this moment the King, who had been for some time busily writing in his note-book, cackled out "Silence!" and read out from his book, "Rule Forty-two. *All persons more than a mile high to leave the court.*"

Everybody looked at Alice.

"*I'm* not a mile high," said Alice.

"You are," said the King.

"Nearly two miles high," added the Queen.

"Well, I shan't go, at any rate," said Alice; "besides, that's not a regular rule: you invented it just now."

"It's the oldest rule in the book," said the King.

"Then it ought to be Number One," said Alice.

The King turned pale, and shut his note-book hastily. "Consider your verdict," he said to the jury, in a low, trembling voice.

"There's more evidence to come yet, please your Majesty," said the White Rabbit, jumping up in a great hurry; "this paper has just been picked up."

"What's in it?" said the Queen.

"I haven't opened it yet," said the White Rabbit, "but it seems to be a letter, written by the prisoner to – to somebody."

"It must have been that," said the King, "unless it was written to nobody, which isn't usual, you know."

"Who is it directed to?" said one of the jurymen.

"It isn't directed at all," said the White Rabbit; "in fact, there's nothing written on the *outside*." He unfolded the paper as he spoke, and added "It isn't a letter, after all: it's a set of verses."

"Are they in the prisoner's handwriting?" asked another of the jurymen.

"No, they're not," said the White Rabbit, "and that's the queerest thing about it." (The jury all looked puzzled.)

"He must have imitated somebody else's hand," said the King. (The jury all brightened up again.)

"Please your Majesty," said the Knave: "I didn't write it, and they can't prove I did: there's no name signed at the end."

"If you didn't sign it," said the King, "that only makes the matter worse. You *must* have meant some mischief, or else you'd have signed your name like an honest man."

There was a general clapping of hands at this: it was the first really clever thing the King had said that day.

"That *proves* his guilt," said the Queen.

"It proves nothing of the sort!" said Alice. "Why, you don't even know what they're about!"

"Read them," said the King.

The White Rabbit put on his spectacles. "Where shall I begin, please your Majesty?" he asked.

"Begin at the beginning," the King said gravely, "and go on till you come to the end: then stop."

These were the verses the White Rabbit read: –

"They told me you had been to her,

And mentioned me to him:
She gave me a good character,
But said I could not swim.

He sent them word I had not gone
(We know it to be true):
If she should push the matter on,
What would become of you?

I gave her one, they gave him two,
You gave us three or more;
They all returned from him to you,
Though they were mine before.

If I or she should chance to be
Involved in this affair,
He trusts to you to set them free
Exactly as we were.

My notion was that you had been
(Before she had this fit)
An obstacle that came between
Him, and ourselves, and it.

Don't let him know she liked them best,
For this must ever be
A secret, kept from all the rest,

Between yourself and me."

"That's the most important piece of evidence we've heard yet," said the King, rubbing his hands; "so now let the jury – "

"If any one of them can explain it," said Alice, (she had grown so large in the last few minutes that she wasn't a bit afraid of interrupting him) "I'll give him sixpence. *I* don't believe there's an atom of meaning in it."

The jury all wrote down on their slates, "*She* doesn't believe there's an atom of meaning in it," but none of them attempted to explain the paper.

"If there's no meaning in it," said the King, "that saves a world of trouble, you know, as we needn't try to find any. And yet I don't know," he went on, spreading out the verses on his knee, and looking at them with one eye; "I seem to see some meaning in them, after all. – '*said i could not swim*' – you can't swim, can you?" he added, turning to the Knave.

The Knave shook his head sadly. "Do I look like it?" he said. (Which he certainly did *not*, being made entirely of cardboard.)

"All right, so far," said the King, and he went on muttering over the verses to himself: " '*We know it to be true* – ' that's the jury of course – '*If she sould push the matter on*' – that must be the Queen – '*What sould become of you?*' – What, indeed! – '*I gave her one, they gave him two*' – why, that must be what he did with the tarts, you know – "

"But, it goes on *'they all returned from him to you.'* " said Alice.

"Why, there they are!" said the King triumphantly, pointing to the tarts on the table. "Nothing can be clearer than that. Then again – *'before she had this fit'* – you never had fits, my dear, I think?" he said to the Queen.

"Never!" said the Queen furiously, throwing an inkstand at the Lizard as she spoke.

(The unfortunate little Bill had left off writing on his slate with one finger, as he found it made no mark; but he now hastily began again, using the ink, that was trickling down his face, as long as it lasted.)

"Then the words don't *fit* you," said the King, looking round the court with a smile. There was a dead silence.

"It's a pun!" the King added in an offended tone, and everybody laughed, "Let the jury consider their verdict," the King said, for about the twentieth time that day.

"No, no!" said the Queen. "Sentence first – verdict afterwards."

"Stuff and nonsense!" said Alice loudly. "The idea of having the sentence first!"

"Hold your tongue!" said the Queen, turning purple.

"I won't!" said Alice.

"Off with her head!" the Queen shouted at the top of her voice.

Nobody moved.

"Who cares for *you*?" said Alice (she had grown to her full size by this time). "You're nothing but a pack of cards!"

At this the whole pack rose up into the air, and came flying down upon her: she gave a little scream, half of fright and half of anger, and tried to beat them off, and found herself lying on the bank, with her head in the lap of her sister, who was gently brushing away some dead leaves that had fluttered down from the trees upon her face.

"Wake up, Alice dear!" said her sister, "Why, what a long sleep you've had!"

"Oh, I've had such a curious dream!" said Alice, and she told her sister, as well as she could remember them, all these strange Adventures of hers that you have just been reading about; and when she had finished, her sister kissed her, and said, "It *was* a curious dream, dear, certainly: but now run in to your tea; it's getting late." So Alice got up and ran off, thinking while she ran, as well she might, what a wonderful dream it had been.

BUT her sister sat still just as she left her, leaning her head on her hand, watching the setting sun, and thinking of little Alice and all her wonderful Adventures, till she too began dreaming after a fashion, and this was her dream: –

First, she dreamed of little Alice herself, and once again the tiny hands were clasped upon her knee, and the bright eager eyes were looking up into hers – she could hear the very tones of her voice, and see that queer little toss of her head to keep back the wandering hair that *would* always get into her eyes – and still as she listened, or seemed to listen, the whole place around her became alive with the strange creatures of her little sister's dream.

The long grass rustled at her feet as the White Rabbit hurried by – the frightened Mouse splashed his way through the neighbouring pool – she could hear the rattle of the teacups as the March Hare and his friends shared their never-ending meal, and the shrill voice of the Queen ordering off her unfortunate guests to execution – once more the pig-baby was sneezing on the Duchess's knee, while plates and dishes crashed around it – once more the shriek of the Gryphon, the squeaking of the Lizard's slate-pencil, and the choking of the suppressed guinea-pigs, filled the air, mixed up with the distant sobs of the miserable Mock Turtle.

So she sat on, with closed eyes, and half believed herself in Wonderland, though she knew she had but to open them again, and all would change to dull reality – the grass would be only rustling in the wind, and the pool rippling to the waving of the reeds – the rattling teacups would change to tinkling sheep-bells and the Queen's shrill cries to the voice of the shepherd boy – and the sneeze of the baby, the shriek of the Gryphon, and all the other queer noises, would change (she knew) to the confused clamour of the busy farm-yard – while the lowing of the cattle in the distance would take the place of the Mock Turtle's heavy sobs.

Lastly, she pictured to herself how this same little sister of hers would, in the after-time, be herself a grown woman; and how she would keep, through all her riper years, the simple and loving heart of her childhood: and how she would gather about her other little children, and make *their* eyes bright and eager with many a strange tale, perhaps even with the dream of Wonderland of long ago: and how she would feel with all their simple sorrows, and find a pleasure in all their simple joys, remembering her own child-life, and the happy summer days.

愛麗絲鏡中奇遇

Through
The
Looking-Glass

第 *1* 章

鏡中的房間

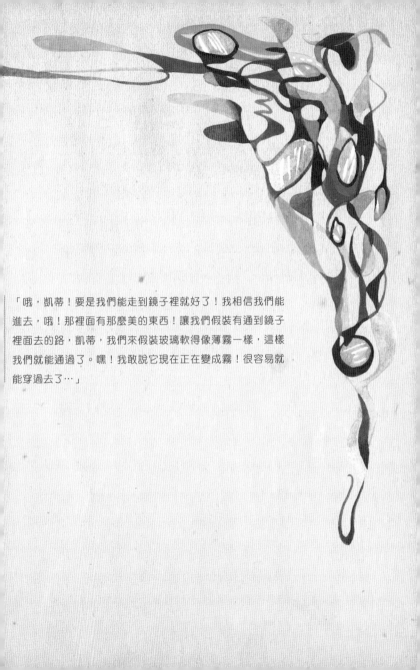

「哦，凱蒂！要是我們能走到鏡子裡就好了！我相信我們能進去，哦！那裡面有那麼美的東西！讓我們假裝有通到鏡子裡面去的路，凱蒂，我們來假裝玻璃軟得像薄霧一樣，這樣我們就能通過了。嘿！我敢說它現在正在變成霧！很容易就能穿過去了…」

有一件事是確定的，就是小白貓和這件事沒關係，全都是小黑貓的錯。因為在剛才的十五分鐘裡，小白貓一直在讓老貓幫牠洗臉（一直都很乖）。所以牠不可能惡作劇。

黛娜是這樣幫牠的孩子們洗臉的：先用一隻爪子抓住惡作劇小貓的耳朵，把牠按下去，接著用另一隻爪子擦個幾遍，然後再換邊，從鼻子開始擦。就像我說的，牠正努力地幫小白貓洗臉，小白貓安安靜靜地躺著，試著發出咕嚕咕嚕的聲音，牠知道這都是為了自己好。

但是下午稍早，小黑貓已經洗完臉了，當愛麗絲蜷縮在大搖椅的一角，一邊自言自語一邊打盹時，這隻小貓正玩著愛麗絲好不容易纏好的毛線球。牠把毛線團滾來滾去，滾到全部散開了。現在這團絨線散落在壁爐前的地毯上，滿是繩結和疙瘩，而小黑貓正站在中間追著自己的尾巴跑。

「哦，可惡的小東西！」愛麗絲喊道，抓起這隻小貓，輕輕地吻了一下，讓牠知道自己不喜歡這樣。「真的，黛娜應該要把你教得更守規矩！你應該這麼做，黛娜，你知道你應該這麼做！」她責備地看著老貓，盡可能用嚴厲的語氣說。接著，她抱著小貓和毛線縮回搖椅上，重新開始纏線團。但是她纏得不是很快，因為她一直在說話，有時和小貓說話，有時自言自語。小貓乖乖地坐在她的膝蓋上，假裝看著她纏毛線，並時不時地伸出爪子輕碰毛線球，好像在說如果可以的話，牠很樂意幫忙。

「凱蒂，你知道明天是什麼日子嗎？」愛麗絲開始說，「要是你剛才和我一起望著窗外的話，你就猜得出來了，只是那時候黛娜正在幫你洗臉，所以你猜不到。我看見男孩們在收集升營火要用的樹枝，那將會需要很多樹枝，凱蒂！可是天氣這麼冷，雪這麼大，他們只好停下來。沒關係，我們明天再去看營火。」說到這裡，愛麗絲把毛線在小貓的脖子上繞了兩三圈，想看看效果如何，這使得小貓掙扎了一下，毛線球又滾到了地板上，散開了好幾碼。

「你知道嗎？我很生氣，凱蒂，」她們又坐好後，愛麗絲繼續說，「當我看到你做的好事時，真想打開窗戶把你扔到雪地裡！你活該，你這個調皮的小東西！你打算為自己辯解嗎？現在別打斷我！」她豎起了一根手指繼續說，「我現在就來告訴你，你都犯了什麼錯。第一：今天早上黛娜幫你洗臉的時候，你叫了兩聲。你別想否認，凱蒂，我聽見了！你說什麼？」（她假裝小貓正在說話。）「牠的爪子戳到了你的眼睛？那是你的不對，因為你一直張開眼睛，要是你閉上眼睛，就不會發生這種事了。現在別再找藉口了，注意聽！第二：我在雪花面前放一碟牛奶的時候，你拉著牠的尾巴，把牠拉走

了！什麼，你口渴了？那你怎麼知道牠不渴呢？第三：你趁我不注意的時候，把毛線團全都弄散了！」

「凱蒂，你一共犯了三個錯，卻還沒有被處罰。你知道，我要把你應該受的處罰累計到下禮拜三一起算……要是他們也把我該接受的處罰累計起來，」她繼續說，大多是自言自語，而不是對小貓說。「到了年底他們會對我怎麼樣呢？我想，到了那天我大概會被送進監獄吧。或者……我想想……要是每罰一次就要少吃一頓飯，那麼，當受罰的日子來臨時，我就得一下子少吃五十頓飯了。嗯，我不在乎！我寧可不吃飯，也不要一下子吃五十頓！」

「凱蒂，你有聽見雪在敲打玻璃窗的聲音嗎？聽起來多麼輕柔悅耳啊！就像有人在外面親吻窗戶。是不是因為白雪愛樹木和田野，所以才那麼輕柔地親吻它們呢？你知道，雪會用白色的被子把樹木和田野暖暖地蓋起來。它可能會說『睡吧，親愛的，直到夏天再次來臨。』當它們在夏天醒來的時候，凱蒂，它們全都換上了綠色的新衣，隨風起舞。噢，那真美！」愛麗絲叫著，放下毛線球拍起手來。「好希望這是真的！我確定樹在秋天看起來很睏，樹葉都變黃了。」

「凱蒂，你會下棋嗎？現在，別笑，親愛的，我是認真地在問你。因為剛才我們下棋的時候，你認真地看著，就像你懂一樣。而且當我說『將軍』的時候，你咕嚕咕嚕地叫了！嗯，那一步很精彩，凱蒂，真的，要不是因為那個討厭的騎士，衝到我的旗子中間，我早就贏了。凱蒂，親愛的，我們來假裝……」這裡我想稍微說明一下愛麗絲最愛說的「我們來假裝……」前一天她才跟姊姊爭論了很久，這都是因為愛麗絲說：「我們來假裝我們是國王和皇后」。而她的姊姊喜歡實事求是，就說辦不到，因為她們只有兩個人。愛麗絲最後讓步說：「好吧，那你來假裝其中一個，我來假裝剩下的。」還有一次，她突然在奶媽的耳邊大吼：「奶媽！我們來假裝我是一條餓狗，你是一根骨頭吧！」這話讓她的奶媽嚇了一大跳。

這把我們從愛麗絲跟小貓的談話扯遠了。「我們來假裝你是紅皇后！你知道嗎？要是你把交叉著的雙手伸直，看起來真的很像紅皇后。現在試試吧，真乖！」愛麗絲把紅皇后從桌上拿走，擺在小貓正前方，讓小貓照著模仿，可是不太成功。愛麗絲說是因為小貓沒有好好地交叉雙腳。為了懲罰牠，她對著鏡子把小貓舉起來，讓牠看看她有多生氣，「要是你不好好表現，」她補充說，「我就把你放到鏡子裡的房間去，你想要那樣嗎？」

「現在，只要你認真點，凱蒂，少說點話，我就告訴你我對鏡子裡的房間的所有看法。首先，你能從鏡子裡看到有個房間，跟我們的休息室一樣，但是所有東西都是反的。當我爬上椅子的時候，我能看到整間鏡中的房間，除了壁爐後面那一區。噢！真希望我能看到那一區！我很想知道他們在冬天是不是也生火。你永遠都看不出來的，你知道，除非我們的火爐冒煙，那時候房間裡才會有煙，但可能只是偽裝，就為了看起來好像他們也在生火一樣。對了，還有，他們的書有點像我們的書，只是字是反的。我曾經把一本書拿到鏡子前面，他們也拿出了一本，所以我知道這件事。」

317

「凱蒂，你覺得住在鏡子裡怎麼樣？我想知道他們會不會給你喝牛奶。也許鏡子裡的牛奶不好喝。但是，哦，凱蒂，我們現在來到走廊了，要是你把客廳的門開大一點，你就能隱約地看見一點鏡中房間的走廊，看起來很像我們的走廊，可是你知道，再遠一點可能會完全不一樣。哦，凱蒂！要是我們能走到鏡子裡就好了！我相信我們能進去，哦！那裡面有那麼美的東西！我們來假裝有通到鏡子裡的路，凱蒂，我們來假裝玻璃軟得像薄霧一樣，這樣我們就能通過了。我敢說它正在變成霧！很容易就能穿過去了……」她說這些話的時候，人已經在壁爐上了，她也不知道自己是怎麼上去的。而且鏡子也的確開始化開了，就像銀色的薄霧。

轉眼間，愛麗絲穿過了玻璃，輕快地跳進了鏡中的房間。她做的第一件事就是去看壁爐裡是不是有火，然後很高興地發現真的有火，燒得就像她剛離開的房間裡的火一樣明亮。「在這裡應該和在之前的房間裡一樣暖和，」愛麗絲想，「說真的，還要更暖和呢，因為這裡沒有人會把我從壁爐邊趕走。哦，當他們從鏡子裡看見我在這裡，卻碰不到我的時候，會有多好玩！」

318

　　她開始東張西望，發現在原本的房間裡能看見的東西都很平凡無趣，但是其他看不見的東西，就完全不一樣了。比如，壁爐旁那面牆上的畫好像都是活的，壁爐上的那個時鐘（你知道，在鏡子外面，你只能看到背面）長著一張小老頭的臉，正朝她微笑。

　　「這個房間打掃得沒有另一間乾淨，」愛麗絲注意到爐灰裡的棋子時在心裡這麼想。但是緊接著，她驚訝地輕輕「哦」了一聲，她在地板上看著那些棋子，那些棋子正成雙成對地在散步！

　　「這是紅國王和紅皇后，」愛麗絲說（很小聲，因為怕嚇到他們），「坐在鐵鏟上的是白國王和白皇后。還有一對挽著手臂散步的城堡，我想他們聽不見我說話，」她繼續說，把頭壓得更低，「而且我幾乎可以確定他們看不見我。我覺得我好像是隱形的……」

　　這時，愛麗絲身後的桌子上有什麼東西開始尖叫起來，她連忙轉過頭去，看見一個白棋滾來滾去，腳踢來踢去。她很驚訝地盯著看，想知道接下來會發生什麼事。

「是我孩子的聲音！」白皇后從國王身邊衝過來的時候大喊，她衝得太過猛烈，把國王都撞翻到爐灰裡了。「我的寶貝莉莉！我的小寶貝！」她開始狂亂地順著壁爐柱杆往上爬。

國王揉著他的鼻子說：「寶貝個頭！」，他摔倒時弄傷了鼻子。他確實有資格對皇后發點牢騷，因為他從頭到腳滿身灰。

愛麗絲非常希望能幫上忙，因為可憐的小莉莉哭到快昏過去了，她急忙地把皇后撿起來放到桌上，靠在她哭鬧著的小女兒旁邊。

皇后氣喘吁吁地坐了下來。這次空中的高速旅行讓她幾乎喘不過氣來，有一、兩分鐘的時間她只能靜靜地抱著小莉莉。等她一喘過氣來，就朝呆坐在爐灰裡的白國王大喊：「小心火山！」

「什麼火山？」國王一面說著，一面急切地檢查爐火，好像他覺得那是最有可能發現火山的地方。

「把我……吹……起來的，」皇后氣喘吁吁，還是有點喘不過氣，「小心……你上來的時候……規規矩矩地走……別被吹起來！」

愛麗絲看著白國王緩慢地沿著一道又一道的欄杆使勁往上爬，最後她說：「按那個速度，你得用幾個鐘頭才能到桌子上。還是我幫幫你吧，怎麼樣？」但是國王沒有理她，很顯然地，他聽不見她說話，也看不見她。

　　於是愛麗絲輕輕地把他撿起來，然後慢慢地提上來，比剛才把皇后提上來慢多了，以免他喘不過氣來。但是，在把他放到桌子上之前，愛麗絲認為最好幫他拍拍身上的灰塵，因為他身上全是灰。

　　後來愛麗絲說，她這輩子從沒見過像國王當時的表情，當他發現自己被一隻看不見的手舉在空中，還給他撣灰的時候，他嚇得都叫不出來了，只剩下眼睛和嘴巴愈張愈大，愈張愈圓。愛麗絲笑得手直發抖，差點害國王掉到地板上。

　　「哦！拜託！不要再擺出這張臉了，親愛的！」愛麗絲叫著，完全忘了國王聽不見她說話：「你讓我笑得都抓不住你了！嘴巴別這麼大，灰塵都跑進去了！嗯，我想現在你夠乾淨了！」她一面替他梳頭一面說，然後把他放在桌子上，讓他靠著皇后。

　　國王立刻躺了下來，一動也不動了。愛麗絲為她做過的事感到有點害怕，於是她走遍了房間，想看看能不能找到一點水來潑醒他，但是她只找到了一瓶墨水。當她拿著墨水回來時，她發現國王已經醒過來了，他正用嚇壞了的語氣和皇后說話，聲音那麼小，愛麗絲幾乎聽不見他們在說什麼。

　　國王正在說：「我保證，我親愛的，我嚇到鬍尖都嚇涼了。」

　　皇后回答說：「你一根鬍子都沒長過。」

「那種恐怖，」國王繼續說，「我永遠，永遠忘不了！」

「你會忘記的，」皇后說，「要是你不寫個備忘錄的話。」

愛麗絲興致勃勃地看著國王從口袋裡拿出一本很大的備忘錄開始寫字。她突然閃過一個念頭，抓住了鉛筆末端，越過了國王的肩膀，開始替他寫起字來。

可憐的國王看起來又困惑又不開心，他不發一語地跟鉛筆奮鬥了好一陣子，可是愛麗絲的力氣比他大多了，最後他氣喘吁吁地說：「親愛的！我真的得找枝細一點的鉛筆了。我根本控制不了這枝筆，它寫的也不是我想的⋯⋯」

「你寫了什麼？」皇后看了看本子（愛麗絲在本子上寫了：「白騎士重心不穩從火鉗上滑下來」），然後說：「那可不是你的經歷！」

愛麗絲旁邊的桌上放著一本書，當她坐著觀察白國王時（她還是有點擔心國王，一直拿著那瓶墨水，做好了只要他再暈倒就朝他潑墨水的準備）順手翻了翻，想找一段她讀得懂的段落，「全都是用我不懂的語言寫的。」她自言自語道。

那上面是這樣寫的：

炸脖狼

・樂歐瀨滑溜的土左漠・
・在茅藜中旋轉翻騰・
・救響屠那謎喃無囉出・
・莊老的棻謎萊齊啊吶・

　　她迷惑了好一陣子，最後忽然靈機一動：「這可是鏡子裡的書！要是我把書拿起來對著鏡子，這些字就會恢復原來的樣子了。」

　　下面是愛麗絲讀的詩：

　　　　　　傑伯沃基
　　燦爛滑動的土武斯，
　　在搖擺中旋轉鑽儀。
　　波羅哥斯慘弱無比，
　　迷茫的萊斯齊吼哨。

　　吾兒，當心傑伯沃基！
　　牠那會咬人的嘴，牠那會抓人的爪。
　　當心加布加鳥，並且閃避
　　憤怒至極的潘達斯奈基！

　　他手持利劍，
　　不斷找尋令人畏懼的仇敵，
　　他倚身嗒嗒樹旁，
　　稍做思索與歇息。

　　就在思緒千頭萬緒之際，
　　有著火焰之眼的傑伯沃基，
　　一路吐氣狂吼不停，
　　大搖大擺穿過幽密之林。

　　一、二！一、二！刺了又刺
　　利劍殺了傑伯沃基！

留下牠的身體，帶走牠的首級
昂首闊步，凱旋歸去。

「當真是你殺了傑伯沃？
吾兒，來我溫暖的臂彎裡，
光榮之日，萬歲！萬歲！」
他笑得如此得意又高興。

燦爛滑動的土武斯，
在搖擺中旋轉鑽儀。
波羅哥斯慘弱無比，
迷茫的萊斯齊吼哨。

「好像寫得很美，」愛麗絲讀完後說，「可是不太好懂！」（你看，就連對她自己，她都不願意承認她根本不懂。）「我的腦子裡好像充滿了各種想法，只是我不太清楚是什麼想法！不過，什麼人殺了什麼東西，一定是這樣沒錯。至少……」

「可是…哎呀！」愛麗絲忽然跳起來了，她想，「要是不快一點的話，還沒看完房子的其他部分長什麼樣子，就得回到鏡子那邊了！先去看看花園吧！」她說完馬上衝出房間，跑下樓梯。其實也不能算是跑，而是她的新發明，可以又快又輕鬆地下樓，愛麗絲自己這麼說。她的手指頭碰著樓梯扶手，腳幾乎不碰地輕飄下去。她用同樣的方式飄過了大廳，要是沒抓住門框，她就會那樣子飄到門外去。這樣在空中飄浮讓愛麗絲頭有點暈，所以當她發現自己又能像平常一樣走路時，她感到非常高興。

第 *2* 章

盛開的花園

「但這不是你的錯，」玫瑰好心地補了一句，
「你知道，你正在凋零，誰都無法讓花瓣整整齊齊的。」

「要是我能爬到那座山的山頂，就能把花園看得更清楚了，」愛麗絲自言自語道，「這條路能直通山上，至少……不，不行……」（在沿著這條路走了好幾碼，拐了好幾個急轉彎後）不過我想它最後會通到山上的，可是這條路太彎了，簡直不像路，更像螺旋！好吧，我想這條路會通到山上的……哎呀，不行！直接通往房子了！好吧，我試試另一個方向。」

她就這樣跑上跑下，轉來轉去，可是不論怎麼走都會回到房子那裡。有一次她還因為轉彎轉得太急，來不及停下來，直接撞上了房子。

「說這個沒用，」愛麗絲望著房子，假裝在爭辯：「我不會再進去了。我知道如果一進去就得回到鏡子那邊，回到原本的房子，那麼一來我的探險就結束了！」

所以，她堅決地轉身背對著房子，再次順著小路往下走，一心向前，直到抵達小山為止。有幾分鐘，一切都進行得很順利。她正想要說：「這次我真的成功了……」，那條小路突然旋轉搖晃了起來（愛麗絲事後形容），下一秒她發現自己正要走進房子裡。

「哦，太糟了！」愛麗絲喊道，「我從沒看過這麼愛擋路的房子！從來沒有！」

但是，小山就在眼前，愛麗絲只好從頭開始。這次她走到了一大片花圃旁邊，四周圍繞著雛菊，中間長著一棵柳樹。

「哦，大百合！」愛麗絲對一朵在微風中優雅擺動的花說，「真希望你會說話。」

「我們會說話，」百合說，「如果遇見值得說話的人。」

愛麗絲驚訝得一時間說不出話來，好像連呼吸都要停了。過了一陣子，大百合繼續搖擺著，她只好膽小地開口、幾乎像耳語似地說：「所有的花都會說話嗎？」

「說得和你一樣好，」大百合說，「而且更大聲。」

「你知道，由我們先開口是很沒禮貌的。」玫瑰說，「我一直在想你什麼時候才要說話呢！我對自己說，『她的臉長得倒有點常識，雖然不是聰明的臉！不過顏色正常，花期還長。』」

「我不在乎顏色，」百合評論道，「如果她的花瓣再捲一點就更好了。」

愛麗絲不喜歡被品頭論足，於是她開始發問：「你們偶爾會害怕從這裡被移出去嗎？你們會害怕沒人照顧你們嗎？」

「中間有棵樹，」玫瑰說，「不然它還有什麼用呢？」

「但是發生危險時，它能做些什麼呢？」愛麗絲問道。

「它會叫。」玫瑰說。

「它『汪！汪！』地叫。」一朵雛菊喊道：「這就是樹枝叫做樹枝的原因！」

「你連那個都不知道嗎？」另一朵雛菊喊道，接著它們開始一起叫了起來，空氣裡好像充滿了她們細微的尖叫聲。「安靜！你們全都安靜下來！」大百合吼道，激動地擺來擺去，氣到發抖。「它們知道我碰不到它們！」大百合氣喘吁吁地說，把顫抖的頭彎向愛麗絲，「否則它們才不敢這樣！」

「沒關係！」愛麗絲安慰她，同時朝著又要七嘴八舌的雛菊彎下腰來，輕聲說道：「你們再不安靜點，我就把你們摘下來。」

它們立刻就安靜了，還有好幾朵粉色的小雛菊嚇得臉色發白。

「這樣就對了，」百合說，「雛菊最壞了。有一朵先說話，它們就全部跟著說，光聽就足以讓花朵枯萎。」

「你們怎麼都這麼會說話呢？」愛麗絲說，她希望用這句讚美的話讓大百合的心情變好，「我以前去過很多花園，從來沒有一朵花會說話。」

「把你的手放在地上，摸摸這裡的泥土，」百合說，「然後你就會明白了。」

愛麗絲照著做了。「土很硬，」她說，「可是我看不出來這跟你們會說話有什麼關係。」

「大部分的花園，」百合說，「都把花圃弄得太軟了，所以花兒們總是在睡覺。」

這聽起來是個很好的理由，愛麗絲很高興自己知道了這一點，「我以前從沒想過這件事！」她說。

「在我看來，你根本就沒有想過。」玫瑰嚴厲地說。

「我沒見過長得比她還笨的人。」紫羅蘭突然開了口。這讓愛麗絲嚇了一跳，因為她之前都沒說話。

「閉嘴！」大百合叫道，「說的好像你們見識很廣一樣！你們一直把頭躲在葉子下面打呼，除了知道自己是個花苞，根本不知道世界長怎樣！」

「花園裡除了我還有別人嗎？」愛麗絲說，決定不去注意玫瑰剛才的評論。

「花園裡有另外一朵像你一樣會動的花，」玫瑰說，「我不知道你們為什麼會動……」（「你什麼都不知道。」大百合說。）「但是她比你長得茂盛多了。」

「她跟我像嗎？」愛麗絲著急地問，腦中想著：「花園裡的某個地方還有一個小女孩！」

「嗯，她長得跟你一樣笨，」玫瑰說，「可是她更紅一些……我想她的花瓣更短。」

「她的花瓣很緊，簡直像朵大理花，」大百合說，「反正不像你的花瓣那樣扭來扭去。」

「但這不是你的錯，」玫瑰好心地補了一句，「你知道，你正在凋零，誰都無法讓花瓣整整齊齊的。」

　　愛麗絲一點都不喜歡這個說法，為了改變話題，她問道：「她來過這裡嗎？」

　　「我敢說你就快看見她了」玫瑰說，「她是帶刺的類型。」

　　「她把刺戴在哪呢？」愛麗絲好奇地問。

　　「當然是戴在頭上啦，」玫瑰回答，「我還在想你怎麼什麼都沒戴，我以為這是規矩呢。」

「她來啦！」一株飛燕草叫道，「我聽到她的腳步聲了，咚！咚！咚！沿著石子路過來啦！」

愛麗絲急忙地東張西望，發現是紅皇后。「她長高了好多！」這是愛麗絲的第一句評論，這是真的，愛麗絲第一次在爐灰裡發現她的時候，她只有三英寸高，現在卻比愛麗絲高出半個頭！

「因為空氣很新鮮，」玫瑰說，「這裡的空氣太好了。」

「我想我應該去迎接她。」愛麗絲說。儘管她認為這些花兒十分有趣，可是她覺得和真正的皇后說話似乎更厲害。

「那是不可能的，」玫瑰說，「我建議你朝另一個方向走。」

愛麗絲覺得這聽起來很沒道理，所以她沒說什麼，立刻朝著紅皇后走去。讓她驚訝的是，皇后一轉眼就從她的視線裡消失了，而她發現自己又要走進房子的前門。

愛麗絲有點生氣，她轉身回來，東張西望尋找皇后（最後她發現皇后在很遠的地方）。愛麗絲想，這次可以試試朝相反方向走。

走不到一分鐘，她就發現計畫成功了，自己正和紅皇后面對面地站著，剛剛找了好久的小山也完整地出現了。

「你是從哪裡來的？」紅皇后說，「你要去哪裡？抬起頭，好好說話，別老是玩你的手指頭。」

愛麗絲聽從了這些命令，盡可能清楚地解釋自己迷路了。

「我不知道你說的『你迷路』是什麼。」皇后說,「這裡所有的路都屬於我,但是你究竟為什麼跑到這裡來呢?」她溫和地說,「在你思考要說什麼的時候行個屈膝禮,可以節省時間。」

愛麗絲有點納悶,但是她太敬畏皇后了,只好相信。「等我回家之後,下次吃飯如果遲到,我也要試試行個屈膝禮。」她在心裡想著。

「現在該你回答了,」皇后邊看著錶邊說,「你說話的時候嘴巴再張大一點,每句話都要說『陛下』。」

「我只是想看看花園長怎什麼樣,陛下……」

「這樣就對了,」皇后說,拍拍愛麗絲的頭,儘管愛麗絲根本不喜歡這樣，「說到『花園』，和我見過的花園相比之下，這裡簡直是荒野。」

愛麗絲不敢和她爭辯，繼續說：「我想我應該試著找到通往山頂的路……」

「如果你是說『小山』，」皇后打斷她，「我可以帶你去看小山，相比之下，這只能叫山谷。」

「不，我不會那麼稱呼的，」愛麗絲說，她終於向皇后頂嘴了，「您知道，小山不會是山谷。這是胡說八道……」

皇后搖搖頭說：「你喜歡的話當然可以說是胡說八道，不過跟我聽過的胡說八道相比之下，這句話就像字典一樣通順。」

愛麗絲又行了個屈膝禮，因為皇后的口氣聽起來有點不高興了。她們繼續默默地走著，來到了小山的山頂。

愛麗絲一聲不響地站了好幾分鐘，望了望四周的原野。這真的是最奇怪的原野了！好多條小溪筆直地從這裡流到那裡，而小溪之間的土地被綠籬笆分成了好多個方塊。

「我看這像一個大棋盤，」她終於開口了，「應該有棋子到處走來走去。……那裡就有！」她愉快地說，心臟因為興奮而噗通噗通地跳了起來。「那裡正在下一盤西洋棋！整個世界就是一盤棋，要是這裡算是全世界的話。太有趣了！我真希望我也是其中的一員！只要我能參加，我不介意當小卒，不過……當然啦，我還是最想當皇后。」

　　她這麼說的時候，害羞地看了看真正的皇后一眼，但是她的同伴只是愉快地微笑著說：「那很簡單。如果你願意，你可以當白皇后的小卒。因為莉莉太小了，不能參加。你從第二格開始，當走到第八格的時候，就可以當皇后了⋯⋯」就在此時，不知道怎麼搞的，她們開始跑了起來。

　　愛麗絲後來回想到這裡時，一直搞不太清楚她們是怎麼開始跑的。她只記得她們手牽著手跑。皇后跑得飛快，愛麗絲只能盡力跟著她，但皇后還是一直喊：「快點！快點！」愛麗絲覺得自己沒辦法快點，但又喘得說不出話來。

　　最奇怪的是，她們周圍的樹和其他東西的位置根本就沒有變，無論她們跑得多快，好像都沒有超越過任何東西。「是不是所有東西都在跑呢？」可憐又困惑的愛麗絲想，皇后好像猜到了愛麗絲的想法，因為她喊道：「快點！別說話！」

　　愛麗絲根本沒有要說話，她覺得自己好像再也說不出話了，她實在太喘了，可是皇后還是喊著：「快點！快點！」，拉著她往前跑。「我們快到那裡了嗎？」愛麗絲終於氣喘吁吁地問了這問題。

　　「快到那裡了！」皇后重複著，「十分鐘前我們就經過那裡了！快點！」她們繼續默默地跑了一會兒。風從愛麗絲耳邊呼嘯而過。她覺得頭髮幾乎要被吹掉了。

　　「快！快！」皇后喊著，「快點！快點！」她們跑得快到腳幾乎碰不到地，彷彿在空中滑行。就在愛麗絲累得筋疲力盡的時候，她們突然停了下來。愛麗絲發現自己癱坐在地上，又暈又喘。

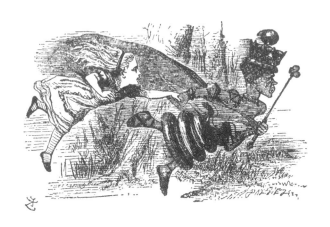

　　皇后把她扶起來，讓她靠著一棵樹，然後和氣地說，「你現在可以休息一會兒了。」

　　愛麗絲非常驚訝地四處張望。「我真的覺得我們好像一直待在這棵樹下面！每樣東西都和剛才一樣！」

　　「當然一樣，」皇后說，「不然你以為是怎麼樣呢？」

　　「嗯，在我們那裡，」愛麗絲說，她還有點喘：「如果快速地跑了很久，像我們剛才那樣，通常都會跑到其他地方去了。」

　　「真是個慢吞吞的地方！」皇后說，「現在，在這裡，你得拼命地跑，才能停在原地。要是想到別的地方，你必須跑得再快一倍！」

「謝謝，我還是不試了！」愛麗絲說，「我很高興能待在這裡，只是我又熱又渴！」

「我知道你想要什麼！」皇后從口袋裡拿出一個小盒子，和藹地說：「要吃餅乾嗎？」

這根本就不是愛麗絲想要的東西，可是她覺得拒絕別人很沒禮貌，於是拿了一塊，勉強吃下去。餅乾很乾，她這輩子第一次覺得自己要噎到了。

「你休息的時候，」皇后說，「我來丈量一下。」接著從口袋裡拿出一條標有尺寸的緞帶，開始丈量土地，並到處插上小木椿。

「再過去兩碼，」她插上一根木椿來表示距離，「我會指示方向。要再吃一塊餅乾嗎？」

「不用了，謝謝，」愛麗絲說，「一片就夠了。」

「我想你不渴了吧？」皇后說。

愛麗絲不知道怎麼回答，幸好皇后沒等她回答就繼續說：「再過去三碼，我會再重複一遍，免得你忘了。然後到第四碼處，我會說再見；到了第五碼的地方，我就走！」

這時她已放好了所有的木椿，愛麗絲很感興趣地看著，她回到樹下，然後沿著那排木椿又開始慢慢走。

到兩碼處的木椿時，皇后轉過頭來說：「你知道，小卒的第一步是走兩格。所以，你應該很快地穿過第三格，我想你得坐火車吧，你會發現你自己立刻就到第四格了。嗯，那一格屬於叮噹和叮叮。第五格全是水，第六格屬於矮胖子……你有沒有記住？」

「我……我不知道得記下……來呢，」愛麗絲結結巴巴地說。

「你應該說，」皇后用責備的口氣低聲繼續說：「『您能告訴我這些真是太好了。』，不過，我就當你說了，第七格全是樹林，但是有一個騎士會為你指路。到了第八格我們就都是皇后了，那裡全是享樂和宴會！」愛麗絲起身來行個屈膝禮，接著坐下。

到了下一個木樁，皇后又轉過身來，這一次她說：「當你想不起英語怎麼說的時候，就講法語。走路的時候把腳尖朝外。還有，記住你是誰！」這次她沒等愛麗絲行屈膝禮，很快地繼續向下一個木樁走去，她回過頭來說了聲「再見」，匆忙地走向最後一個木樁。

愛麗絲不知道是怎麼發生的，當皇后走到最後一個木樁時就不見了。愛麗絲猜不出她究竟是消失在空氣中，或者飛奔進樹林（「她跑得非常快！」），反正皇后就是消失了。接著她想起來自己是小卒，很快就輪到她走了。

第 *3* 章

鏡中的昆蟲

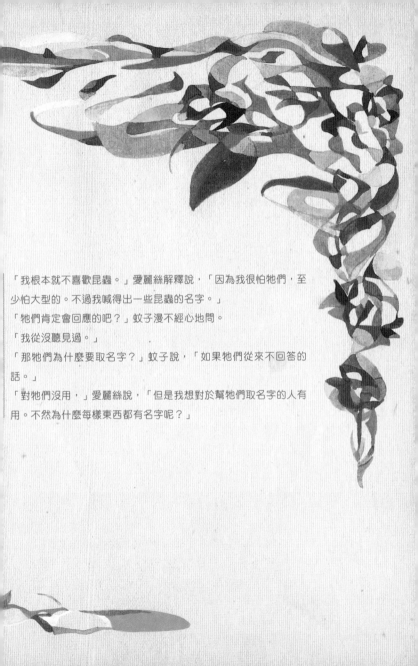

「我根本就不喜歡昆蟲。」愛麗絲解釋說，「因為我很怕牠們，至少怕大型的。不過我喊得出一些昆蟲的名字。」

「牠們肯定會回應的吧？」蚊子漫不經心地問。

「我從沒聽見過。」

「那牠們為什麼要取名字？」蚊子說，「如果牠們從來不回答的話。」

「對牠們沒用，」愛麗絲說，「但是我想對於幫牠們取名字的人有用。不然為什麼每樣東西都有名字呢？」

當然，第一件要做的事是調查她要行經的地方。「真像在學地理，」為了能看得更遠一點，愛麗絲踮起了腳尖，心裡想著：「主要河流……沒有。主要山脈……我站在唯一的一座山上，不過我想它沒有名字。主要城市……在那採蜜的那些是什麼？牠們不可能是蜜蜂……沒有人能看到一英里外的蜜蜂……」她安靜地站了一會兒，看見其中一個正忙著把鼻子伸進花朵中，「跟一般的蜜蜂沒什麼兩樣。」她想。

可是，牠們絕對不可能是蜜蜂，牠們是大象！愛麗絲很快就發現了，儘管一開始這個想法讓她驚訝得喘不過氣來。「那些花一定很巨大！」這是她的第二個想法。「看起來就像把茅屋的屋頂拿掉，再放到花莖上面，裡面會有多少花蜜呢！我要下去……不，我現在還不要去。」她跑下山時想著，想為自己突如其來的畏縮找藉口。

「要是沒有長樹枝能把牠們趕走的話,我絕不下去……要是牠們問我覺得散步怎麼樣,這該有多好玩啊,『我覺得很好……』」(她甩了甩頭,這是她最喜歡的動作)。「只是那裡灰塵很多又很熱,而且那些大象太吵了!」

「我想還是從另一條路走下去,」她停了一會兒說,「也許晚點再去看大象。再說,我的確該去第三格了!」

利用這個藉口,她跑下了小山,跳過了六條小溪中的第一條。

「請出示車票!」警衛把頭伸進車窗說。大家立刻把車票拿了出來。票和人差不多大,好像都要把車廂塞滿了。

「喂,小孩,你的票!」警衛生氣地看著愛麗絲說。許多聲音一起喊著(「像合唱一樣。」愛麗絲想),「別讓他等,小孩!嘿,

他一分鐘值一千鎊呢！」

「我沒有票，」愛麗絲用被嚇壞了的語調說，「我來的地方沒有售票處。」合音又響起來了：「她來的地方沒有售票處，那裡的地一英寸值一千鎊呢！」

「別找藉口，」警衛說，「你應該和火車司機買一張的。」合音再次響起：「開火車的那個人。光是火車噴的煙就值一千鎊！」

愛麗絲心想：「看來說什麼都沒用。」這一次愛麗絲沒發出聲來，所以沒有合唱聲，但是讓她非常驚訝的是，他們都齊聲想著（我希望你們能懂「齊聲想著」是什麼意思。我必須承認我不懂），「最好什麼都別說，一個字值一千鎊呢！」

「我今天晚上一定會夢到『一千鎊』，一定！」愛麗絲想。

這段時間，警衛一直看著愛麗絲，先是用望遠鏡，接著用顯微鏡，之後用看歌劇用的單片鏡，最後他說：「你坐錯車了。」，就關上車窗走了。

「這麼小的孩子，」坐在她對面的紳士說（他穿著白紙做的衣服）：「就算她不知道自己的名字，也該知道要走哪條路啊。」

坐在白衣紳士旁的山羊閉著眼睛大聲地說，「就算她不認識字，也應該知道去售票處的路啊！」

山羊旁邊坐著一隻甲蟲（車裡全是非常奇怪的乘客）好像有規定好像他們應該輪流說話似的，甲蟲繼續說：「得把她當成行李從這裡運回去！」

愛麗絲看不見坐在甲蟲旁邊的乘客，只聽到一個粗啞的聲音接著說：「更換火車頭……」他說到這被迫停住了。

「聽起來很像馬。」愛麗絲心裡想。這時一個非常小的聲音在她耳邊說，「你知道，你可以用「馬」和「啞」開個玩笑。」

然後遠處一個很溫柔的聲音說，「得幫她貼上『小心輕放』……」

後面又有其他的聲音傳來（「車廂裡怎麼這麼多乘客！」愛麗絲想），「她有一個頭，所以得用郵寄的……」「得把她當成消息發個電報回去……」「剩下的路途她應該自己拉火車……」等等。

但穿白紙衣服的紳士俯身向前，在她耳邊輕聲說：「親愛的，別理他們說的話，但是每當火車停下來時，你就要買張回程車票。」

「我才不要！」愛麗絲有點不耐煩地說，「我根本就不屬於這趟火車之旅，我剛才還在樹林裡！而且我希望我能回去那裡。」

「你可以拿這個開玩笑，」那小小的聲音在她耳邊說，「譬如『要是你做得到你就想要做』。」

「別煩了，」愛麗絲說，並且徒勞地四處張望，想知道聲音是從哪傳來的，「要是你這麼想編笑話，為什麼不自己編一個？」

那個小小的聲音深深地嘆了一口氣。顯然很不開心。愛麗絲本來想說些同情的話安慰他，「要是牠能夠像別人那樣嘆氣就好了。」

愛麗絲想。但是那嘆息聲這麼輕，要不是緊貼在她耳朵旁，她根本就聽不見。這聲嘆息讓她的耳朵很癢，使她完全沒心思安慰這可憐的小生物了。

「我知道你是朋友，」小聲音繼續說，「親愛的朋友，老朋友。你不會傷害我，即使我是昆蟲。」

「哪種昆蟲？」愛麗絲有點好奇地打聽。她真正想知道的是他會不會咬人，但又覺得那樣問不太禮貌。

「什麼？這麼說你不……」小小的聲音說到一半就被火車引擎發出的尖銳聲響打斷了。所有人都慌張地跳了起來，愛麗絲也一樣。

那匹把頭伸出車窗外的馬，安靜地把頭放進車廂說，「我們只不過是要跳過一條小溪。」大家似乎都對這個說法很滿意。只有愛麗絲對火車會跳感到有些不安。「但是，它會把我們帶到第四格，也還算是安慰！」她對自己說。過了一會兒，她覺得火車似乎要直衝天際，驚慌之中她抓住了離她最近的東西，正好是山羊的鬍鬚。

但鬍鬚似乎在她碰到的瞬間就融化了，然後她發現自己正安靜地坐在樹下。這時那隻蚊子（剛剛跟她說話的昆蟲）正停在她頭頂的樹梢上，用翅膀幫她搧風。

牠的確是一隻很大的蚊子。「和雞一樣大，」愛麗絲想，不過因為他們已經聊了那麼久，她並沒有感到特別不安。

「……所以你不喜歡所有的昆蟲？」蚊子接著說，平靜得好像什麼事都沒發生過一樣。

「要是牠們會說話，我就喜歡，」愛麗絲說，「我住的地方沒有昆蟲會說話。」

「在你來的那個地方，你喜歡哪種昆蟲？」蚊子問。

「我根本就不喜歡昆蟲。」愛麗絲解釋說，「因為我很怕牠們，至少怕大型的。不過我喊得出一些昆蟲的名字。」

「牠們肯定會回應的吧？」蚊子漫不經心地問。

「我從來沒聽過。」

「那牠們為什麼要取名字？」蚊子說，「如果牠們從來不回答的話。」

「對牠們沒用，」愛麗絲說，「但是我想對於幫牠們取名字的人有用。不然為什麼每樣東西都有名字呢？」

「我不知道。」蚊子回答，「對了，那邊樹林裡的東西就沒有名字。不過，繼續說你那裡有什麼昆蟲吧，你們這樣是在浪費時間。」

「嗯，有馬蠅。」愛麗絲開始扳著手指頭數起來。

「好，」蚊子說，「要是往那個樹叢裡看，你會看見一隻木馬

349

蠅，全身都是木頭做的，在樹枝間搖來搖去。」

「牠都吃什麼維生呢？」愛麗絲很好奇地問。

「樹液和木屑，」蚊子說，「繼續列出你那裡的昆蟲吧。」

愛麗絲好奇地朝木馬蠅那張臉望過去，認為牠一定剛剛才重新上過油漆，因為牠看起來又亮又黏。接著她繼續說：

「還有蜻蜓。」

「看看你頭上的樹枝，」蚊子說，「你會看到一隻火蜻蜓。牠的身體是聖誕布丁，翅膀是冬青樹葉，頭是浸了白蘭地燃燒著的葡萄乾。」

「牠都吃什麼維生呢？」愛麗絲問了和剛剛一樣的問題。

「小麥粥和肉餅。」蚊子回答，「牠住在聖誕禮盒裡。」

她仔細看了看那隻頭上燃著火燄的昆蟲，心裡想著，「這會不會就是昆蟲老愛飛到蠟燭上的原因呢？因為牠們想變成聖誕蜻蜓！」她接著說，「我們那裡還有蝴蝶。」

「在你腳邊爬的，」蚊子說（愛麗絲趕緊把腳縮回來），「你看得出來是一隻麵包蝴蝶，牠的翅膀是兩片塗了奶油的麵包薄片，身體是麵包皮，頭是一塊方糖。」

「牠都吃什麼維生呢？」

「奶油紅茶。」

　　愛麗絲想到了一個新的難題，「要是找不到奶油紅茶怎麼辦呢呢？」她說。

　　「當然就餓死啦。」

　　「但這種事一定常常發生。」愛麗絲思索著說。

　　「總是會發生的。」蚊子說。

　　愛麗絲沉默地思考了一兩分鐘，這時蚊子繞著她的頭嗡嗡地飛來飛去。最後，牠停下來說：「你不想失去你的名字吧？」

　　「當然不想，」愛麗絲有點不安地說。

　　「這很難說，」蚊子漫不經心地繼續說：「你想想，要是沒有名字也能回家，那有多方便啊！比方說，老師想叫你回答問題，她只說『過來……』就說不下去了，因為她叫不出你的名字，你當然就不用回答問題了。」

　　「我很確定那是不可能的，」愛麗絲說，「老師絕對不會因為這樣就放過我。要是她忘了我的名字，她就會叫我『密斯！』，就像叫傭人那樣。」

　　「好，要是她叫你『密斯』，」蚊子說，「你當然可以『迷失』這堂課了。這只是玩笑話，我希望你開過這個玩笑。」

　　「為什麼你希望我開過這個玩笑？」愛麗絲問，「這個笑話非常糟糕。」

但是蚊子只是深深地嘆了氣，兩顆斗大的淚珠從牠的臉頰滑落。

「要是說笑話讓你這麼不開心，那還是別說了。」愛麗絲說。

接下來又是一聲憂鬱而細微的嘆息。可憐的蚊子這次好像真的嘆氣嘆到消失不見了，因為當愛麗絲抬頭看的時候，樹梢上什麼也沒有。而且，由於坐太久了，她感到越來越冷，於是她起身繼續向前走。

很快地，她來到了開闊的田野，田野的另一邊是樹林。這片樹林看上去比剛才的陰暗很多，愛麗絲有點害怕，不敢走進去。可是下一秒，她就下定了決心，「我不想走回頭路，」她心想，而且這是通往第八格唯一的路。

「這一定就是什麼東西都沒有名字的樹林，」她邊想邊自言自語，「我走進去之後名字會變怎樣呢？我不想要失去名字，因為這樣人們就要再幫我取個新的名字了，一定會很難聽。不過到那時候，我要想辦法找到拿走我原本名字的人，這就蠻有意思！看，就像人們的狗走丟的時候『戴著銅項圈，叫牠牠許會回應。』。想想看，我每遇到一個東西，就叫一聲『愛麗絲』，直到有人回應為止！但是夠聰明的人根本就不會回應。」

她沿著這條路走到了樹林，那裡看起來既冷又暗。「嗯，不管怎樣，這裡很舒服，」她邊說邊走到了樹下，「剛剛走到好熱，我到了……到了哪裡呀？」她很訝異自己竟然想不起要說的字。「我是指到了……到了……到了這個下面！」她把手放到了樹幹上。「它怎麼稱呼自己呢？我相信它沒有名字……我確定它沒有名字！」

　　她安靜地站著想了一會兒，突然又開始說話了：「這竟然真的發生了！我是誰呢？只要我想，我一定能想起來的，我一定要想起來！」但是這股決心也幫不了太大的忙，在苦惱了一陣子之後，她只能說：「麗，我知道是麗開頭的名字！」

　　這時一隻小鹿從旁邊經過，牠用溫柔的大眼睛看著愛麗絲，好像根本就不害怕。「來呀，來呀。」愛麗絲一邊說，一邊伸出手去想拍拍牠，牠只是往後退了一點，然後又站著看她。

　　「你叫什麼名字？」小鹿終於說話了，聲音又柔和、又甜美。

　　「我希望我知道！」可憐的愛麗絲想。她有些傷心地回答道，「我現在什麼都想不起來。」

　　「再想想吧，」小鹿說，「不可能想不起來的。」

　　愛麗絲想了想，可是什麼都想不起來。「請問，你願意告訴我你叫什麼嗎？」她不好意思地說，「我想那可能會有些幫助。」

　　「要是你願意再走過去一點，我就能告訴你了，」小鹿說，「在這裡我想不起來。」

　　於是她們一起穿過了樹林，愛麗絲親密地用手臂摟著小鹿柔軟的脖子。她們一直走出樹林，到了另一片開闊的田野。小鹿突然跳了起來，從愛麗絲的手臂中掙脫出來，「我是小鹿！」牠開心地叫道，「我的天啊！你是一個人類的小孩！」牠那美麗的棕色大眼睛突然閃過一絲恐懼，飛快地跑掉了。

愛麗絲站在那目送牠走遠。突然間失去了旅伴,她難過得幾乎要哭出來了。「不過,我現在知道自己的名字了,」她說,「這也算是安慰,愛麗絲,愛麗絲,我再也不會忘記了。現在我究竟該照哪個路標走呢?」

這個問題不會太難回答,因為只有一條路能穿過樹林,而兩個路標都指向了同一個方向。愛麗絲對自己說,「等到有岔路,路標又指向不同方向的時候,我再來解決這個問題。」

但是,這種情況好像不可能發生。她一直走了很遠,只要有岔路,就一定會出現兩個指著同一個方向的路標,一個寫著「通往叮噹家」,另一個寫著「通往叮叮家」。

　　「我相信，」愛麗絲最後說，「他們一定住在同一間房子裡！真奇怪，剛才我怎麼沒想到。可是我不能在那裡停留太久，我只要打聲招呼說『你們好。』，然後再問他們離開樹林的路怎麼走。要是能在天黑之前抵達第八格就好了！」於是她繼續向前走，邊走邊自言自語，就在她轉了一個急轉彎後，她看到了兩個小胖子，他們出現得這麼突然，嚇得愛麗絲直往後退。但是她很快地就恢復正常，她確定他們一定是……

第 4 章

叮噹與叮叮

「我是真的！」愛麗絲說，開始哭了起來。

「哭也不會讓你變得更真實，」叮叮說，「沒什麼好哭的。」

「如果我不是真的，」愛麗絲說，哭中還帶著笑，因為這一切

都如此荒唐：「我就不能哭了。」

他們正站在一棵樹下,用手臂摟著對方的脖子。愛麗絲立刻就知道誰是誰了,因為一個的衣領上繡著「噹」,另一個的繡著「叮」。「我想他們每個人的衣領後面都繡著『叮』。」她對自己說。

他們那麼安靜地站著,使她幾乎忘了他們還活著。她正想要到後面看看他們衣領後面是不是繡有「叮」字,繡著「噹」字的那個突然發出聲音,嚇了她一跳。

「要是你以為我們是蠟像,」他說,「那你就應該付錢。你知道,蠟像可不是讓人免費觀賞的,絕對不是!」

「相反的,」衣領上繡著「叮」字的那個補充道,「如果你認為我們是活人,你就應該說話。」

「我感到非常抱歉,」愛麗絲只能這麼說了。因為那首老歌的歌詞一直在她腦海裡,像鐘擺一樣滴答滴答地響著,她幾乎忍不住要大聲唱出來了:

> 「叮噹與叮叮，
> 同意打一架。
> 因為叮噹說，
> 叮叮弄壞了，
> 新的波浪鼓。
>
> 這時大烏鴉，
> 從天空而降，
> 黑得像瀝青，
> 嚇著英雄倆，
> 爭執全忘光。」

「我知道你在想什麼，」叮噹說，「但不是那樣的，絕對不是。」

「相反的，」叮叮接著說，「如果是那樣，就可能是；如果曾經是那樣，就曾經是那樣；但是因為不是，所以就不是。這是邏輯。」

「我在想，」愛麗絲非常禮貌地說，「哪條是走出樹林最好的路。天都變這麼黑了。可以請你們告訴我嗎？」

但是這兩位只是你看我、我看你，嘿嘿地笑。

他們看起來真的很像一對小學生，愛麗絲忍不住像老師那樣指著叮噹說，「你先說！」

「絕對不說！」叮噹大叫著，然後立刻就閉緊了嘴巴。

「你說！」愛麗絲指著叮叮說，很確定他會喊一句「相反！」

而他確實那麼喊了。

「你從一開始就錯了！」叮噹喊道，「拜訪別人要做的第一件事是說『你好』和握手！」說到這裡，兩兄弟互相擁抱了一下，然後伸出空著的手和愛麗絲握手。

愛麗絲不想和任何一個先握手，害怕會讓另一個不高興。擺脫困境最好的方法就是同時握住兩個人的手。接著，他們轉著圈跳起舞來。這好像很自然（愛麗絲後來回憶說），她甚至沒有因為聽到音樂而感到驚訝。音樂彷彿是從他們頭上的樹木發出來的，她聽得出來，那是樹枝互相摩擦發出的聲音，就像琴弓和琴弦一樣。

「不過那可真有趣（愛麗絲後來跟姊姊描述這一切的時候說），我發現自己正在唱『我們圍著桑樹叢跳舞』。我不知道是什麼時候開始的，但我覺得自己好像已經唱了好久！」

另外兩位舞者很胖，他們很快就喘不過氣來了。「一支舞跳四圈就夠了。」叮噹氣喘吁吁地說。他們停了下來，像開始跳舞時一樣突然，音樂也跟著停了。

接著他們鬆開愛麗絲的手，站在那盯著她看，這一陣靜默讓人覺得尷尬，因為愛麗絲不知道該如何跟剛剛一起跳過舞的人交談。「現在不用再說『你好』了吧，」她自言自語地說，「我們好像不是初次見面了。」

「希望你們不會累？」最後她說。

「絕對不累。非常感謝你的關心。」叮噹說。

「非常感激！」叮叮說，「你喜歡詩嗎？」

「喜⋯⋯喜歡⋯⋯非常喜歡⋯⋯某些詩，」愛麗絲遲疑地說，「你可以告訴我哪條路能夠走出樹林嗎？」

「我該為她背哪首詩呢？」叮叮非常嚴肅地看著叮噹說，沒有注意到愛麗絲的問題。

「《海象和木匠》是最長的。」叮噹回答，同時給了他的兄弟一個熱情的擁抱。

叮叮馬上開始背了起來：

　　「太陽照耀著⋯⋯」

這時，愛麗絲斗膽打斷了他，「要是很長的話，」她盡可能禮貌地說，「可以請你先告訴我哪條路⋯⋯」

叮叮溫和地微笑著，繼續背下去：

　　「太陽照耀著海洋，
　　用盡了全部的力量。
　　它盡力想要讓，
　　海上碧波蕩漾。
　　說來真奇怪，
　　因為正是午夜時光。

　　月亮生氣地閃著光，

因為它認為太陽，
不該在此時發光，
它已經佔用了白天，
它說：『它實在太過無禮，
來這裡讓人掃興！』
大海潮得不能再潮，
沙灘乾得不能再乾。
你看不到雲彩是因為，
天空中沒有雲彩。
沒有鳥飛過頭頂，
因為沒有鳥在飛。

海象和木匠，
在附近散步。
看見那麼多沙子，
他們淚流滿面。
『如果能把它們掃掉，』
他們說，『那可真妙！』

『七個女傭七把掃把，
花半年時光來清掃，
你想想看，』海象說，
『沙子能否全被掃光？』
『我很懷疑。』木匠說，
一滴熱淚流下。

『哦，牡蠣們，來和我們一起散步！』
海象發出邀請。
『愉快地走，愉快地聊
沿著這個海灘，
我們只能拉著四個，
一隻手拉一個』

最老的牡蠣看著牠，
卻一言不發；
最老的牡蠣眨眨眼，
搖著沉重的頭，
表示牠不會，
離開牡蠣的家。

有四隻小牡蠣趕了上來，
盼著能接受款待。
牠們熨了衣服洗了臉，
牠們的鞋子乾淨又整潔。
說到鞋子真奇怪，
牠們又沒長腳。

後頭還跟著四隻，
後頭還有四隻。
最後來了一大群，
越來越多，越來越多，
一起跳過了白浪，

爬到了岸上。

海象和木匠,
走了大概一英里。
他們在矮石頭上休息。
小牡蠣都站著,
排成一隊在等待。

『是時候了,』海象說,
我們來東拉西扯,
談談鞋子、船和密封蠟;
還有白菜和國王。
海水為什麼滾燙,
小豬是否有翅膀。』

『但是等一下,』牡蠣們叫道
『在聊天開始前,
我們全部都很胖,
有的已經喘不過氣!』
木匠說:『不急!』
小牡蠣為此非常感激。

『一條麵包,』海象說道,
『正是我們最需要,
還有辣椒和醋,
我們也很需要,
要是牡蠣們準備好,

我倆就要吃個飽。』

『但是別吃我們！』牡蠣們在叫，
全都嚇到臉色發青。
『剛才對我們那麼好，
現在真可怕！』
『夜色真美妙』海象說，
『喜歡這風景嗎？
你們能來真好，
你們的味道真好。』
木匠只說了：
『給我們再切片麵包，
希望你還沒太聾，
我已經說了兩次！』

『好像有點可恥，』海象說，
『這樣欺騙牠們，
我們已經把牠們帶到這麼遠，
讓牠們跑得這麼快！』
木匠只說了，
『奶油塗得太厚了！』

『我為你們哭泣，』海象說：
『我深感同情。』
牠涕淚交加，
掏出一條手帕，

掩住了牠的淚眼。」

『噢，牡蠣們，』木匠說，
『你們愉快地跑了一圈，
我們再跑回家吧？』
但是沒有人回答，
這一點都不奇怪，因為，
他們吃光了所有牡蠣。」

「我最喜歡海象，」愛麗絲說，「因為你看，牠對可憐的牡蠣還有點內疚。」

「相反，牠吃得比木匠多，」叮叮說，「你瞧，他把手帕擋在面前，這樣木匠就數不清他吃了多少。」

「原來是這樣！」愛麗絲憤怒地說，「那我喜歡木匠，如果他吃的沒有海象那麼多的話。」

「但他已經吃得再也吃不下了。」叮噹說。

這是個難題。過了一會兒愛麗絲說：「哼，他們兩個都是討厭的東西……」說到這裡她驚慌地停住了，因為她聽見一個聲音，旁邊的樹林裡，有像蒸氣火車在噴氣的聲音。她更擔心那可能是頭野獸。「這附近有獅子或老虎嗎？」她害怕地問。

「那只不過是紅國王在打呼。」叮叮說。

「走，去看看他！」兄弟倆叫著，他們各自拉著愛麗絲的其中一隻手，把她帶到了國王熟睡的地方。

「他的樣子很可愛吧？」叮噹說。

說實話，愛麗絲可不這麼想。國王戴著一頂有流蘇、高高的紅色睡帽。他躺在那，縮成亂七八糟的一團，大聲地打呼。「都要把他的頭呼掉了！」叮噹這樣說。

「我怕他這樣躺在潮濕的草地上會感冒。」愛麗絲說。她是心思細膩的小女孩。

「他正做夢，」叮叮說，「你猜他夢見什麼了？」

愛麗絲說：「沒人能猜得到。」

「怎麼會，他夢見的就是你！」叮叮得意地拍手叫道，「要是他沒夢見你，你想你現在會在哪裡？」

「當然是在這裡！」愛麗絲說。

「才不是！」叮叮輕蔑地反駁，「你就會消失，你只不過是他夢裡的一樣東西罷了！」

「國王要是醒了，你就無影無蹤了。」叮噹接著說，「『砰』地一聲，像支蠟燭一樣。」

「我才不會呢！」愛麗絲生氣地喊道，「再說，如果我只是他夢裡的一樣東西，我很想知道，那你們會是什麼？」

「和你一樣。」叮噹說。

「一樣，一樣。」叮叮喊。

他叫得那麼大聲，愛麗絲忍不住說：「噓！你發出這麼大的聲響會吵醒他的。」

「哼！吵醒他也沒用。」叮噹說，「你只是他夢裡的一樣東西，你明知道你不是真的。」

「我是真的！」愛麗絲說，開始哭了起來。

「哭也不會讓你變得更真實，」叮叮說，「沒什麼好哭的。」

「如果我不是真的，」愛麗絲說，哭中還帶著笑，因為這一切都如此荒唐：「我就不能哭了。」

「我說，你該不會以為那是真的眼淚吧？」叮噹用非常輕蔑的語氣打斷她。

「我知道他們是在胡說八道。」愛麗絲心裡想，「為了這個哭可真傻。」於是她擦乾了眼淚，儘量開心地繼續說：「無論如何，我最好還是走出樹林，因為天色變得非常黑了。你們覺得會下雨嗎？」

叮噹撐開一把大傘，遮住他和他的兄弟，然後抬頭看著傘說，「不，我覺得不會下雨，至少在這下面不會。絕對不會。」

「但是外面可能下雨？」

「要是老天想下雨，那就會下。」叮叮說，「我們沒有意見，反之亦然。」

「自私的東西！」愛麗絲想。她正想說聲「再見」離開他們，這時叮噹從傘下跳了出來，抓住她的手腕。

「你看見了嗎？」他激動得聲音都在顫抖，他的眼睛變得又大又黃，用發抖的手指，指著樹下躺著的一個白色小東西。

「那只是波浪鼓，」愛麗絲仔細看了看，「你看，不是響尾蛇。」愛麗絲以為他被嚇到了，急忙補充說，「只是個舊波浪鼓，又舊又破了。」

「我知道！」叮噹叫道，開始發瘋般地邊跺腳邊拉自己的頭髮，「它當然壞了！」說到這裡他看著叮叮，叮叮立刻坐到地上，想要躲到傘裡去。

愛麗絲把手放在他的手臂上，安慰他說：「你不用因為一個舊波浪鼓生這麼大的氣。」

「它不是舊的！」叮噹更生氣地大喊，「它是新的，我告訴你！是我昨天買的，新的波浪鼓！」他提高了嗓門尖叫著。

這段時間裡，叮叮正盡力地把傘收攏，好把自己包在裡面。這太奇妙了，愛麗絲的注意力從生氣的叮噹身上被吸引過去了。但是叮叮不太成功，最後連人帶傘在地上滾來滾去，只有頭露在外面。他躺在那，嘴巴和大眼睛一會兒開一會兒合的。「看起來好像一條魚，」愛麗絲想。

「你同意打一架嗎？」叮噹用稍微冷靜下來的語調問。

「我想是的，」叮叮從傘裡爬了出來，不高興地回答。「可是她必須幫我們穿好衣服。」於是兩兄弟手拉手地進了樹林，不到一分鐘又回來了，懷裡抱著一大堆東西，比如墊子、毯子、地毯、桌布、碗罩和煤桶。「你能把東西別起來和繫起來吧？」叮噹問，「這些東西都得穿上。」

愛麗絲後來說，她這輩子從沒經歷過那麼亂七八糟的事情。這兩兄弟忙亂極了，他們戴著那麼多東西，要她忙著繫帶子和扣鈕釦。「當他們裝扮好之後，看起來一定很像一團破布！」愛麗絲自言自語地說，這時她把一個墊子圍到了叮叮的脖子上，叮叮說：「這是為了防止頭被砍下來。」

「你知道，頭被砍下來，」他嚴肅地接著說下去，「這是在戰鬥中可能遇到的最嚴重的事。」

愛麗絲大聲笑了出來，但是她設法把笑聲變成了咳嗽聲，怕他聽

了不高興。

叮噹走過來讓她替他綁頭盔（他認為那叫頭盔，但實際上那東西看起來更像個湯鍋）。「我看起來很蒼白嗎？」他問。

「嗯，是的……有一點……」愛麗絲溫柔回答。

「我平常非常勇敢，」他低聲說，「不過剛好我今天頭痛。」

「我牙痛！」叮叮聽到這話說，「我比你更糟！」

「那麼你們今天最好別打架，」愛麗絲說，她認為這是講和的好機會。

「我們必須打一架，但是我不想打太久。」叮噹說，「現在幾點？」

叮叮看著他的表說：「四點半。」

「我們打到六點，然後去吃晚餐。」叮噹說。

「很好，」叮叮有點難過地說，「她可以看我們打架，不過最好別太靠近。」他又補充說，「我真正激動起來的時候，看到什麼就打什麼。」

「我碰到什麼就打什麼，」叮噹喊道，「不管我看不看得見！」

愛麗絲笑了，「你一定常常打那些樹。」她說。叮噹帶著得意的微笑環視著周圍。「我想，」他說，「等我們打完的時候，這附

371

近就一棵樹都不剩了。」

「就為了一個波浪鼓！」愛麗絲說，她還是希望能讓他們知道不值得為這點小事打架。

「要不是那是新的，我就不會那麼在乎了。」叮噹說。

「我希望那隻大烏鴉快來！」愛麗絲想。

「只有一把劍，你知道，」叮噹對叮叮說，「不過你還有傘，它也一樣鋒利。但是我們必須快點開始，天太黑了。」

「越來越黑了。」叮叮說。

天突然就變黑了，愛麗絲還以為會有一場雷雨呢。「這烏雲真厚！」她說，「而且來得真快！嘿！我絕對相信它是有翅膀的！」

「那是烏鴉！」叮噹驚慌地尖叫，兄弟倆一眨眼就跑得不見人影了。

愛麗絲跑進了樹林，躲在一棵大樹下。「在這裡牠就抓不到我了，」她想，「烏鴉太大了，不能擠到樹中間來。我希望牠別揮動翅膀，牠在樹林裡掀起了這麼大的風……有人的披肩被吹走了！」

第 5 章
羊毛與小河

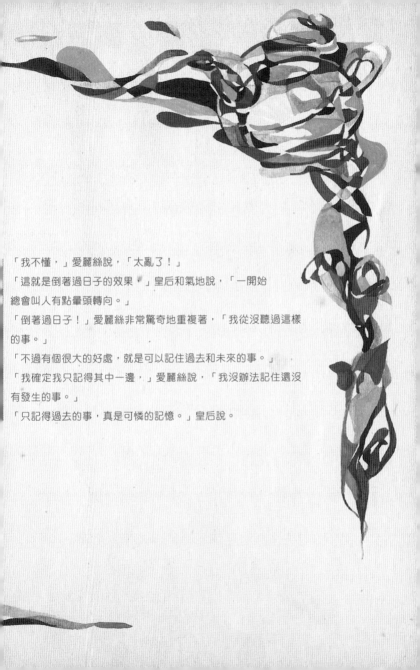

「我不懂，」愛麗絲說，「太亂了！」

「這就是倒著過日子的效果，」皇后和氣地說，「一開始
總會叫人有點暈頭轉向。」

「倒著過日子！」愛麗絲非常驚奇地重複著，「我從沒聽過這樣
的事。」

「不過有個很大的好處，就是可以記住過去和未來的事。」

「我確定我只記得其中一邊，」愛麗絲說，「我沒辦法記住還沒
有發生的事。」

「只記得過去的事，真是可憐的記憶。」皇后說。

愛麗絲一邊說一邊抓住了披肩，東張西望想找到它的主人，過了一會，白皇后張開雙臂狂奔過樹林，就像在飛一樣，於是愛麗絲很有禮貌地拿著披肩去找她。

「我很高興剛好撿到了您的披肩。」愛麗絲邊說邊幫她披上披肩。

皇后用無助又害怕的表情看著她，一直小聲地喃喃自語，聽起來像是「奶油麵包、奶油麵包」。愛麗絲認為，如果想要對話，必須自己找話題，於是她有點靦腆地說：「我是在參見白皇后嗎？」

「哦，是的，如果你認為這叫『穿』的話，」白皇后說，「我想的穿衣服可不是這樣。」

愛麗絲心想不該在談話開始時就發生爭執，於是她微笑著說：「如果陛下告訴我怎麼做，我願意盡力做好。」

「可是我根本不想做！」可憐的皇后呻吟著，「從剛才開始的兩個小時，我一直在穿衣服。」

在愛麗絲看來，白皇后最好找個人來幫她穿衣服，她穿得實在太不整齊了。「每樣東西都皺巴巴的。」愛麗絲心裡想。「全是別針……我可以幫您整理披肩嗎？」她大聲地說。

「我不知道它是怎麼回事，」皇后憂鬱地說，「我想它一定是在鬧脾氣，我在這別個別針，在那也別個別針，都無法讓它滿意。」

「要是您全別在同一邊，是不可能把它披好的。」愛麗絲說，同時輕輕地幫皇后把披肩別好：「我的老天！您的頭髮怎麼變成這樣了！」

「頭髮被梳子纏住了！」皇后嘆息了一聲說，「我昨天又弄丟梳子了。」

愛麗絲小心地拿出梳子，盡力把她的頭髮梳好，又把大多數的別針換了地方，然後愛麗絲說：「好啦！您現在看起來好多了。不過您真該有個侍女！」

「我很樂意讓你當我的侍女，」皇后說，「一星期兩便士，每隔一天吃一次果醬。」

愛麗絲忍不住笑了起來，她說：「我不想讓您雇用我，而且我不喜歡果醬。」

「那是非常好的果醬。」皇后說。

「嗯，至少我今天不想吃。」

「你就是今天想吃也吃不到，」皇后說，「規矩是，明天有果醬，昨天有果醬，但是今天絕不會有果醬。」

「『今天有果醬』的那天一定會到的。」愛麗絲反駁說。

「不，不可能，」皇后說，「它是每隔一天果醬，今天不是每隔一天，你懂的。」

「我不懂，」愛麗絲說，「太亂了！」

「這就是倒著過日子的效果，」皇后和氣地說，「一開始總會叫人有點暈頭轉向。」

「倒著過日子！」愛麗絲非常驚訝地重複，「我從沒聽過這樣的事。」

「不過有個很大的好處，就是可以記住過去和未來的事。」

「我確定我只記得其中一邊，」愛麗絲說，「我沒辦法記住還沒有發生的事。」

「只記得過去的事，真是可憐的記憶。」皇后說。

「哪種事您記得最清楚呢？」愛麗絲斗膽問了一句。

「哦，下下星期發生的事，」皇后隨便地回答，「比如說，現在，」她接著說，邊說邊把一大塊膠布黏到她的手指上，「有個國王的信差現在正在牢裡接受懲罰，審判下週三才開始，那他當然得在那之後犯罪。」

「如果他從不犯罪呢？」愛麗絲

問。

「那就更好了，不是嗎？」皇后說，同時用緞帶把纏在手指上的膠布綁得更緊。

愛麗絲覺得這沒什麼好否認的。「那樣當然更好了，」她說，「但是因為那個信差已經受罰了，所以就沒那麼好。」

「你又錯了，」皇后說，「你被處罰過嗎？」

「只有當我犯錯的時候。」愛麗絲說。

「因為受罰所以你變得更好了，我就知道！」皇后得意地說。

「對，但是我是因為做錯什麼事而被處罰，」愛麗絲說，「那完全不一樣。」

「可是就算你沒做錯事，」皇后說，「處罰還是會讓你更好。更好！更好！更好！」每說一個「更好」，她的嗓門就提高一點，最後變成在尖叫。

愛麗絲正想要說「有什麼地方不對……」時，皇后大聲尖叫了起來，害她話只說到一半。「哦！哦！哦！」皇后邊喊邊甩手，好像要把手甩掉一樣，「我的手指頭在流血！哦，哦，哦，哦！」

她的叫聲真像火車頭的汽笛聲，愛麗絲只好用雙手搗住耳朵。

「怎麼了？」一有機會說話，愛麗絲立刻問，「您刺傷手指了嗎？」

「還沒有，」皇后說，「可是就快了。哦，哦，哦！」

「您認為什麼時候會發生呢？」愛麗絲問，差點笑了出來。

「在我別披肩別針的時候，」可憐的皇后呻吟著說，「別針馬上就要鬆開了。哦，哦！」說這些話的同時，別針鬆開了，皇后一把抓住它，想把它再別好。

「當心！」愛麗絲叫道，「您把它都弄彎了！」她抓住了別針，但太遲了，別針已經戳了出來，弄傷了皇后的手指。

「你看，流血了。」她微笑著對愛麗絲說，「現在你明白這裡的事情是怎麼發生的了。」

「但是您現在為什麼不叫了呢？」愛麗絲問，並且準備好隨時再用手捂耳朵。

「哦，我剛才已經全都叫完了，」皇后說，「再從頭叫一遍有什麼好處呢？」

這時候，天逐漸亮起來了。「我想那隻烏鴉一定已經飛走了，」愛麗絲說，「牠走了我真高興，我還以為天黑了呢！」

「我希望能想辦法高興起來！」皇后說，「可我老是記不住規則。住在這樹林裡，你一定要非常快樂，想快樂就快樂。」

「可是在這裡真孤單！」愛麗絲悲傷地說，想到自己孤伶伶的，兩顆斗大的淚珠從她的臉頰落了下來。

「哦，別那樣！」可憐的皇后絕望地緊握著手叫道，「想想你自己是個多棒的女孩，想想你今天走了多少路，想想現在幾點，想點別的事，就是不要哭！」

愛麗絲忍不住笑了起來，眼淚還在眼眶中打轉：「您能靠著想些別的事情讓自己不哭嗎？」她問。

「我就是那麼做的，」皇后肯定地說，「沒人能同時做兩件事。讓我們先從你的年齡開始。你多大了？」

「準確地說，我七歲半了。」

皇后說：「你不用說『準確地說』，不那麼說我也信。現在換我說些你會相信的事。我一百零一歲五個月又一天了。」

「我不相信！」愛麗絲說。

「你不相信嗎？」皇后遺憾地說，「再試試看：深深地吸一口氣，然後閉上雙眼。」

愛麗絲笑了。她說：「試也沒用，一個人不會相信不可能發生的事。」

「我敢說是你練習得不夠，」皇后說，「我像你這麼大的時候，一天要練習半個小時呢。有時候，我吃早餐之前就能相信六件不可能的事。披肩又飛走了！」

皇后說話的時候披肩又鬆了，突如其來的一陣風把披肩吹過了

小溪。皇后又張開了雙臂,飛一樣地追了過去。這次她成功地自己
抓住了披肩。「我抓到了!」皇后得意洋洋地叫道,「你看,我又
把它別好了,全靠自己!」

「我希望您的手指頭現在好多了。」愛麗絲非常禮貌地說,同
時跟在皇后身後穿過了小溪。

「哦,好多了!」皇后叫道,她
的音調越來越高,最後變成了尖叫。
「好多了!好!好!好!」最後一個
字的尾音拖得很長,就像一隻綿羊在
叫,愛麗絲嚇了一跳。

她看著皇后,皇后好像突然把自
己裹到一團羊毛裡了。愛麗絲揉了揉
眼睛,再仔細看了看,她說不上來到
底發生了什麼事。她是在一間商店裡
嗎?真的是一隻綿羊坐在櫃檯裡嗎?不論她怎麼揉眼睛,看到的都
是:她在一間漆黑的小店,手肘撐在櫃檯上,對面是隻老綿羊,正
坐在椅子上打毛線,並不時地停下來,透過一副大眼鏡看著她。

終於,綿羊停下手邊的毛線活,看了愛麗絲一會,問道:「你
想買什麼?」

「我現在還不知道,」愛麗絲非常輕聲地說,「要是可以的話,
我想先四處看看。」

「要是你願意，你可以看看你的前面，也可以看看你的兩邊；」綿羊說，「可是你無法『四處』看，除非你腦袋後面有長眼睛。」

但是愛麗絲腦袋後面沒有長眼睛，她只能轉動身體走向貨架一一瀏覽。

這間小店好像放滿了各式各樣奇怪的東西，但最奇怪的是，只要她認真地看著某個貨架，想弄清楚上面有什麼東西時，那個貨架總是空蕩蕩的，而旁邊的其他貨架卻擺得滿滿的。

「這裡的東西真愛到處跑！」愛麗絲花了幾分鐘徒勞地追著一個又大又亮的東西，它有時候看起來像個洋娃娃，有時候像個針線盒，總是出現在她盯著看的隔壁貨架上。最後她說：「真是氣死人了……不過我告訴你……」她突然靈機一動，接著說：「我要一直跟著它到最上面的貨架，我想它是沒辦法穿過天花板的！」

但是，就連這個計畫也失敗了，那個東西無聲無息地穿過了天花板，好像很習慣了。

「你是個小孩還是陀螺？」綿羊一邊取出另一對棒針，一邊問道：「要是你一直像那樣轉來轉去，我很快就會被你弄暈了。」她現在正同時用十四對棒針打毛線，愛麗絲非常驚訝地看著她。

「她怎麼能用那麼多針打毛線？」這個感到迷惑的小朋友心想，「她現在越來越像一頭豪豬了！」

「你會划船嗎？」綿羊問，同時拿給她一對棒針。

「會，就一點……但不是在陸地上……也不是用棒針……」愛麗絲剛開口，手裡的棒針突然變成了槳，而且她發現自己和綿羊正坐在一艘小船上，在河面漂浮，因此她只能盡力地划船。

「平槳！」綿羊叫道，同時又拿出一對棒針。

這聽起來不像一句需要回答的話，所以愛麗絲什麼都沒說，認真地划船。她想，這裡的水非常奇怪，船槳會不時地卡在裡面，很難再拉出來。

「平槳！平槳！」綿羊又叫了起來，拿出了更多的棒針。「你的船槳會直接卡住。」

「我倒希望抓住一隻可愛的小螃蟹！」愛麗絲想。

「你沒聽見我說『平槳』嗎？」綿羊生氣地喊，又取出了一捆棒針。

「我的確聽到了，」愛麗絲說，「你說了好多遍，而且非常大聲。請問你，螃蟹在哪裡？」

「當然在水裡！」綿羊說，又取出一些棒針插進她的頭髮裡，因為她手裡已經拿滿了。「我說，平槳！」

「為什麼你一直說羽毛呢？」愛麗絲有點生氣地問，「我又不是鳥！」

「你是，」綿羊說，「你是一隻小笨鵝。」

這讓愛麗絲有點不高興，所以有一、兩分鐘她們沒有繼續談話。小船繼續輕輕地前進，有時滑進了水草叢（這些水草讓船槳卡在水裡，比剛才卡得更緊），有時又從樹下滑過，但是她們頭上始終是高高的河岸。

「啊，拜託！有一些很香的燈心草！」愛麗絲突然開心地喊道，「真的……好漂亮！」

「你不用為了燈心草對我說『拜託』，」綿羊打著毛線，頭也不抬地說，「我沒在這裡種燈心草，我也不打算把它們拿走。」

「不，我的意思是，拜託，我們能停下來摘些草嗎？」愛麗絲請求著，「如果你不介意把船停下來一分鐘的話。」

「我要怎麼讓它停下來？」綿羊說，「如果你不划，它自己就會停了。」

於是愛麗絲停了下來，讓小船順水漂流在燈心草搖曳的小溪上。然後，愛麗絲捲起袖子，把手臂伸到水裡摘燈心草，她摘了很久，有一陣子完全忘了綿羊和打毛線的事。她把身子俯過船舷，捲髮的髮梢浸入了水中，眼神既明亮又熱切，摘下一束一束可愛芳香的燈心草。

「我只希望不會翻船！」她對自己說，「哦！多可愛啊！可惜我摘不到。」這確實讓人有點著急（「簡直就像是故意的」，她想），雖然愛麗絲已經努力地在小船漂過的地方，摘了很多美麗的燈心草，卻摘不到其他更可愛的草。

「最好看的總是離得更遠！」她最後說，為這些長得很遠的燈心草嘆了一口氣。然後，帶著發紅的臉頰、浸濕的頭髮和雙手爬回了原本的位子，開始整理她新發現的寶貝。

很可惜的是，這些燈心草摘下來後就開始枯萎，失去香氣和美麗。你知道，即使是真正的燈心草，香氣和美麗也只能維持很短的時間，而這些夢裡的燈心草，就像雪一般地在他腳下融化了。可是愛麗絲幾乎沒有注意到這件事，因為有太多奇怪的事要想了。

她們還沒走多遠，一隻槳就卡在水裡，再也不願意出來了（愛麗絲事後是這麼解釋的）。結果槳柄打到了她的下巴，可憐的愛麗絲不斷發出「哦！哦！哦！」的叫聲，從座位上跌到了燈心草堆裡。

然而，她沒受傷，很快就又爬了起來。綿羊這段時間一直繼續打著毛線，好像什麼事都沒發生一樣。「你抓到了一隻大螃蟹！」她說。這時愛麗絲回到了原來的座位，發現自己還在小船上，頓時鬆了口氣。

「是嗎？我沒看見。」愛麗絲說，一面彎腰仔細地往黑水裡瞧，「我希望牠沒逃走，我好想帶一隻小螃蟹回家！」但是綿羊只是輕蔑地笑著，繼續打毛線。

「這裡有很多螃蟹嗎？」愛麗絲問。

「有，什麼東西都有，」綿羊說，「夠你挑的，不過你得下定決心，來，你到底要買什麼？」

「要買？」愛麗絲又詫異而又害怕地重複著，因為船、船槳和河流全都在一瞬間消失了，她又回到了那個陰暗的小店裡。

「我想買一個雞蛋。」她怯生生地說，「你這裡雞蛋怎麼賣？」

「五便士一個，兩便士兩個。」綿羊回答。

「兩個比一個便宜？」愛麗絲一邊拿出錢包，一邊驚訝地問。

「但是買兩個的話，必須全部吃掉！」綿羊說。

「那我就買一個吧！」愛麗絲說著，同時把錢放在櫃檯上，她心想，「這些蛋不一定都是好的。」

綿羊拿了錢，放到一個盒子裡，然後說：「我從不把東西放到人們的手裡，永遠都不，你得自己拿。」說著說著，她走到了小店的另一邊，把一個雞蛋立在貨架上。

「我不知道為什麼不能放到人們的手裡？」愛麗絲想著，因為店裡非常暗，她只好在桌椅之間摸索著前進。「好像我越朝它走去，那顆蛋就離我越遠。讓我看看，這是把椅子嗎？哎喲，有樹枝，真的！有樹長在這裡真是太怪了，還有一條小溪！哦，這真是我見過最奇怪的商店了！」

她就這樣繼續往前走，每走一步她就感到越來越驚奇，因為在她走近的時候，所有東西都變成了一棵樹。她相信那顆蛋肯定也是如此。

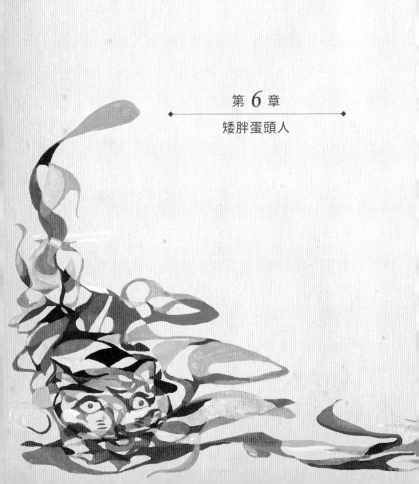

第 6 章

矮胖蛋頭人

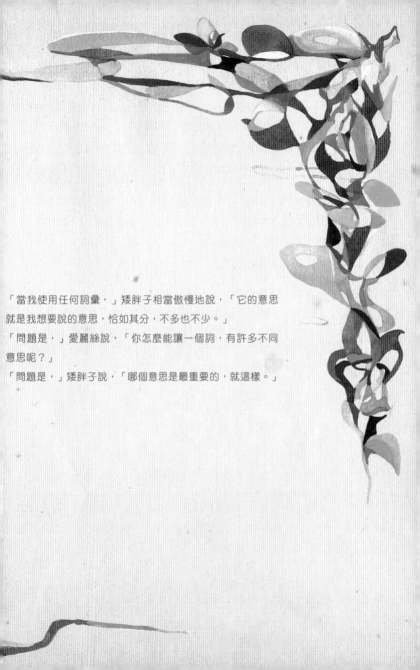

「當我使用任何詞彙，」矮胖子相當傲慢地說，「它的意思就是我想要說的意思，恰如其分，不多也不少。」

「問題是，」愛麗絲說，「你怎麼能讓一個詞，有許多不同意思呢？」

「問題是，」矮胖子說，「哪個意思是最重要的，就這樣。」

然而，那顆蛋不但越來越大，而且越來越像人了。當愛麗絲走到離他只有幾步遠的時候，她看到蛋有眼睛、鼻子和嘴巴。而當她更靠近時，她清楚地看到這就是「矮胖子」本人。「這不可能是別人！」她對自己說，「我確定，就像他的臉上寫了名字一樣地確定。」

他的臉大得可以輕易地寫上一百個名字了。矮胖子像土耳其人一樣，正盤腿坐在一座高牆上。愛麗絲很疑惑他要如何在那麼窄的牆上保持平衡。還有，他的眼睛一動也不動地盯著對面，完全沒注意到她，所以她想矮胖子一定只是個填充玩具。

「他實在太像一顆蛋了！」愛麗絲大聲地說，並準備好用手抓住他，因為她時時刻刻都擔心矮胖子會掉下來。

「真是氣死人了，」矮胖子沉默了很久之後說，而且說話時故意不看愛麗絲，「竟然被說是蛋！」

「先生，我是說你看起來像一顆蛋，」愛麗絲溫和地解釋，「你也知道，有些蛋是相當漂亮的。」她補了一句，希望把她的評論變成一種恭維。

「有些人，」矮胖子還是不看愛麗絲，「比嬰兒還沒常識！」

愛麗絲不知道該說什麼，這根本不像談話，因為他從不對著她說話。事實上，他最後那句話，顯然是對著一棵樹說的。於是，愛麗絲站起來，輕輕地背誦著：

　　「矮胖子坐在牆上，
　　　矮胖子摔得很慘，

國王全部的駿馬和勇士，

都無法把矮胖子放回去。」

「這首詩的最後一行太長了。」愛麗絲說，她幾乎就是在大喊，忘了矮胖子會聽到。

「別站在那對自己說話，」矮胖子第一次看著她說話，「告訴我你的名字還有你是做什麼的。」

「我的名字是愛麗絲，但是……」

「真夠蠢的名字！」矮胖子不耐煩地打斷說，「有什麼意思？」

「名字一定要有意思嗎？」愛麗絲懷疑地問。

「當然要有啊，」矮胖子笑了一聲說，「我的名字就是指我的體型，又好又漂亮的體型。像你這樣的名字，簡直可以是任何形狀。」

「為什麼你自己坐在這裡呢？」愛麗絲問，不想跟他爭論。

「哦，因為沒有人和我一起啊！」矮胖子喊道，「你以為我不知道你的問題的答案嗎？再問點別的。」

「你不認為站在地上更安全嗎？」愛麗絲繼續說，她沒想過要再提什麼問題，只是出於善意擔心這個奇怪的傢伙。「那道牆實在太窄了！」

「你問的謎題未免也太簡單了！」矮胖子大喊起來，「當然不！如果我曾經從這裡摔下去過，當然這是不可能的，我是說如

果……」說到這裡他噘起了嘴，那麼嚴肅認真，愛麗絲忍不住笑了出來，「如果我真的跌下來，」他繼續說，「國王已經答應我了，他親口說要……」

「派出所有的駿馬和勇士。」愛麗絲打斷了他，這是很不聰明的舉動。

「真是太可惡了！」矮胖子突然激動地喊道：「你一定是在門口、樹後面和煙囪下偷聽了，否則你不可能會知道！」

「我絕對沒有！」愛麗絲非常溫和地說，「書上是這麼寫的。」

「啊，對！他們可能會把這種事寫進書裡，」矮胖子稍微平靜了點，「那就是你們說的英格蘭歷史，就是這樣。現在，好好看看我！我是跟國王說過話的人，是我！或許你再也不會遇到另外一個這樣的人了。為了表示我並不傲慢，你可以和我握手！」矮胖子咧嘴笑了起來，大嘴巴幾乎要裂到耳朵旁邊了。他俯身向前（幾乎快從牆上摔下來了），向愛麗絲伸出了手。愛麗絲握著他的手時有點擔心地看著他。「他要是笑得再開一點，嘴角可能會碰到後腦勺，」她想，「不知道那時他的頭會變成什麼樣子，恐怕要斷成兩半了！」

「是的，國王全部的駿馬和勇士，」矮胖子繼續說，「他們會立刻把我再扶起來。他們會的！不過，這次談話進行得太快了，讓我們回到上一個話題吧。」

「我恐怕不太記得了。」愛麗絲很禮貌地說。

「那我們就重新開始吧，」矮胖子說，「現在輪到我來選擇話題了。」（愛麗絲想：「他把談話說得像個遊戲一樣！」）「這裡有個問題要問你，你剛剛說你幾歲了？」

愛麗絲算了一下，然後說：「七歲零六個月。」

「錯了！」矮胖子得意地喊著，「你本來不是這麼說的！」

「我想你的意思是『你現在幾歲了？』」愛麗絲解釋說。

「如果我是那個意思，我會那樣說。」矮胖子說。

愛麗絲不想再起爭執，所以什麼都沒說。

「七歲零六個月！」矮胖子沉思著重複道：「這個年齡多不舒服啊。如果你徵求我的意見，我會說『就停在七歲』，但是現在太遲了。」

「我從不針對長大這件事徵求意見。」愛麗絲憤怒地說。

「因為你太驕傲了？」矮胖子問。

聽到這句話，愛麗絲更生氣了，「我的意思是，」她說，「一個人不能阻止年齡增長。」

「一個人或許不能，」矮胖子說，「但是兩個人就能了。有了適當的幫助，你就可以停在七歲了。」

「你的皮帶真漂亮！」愛麗絲突然說。（她想，年齡的問題已經談得夠多了，要是他們真的要按順序來選擇話題的話，現在該輪到她了。）「至少，」她趕緊糾正說，「是漂亮的領帶，我該這麼說……哦，不是皮帶，我想說……請原諒！」愛麗絲有點慌了，因為矮胖子看起來澈底被激怒了，她開始後悔選了這個話題。「要是我能知道哪裡是脖子，哪裡是腰就好了！」她在心裡想。

矮胖子非常地憤怒，他沉默了一、兩分鐘，當他再次開口時，簡直是在咆哮。

「這是最令人憤怒的事！」他最後說，「竟然有人分不清楚領帶和皮帶！」

「我知道我很無知。」愛麗絲很謙卑地說，矮胖子變得溫和了一點。

「這是領帶，孩子，正像你說的，是一條漂亮的領帶。是白國王和白皇后送的。你看！」

「真的？」愛麗絲說，她非常高興自己原來選了個好話題。

「他們送給我的，」矮胖子翹起了二郎腿，用雙手抱住膝蓋，繼續沉思著說：「他們送給我的，我的非生日禮物。」

「抱歉，你說什麼？」愛麗絲困惑地說。

「我沒生氣。」矮胖子說。

「我的意思是,什麼是『非』生日禮物?」

「當然是在不是你生日的時候,別人送的禮物了。」

愛麗絲想了想,最後說:「我最喜歡生日禮物了。」

「你不懂你在說什麼!」矮胖子叫道,「一年有多少天呀?」

「三百六十五天。」愛麗絲說。

「你一年有多少個生日呢?」

「一個。」

「如果從三百六十五裡減掉一,還剩多少?」

「當然是三百六十四。」

矮胖子看起來好像有點懷疑,他說:「我倒要看看在紙上是怎麼算的。」

愛麗絲不禁笑了起來,她拿出了她的本子,為他列了算式:

$$
\begin{array}{r}
365 \\
-1 \\
\hline
364
\end{array}
$$

矮胖子拿著本子，仔細地看了看之後說：「看起來是算對了……」

「你拿反了！」愛麗絲打斷他說。

「我真的拿反了！」當愛麗絲把本子轉過來後，矮胖子很高興地說，「我還在想它看起來有點怪，就像我說的：『看起來』是算對了。雖然我現在沒時間仔細看，不過這說明有三百六十四天可以得到非生日禮物。」

「當然。」

「你看，只有一天可以收生日禮物。這對你多光榮呀！」

「我不明白你說的『光榮』是什麼意思。」愛麗絲說。

矮胖子輕蔑地笑了：「你當然不懂，得等我告訴你。我的意思是『你在這場辯論中徹底輸了！』」

「但是『光榮』的意思並不是『在辯論中徹底失敗』。」愛麗絲反駁說。

「當我使用任何詞彙，」矮胖子相當傲慢地說，「它的意思就是我想要說的意思，恰如其分，不多也不少。」

「問題是，」愛麗絲說，「你怎麼能讓一個詞，有許多不同意思呢？」

「問題是，」矮胖子說，「哪個意思是最重要的，就這樣。」

　　愛麗絲疑惑到無話可說。過了一會兒，矮胖子又開口了：「這些詞有自己的脾氣，特別是動詞，他們是最驕傲的。你可以隨意使喚形容詞，但動詞不行。不過，我能夠使喚所有的詞！我簡直太高深莫測了！這就是我要說的！」

　　「請問，你願意告訴我那是什麼意思嗎？」愛麗絲說。

　　「現在你說起話來像個懂事的孩子了，」矮胖子看起來非常高興，他說：「我說『高深莫測』是指這個話題我們已經談得夠多了，我不認為你想把下半輩子都耗在這裡，所以你可以接著說你下一步的打算。」

　　「讓一個詞有意思真麻煩。」愛麗絲沉思著說。

　　「當我讓一個詞像剛才那樣有很多意思時，」矮胖子說，「我總是會多付點錢。」

　　「哦！」愛麗絲說。她疑惑得都不知道說什麼了。

　　「哎，星期六晚上你就能看到他們圍著我，」矮胖子繼續說著，同時把頭搖來搖去，「你知道，他們是來拿工資的。」（愛麗絲不敢問他為什麼要付工資。所以你看，我無法告訴你了。）

　　「先生，你好像很會解釋字詞的意義，」愛麗絲說，「你願意告訴我《傑伯沃基》那首詩的意思嗎？」

　　「讓我聽聽，」矮胖子說，「我能解釋所有已經創作出來的詩，也能解釋很多還沒創作出來的詩。」

愛麗絲聽到這句話覺得充滿希望，於是背了第一節：

「燦爛滑動的土武斯，
在搖擺中旋轉鑽儀，
波羅哥斯慘弱無比，
迷茫的萊斯齊吼哨。」

「這個開頭就夠了，」矮胖子插話說：「這裡有很多難懂的詞。『燦爛』指的是下午四點鐘，開始準備晚飯，把『菜』燉『爛』的時間。」

「解釋得真好，」愛麗絲說，「那『滑動』呢？」

「嗯，『滑動』指的是『滑溜』和『流動』，『滑溜』和『活潑』的意思一樣。你看，這就像合成詞，把兩個意思放在一個詞裡。」

「我現在明白了，」愛麗絲沉思著說，「那什麼是『土武斯』？」

「嗯，『土武斯』是像獾的東西，有點像蜥蜴，也有點像開瓶器。」

「他們看起來一定很奇怪。」

「他們是很怪，」矮胖子

說，「他們在日晷下面築巢，還靠乳酪維生。」

「那麼『旋轉』和『鑽儀』是什麼呢？」

「『旋轉』就是像陀螺一樣一圈圈地轉，『鑽儀』就是像鑽子那樣打洞。」

「我猜，『搖擺』一定是繞著日晷的草地了？」愛麗絲邊說邊為自己的機靈感到驚訝。

「當然是啊，你知道，它叫做『搖擺』，是因為走路起來前後搖晃。」

「搖晃時還往上翹。」愛麗絲補充說。

「確實如此。接下來，『慘弱無比』，就是『脆弱的』和『悲慘的』（又是一個合成詞。）而『波羅哥斯』是一種又瘦又醜的鳥，他的羽毛都向外豎著，有點像抹布。」

「那麼『迷茫的萊斯』呢？」愛麗絲說，「恐怕給你添太多麻煩了。」

「嗯。『萊斯』是一種綠色的豬。但是『迷茫』的意思我不確定，我想可能是『離家』的縮寫，表示迷路了。」

「那『吼哨』是什麼意思？」

「嗯，『吼哨』是介於『吼叫』和『口哨』的聲音，中間還有噴嚏聲。你要是在樹林那邊就聽得到了，當你聽到你就懂了。誰讓你背這些難懂的東西的？」

「我在一本書裡讀到的，」愛麗絲說，「但是我還唸過一些詩，比這首容易多了，我想是叮噹寫的。」

「說到詩，」矮胖子伸出一隻大手說，「我能背得和別人一樣好……」

「哦，不需要！」愛麗絲急忙地說，希望他不會從頭背起。

「我要背一首，」他沒注意到她的話，繼續說，「完全是為了讓你開心而寫的詩。」

愛麗絲覺得在這種情況下，她實在應該聽聽。於是她坐了下來，有點難過地說了聲「謝謝」。

　　「冬天，田野一片雪白，
　　我唱此歌使你歡欣。」

「不過我不是真的要唱。」他補充說，作為解釋。

「我知道。」愛麗絲說。

「要是你能夠看出來我是不是在唱，你就比大多數人都厲害了。」矮胖子嚴肅地說。愛麗絲沒有說話。

　　「春天，樹木一片青翠，
　　我將對你訴說一切。」

「非常感謝。」愛麗絲說。

「夏天，白天如此漫長，
也許你會懂這首歌。」

秋天，樹葉一片金黃，
備好筆墨記下一切。」

「我會的，要是我能記那麼久的話。」愛麗絲說。

「你不需要像這樣回應，」矮胖子說，「既沒意思又打擾我。」

「我給魚群捎了信息，
告訴他們『此為我所希冀』。」
大海裡的小魚，
為我送回了音訊。

小魚們如此回應：
『我們不能，先生，因為……』」

「我恐怕不太明白。」愛麗絲說。

「後面就簡單了。」矮胖子回答說。

「我給他們再次捎了封信，
說『你們應該服從命令。』

魚兒微笑著回應，
『哎呀，你好大的脾氣！』

我說了一遍又一遍，

401

他們不聽我的勸。

我拿個新的大茶壺，
正好派上用處。

我的心怦怦地跳，
用水泵裝水注滿茶壺。

然後有人來對我說，
『小魚們已經睡了。』

我清楚地對他說，
『那你必須把牠們叫醒。』

我說得又響又清楚，
我對著他的耳朵高聲吼。」

矮胖子唸到這一節時，聲調提高到幾乎在尖叫。愛麗絲顫抖了
一下，心想：「我才不要當信差！」

「但他如此固執和驕傲，
他說『你不必大聲吼叫！』

他是如此驕傲和固執，
他說『如果需要我會叫。』

我從架子上拿了開瓶器，
我要親自去叫醒他們。」

當我發現門已被鎖上，
我又拉又推，又踢又敲。

當我發現門已被關上，
我想轉動門把，但……」

然後是一陣沉默。

「就這樣？」愛麗絲膽怯地問。

「就這樣，」矮胖子說，「再見。」

這有點突然，愛麗絲想。但是他已經給了這麼強烈的暗示，她
也應該離開，再待下去就太沒禮貌了。因此她站起來，伸出手說：

「再見，我們下次再碰面吧！」她儘量以高聲的語調說。

「如果我們真的碰面的話，我應該也認不得你，」矮胖子不滿地說，伸出一根手指來和她握手，「你長得和別人太像了。」

「通常是靠臉來分辨人的。」愛麗絲若有所思地說。

「這正是我抱怨的，」矮胖子說，「你的臉和其他人一樣，兩個眼睛（他用大拇指在空中比劃著臉的形狀），中間是鼻子，鼻子下面是嘴巴。都長一樣。假如你的雙眼和鼻子長在同一個地方，或者嘴在頭頂上，那就好分辨了。」

「那就不好看了。」愛麗絲反對說。但矮胖子只是閉著眼睛說：「等你試試看再說吧。」

愛麗絲等了一下子，想看看他是不是還要說些什麼。但是矮胖子再也不睜開眼睛，也不再注意她了。愛麗絲又說了聲「再見」，沒有人回答，於是她靜靜地離開了。離開時她不禁自言自語：「在所有惹人厭的……」（她大聲重複著，好像能說出這麼長的句子，是一種很大的安慰）「在我所遇見的所有惹人厭的人當中……」她話還沒說完，就聽見一聲巨響撼動了整個樹林。

第 7 章
獅子與獨角獸

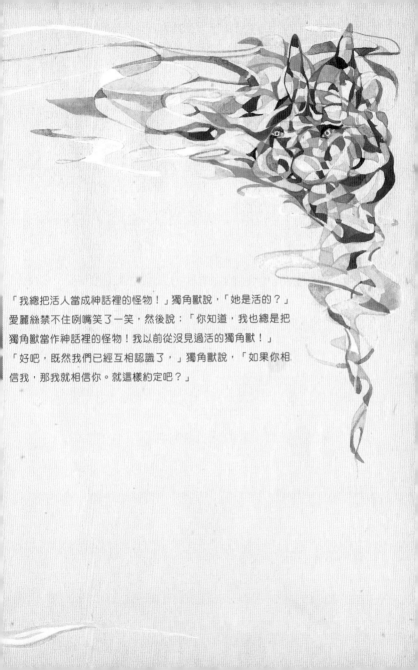

「我總把活人當成神話裡的怪物！」獨角獸說，「她是活的？」
愛麗絲禁不住咧嘴笑了一笑，然後說：「你知道，我也總是把
獨角獸當作神話裡的怪物！我以前從沒見過活的獨角獸！」
「好吧，既然我們已經互相認識了，」獨角獸說，「如果你相
信我，那我就相信你。就這樣約定吧？」

士兵們很快地穿過樹林跑了過來，起初只有兩三個，接著十幾、二十個，最後變成一整群，好像要把整座樹林都塞滿了。愛麗絲怕被他們踩扁，躲在一棵樹後面，看著他們走過去。

愛麗絲這輩子從沒見過像這樣連路都走不穩的士兵，他們總是被東西絆倒，而且只要一個倒下，就會有好幾個接二連三倒在他身上，地上很快就倒了一堆人。

接著過來的是馬。馬有四條腿，所以比步兵好一點。但即使如此，**牠們**也是不時地被絆倒。而且好像有規律似的，只要一匹馬被絆倒，騎士就會立刻摔下來。這種混亂隨時都在發生，情況越來越糟。愛麗絲很慶幸自己走出樹林，來到了一片空地，在這裡，她發現白國王坐在地上，忙著在筆記本上書寫。

「我把他們都派出去了！」國王一見到愛麗絲就高興地喊：「親愛的，你走過樹林的時候，有沒有碰見士兵們？」

「是的，我看見了，」愛麗絲說，「我想有幾千人吧。」

「確切的數字是四千二百零七個。」國王看著他的本子說，「你知道，我不能把所有的駿馬都派出去，因為有兩匹需要參加比賽，而且我也沒把兩名信差派出去，他們都到鎮上去了。看看那條路，要是你看見信差就告訴我。」

「沒有人。」愛麗絲說。

「我真希望我有一雙能看見沒有人的眼睛，」國王煩躁地說，「就算再遠也能看見！嗯，在這樣的光線下，我只能看見真正的人！」

愛麗絲沒聽到這些話，她專心地往小路的方向看，一隻手遮在眼睛上。「現在我看見人了！」她最後喊道，「可是他走得非常慢，姿勢真奇怪！」（那個信差一直跳上跳下，還像鰻魚似地扭來扭去，邊走還邊伸出了兩隻大手，好像兩把大扇子。）

「一點都不奇怪。」國王說，「他是盎格魯撒克遜人，這是盎格魯撒克遜姿勢。他只在高興的時候這樣走。他的名字是海發。」（他像朗誦般地唸出這個名字。）

「我喜歡『ㄏ』這個字，」愛麗絲不禁說：「因為就像『嗨』，聽起來很快樂。不過我也討厭它，因為他和「害」差不多。他應該吃火腿三明治和海草。他的名字叫海發，他住在……」

「住在海山上，」國王簡單地說，完全沒想到他也參與了愛麗絲關於「ㄏ」的遊戲，這時愛麗絲還在思索著「ㄏ」開頭的字。「另一個信差叫海他。我必須有兩個信差，你知道，一個回來，一個過去。」

「不好意思？」愛麗絲說。

「沒什麼不好意思的。」國王說。

「我只是說我不懂，」愛麗絲說，「為什麼要一個來，一個去呢？」

「我沒告訴你嗎？」國王不耐煩地重複說，「我必須有兩個，一個把信拿回來，一個把信帶過去。」

這時，那個信差到了，他喘得說不出話來，只能揮動雙手，對著可憐的國王做出最可怕的表情。

「這位年輕女士喜歡你，因為你的名字有個『ㄏ』，」國王把愛麗絲介紹給他，希望信差的注意力能從自己身上移開，但是沒有用。所謂的盎格魯撒克遜姿勢變得越來越特別了：他斗大的眼睛飛快地轉來轉去。

「你嚇到我了！」國王說，「我頭昏了，給我一塊火腿三明治！」

讓愛麗絲感到十分新奇的是，信差打開繞在脖子上的袋子，拿出三明治，國王立即貪婪地狼吞虎嚥了起來。

「再一塊！」國王說。

「沒有了，現在就剩海草了。」信差看了看口袋說。

「那就海草吧。」國王

有氣無力地嘀咕著。

　　看到海草讓國王的精神振作了許多，愛麗絲感到很高興。「當你頭昏時，沒有別的東西能像海草一樣好了。」國王一面大口吃著，一面對愛麗絲說。

　　「我認為潑點冷水會更好，」愛麗絲提議，「或者來點提神藥。」

　　「我說的不是『沒有更好了』，」國王回答，「我說的是『沒有一樣好了』。」愛麗絲不敢反駁。

　　「你在路上遇見誰了？」國王繼續問，又向信差要了點海草。

　　「沒有人。」信差說。

　　「太正確了，」國王說，「這位年輕女士也看到沒有人了，當然，沒有人走得比你慢。」

　　「我盡力了，」信差不高興地說，「我肯定沒有人走得比我快！」

　　「他不會走得比你更快的。」國王說，「不然他早就到這裡了。不過，既然現在你已經喘過氣來了，可以告訴我們城裡發生什麼事了吧。」

　　「我要小聲地跟您說，」信差說，他把手放在嘴邊，做成喇叭狀圈住嘴，彎腰靠近國王的耳朵。愛麗絲對此有點不高興，因為她也想聽。但是信差並沒有小聲地說，反而是用最大的音量喊道：「牠們又在那裡了！」

「你認為這樣叫小聲？」可憐的國王跳了起來，發抖著喊道：「你要是再這樣，我要把你用油煎了！你的叫聲像地震一樣穿過了我的腦袋。」

「這可是場小地震！」愛麗絲想，「誰又在那裡了？」她鼓起勇氣問。

「當然是獅子和獨角獸了。」國王說。

「爭奪王冠嗎？」

「當然啦！」國王說，「最可笑的是，王冠一直都是我的！讓我們跑去看看牠們吧。」說著，他們就小跑步過去了。愛麗絲跑的時候，為自己背誦了一首古老的歌曲，歌詞是：

　　「獅子和獨角獸為王冠而鬥，

　　　獅子一直在打獨角獸。

　　　有人給牠們白麵包，有人給牠們黑麵包，

　　　有人給了葡萄乾蛋糕並趕牠們走。」

「那麼……那個……贏的人……得到……王冠……了嗎？」愛麗絲跑得上氣不接下氣地問。

「親愛的，當然沒有！」國王說，「你怎麼會這樣想！」

又跑了一小段路，愛麗絲氣喘吁吁地說：「能停下來……歇一口氣嗎？」

「你能……你願意……」又跑了一會兒，愛麗絲上氣不接下氣地說，「停一會兒……好讓人喘口氣嗎？」

「我願意，」國王說，「我很好，只是我不夠強壯。你看，一分鐘過得這麼快。你應該設法讓潘達斯奈基停下來！」

愛麗絲喘得說不出話，因此，他們沉默地跑著，直到看見了一大群人。獅子和獨角獸在人群中搏鬥，牠們打得塵土飛揚，讓愛麗絲分辨不出誰是誰，不過她很快就根據角認出了獨角獸。

他們走近了另一位叫做海他的信差，海他正站著觀看這場搏鬥，一隻手拿著茶，另一隻手拿著奶油麵包。

「他才剛從監獄裡被釋放出來，還沒喝完茶就被派來了。」海發低聲告訴愛麗絲，「監獄裡只給他吃牡蠣殼，所以你看，他又渴又餓。」海發說著，親切地用手臂勾住了海他的脖子，對他說：「親愛的，你好嗎？」

海他轉過頭來，點了點頭，繼續吃他的奶油麵包。

「你在監獄裡好嗎，親愛的？」海發問。

海他又把頭轉了過來，這次有一兩滴淚珠順著他的臉頰滑落了下來，但他還是不發一語。

「你不會說話嗎？」海發不耐煩地喊道。但海他只是大口地嚼著，又喝了幾口茶。

「說話啊你！」國王喊道，「牠們打得怎麼樣了？」

海他用盡了力氣，吞下一大片奶油麵包。「牠們打得真棒，」他嗓子裡還嘻著麵包，「雙方都被彼此打倒了大概八十七次了。」

「那我想牠們就快拿到白麵包和黑麵包了吧？」愛麗絲鼓起勇氣問。

「這就是為牠們準備的，」海他說，「我現在吃的就是。」

這時候搏鬥暫停了一會兒，獅子和獨角獸氣喘吁吁地坐了下來。國王宣佈：「休息十分鐘！」海發和海他立即開始工作，端上了盛滿白麵包和黑麵包的盤子。愛麗絲嚐了一片，她覺得麵包太乾了。

「我想牠們今天不會再打了，」國王對海他說，「去叫他們開

414

始擊鼓。」海他像蚱蜢似地跳走了。

愛麗絲望著海他靜靜地站了一兩分鐘。突然，她高興起來，「快看，快看！」她大喊，興奮地指指點點，「白皇后穿過田野跑過來了！她飛也似地從那邊的樹林跑了出來，皇后跑得多快呀！」

「毫無疑問，有敵人在追趕她，」國王頭也不回地說，「那片樹林裡全是敵人。」

「但是你不用去救她嗎？」愛麗絲問，她對國王的不在乎感到非常訝異。

「不用，不用！」國王說，「她跑得太快了，和救她比起來，你最好去抓潘達斯奈基！但是如果你想的話，我會把她記在備忘錄。她是個可愛的好傢伙。」他溫和地重複，同時打開了他的備忘錄，「『傢伙』這兩個字有人字旁嗎？」

這時，獨角獸遛躂到他們身邊，手插在口袋裡，「我這次贏了吧？」牠經過的時候這麼問，還瞄了一下國王。

「一點點……一點點。」國王緊張地回答，「你不應該用角刺穿牠。」

「沒傷到牠。」獨角獸滿不在乎地說，繼續往前走。這時，牠的眼光恰巧落在了愛麗絲身上。牠轉過來站了一會兒，以厭惡的眼神看著她。

「這是……什麼？」牠終於開口問道。

415

「這是個孩子！」海發急忙回答，跑到愛麗絲前面介紹，他朝愛麗絲伸出了雙手，擺出盎格魯撒克遜姿勢，「我們今天發現的。她的大小跟活人一樣，是我們這裡一般人的兩倍！」

「我總把活人當成神話裡的怪物！」獨角獸說，「她是活的？」

「她會說話。」海發嚴肅地說。

獨角獸迷茫地看著愛麗絲，說：「說話，孩子。」

愛麗絲禁不住咧嘴笑了一笑，然後說：「你知道，我也總是把獨角獸當作神話裡的怪物！我以前從沒見過活的獨角獸！」

「好吧，既然我們已經互相認識了，」獨角獸說，「如果你相信我，那我就相信你。就這樣約定吧？」

「好的，如果你喜歡的話。」愛麗絲說。

「來吧，把葡萄乾蛋糕拿出來，老頭！」獨角獸從愛麗絲這裡轉向國王繼續說，「別把你的黑麵包給我！」

「當然……當然！」國王咕噥著，然後和海發說，「打開口袋！」他低聲說，「快！不是那個……那個裝的都是海草！」

海發從口袋裡取出了一塊蛋糕，交給愛麗絲，這時他拿出了盤子和切肉用的刀子。愛麗絲猜不到這些東西是怎麼出現的，就像在變魔術。

這時候獅子也加入了，牠看起來又累又睏，眼睛半閉著。「這是什麼！」牠懶洋洋地看著愛麗絲說，牠的聲音很低沉，聽起來就像一口大鐘的聲響。

「哦，你問這是什麼嗎？」獨角獸連忙喊了起來，「你永遠都猜不出來！我就沒猜到。」

獅子疲倦地看著愛麗絲：「你是動物……植物……還是礦物？」牠每說一個字都要打呵欠。

「牠是神話裡的怪物！」沒等愛麗絲回答，獨角獸就喊出來了。

「那來分葡萄乾蛋糕吧，怪物。」獅子說著趴了下來，用爪子撐著下巴。「你們倆個，坐下，」（牠對國王和獨角獸說）：「平分這塊蛋糕！」

國王坐在這兩個大傢伙之間，顯得很不自在，但又沒別的地方可以坐。

「我們應該為這頂王冠打一場，就現在吧！」獨角獸說著，狡猾地看著王冠。可憐的國王開始顫抖，差點把王冠從頭上抖下來。

「我會輕鬆獲勝的。」獅子說。

「我看不一定。」獨角獸說。

「什麼，我把你打得在全城團團轉還不夠，你這膽小鬼！」獅子憤怒地回答，說話的時候半支起了身子。

國王在這時打斷了牠們，想制止住爭吵，他很不安，聲音抖得厲害:「在全城團團轉?」他說,「那條路可真長。你們路過舊橋了嗎?還是經過了市場?在舊橋上看到的景色最好。」

「我真的不知道。」獅子又趴了下來,同時咆哮著說,「到處都是灰塵,什麼也看不見。怪物,都什麼時候了,切蛋糕!」

愛麗絲已經坐在溪邊,膝蓋上放著大盤子,認真地用刀切著。「太氣人了!」她回答獅子說(她已經很習慣被叫做怪物了),「我已經切開好幾塊了,可是它們又會重新合起來!」

「你不懂得怎麼對付鏡子裡的蛋糕,」獨角獸說,「先拿著它轉一圈,然後再切。」

這話聽起來很荒唐,但是愛麗絲非常順從地站起來,端著盤子轉了一圈,這時蛋糕就自動分成了三片。「現在切開了吧。」愛麗絲拿著空盤子回到原位上時,獅子這麼說。

「這不公平！」獨角獸喊道，這時愛麗絲手裡拿著刀坐著，對蛋糕是怎麼切開的還十分迷惑不解。「怪物分給獅子的蛋糕，比我的多了兩倍！」

「她都沒給自己留一點呢，」獅子說，「怪物，你喜歡葡萄乾蛋糕嗎？」

愛麗絲還沒回答，鼓聲就開始響了。

她不知道聲音是從哪裡來的。空氣中彷彿充滿了鼓聲，而且在她腦袋瓜裡轟隆作響，她覺得自己快聾了。她恐懼地站起來，跳過了小溪。就在此時，她看到獅子和獨角獸也站了起來，因為宴會被打斷而怒氣沖沖。接著她跪了下來，用手捂著耳朵，徒勞地想避開這可怕的噪音。

「如果不是『鼓聲驅逐』，恐怕還無法趕走牠們呢！」

第 8 章

「這是我自己的發明」

「所以，那根本不是做夢，」她自言自語地說，「除非……
除非我們全都在同一個夢裡，不過我真希望這是我的夢，而不
是紅國王的夢！我不喜歡在別人的夢裡。」她用帶點埋怨的口
氣繼續說，「我得去叫醒他，看看發生了什麼事！」

過了一會，鼓聲漸漸消失了，最後變成一片死寂。愛麗絲驚魂未定地抬起頭，發現周圍一個人也沒有了。她的第一個念頭是，剛才一定是做夢，夢見了獅子和獨角獸，但她腳邊還放著那個盛裝葡萄乾蛋糕的大盤子。「所以，那根本不是做夢，」她自言自語地說，「除非……除非我們全都在同一個夢裡，不過我真希望這是我的夢，而不是紅國王的夢！我不喜歡在別人的夢裡。」她用帶點埋怨的口氣繼續說，「我得去叫醒他，看看發生了什麼事！」

這時她的思路被一聲高喊打斷。「喂，喂，停下來！」一位穿著紅盔甲的騎士朝她飛馳而來，還揮舞著一根大棍子。到了愛麗絲跟前的時候，馬突然停了下來，「你是我的俘虜了！」騎士喊著，從馬上摔了下來。

愛麗絲吃了一驚，倒不是為她自己，而是被騎士摔下馬給嚇了一跳。她有些著急地看著他重新上了馬。他在馬鞍上一坐穩，就又開始喊：「你是我的……」就在這時候，又有個聲音冒出來：「喂！喂！停下來！」愛麗絲為來了新的敵人感到有些驚奇，東張西望起來。

這次是一位白騎士。他停在愛麗絲身邊，像紅騎士一樣從馬上摔了下來，然後又重新上馬。兩位騎士互相盯著彼此好一陣子，不發一語。愛麗絲看看這個，又看看那個，感到很困惑。

「她是我的俘虜！」紅騎士終於開口了。

「是的，但是後來我救走她了！」白騎士回答。

「好吧，那麼我們必須為她打一仗了。」紅棋騎士邊說邊把頭盔戴上（就掛在馬鞍旁，形狀有點像馬的頭）。

「你會遵守戰鬥規則吧？」白棋騎士也戴上頭盔說。

「我一直都遵守規則。」紅騎士說，然後他們開始狂怒地打了起來，嚇得愛麗絲躲到樹後面，以免被打中。

「我想知道戰鬥規則是什麼？」愛麗絲自言自語，同時從藏身處膽怯地窺伺著這場戰鬥，「看來有一條規則是，如果一個騎士擊中對方，對方就會落馬；如果沒有擊中，他自己就得摔下馬來。還有一條規則好像是，他們得用手臂夾著棍棒，就像『龐奇與茱蒂』一樣。他們摔下馬時會發出很大的聲音，就像火鉗掉在鐵欄杆上一樣！然而他們的馬卻那麼安靜，任憑他們上上下下，彷彿像兩張桌子！」

還有一條愛麗絲沒有注意到的戰鬥規則，好像是這樣的：他們摔下來時總是頭先落地。這場戰鬥就以雙方肩並肩摔下來而告終。當他們再爬起來的時候，彼此握握手，然後紅騎士上馬奔馳離去。

「這是一次光榮的勝利，對吧？」白騎士氣喘吁吁地說。

「我不知道，」愛麗絲含糊地說，「我不想做任何人的俘虜。我想當皇后。」

「你穿過下一條小溪，就會成為皇后了。」白騎士說，「我要把你安全地送到樹林盡頭，然後我必須回來。按規矩我不能再往那邊走了，你知道的。」

「非常感謝你，」愛麗絲說，「要我幫你脫掉頭盔嗎？」很明顯，他自己就能把頭盔脫下來，但愛麗絲最後還是幫他把頭盔脫了下來。

「現在呼吸順暢多了。」騎士說著用雙手整理了一頭亂髮，將平靜的臉孔轉過來，張著溫柔的大眼睛望著愛麗絲。愛麗絲心想，這輩子從沒見過長的這麼奇怪的士兵。

他穿著一身錫盔甲，看上去非常不合身，肩膀上還掛著一個形狀很怪異的箱子：箱子上下顛倒，蓋子還開著。愛麗絲充滿好奇地看著它。

「我知道你很羨慕我的小箱子。」騎士友善地說，「這是我自己的發明，用來放衣服和三明治。你看，我把它倒著放，這樣雨水就不會跑進去了。」

「但是東西會掉出來的，」愛麗絲溫和地說，「你不知道蓋子是開著的嗎？」

424

「我不知道。」騎士說，一絲煩惱掠過他的臉，「那麼所有的東西都掉出去了！東西沒了，箱子就沒用了。」他邊說著邊卸下箱子，打算扔到樹叢裡。此時，他突然有了個想法，於是他小心翼翼地把箱子掛在樹上。「你猜得到我為什麼這樣做嗎？」他問愛麗絲。

愛麗絲搖搖頭。

「我希望會有些蜜蜂在箱子裡築巢，那樣就有蜂蜜了。」

「但是你已經把蜂箱……或者是類似的東西，繫在馬鞍上了。」愛麗絲說。

「是的，這是個非常好的蜂箱，」騎士不滿足地說，「最好的那種。可是沒有任何一隻蜜蜂靠近。它也能當捕鼠器用。我想是老鼠把蜜蜂趕走了，要不就是蜜蜂把老鼠趕走了。我分不清是哪種情況。」

「我不知道捕鼠器要做什麼，」愛麗絲說，「馬背上不可能會有老鼠。」

「或許是不可能，」騎士說，「但是如果牠們真的來了，我不能讓牠們跑掉呀。」

「你看，」他停了一會之後繼續說，「還是應該做好各種準備。這就是我的馬戴腳環的緣故。」

「用途是什麼呢？」愛麗絲非常好奇地問。

「防止被鯊魚咬。」騎士回答,「這是我自己的發明。現在幫我上馬,我會跟你走到樹林盡頭。那個盤子是做什麼用的?」

「盛葡萄乾蛋糕的。」愛麗絲說。

「我們最好帶著它,」騎士說,「如果我們找到了葡萄乾蛋糕,它就能派上用場了。來,幫我把它放進口袋裡。」

這件事花了很長時間。雖然愛麗絲非常小心地撐開了口袋,但是因為騎士放盤子時笨手笨腳的,前兩、三次他自己掉了進去。「你看,口袋太小了,」當他們終於把盤子放進去時,他說:「口袋裡還有很多燭台呢。」他把口袋掛在馬鞍上,而馬鞍上早就掛滿了好幾捆胡蘿蔔、火鉗和很多別的東西。

「我希望你把頭髮好好地固定在頭上。」出發時騎士這麼說。

「像平常一樣就行了。」愛麗絲笑著說。

「差遠了,」騎士著急地說,「你看這裡的風非常大,和滾燙沸騰的濃湯一樣大。」

「你有沒有發明過能讓頭髮別被吹亂的辦法呢?」愛麗絲問。

「還沒有,」騎士回答,「不過我有個辦法,能不讓頭髮脫落。」

「我很想聽聽看。」

「首先,你拿根向上直立的棍子。」騎士說,「然後讓頭髮順著棍子往上爬,就像葡萄爬藤一樣。頭髮吹掉是因為它們向下倒掛，你知道，向上的東西是永遠不會掉下來的。這是我自己的發明。要是你喜歡的話，可以試試。」

這聽起來不是個好辦法，愛麗絲想。她默默地走了幾分鐘，苦思著這個辦法，還不時停下來幫助這位可憐的騎士，他確實不太會騎馬。

只要馬停下來（馬經常停下來），騎士就會往前滾下來；只要馬又開始走了（馬總是突然起步），騎士就會向後滾下來。要是他沒有時不時掉下來的毛病，倒也稱得上是個好騎士。而且他老是在往愛麗絲這邊走的時候摔倒，愛麗絲很快就發現了，最好的辦法就是別走得離馬太近。

「恐怕你不常練習騎馬。」愛麗絲冒昧地說，同時把摔了第五次的騎士扶上馬。

騎士看起來非常吃驚，對此有點不高興。「你怎麼會這樣說？」他爬回馬鞍時說，一隻手還抓著愛麗絲的頭髮，以免從另一邊跌下去。

「因為經常練習的人不會老是跌下來的。」

「我有非常豐富的經驗，」騎士鄭重地說，「非常豐富的經驗！」

愛麗絲只能盡量熱情地說「真的嗎？」，因為她想不出更合適的話。之後他們默默地走了一小段路，騎士閉著眼睛喃喃自語，愛麗絲則是提心吊膽地看著，很怕他又摔下來。

「騎馬的精妙之處，」騎士突然揮了揮右手臂，大聲地說：「就是要保持……」話說到這裡突然結束了，就像開始時一樣突然，原來是騎士重重地摔到了路上。這次愛麗絲很害怕，扶他起來時著急地問：「骨頭沒摔斷吧？」

「完全沒事。」騎士說，好像摔斷兩三根骨頭根本不值得一提，「我正要說，騎馬的精妙之處，就是要……使自己完美地保持平衡，就像這樣，你看……」

他鬆開了韁繩，張開雙臂，示範他所說的平衡，而這次他的背著地，正好摔在馬蹄下方。

「豐富的經驗！」他繼續反覆說著，愛麗絲再一次把他扶起來，「豐富的經驗！」

「太可笑了！」這次愛麗絲完全失去了耐心，她叫道，「你應該弄匹有輪子的木馬，你應該騎那個！」

「那種馬跑得穩嗎？」騎士充滿興趣地發問，同時用兩隻手臂緊摟著馬的脖子，總算及時地避免了自己再摔下來。

「比真的馬穩多了。」愛麗絲說，她的聲音裡帶著一絲笑意，並努力克制自己大聲笑出來。

「我要弄一匹，」騎士深思熟慮地說，「一、兩匹……好幾匹。」

一陣短暫的沉默之後，騎士又繼續說：「我是發明東西的專家。現在，我敢說你注意到了，上次你扶我起來的時候，我是不是看上去正在思考？」

「你確實是有點認真。」愛麗絲說。

「對，那時候我正在發明一種跨過大門的新方法。你願意聽嗎？」

「非常想聽，真的。」愛麗絲禮貌地回答。

「我會告訴你我是怎麼想到這些的。」騎士說，「我對自己說，『頭已經夠高了，唯一困難的是腳。』現在，我先把頭放到門頂，接著我站在自己的頭上，那麼腳就夠高了，你看，然後我就可以跨過大門了。」

「是的，我想你能做到這樣的話就可以跨過大門了」愛麗絲思索著說，「但是你不認為這很困難嗎？」

「我還沒試過，」騎士嚴肅地說，「所以我不能肯定地告訴你。不過恐怕是有點困難。」

騎士好像感到很苦惱，於是愛麗絲趕快轉換了話題。「你拿的頭盔好特別哦！」她高興地說，「這也是你的發明嗎？」

騎士驕傲地看著掛在馬鞍上的頭盔。「是的，」他說，「不過我還發明了一個比這個更好的，就像一個錐形糖塊。當我戴著它時，要是從馬上掉下來，總是頭盔先著地，所以我很少摔傷。

但是確實有掉進頭盔裡的風險，這是肯定的，我就發生過一次，最糟糕的是，我還沒有從頭盔裡出來，另一個白騎士就過來就把它戴上了。他以為是自己的頭盔呢。」

騎士很認真，所以愛麗絲不敢笑出聲來。「你在他的頭頂上，我想他一定會受傷。」愛麗絲擔心地說。

「當然，我只能踢他了。」騎士說得很嚴肅，「然後他就又把頭盔拿掉了。我花了好幾個小時，才從頭盔裡爬出來。我可是快得跟……跟……閃電一樣。」

「這種快法不一樣。」愛麗絲反駁說。

騎士搖了搖頭。「我敢向你保證，那是我最快的了！」他說話的時候，激動得舉起了雙手，然後立刻從馬鞍上滾下來，栽進路邊的一條深溝。

愛麗絲跑到溝邊去看他。她這次有點擔心，雖然前幾次騎士都沒摔傷，但愛麗絲擔心他這次真的會受傷。然而，儘管她只能看到

騎士的鞋底,當她聽到他用平常的語調說話時,她就放心了。「最快的了。」騎士重複說。「但是那個騎士也太粗心了,竟然戴了別人的頭盔,而裡面還有人。」

「你頭都朝下了,語氣怎麼還這麼平靜呢?」愛麗絲邊問邊拉著他的腳把他拖出來,然後把他放到岸邊的土堆上。

騎士似乎對這個問題很驚訝。「這跟我的身體發生了什麼事,有什麼關係呢?」他說,「我的腦袋一樣在活動。事實上,越是頭朝下,我就越能發明新東西。」

「我做過最聰明的一件事,」他停了一會兒繼續說,「就是在做肉類主菜時發明了一種新式布丁。」

「那麼我們趕快做一個,下一頓吃吧?」愛麗絲說。「嗯,不是下一頓吃的。」騎士若有所思地慢慢說,「不,當然不是下一頓吃的。」

「那就是明天要吃的吧。我想你不會一頓飯吃兩道布丁吧?」

「嗯,不是明天吃的。」騎士還是那樣重複著說,「不是明天吃的。事實上,」他繼續說,低著頭,而且聲音越來越小,「我不相信布丁有被做出來過!事實上,我也不相信以後有人可以把布丁做出來!不過那真是道十分聰明的布丁。」

「布丁要用什麼做呢?」愛麗絲問,希望騎士能高興起來,因為可憐的騎士看起來情緒非常低落。

「先用吸水紙。」騎士呻吟了一聲後回答。

「這恐怕不太好。」

「如果只有這樣，當然不好，」騎士急忙插話，「但是你不曉得，如果混合了其他東西後，會有多大的區別，比如混合了火藥還有石蠟。在此我必須向你告辭了。」他們已經到了樹林盡頭。

愛麗絲看起來很困惑，她還在想著那個布丁。

「你很難過，」騎士不安地說，「讓我唱首歌安慰你吧。」

「很長嗎？」愛麗絲問，因為她一天之中已經聽太多詩歌了。

「是很長，」騎士說，「但是真的非常美。聽我唱過這首歌的人，不是流淚，就是⋯⋯」

「就怎麼樣？」愛麗絲問，因為騎士突然不說話了。

「就是不流淚，你知道的。歌名叫做《鱈魚的眼睛》。」

「哦，那首歌的名字，是嗎？」愛麗絲問，盡力裝出很感興趣的樣子。

「不，你不懂，」騎士看上去有點惱怒地說，「別人是這麼叫它的，但它真正的名字是《上了年紀的人》。」

「那麼我應該說『那是別人叫它的名字』囉？」愛麗絲糾正自己。

「不，不應該，這完全是兩回事！這首歌還叫《方法和手段》。不過你知道那是別人說的。」

「哦，那麼這首歌到底是什麼呢？」愛麗絲完全被搞糊塗了。

「我正要說呢。」騎士說，「這歌真正的名字應該是《坐在門口》，曲子是我創作的。」

說到這裡，他穩住了馬，讓韁繩落在馬的脖子上。然後，用一隻手慢慢地打著拍子，溫柔憨厚的臉上露出淡淡的微笑，好像在欣賞自己的音樂一樣，就這樣，他開始唱了。

愛麗絲在穿越鏡子的旅程中，遇到了無數的奇異事件，但這是她記得最清楚的一次了。多年以後，她還是能夠回想起全部的景象，彷彿就像昨天才發生一樣：騎士溫柔的藍眼睛與溫和的微笑；落日餘暉穿過他的髮際，照得盔甲閃閃發亮，使她目眩；馬兒安靜地踱步，吃著愛麗絲腳邊的青草，脖子上鬆散地垂著韁繩。還有後面樹林的黑色陰影，所有的景象構成了一幅圖畫。這時愛麗絲單手遮在眼前，背靠著樹，注視著那奇怪的騎士和馬，似夢非夢地聽著那首憂鬱的歌曲。

「可是曲子不是騎士自己創作的，」愛麗絲自言自語說，「它是《我奉獻一切，毫無保留》。」她站著，很仔細地聽，但沒有落淚。

> 「我會把一切告訴你，
> 雖然沒多大的關聯，
> 我見到一位老人，

就坐在門口。
我問，『老人家，你是誰？
你怎麼過生活？』
他的回答流進我的腦海，
就像水穿過篩子。

他說，『我要找蝴蝶，
牠們睡在麥子上。
我把牠們做成羊肉餡餅，
再拿到街上去賣。
我要賣給那些，
在狂暴大海中航行的人，
我就靠這換來我的麵包，
不好意思，這只是個玩笑。

但我正在想辦法，
把某人的鬍子給染綠。
總要用把大扇子，
這樣就沒人會看到。』

對老人的話，
我沒話可答。
我大聲喊道：
『快告訴我你怎麼生活？』

他溫和地講起了故事：
『我有我的法子，

當我發現山間小溪，
就讓它閃閃生光輝。
從此他們有了資源，
稱之為羅蘭德髮油。
然後付給我兩便士，
當作我勞苦的酬勞。

但我想出了一個辦法，
餵食用奶油當乾糧，
每天都如此，
他開始長胖。』

我把他左右搖晃，
直到他臉色陰鬱。
我喊：『快告訴我你怎麼生活，
你做了些什麼？』

他說：『我尋找鱈魚的眼睛，
在石南草叢中間。
寂靜的夜裡，
把魚眼製成西服背心的扣子。
我不用這些換金子，
或是閃光的銀幣；
只要銅幣半便士，
就能買到九隻。

有時我挖洞找奶油捲，

435

或者把螃蟹黏上樹枝；
有時我在綠色的小山上，
尋找小馬車的車輪。
就這樣（他眨了眨眼），
我得到了財富，
所以非常高興，
我要為您的健康乾杯痛飲。』

我聽他把話說完，
剛好完成了我的設計，
要防止麥南大橋生銹，
可以用酒煮沸它。
非常感謝他告訴我，
他如何得到財寶，
但我更要感謝，
他為我的健康乾杯。

現在，如果我偶然地，
把手指放進膠水，
或者發瘋似地，
把右腳擠進左靴，
或者用非常重的東西，
砸我的腳趾，
我悲泣，因為這讓我想起，
我曾認識的那位長者，
他的外貌慈祥，

他的談吐文雅，
他的頭髮比雪還白，
他的臉色黑如烏鴉，
他的眼睛紅過爐渣，
他似乎悲傷又不安，
他的身子前後搖晃，
他不斷地低聲嘟喃，
好像嘴裡塞滿麵團；
鼻子哼氣像頭水牛。
很久之前的夏日午後，
他就坐在門口。」

當騎士唱完了最後一句，他收起韁繩，掉轉馬頭，朝向他們來的那條路。「只有幾步路了，」他說，「下了小山，過了小溪，你就會成為皇后了。但是你願意留在這裡看著我先走嗎？」愛麗絲以殷切的眼光看著騎士所指的方向，這時騎士補充說：「不會太久的，當我走到路上那個轉角時，你願意向我揮揮手帕嗎？我想這會鼓舞我的。」

「當然，我會在這裡等，」愛麗絲說，「非常感謝你送了我這麼遠，還有那首歌，我非常喜歡。」

「但願如此，」騎士有些懷疑地說，「不過我以為你會哭得更厲害。」

於是他們握了握手，騎士騎著馬緩緩地走進了森林。「我希望目送他離開不會花太多時間，」愛麗絲看著騎士遠去，自言自語

437

地說，「他到那了！和平常一樣頭朝下！不過他很輕鬆地又爬上去了，這是因為馬上掛了太多東西。」她繼續自言自語，一邊看著那匹馬沿著小路悠閒地走著，而騎士一下從這邊，一下從那邊摔下來。連摔了四、五次以後，騎士到了拐彎處，愛麗絲向他揮了手帕，直到看不見他為止。

「我希望這可以鼓舞他。」愛麗絲說完轉身跑下山，「現在是最後一條小溪了，我就要成為皇后了！聽起來真了不起！」沒幾步她就到了小溪邊。「終於到第八格了！」她邊喊邊跳了過去，在一片軟得像苔蘚的草地上躺下休息，周圍滿是小花圍。

「噢，到這裡真開心！我頭上是什麼？」她驚慌地喊了起來，這時她摸到了一個重物緊緊套在她頭上。

「可是怎麼會不知不覺中就跑到我頭上呢？」她一邊自言自語，一邊把它拿下來放在膝蓋上，想知道究竟是什麼。

結果是一頂黃金王冠。

第 9 章

愛麗絲皇后

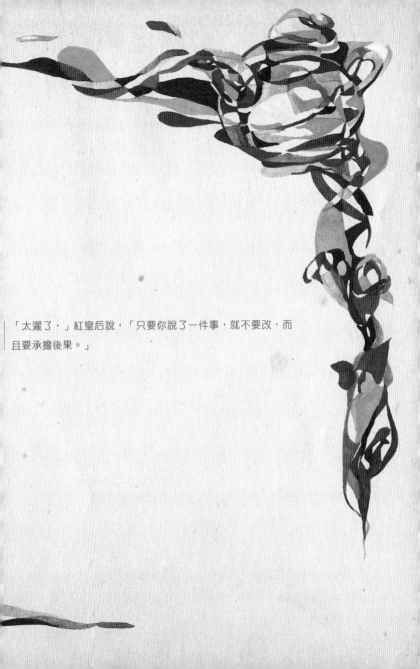

「太遲了，」紅皇后說，「只要你說了一件事，就不要改，而且要承擔後果。」

「**哦**，這真了不起！」愛麗絲說，「我從沒想過會這麼快成為皇后。我要告訴你，陛下，」她繼續嚴肅地說（她老愛責備自己），「你永遠不該這樣懶散地躺在草地上！皇后得威嚴一點！」

於是她站了起來，在周圍走了走。起初相當不自然，因為她怕王冠會掉下來，不過一想到沒有人會看見她，她就放鬆了。「要是我真的是皇后，」她再次坐下來的時候說，「我遲早會習慣的。」

一切都那麼奇怪，所以當她發現紅皇后和白皇后正一左一右坐在她身旁時，她竟然一點都不驚訝。她很想問她們是怎麼來這裡的，但又怕這樣太像平民。不過她想，問問比賽是否結束了應該沒關係。「請問，你願意告訴我……」她膽怯地看著紅皇后，開始說。

「別人跟你說話的時候你再說話！」紅皇后立刻打斷她。

「但是如果每個人都遵守這條規矩，」愛麗絲已經準備好進行一場小小的辯論了，她說：「而且如果你只在別人跟你說話的時候才說話，別人又總是等你先說，你想，那就沒人說話了，這樣會……」

「可笑！」紅皇后喊道，「怎麼，你不知道嗎，孩子……」說到這裡，她皺起眉頭想了一會，然後突然轉換了話題：「你說『要是我真的是皇后』，這是什麼意思？你有什麼權利說自己是皇后？

你不可能成為皇后的，除非你通過了適當的測驗，你知道嗎？而且越早開始測驗越好。」

「我只是說『如果』。」可憐的愛麗絲用哀求的語氣說。

兩個皇后互相看了看，紅皇后有點發抖地說：「她說，她只是說『如果』。」

「可她說的比這多太多了！」白皇后抖著手哼了一聲說，「哦，比這多太多了！」

「所以你看，你確實說了，」紅皇后對愛麗絲說，「永遠都要說實話……想好了以後再說……說過就寫下來。」

「我絕對沒有這個意思……」愛麗絲剛開頭，紅皇后就不耐煩地打斷了她。

「這正是我討厭的！你就是這個意思！你想想沒有意思的孩子有什麼用呢？即使一個笑話都要有些意思的，我想孩子比笑話更重要。你別否認了，就算用雙手也否認不了。」

「我沒有用雙手否認。」愛麗絲反駁。

「沒人說你用了，」紅皇后說，「我是說就算你用也不行。」

「她心裡是這麼說的，」白皇后說，「她想否認，但是她不知道要否認什麼！」

「真是討厭又惡毒的脾氣，」紅皇后評論說，然後是一、兩分鐘令人不安的沉默。

紅皇后先打破了沉默，對白皇后說：「我邀請你今天下午參加愛麗絲的晚宴。」

白皇后淡淡一笑說：「我也邀請你。」

「我根本不知道我要舉辦宴會，」愛麗絲說，「但如果有宴會的話，我想應該是由我來邀請客人。」

「我們給了你機會做這件事，」紅皇后說，「但我敢說你還沒有上過多少禮儀方面的課吧？」

「課堂上不教禮儀，」愛麗絲說，「課堂上教的是算術之類的東西。」

「你會加法嗎？」白皇后問，「一加一加一加一加一加一加一加一加一是多少？」

「我不知道，」愛麗絲說，「我沒數。」

「她不會加法，」紅皇后插嘴說，「那你會減法嗎？八減掉九。」

「我不會八減九，」愛麗絲很快回答說，「但……」

「她不會減法，」白皇后說，「你會除法嗎？一把刀子除以一條麵包，答案是什麼？」

「我想……」愛麗絲剛開始說，紅皇后就替她回答了，「當然是奶油麵包了。再做一題減法問題吧。一隻狗減去一根骨頭，還剩什麼？」

愛麗絲想了想，「當然不會剩下骨頭，如果我把骨頭拿走，那狗也不會留下來，牠會跑來咬我，我肯定也不會留在那裡！」

「所以你認為是什麼都不剩囉？」紅皇后問。

「我想這就是答案。」

「錯了，」紅皇后說，「和平常一樣，會剩下狗的脾氣。」

「我不明白，怎麼……」

「聽著！」紅皇后叫道，「狗會把脾氣留下，不是嗎？」

「或許是的。」愛麗絲小心地回答，

「如果狗跑掉了，牠的脾氣就留下了！」那個皇后得意地宣佈。

愛麗絲盡可能鄭重地說：「狗和狗的脾氣是兩回事，」但她又忍不住在心裡想：「我們談論的事情真無聊！」

「她完全不會算術。」兩個皇后一起說，她們特別強調了「不會」兩個字。

「你會算術嗎？」愛麗絲突然轉向對白皇后說，因為她不喜歡別人這樣挑錯。

皇后倒抽一口氣，閉上了眼睛。「我會加法，」她說，「如果給我時間的話……不過無論在什麼情況下，我都不會減法。」

「你應該認識英文字母？」紅皇后問。

「當然知道。」愛麗絲說。

「我也是，」白皇后低聲說，「我們經常一起說的，哦，我告訴你一個秘密，我只會唸一個字母的單字！很了不起對嗎？別氣餒，到時候你也能辦到的。」

這時紅皇后又開始說話了：「你會回答常識問題嗎？」她說，「麵包是怎麼做的？」

「我知道！」愛麗絲急忙喊道：「拿些麵粉……」

「你在哪裡摘花？」白皇后問，「花園還是樹林裡？」

「哦，根本不是摘的，」愛麗絲解釋說，「是磨……」

「那有多少畝？」白皇后說，「你不能漏掉這麼多事。」

「替她的頭搧搧風吧！」紅皇后急忙打斷說：「動了這麼多腦筋，她就要發燒了。」於是她們開始用一把樹葉幫她搧風，直到愛麗絲請求她們停下來，因為她的頭髮已經被吹亂了。

「她現在又痊癒了，」紅皇后說，「你懂語言嗎？ fiddle-de-dee 的法語怎麼說？」

「fiddle-de-dee 不是英語。」愛麗絲認真地回答。

「誰說是英語了？」紅皇后說。

愛麗絲想到個辦法可以擺脫現在的窘境。「如果你告訴我 fiddle-de-dee 是什麼語言，我就告訴你這個字用法語怎麼說！」她得意地說。

紅皇后僵著身子站起來說：「皇后們從不討價還價。」

愛麗絲心想：「我希望皇后們從不問問題。」

「我們別吵，」白皇后不安地說：「你知道為什麼會有閃電嗎？」

「為什麼會有閃電，」愛麗絲非常肯定地說，因為她覺得自己對這個問題很有把握，「是由於打雷……不！不！」她趕快糾正自己，「我講反了。」

「太遲了，」紅皇后說，「只要你說了一件事，就不要改，而且要承擔後果。」

「這讓我想到，」白皇后說，她低頭看著地上，神經質地擺弄著手：「上星期二我們遇到了一場多麼大的雷雨呀！我指的是上星期二裡的一天，你知道。」

愛麗絲感到很疑惑。「在我們國家，」她說，「一次只有一天。」

紅皇后說：「那樣做事可憐又膚淺。在這裡，我們大多數情況下同時擁有兩個或三個白天和晚上。在冬天，為了要暖和點，我們有時會把五個晚上放在一起，你懂嗎？」

「那麼五個晚上比一個晚上還要溫暖嗎？」愛麗絲大膽地問。

「當然，溫暖五倍呢。」

「但是，同樣的道理，也會冷五倍啊。」

「就是這樣！」紅皇后大喊：「溫暖五倍，也冷五倍。就像我有比你有錢五倍，也比你聰明五倍！」

愛麗絲嘆了口氣，不說話了，她想：「真像沒有謎底的謎語。」

「矮胖子也懂，」白皇后繼續小聲說，更像是對她自己說的，「他曾經手裡拿著開瓶器來到門口⋯⋯」

「他想要幹什麼？」紅皇后問。

「他說要進來，」白皇后接著說，「因為他在找一頭河馬。可是碰巧那天上午屋裡沒有河馬。」

「平常有嗎？」愛麗絲驚訝地問。

「哦，只有星期四有，」白皇后答道。

「我知道他為什麼會過來，」愛麗絲說，「他要懲罰那些魚，因為⋯⋯」

這時，白皇后又開始說話了：「那天的暴雨有多大，你一定想像不到！（紅皇后說：「你知道，她永遠都想像不出來的。」）屋頂塌了一部分，那麼多雷進來了，然後變成一大團在屋子裡轉，打翻了桌子和別的東西，我被嚇得連自己的名字都不記得了！」

愛麗絲心想：「這種時候，我從不會去想自己叫什麼名字！那有什麼用呢？」但是她沒有大聲說出來，怕惹這位可憐的皇后不高興。

「陛下必須原諒她，」紅皇后對愛麗絲說，同時拉起了白皇后的一隻手，溫和地拍著，「她沒有惡意，但老是說傻話，一直都這樣。」

白皇后膽怯地看看愛麗絲，愛麗絲覺得應該說些好話，可是一時又真的想不出什麼話來。

「她從沒真正受過良好的教育，」紅皇后繼續說，「但令人驚訝的是她的脾氣那麼好！拍拍她的頭吧，看看她會多麼高興！」可是愛麗絲不敢這樣做。

「對她好一點，用紙捲幫她捲頭髮，她會很高興的。」

白皇后深深地嘆了口氣，把頭靠在愛麗絲的肩上。「我怎麼這麼睏？」她呻吟著說。

「她累了，可憐的傢伙！」紅皇后說，「順順她的頭髮，把你的睡帽借給她，為她唱首溫柔的催眠曲吧。」

「我沒帶著睡帽，」愛麗絲說，這時她正盡力服從紅皇后的第一個命令：「我連一首溫柔的催眠曲都不會唱。」

「那只能由我來唱了。」紅皇后說完就開始唱：

「乖乖睡吧，夫人，在愛麗絲的膝旁！
宴會以前，我們還有小睡的時光。
等宴會結束，我們還要參加舞會，
紅皇后、白皇后、愛麗絲，所有人一起！」

「現在你知道歌詞了，」紅皇后接著說，一邊把頭靠在愛麗絲的另一個肩膀上，「唱給我聽吧，我也睏了。」不一會的工夫，兩位皇后就睡著了，並大聲地打呼。

「我該怎麼辦？」愛麗絲喊道，不知所措地左顧右盼，這時先是一個腦袋，接著又是一個腦袋，從她肩上滑了下來，像兩個小土堆重重地壓在她的膝蓋上。「我想以前從沒發生過這種事，一個人得同時照顧兩位睡著的皇后！不會有的，整個英國歷史中都沒有，你知道，這不可能，因為同一個時期只會有一個皇后。醒醒吧！你們這些笨重的東西！」她不耐煩地繼續說，但是除了有節奏的鼾聲外，沒有任何回答。

鼾聲越來越清晰，而且聽上去越來越像一種曲調，最後愛麗絲甚至能分辨出它的歌詞。愛麗絲急切地聽著，以至於當這兩個大腦袋從她膝蓋上消失時，她根本抓不住。

她現在站在一座拱門門口，門上用大字寫著「愛麗絲皇后」。拱門兩邊各有一個拉鈴的把手，一個寫著「賓客之鈴」，另一個寫

著「僕人之鈴」。

「我得等歌唱完，」愛麗絲想，「那時候我再拉鈴。我該拉……哪個鈴呢？」她被把手上的字給困住了，「我不是賓客，也不是僕人，應該要有一個標著『皇后』的才對啊。」

就在這時，大門開了一點，有一個長嘴動物把頭探了出來，說：「下下星期之前不准進入！」然後砰的一聲又把門關上了。

愛麗絲又敲門，又拉鈴，都是白忙一場。不過最後，坐在樹下的老青蛙站了起來，一跛一跛地慢慢朝她走了過來。青蛙穿著淺黃色的衣服，腳上蹬著一雙大靴子。

「現在怎麼了？」青蛙用低啞的聲音小聲問。

愛麗絲轉過來，她現在正存心想找碴。「應門的僕人在哪？」她開始發怒了。

「哪個門？」青蛙問。

他說話時那種慢吞吞、懶洋洋的樣子，幾乎讓愛麗絲氣得跺腳。「當然是這個門！」

青蛙用呆滯的大眼睛看了大門一會兒，然後又靠近了點，用大拇指在門上擦了擦，好像在看油漆能不能擦掉，然後牠看著愛麗絲。

「應門？」牠說，「你問了什麼問題要門來回應？」他的聲音那麼啞，愛麗絲幾乎聽不清楚。

「我不知道你在說什麼。」愛麗絲說。

「我說的是英語，不是嗎？」青蛙繼續說，「還是你聾了？大門問了你什麼問題？」

「什麼也沒問！」愛麗絲不耐煩地說，「我一直在敲門。」

「不該這麼做，不該這麼做，」青蛙嘟嚷著，「你知道，你惹惱它了。」然後牠走過去用大腳踢了門一下，「你別理它，」牠喘著氣說，一瘸一拐地走回到樹下，「那樣它也不會理你。」

就在這時，門突然開了，然後聽到一個尖尖的嗓音唱著歌：

> 「愛麗絲對鏡中世界說：
> 『我手執權杖、頭戴王冠，
> 鏡中的眾生啊，無論哪個，
> 跟紅白皇后一同與我共餐。』」

接著是上百個聲音的合聲：

> 「趕快倒滿你的酒杯，
> 桌上撒著鈕釦和米糠，
> 咖啡裡放貓，茶裡放老鼠，
> 三十乘三遍地歡迎愛麗絲皇后。」

接著是吵雜的歡呼聲，愛麗絲心裡想：「三十乘三是九十，我懷疑是不是有人會算術？」很快又恢復了寂靜，然後同樣的尖聲唱起了另一段：

「『哦，鏡中的眾生，』愛麗絲說，『圍攏來！
見到我是榮耀，聽我說話是受寵，
跟紅白皇后還有我一起，
用餐和飲茶，是最大的榮幸！』」

然後又是合唱：

「糖漿和墨水倒滿杯，
或者暢飲點別的。
蘋果酒加沙子，葡萄酒加羊毛，
九十乘九遍歡迎愛麗絲皇后！」

「九十乘九遍！」愛麗絲絕望地重複著，「哦，絕對不行！我最好立刻就走……」這時，四周一片死寂，她又到了另一個地方。

愛麗絲在大廳裡邊走邊不安地看了桌子一眼，她注意到大約有五十位賓客，什麼樣的都有：有些是動物，有些是鳥類，甚至還有幾朵花。「我很高興牠們沒等邀請就來了，」她想，「我完全不知道該請什麼人！」

桌子的最前面放著三張椅子，紅皇后和白皇后已經占了其中的兩張，中間一張是空的，愛麗絲坐到了那張椅子上，她對大廳的寂靜感到有些不安，希望有人能開口說話。

最後，紅皇后開口了。「你已經錯過湯和魚了，」她說，「把大塊肉端上來吧！」然後侍者在愛麗絲面前放上一隻羊腿，愛麗絲有點焦慮地看著羊腿，因為她從來沒切過大塊肉。

「你看起來有點害羞，讓我把你介紹給那隻羊腿吧，」紅皇后說，「愛麗絲，羊肉，羊肉，愛麗絲。」那隻羊腿從盤子裡站了起

來，向愛麗絲鞠躬。愛麗絲不知道該覺得害怕還是好玩，也回了禮。

「我來給你們切一片吧？」愛麗絲說著，拿起了刀叉，看看這位皇后，又看看那位皇后。

「當然不行，」紅皇后非常堅決地說：「去切剛剛才介紹給你的那一位是不禮貌的，把大塊肉端走！」侍者端走了羊腿，拿來了大的葡萄乾布丁。

「對不起，我不想被介紹給布丁了，」愛麗絲急忙說，「不然我們根本就不能吃東西了。我給你一些吧？」

但是紅皇后看上去很生氣，吼道：「布丁，愛麗絲，愛麗絲，布丁。把布丁端走！」侍者很快就端走了布丁，愛麗絲都沒來得及回禮。

愛麗絲不明白為什麼紅皇后是唯一發號施令的人，於是，為了實驗，她喊了聲「侍者！把布丁送回來！」，像變魔術一樣，布丁立刻又出現在桌子上了。布丁那麼大，愛麗絲不禁有點畏縮，和剛

才面對羊腿時一樣。但是，她努力克服了她的膽怯，切了一片布丁遞給紅皇后。

「真無禮！」布丁說，「要是我從你身上切下一片來，我看你會怎麼樣？你這東西！」

布丁用油膩膩的聲音說著，愛麗絲不知道怎麼回答，只能坐下來，驚訝地望著它。

「說點什麼吧，」紅皇后說：「所有的話都讓布丁說了多可笑！」

「你知道嗎，我今天聽別人背了這麼多的詩，」愛麗絲開始說，有點惶恐地發現，她一開口，周圍就一片死寂，所有的眼睛都盯著她，「我覺得這很奇怪，每首詩或多或少都和魚有關，你知道為什麼這裡的人這麼喜歡魚嗎？」

她是對紅皇后說的，但是紅皇后的回答卻毫不相關。「說到魚，」紅皇后非常緩慢而嚴肅地湊到愛麗絲耳邊說，「白皇后陛下知道一個可愛的謎語，全是用詩來表示的，說的都是魚。要她背來聽聽嗎？」

「紅皇后陛下好意地提到這件事，」白皇后在愛麗絲的另一邊用像鴿子咕咕叫的聲音說，「是有這回事！我可以唸嗎？」「請吧。」愛麗絲很有禮貌地說。

白皇后高興地笑了，摸了一下愛麗絲的臉，然後開始背：

「『首先，一定要捉到魚。』
那不難，我想一個嬰孩就可以。

『其次，一定要買到魚。』
那不難，我想一個便士就可以。

『現在給我煎魚！』
那不難，用不了一分鐘。
『把魚盛在盤裡。』
那不難，它本來就在那裡。

『拿這裡來！讓我嚐嚐！』
那不難，只要把盤子放在桌上。
『把盤子蓋打開！』
啊，那太難，我怕辦不到！

因為蓋子好像黏在盤子上。
那就把魚裝在蓋子上，讓它躺在正中央。
這最容易了，
究竟，盤子是蓋住了魚，還是蓋住了謎語？」

「花一分鐘想一想之後再猜，」紅皇后說，「同時，我們為你的健康乾杯，祝愛麗絲皇后健康！」她用最高的嗓門尖叫，所有的客人都開懷暢飲，他們喝酒的樣子非常奇怪：有的把酒杯放在頭上，就像滅火器，去喝沿著臉流下來的酒；有的把酒瓶倒過來，等酒順著桌邊流的時候再喝；其中有三隻動物（看上去像袋鼠）動物爬進了盛著烤羊肉的盤子，開始貪婪地舔著肉汁。「就像豬對著食槽一樣！」愛麗絲想。

「你應該用些優雅的話來答謝。」紅皇后皺著眉對愛麗絲說。

「我們一定支持你，你知道的。」當愛麗絲起身要講話時，白皇后低聲說，態度非常恭順，但又有點膽怯。

「非常感謝，」愛麗絲低聲回答說：「不過沒有你們的支持，我也能講得非常好。」

「根本不是那麼回事。」紅皇后非常肯定地說。對此，愛麗絲願意讓步。

（「她們一直擠！」後來愛麗絲講宴會的這段故事給姊姊聽時說，「你會以為她們想把我擠扁！」）

事實上，愛麗絲在致辭時想要使自己平穩地保持在原位，但確實有點困難。兩位皇后一邊一個使勁地擠她，差一點把她擠到了空中。「我起身答謝……」愛麗絲開始講話了，在她講話時真的上升了幾英寸，她抓住了桌腳，努力把自己拉回原處。

「你當心！」白皇后雙手抓住愛麗絲的頭髮尖叫道：「有事情要發生了！」

然後（就像愛麗絲後來說的那樣），一下子發生了好多事。蠟燭全都長高到了天花板，看起來像頂上放著焰火的燈心草花壇。至於酒瓶，它們每個都拿出了兩塊盤子，就像替自己裝了一對翅膀。還有長了腿的叉子到處亂跑。「它們看上去真像鳥。」愛麗絲心裡想，然而，在這場可怕的混亂中，這只是個開始。

就在這時，她聽到旁邊有嘶啞的笑聲，就轉過來看看白皇后出了什麼事，卻見到那隻羊腿代替白皇后坐在椅子上。「我在這裡！」

湯碗裡發出了聲音，愛麗絲又轉過去，正好看到白皇后寬闊而忠厚的臉在湯碗邊對她笑著，然後很快地消失在湯裡。

不一會的工夫，一切都亂七八糟，已經有好幾位客人倒在盤子裡了，而湯勺正沿著餐桌向愛麗絲走來，並且不耐煩地向她揮手，要她讓路。

「我再也受不了了。」愛麗絲喊道，同時跳了起來，雙手抓住桌布，用力一拉，盤子、菜餚、客人和蠟燭全都撞在一起摔下來，倒在地板上。

「至於你，」愛麗絲轉過身來對紅皇后嚴厲地說，她認為紅皇后是一切惡作劇的根源，但是那位皇后已經不在愛麗絲身旁了。她已經縮成一個小洋娃娃大小，正在桌子上歡樂地追著拖在她身後的圍巾轉圈。

要是在別的時候，愛麗絲一定會大吃一驚，但是她現在太興奮，對於任何事情都不會感到驚訝了。

「至於你，」當這個小東西剛好跳過一個倒在桌上的瓶子時，愛麗絲捉住了她，重複說著：「我要把你變成一隻小貓，我說到做到！」

458

第 10 章

搖搖晃晃

「至於你，」當這個小東西剛好跳過一個倒在桌上的瓶子時，愛麗絲捉住了她，重複著說：「我要把你變成一隻小貓， 我說到做到！」

愛麗絲說話的同時，把紅皇后從桌上拿起來，用盡全身的力氣前後搖晃著她。

　　紅皇后完全沒有反抗，她的臉變得很小，眼睛變得又大又綠。愛麗絲繼續搖晃著她，她繼續變得更矮……更胖……更軟……更圓……更……

第 *11* 章

醒來

┃……她繼續變得更矮……更胖……更軟……更圓……更……

……原來真的是一隻貓。

第 *12* 章

是誰做了夢？

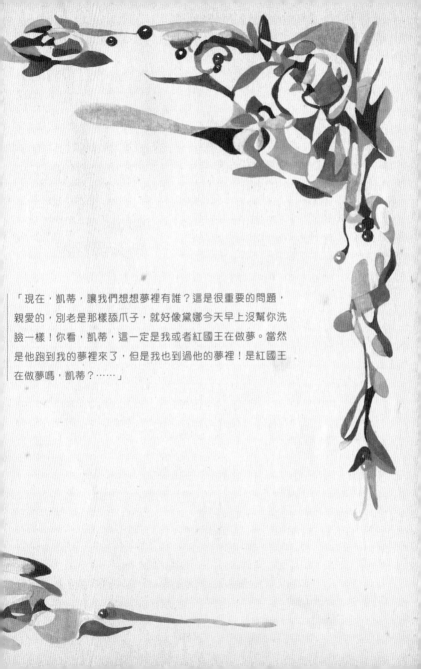

「現在，凱蒂，讓我們想想夢裡有誰？這是很重要的問題，親愛的，別老是那樣舔爪子，就好像黛娜今天早上沒幫你洗臉一樣！你看，凱蒂，這一定是我或者紅國王在做夢。當然是他跑到我的夢裡來了，但是我也到過他的夢裡！是紅國王在做夢嗎，凱蒂？……」

「陛下不應該發出這麼大的咕嚕聲，」愛麗絲揉了揉眼睛，尊敬又有些嚴厲地對這隻小貓說，「你把我從美夢中吵醒了！凱蒂，你一直跟著我經歷了鏡中世界。你知道嗎，親愛的？」

小貓們有一種非常不恰當的習慣（愛麗絲有一次這樣說），無論你對牠們說什麼，牠們總是咕嚕咕嚕地叫。「要是牠們能把咕嚕當作『是』，把喵喵當作『不是』，或者類似這樣規則的話，」愛麗絲說，「就可以跟牠們談話了！但是，要是牠們總是說一樣的話，要怎麼交談呢？」

在這種場合下，小貓還是只會咕嚕咕嚕叫，猜不出牠在說「是」還是「不是」。於是愛麗絲從桌上的棋子中找出了紅皇后，她跪在地毯上，把小貓和紅皇后放在一起，讓她們對望。「好了，凱蒂，」她得意地拍手叫道，「承認吧，你變成這樣了！」

（「但是小貓不願意看皇后，」後來愛麗絲在對她姊姊解釋的時候說，「牠把頭轉開了，假裝沒看見，看來小貓有點害羞，所以我想牠一定就是變成紅皇后了。」）

「再坐直一點，親愛的！」愛麗絲快樂地笑著說，「行個屈膝禮吧，我知道你在想……想要用咕嚕表示什麼意思才好。記住，別浪費時間了！」愛麗絲把貓咪舉起來輕輕吻了一下，「這是為了慶祝你當過了紅皇后。」

「小雪花，親愛的！」她回頭看著小白貓，看見牠正在耐心地梳妝打扮，愛麗絲繼續說，「什麼時候黛娜能幫您這位白皇后陛下打扮好呢？這一定就是你在我的夢裡那麼不整潔的原因了。黛娜！你知道你是在幫白皇后擦臉嗎？真是，你這樣太失禮了！」

「我想想，黛娜變成什麼了呢？」愛麗絲一面繼續嘮叨著，一面舒服地躺下，用一隻手臂撐在地毯上，手托著下巴，看著這些貓。「告訴我，黛娜，你是變成矮胖子了嗎？我想你是。不過你最好先別對你的朋友們提起，因為我還不確定。」

「順便說一下，凱蒂，如果你們真的和我一起經歷了那場夢境，有一件事你們一定會很高興，我聽人家唸了很多詩，全都提到了魚！明天早上你們應該有頓大餐了。在你們吃早餐的時候，我給你們背《海象和木匠》這首詩，你們就能想像出裡面的牡蠣了，親愛的！」

「現在，凱蒂，讓我們想想夢裡有誰？這是重要的問題，親愛的，別老是那樣舔爪子，就好像黛娜今天早上沒幫你洗臉一樣！你看，凱蒂，這一定是我或者紅國王在做夢。當然是他跑到我的夢裡來了，但是我也到過他的夢裡！是紅國王做夢嗎，凱蒂？你曾經是他的妻子，親愛的，所以你應該知道。哦，凱蒂，幫我弄清楚吧！等一下再舔你的爪子吧！」但是那隻氣人的小貓只是換了一隻爪子來舔，假裝沒聽到愛麗絲提的問題。

你認為是誰做的夢呢？

晴空下的小船，
夢幻般蕩漾前行，
就在七月的黃昏。

三個孩子相互依偎，
熱切的眼睛，期待的耳朵，
高興地聽簡單的故事。

晴空早已蒼白，
回聲和記憶都消逝，
秋霜取代了七月。

她的幻影依舊縈繞，
愛麗絲在世間移動，
儘認為清醒的眼睛從未看見。

孩子們還要聽故事，
熱切的眼睛，期待的耳朵，
親熱地相互依偎。

他們置身於仙境中，
白日在夢幻中過去，
夏天在夢幻中消逝。

沿著小溪漂流而下，
在金色的餘暉中蕩漾，
生活，只是一場夢嗎？

Chapter 1

Looking-Glass House

"Oh, Kitty! how nice it would be if we could only get through into Looking-glass House! I'm sure it's got, oh! such beautiful things in it! Let's pretend there's a way of getting through into it, somehow, Kitty. Let's pretend the glass has got all soft like gauze, so that we can get through. Why, it's turning into a sort of mist now, I declare! It'll be easy enough to get through – "

One thing was certain, that the WHITE kitten had had nothing to do with it: – it was the black kitten's fault entirely. For the white kitten had been having its face washed by the old cat for the last quarter of an hour (and bearing it pretty well, considering); so you see that it *couldn't* have had any hand in the mischief.

The way Dinah washed her children's faces was this: first she held the poor thing down by its ear with one paw, and then with the other paw she rubbed its face all over, the wrong way, beginning at the nose: and just now, as I said, she was hard at work on the white kitten, which was lying quite still and trying to purr – no doubt feeling that it was all meant for its good.

But the black kitten had been finished with earlier in the afternoon, and so, while Alice was sitting curled up in a corner of the great arm-chair, half talking to herself and half asleep, the kitten had been having a grand game of romps with the ball of worsted Alice had been trying to wind up, and had been rolling it up and down till it had all come undone again; and there it was, spread over the hearth-rug, all knots and tangles, with the kitten running after its own tail in the middle.

"Oh, you wicked little thing!" cried Alice, catching up the kitten, and giving it a little kiss to make it understand that it was in disgrace. "Really, Dinah ought to have taught you better manners! You *ought*, Dinah, you know you ought!" she added, looking reproachfully at the old cat, and speaking in as cross a voice as she could manage –

and then she scrambled back into the arm-chair, taking the kitten and the worsted with her, and began winding up the ball again. But she didn't get on very fast, as she was talking all the time, sometimes to the kitten, and sometimes to herself. Kitty sat very demurely on her knee, pretending to watch the progress of the winding, and now and then putting out one paw and gently touching the ball, as if it would be glad to help, if it might.

"Do you know what tomorrow is, Kitty?" Alice began. "You'd have guessed if you'd been up in the window with me – only Dinah was making you tidy, so you couldn't. I was watching the boys getting in sticks for the bonfire – and it wants plenty of sticks, Kitty! Only it got so cold, and it snowed so, they had to leave off. Never mind, Kitty, we'll go and see the bonfire to-morrow." Here Alice wound two or three turns of the worsted round the kitten's neck, just to see how it would look: this led to a scramble, in which the ball rolled down upon the floor, and yards and yards of it got unwound again.

"Do you know, I was so angry, Kitty,"Alice went on as soon as they were comfortably settled again, "when I saw all the mischief you had been doing, I was very nearly opening the window, and putting you out into the snow! And you'd have deserved it, you little mischievous darling! What have you got to say for yourself? Now don't interrupt me!" she went on, holding up one finger. "I'm going to tell you all your faults. Number one: you squeaked twice while Dinah was washing your face this morning. Now you can't deny it, Kitty: I heard you! What that you say?" (pretending that the kitten was speaking.) Her paw went into your eye? Well, that's *your* fault, for keeping your eyes open – if you'd shut them tight up, it wouldn't have happened. Now don't make any more excuses, but listen! Number two: you pulled Snowdrop away by the tail just as I had put down the saucer of milk before her! What, you were thirsty, were you? How do you know she wasn't thirsty too? Now for number three: you unwound every bit of the worsted while I wasn't looking!

"That's three faults, Kitty, and you've not been punished for any of them yet. You know I'm saving up all your punishments for Wednesday week – Suppose they had saved up all *my* punishments!" she went on, talking more to herself than the kitten. "What *would* they do at the end of a year?" I should be sent to prison, I suppose, when the day came. Or – let me see – suppose each punishment was to be going without a dinner: then, when the miserable day came, I should have to go without fifty dinners at once! Well, I shouldn't mind *that* much! I'd far rather go without them than eat them!

"Do you hear the snow against the window-panes, Kitty? How nice and soft it sounds! Just as if some one was kissing the window all over outside. I wonder if the snow LOVES the trees and fields, that it kisses them so gently? And then it covers them up snug, you know, with a white quilt; and perhaps it says, "Go to sleep, darlings, till the summer comes again." And when they wake up in the summer, Kitty, they dress themselves all in green, and dance about – whenever the wind blows – oh, that's very pretty!" cried Alice, dropping the ball of worsted to clap her hands. And I do so *wish* it was true! I'm sure the woods look sleepy in the autumn, when the leaves are getting brown.

"Kitty, can you play chess? Now, don't smile, my dear, I'm asking it seriously. Because, when we were playing just now, you watched just as if you understood it: and when I said 'Check!' you purred! Well, it WAS a nice check, Kitty, and really I might have won, if it hadn't been for that nasty Knight, that came wiggling down among my pieces.

"Kitty, dear, let's pretend – " And here I wish I could tell you half the things Alice used to say, beginning with her favourite phrase "Let's pretend." She had had quite a long argument with her sister only the day before – all because Alice had begun with "Let's pretend we're kings and queens;" and her sister, who liked being very exact, had argued that they couldn't, because there were only two of them, and Alice had been reduced at last to say, "Well, *you* can be one of them

479

then, and I'LL be all the rest." And once she had really frightened her old nurse by shouting suddenly in her ear, "Nurse! Do let's pretend that I'm a hungry hyaena, and you're a bone."

But this is taking us away from Alice's speech to the kitten. "Let's pretend that you're the Red Queen, Kitty! Do you know, I think if you sat up and folded your arms, you'd look exactly like her. Now do try, there's a dear!" And Alice got the Red Queen off the table, and set it up before the kitten as a model for it to imitate: however, the thing didn't succeed, principally, Alice said, because the kitten wouldn't fold its arms properly. So, to punish it, she held it up to the Looking-glass, that it might see how sulky it was "– and if you're not good directly," she added, "I'll put you through into Looking-glass House. How would you like *that*?"

Now, if you'll only attend, Kitty, and not talk so much, I'll tell you all my ideas about Looking-glass House. First, there's the room you can see through the glass – that's just the same as our drawing room, only the things go the other way. I can see all of it when I get upon a chair – all but the bit behind the fireplace. Oh! I do so wish I could see *that* bit! I want so much to know whether they've a fire in the winter: you never can tell, you know, unless our fire smokes, and then smoke comes up in that room too – but that may be only pretence, just to make it look as if they had a fire. Well then, the books are something like our books, only the words go the wrong way; I know that, because I've held up one of our books to the glass, and then they hold up one in the other room.

"How would you like to live in Looking-glass House, Kitty? I wonder if they'd give you milk in there? Perhaps Looking-glass milk isn't good to drink – But oh, Kitty! now we come to the passage. You can just see a little PEEP of the passage in Looking-glass House, if you leave the door of our drawing-room wide open: and it's very like our passage as far as you can see, only you know it may be quite different on beyond. Oh, Kitty! how nice it would be if we could only get through into Looking-glass House! I'm sure it's got, oh! such beautiful things in it! Let's pretend there's a way of getting through into it, somehow, Kitty. Let's pretend the glass has got all soft like gauze, so that we can get through. Why, it's turning into a sort of mist now, I declare! It'll be easy enough to get through – " She was up on the chimney-piece while she said this, though she hardly knew how she had got there. And certainly the glass WAS beginning to melt away, just like a bright silvery mist.

In another moment Alice was through the glass, and had jumped

481

lightly down into the Looking-glass room. The very first thing she did was to look whether there was a fire in the fireplace, and she was quite pleased to find that there was a real one, blazing away as brightly as the one she had left behind. "So I shall be as warm here as I was in the old room," thought Alice: "warmer, in fact, because there'll be no one here to scold me away from the fire. Oh, what fun it'll be, when they see me through the glass in here, and can't get at me!"

Then she began looking about, and noticed that what could be seen from the old room was quite common and uninteresting, but that all the rest was as different as possible. For instance, the pictures on the wall next the fire seemed to be all alive, and the very clock on the chimney-piece (you know you can only see the back of it in the Looking-glass) had got the face of a little old man, and grinned at her.

"They don't keep this room so tidy as the other," Alice thought to herself, as she noticed several of the chessmen down in the hearth among the cinders: but in another moment, with a little "Oh!" of surprise, she was down on her hands and knees watching them. The chessmen were walking about, two and two!

"Here are the Red King and the Red Queen," Alice said (in a whisper, for fear of frightening them), "and there are the White King and the White Queen sitting on the edge of the shovel – and here are two castles walking arm in arm – I don't think they can hear me," she went on, as she

put her head closer down, "and I'm nearly sure they can't see me. I feel somehow as if I were invisible – "

Here something began squeaking on the table behind Alice, and made her turn her head just in time to see one of the White Pawns roll over and begin kicking: she watched it with great curiosity to see what would happen next.

"It is the voice of my child!" the White Queen cried out as she rushed past the King, so violently that she knocked him over among the cinders. "My precious Lily! My imperial kitten!" and she began scrambling wildly up the side of the fender.

"Imperial fiddlestick!" said the King, rubbing his nose, which had been hurt by the fall. He had a right to be a *little* annoyed with the Queen, for he was covered with ashes from head to foot.

Alice was very anxious to be of use, and, as the poor little Lily was nearly screaming herself into a fit, she hastily picked up the Queen and set her on the table by the side of her noisy little daughter.

The Queen gasped, and sat down: the rapid journey through the air had quite taken away her breath and for a minute or two she could do nothing but hug the little Lily in silence. As soon as she had recovered her breath a little, she called out to the White King, who was sitting sulkily among the ashes, "Mind the volcano!"

"What volcano?" said the King, looking up anxiously into the fire, as if he thought that was the most likely place to find one.

"Blew – me – up," panted the Queen, who was still a little out of breath. "Mind you come up – the regular way – don't get blown up!"

Alice watched the White King as he slowly struggled up from bar to bar, till at last she said, "Why, you'll be hours and hours getting to the table, at that rate. I'd far better help you, hadn't I?" But the King took no notice of the question: it was quite clear that he could neither hear her nor see her.

So Alice picked him up very gently, and lifted him across more slowly than she had lifted the Queen, that she mightn't take his breath away: but, before she put him on the table, she thought she might as well dust him a little, he was so covered with ashes.

She said afterwards that she had never seen in all her life such a face as the King made, when he found himself held in the air by an invisible hand, and being dusted: he was far too much astonished to cry out, but his eyes and his mouth went on getting larger and larger, and rounder and

rounder, till her hand shook so with laughing that she nearly let him drop upon the floor.

"Oh! PLEASE don't make such faces, my dear!" she cried out, quite forgetting that the King couldn't hear her. "You make me laugh so that I can hardly hold you! And don't keep your mouth so wide open! All the ashes will get into it – there, now I think you're tidy enough!' she added, as she smoothed his hair, and set him upon the table near the Queen.

The King immediately fell flat on his back, and lay perfectly still; and Alice was a little alarmed at what she had done, and went round the room to see if she could find any water to throw over him. However, she could find nothing but a bottle of ink, and when she got back with it she found he had recovered, and he and the Queen were talking together in a frightened whisper – so low, that Alice could hardly hear what they said.

The King was saying "I assure, you my dear, I turned cold to the very ends of my whiskers!"

To which the Queen replied, "You haven't got any whiskers."

"The horror of that moment," the King went on, "I shall never, *never* forget!"

"You will, though," the Queen said, "if you don't make a memorandum of it."

Alice looked on with great interest as the King took an enormous memorandum-book out of his pocket, and began writing. A sudden thought struck her, and she took hold of the end of the pencil, which came some way over his shoulder, and began writing for him.

The poor King *look* puzzled and unhappy, and struggled with the pencil for some time without saying anything; but Alice was too strong for him, and at last he panted out, "My dear! I really *must* get a thinner pencil. I can't manage this one a bit; it writes all manner of things that I don't intend – "

"What manner of things?" said the Queen, looking over the book (in which Alice had put 'THE WHITE KNIGHT IS SLIDING DOWN THE POKER. HE BALANCES *very* BADLY') "That's not a memorandum of *your* feelings!"

486

There was a book lying near Alice on the table, and while she sat watching the White King (for she was still a little anxious about him, and had the ink all ready to throw over him, in case he fainted again), she turned over the leaves, to find some part that she could read, "– for it's all in some language I don't know," she said to herself.

It was like this.

YKCOWREBBAJ

sevot yhtils eht dna ,gillirb saw T'
ebaw eht ni elbmig dna eryg diD
,sevogorob eht erew ysmim llA
.ebargtuo shtar emom eht dnA

She puzzled over this for some time, but at last a bright thought struck her. "Why, it's a Looking-glass book, of course! And if I hold it up to a glass, the words will all go the right way again."

This was the poem that Alice read.

JABBERWOCKY

'T was brillig, and the slithy toves
Did gyre and gimble in the wabe;
All mimsy were the borogoves,
And the mome raths outgrabe.

"Beware the Jabberwock, my son!
The jaws that bite, the claws that catch!

Beware the Jubjub bird, and shun
The frumious Bandersnatch!"

He took his vorpal sword in hand:
Long time the manxome foe he sought-
So rested he by the Tumtum tree,
And stood awhile in thought.

And, as in uffish thought he stood,
The Jabberwock, with eyes of flame,
Came whiffling through the tulgey wood,
And burbled as it came!

One, two! One, two! And through and through
The vorpal blade went snicker-snack!
He left it dead, and with its head
He went galumphing back.

"And has thou slain the Jabberwock?
Come to my arms, my beamish boy!
O frabjous day! Callooh! Callay!"
He chortled in his joy.

'Twas brillig, and the slithy toves
Did gyre and gimble in the wabe;
All mimsy were the borogoves,
And the mome raths outgrabe.

"It seems very pretty," she said when she had finished it, "but it's

RATHER hard to understand!" (You see she didn't like to confess, ever to herself, that she couldn't make it out at all.) "Somehow it seems to fill my head with ideas – only I don't exactly know what they are! However, *somebody* killed s*omething*: that's clear, at any rate – "

"But oh!" thought Alice, suddenly jumping up, "if I don't make haste I shall have to go back through the Looking-glass, before I've seen what the rest of the house is like! Let's have a look at the garden first!" She was out of the room in a moment, and ran down stairs – or, at least, it wasn't exactly running, but a new invention of hers for getting down stairs quickly and easily, as Alice said to herself. She just kept the tips of her fingers on the hand-rail, and floated gently down without even touching the stairs with her feet; then she floated on through the hall, and would have gone straight out at the door in the same way, if she hadn't caught hold of the door-post. She was getting a little giddy with so much floating in the air, and was rather glad to find herself walking again in the natural way.

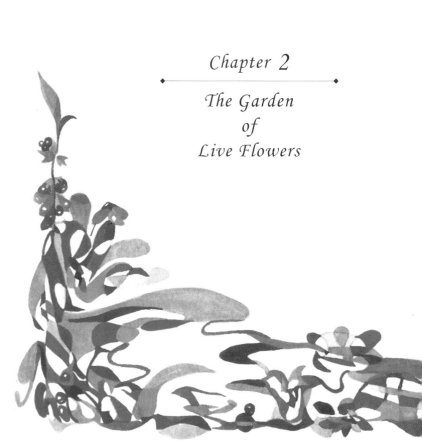

Chapter 2

*The Garden
of
Live Flowers*

"But that's not your fault," the Rose added kindly.
"You're beginning to fade, you know – and then one
can't help one's petals getting a little untidy."

"I should see the garden far better," said Alice to herself, "if I could get to the top of that hill: and here's a path that leads straight to it – at least, no, it doesn't do that – " (after going a few yards along the path, and turning several sharp corners), "but I suppose it will at last. But how curiously it twists! It's more like a corkscrew than a path! Well, THIS turn goes to the hill, I suppose – no, it doesn't! This goes straight back to the house! Well then, I'll try it the other way."

And so she did: wandering up and down, and trying turn after turn, but always coming back to the house, do what she would. Indeed, once, when she turned a corner rather more quickly than usual, she ran against it before she could stop herself.

"It's no use talking about it," Alice said, looking up at the house and pretending it was arguing with her. "I'm *not* going in again yet. I know I should have to get through the Looking-glass again – back into the old room – and there'd be an end of all my adventures!"

So, resolutely turning her back upon the house, she set out once more down the path, determined to keep straight on till she got to the hill. For a few minutes all went on well, and she was just saying, "I really *shall* do it this time – " when the path gave a sudden twist and shook itself (as she described it afterwards), and the next moment she found herself actually walking in at the door.

"Oh, it's too bad!" she cried. "I never saw such a house for getting in the way! Never!"

However, there was the hill full in sight, so there was nothing to be done but start again. This time she came upon a large flower-bed, with a border of daisies, and a willow-tree growing in the middle.

"O Tiger-lily," said Alice, addressing herself to one that was waving gracefully about in the wind, "I wish you *could* talk!"

"We *can* talk," said the Tiger-lily, "when there's anybody worth talking to."

Alice was so astonished that she could not speak for a minute: it quite seemed to take her breath away. At length, as the Tiger-lily only went on waving about, she spoke again, in a timid voice – almost in a whisper. "And can *all* the flowers talk?"

"As well as *you* can," said the Tiger-lily. "And a great deal louder."

"It isn't manners for us to begin, you know," said the Rose, "and I really was wondering when you'd speak! Said I to myself, 'Her face has got *some* sense in it, thought it's not a clever one!' Still, you're the right colour, and that goes a long way."

"I don't care about the colour," the Tiger-lily remarked. "If only her petals curled up a little more, she'd be all right."

Alice didn't like being criticised, so she began asking questions. "Aren't you sometimes frightened at being planted out here, with nobody to take care of you?"

"There's the tree in the middle," said the Rose. "what else is it good for?"

"But what could it do, if any danger came?" Alice asked.

"It could bark," said the Rose.

"It says 'Bough-wough!'" cried a Daisy: "That's why its branches are called boughs!"

"Didn't you know *that?*" cried another Daisy, and here they all began shouting together, till the air seemed quite full of little shrill voices. "Silence, every one of you!" cried the Tigerlily, waving itself passionately from side to side, and trembling with excitement. "They know I can't get at them!" it panted, bending its quivering head towards Alice, "or they wouldn't dare to do it!"

"Never mind!" Alice said in a soothing tone, and stooping down to the daisies, who were just beginning again, she whispered, "If you don't hold your tongues, I'll pick you!"

There was silence in a moment, and several of the pink daisies turned white.

"That's right!" said the Tiger-lily. "The daisies are worst of all. When one speaks, they all begin together, and it's enough to make one wither to hear the way they go on!"

"How is it you can all talk so nicely?" Alice said, hoping to get it into a better temper by a compliment. "I've been in many gardens before, but none of the flowers could talk."

"Put your hand down, and feel the ground," said the Tiger-lily. "Then you'll know why."

Alice did so. It's very hard," she said; "but I don't see what that has to do with it."

"In most gardens," the Tiger-lily said, "they make the beds too soft – so that the flowers are always asleep."

This sounded a very good reason, and Alice was quite pleased to know it. "I never thought of that before!" she said.

"It's *my* opinion that you never think *at all*," the Rose said in a rather severe tone.

"I never saw anybody that looked stupider," a Violet said, so suddenly, that Alice quite jumped; for it hadn't spoken before.

"Hold *your* tongue!" cried the Tiger-lily. "As if *you* ever saw anybody! You keep your head under the leaves, and snore away there, till you know no more what's going on in the world, than if you were a bud!"

497

"Are there any more people in the garden besides me?" Alice said, not choosing to notice the Rose's last remark.

"There's one other flower in the garden that can move about like you," said the Rose. "I wonder how you do it – " ("You're always wondering," said the Tiger-lily), "but she's more bushy than you are."

"Is she like me?" Alice asked eagerly, for the thought crossed her mind, "There's another little girl in the garden, somewhere!"

"Well, she has the same awkward shape as you," the Rose said, "but she's redder – and her petals are shorter, I think."

"They're done up close, almost like a dahlia," said the Tiger-lily: "not tumbled about anyhow, like yours."

"But that's not your fault," the Rose added kindly. "You're beginning to fade, you know – and then one can't help one's petals getting a little untidy."

Alice didn't like this idea at all: so, to change the subject, she asked "Does she ever come out here?"

"I dare say you'll see her soon," said the Rose. "She's one of the thorny kind."

"Where does she wear the thorns?" Alice asked with some curiosity.

"Why all round her head, of course," the Rose replied. "I was wondering *you* hadn't got some too. I thought it was the regular rule."

"She's coming!" cried the Larkspur. "I hear her footstep, thump, thump, thump, along the gravel-walk!"

Alice looked round eagerly, and found that it was the Red Queen. "She's grown a good deal!" was her first remark. She had indeed: when Alice first found her in the ashes, she had been only three inches high – and here she was, half a head taller than Alice herself!

"It's the fresh air that does it," said the Rose: "wonderfully fine air it is, out here."

"I think I'll go and meet her," said Alice, for, though the flowers were interesting enough, she felt that it would be far grander to have a talk with a real Queen.

"You can't possibly do that," said the Rose: "*I* should advise you to walk the other way."

This sounded nonsense to Alice, so she said nothing, but set off at once towards the Red Queen. To her surprise, she lost sight of her in a moment, and found herself walking in at the front-door again.

A little provoked, she drew back, and after looking everywhere for the queen (whom she spied out at last, a long way off), she thought she would try the plan, this time, of walking in the opposite direction.

It succeeded beautifully. She had not been walking a minute before she found herself face to face with the Red Queen, and full in sight of the hill she had been so long aiming at.

"Where do you come from?" said the Red Queen. "And where are you going? Look up, speak nicely, and don't twiddle your fingers all the time."

Alice attended to all these directions, and explained, as well as she could, that she had lost her way.

"I don't know what you mean by *your* way," said the Queen: "all the ways about here belong to ME – but why did you come out here at all?" she added in a kinder tone. "Curtsey while you're thinking what to say, it saves time."

Alice wondered a little at this, but she was too much in awe of the Queen to disbelieve it. "I'll try it when I go home," she thought to herself. "the next time I'm a little late for dinner."

"It's time for you to answer now," the Queen said, looking at her watch: "open your mouth a *little* wider when you speak, and always say 'your Majesty.'"

"I only wanted to see what the garden was like, your Majesty –"

"That's right," said the Queen, patting her on the head, which Alice didn't like at all, though, when you say 'garden,' – "*I've* seen gardens, compared with which this would be a wilderness."

Alice didn't dare to argue the point, but went on: – "and I thought I'd try and find my way to the top of that hill – "

"When you say 'hill,'" the Queen interrupted, "*I* could show you hills, in comparison with which you'd call that a valley."

"No, I shouldn't," said Alice, surprised into contradicting her at last: a hill *can't* be a valley, you know. That would be nonsense – "

The Red Queen shook her head, "You may call it 'nonsense' if you like," she said, "but *I've* heard nonsense, compared with which that would be as sensible as a dictionary!"

Alice curtseyed again, as she was afraid from the Queen's tone that she was a *little* offended: and they walked on in silence till they got to the top of the little hill.

For some minutes Alice stood without speaking, looking out in all directions over the country – and a most curious country it was. There were a number of tiny little brooks running straight across it from side to side, and the ground between was divided up into squares by a number of little green hedges, that reached from brook to brook.

"I declare it's marked out just like a large chessboard!" Alice said at last. "There ought to be some men moving about somewhere – and so there are!" She added in a tone of delight, and her heart began to beat quick with excitement as she went on. "It's a great huge game of chess that's being played – all over the world – if this IS the world at all, you know. Oh, what fun it is! How I *wish* I was one of them! I wouldn't mind being a Pawn, if only I might join – though of course I should LIKE to be a Queen, best."

She glanced rather shyly at the real Queen as she said this, but her companion only smiled pleasantly, and said, "That's easily managed. You can be the White Queen's Pawn, if you like, as Lily's too young to play; and you're in the Second Square to began with: when you get to the Eighth Square you'll be a Queen – " Just at this moment, somehow or other, they began to run.

Alice never could quite make out, in thinking it over afterwards, how it was that they began: all she remembers is, that they were running hand in hand, and the Queen went so fast that it was all she could do to keep up with her: and still the Queen kept crying "Faster! Faster!" but Alice felt she *could not* go faster, though she had not breath left to say so.

The most curious part of the thing was, that the trees and the other things round them never changed their places at all: however fast they went, they never seemed to pass anything. "I wonder if all the things move along with us?" thought poor puzzled Alice. And the Queen seemed to guess her thoughts, for she cried "Faster! Don't try to talk!"

Not that Alice had any idea of doing *that*. She felt as if she would never be able to talk again, she was getting so much out of breath: and still the Queen cried "Faster! Faster!" and dragged her along. "Are we nearly there?" Alice managed to pant out at last.

"Nearly there!" the Queen repeated. "Why, we passed it ten

minutes ago! Faster!" And they ran on for a time in silence, with the wind whistling in Alice's ears, and almost blowing her hair off her head, she fancied.

"Now! Now!" cried the Queen. "Faster! Faster!" And they went so fast that at last they seemed to skim through the air, hardly touching the ground with their feet, till suddenly, just as Alice was getting quite exhausted, they stopped, and she found herself sitting on the ground, breathless and giddy.

The Queen propped her up against a tree, and said kindly, "You may rest a little now."

Alice looked round her in great surprise. "Why, I do believe we've been under this tree the whole time! Everything's just as it was!"

"Of course it is," said the Queen, "what would you have it? "

"Well, in *our* country," said Alice, still panting a little, "you'd generally get to somewhere else – if you ran very fast for a long time, as we've been doing."

"A slow sort of country!" said the Queen. "Now, *here*, you see, it takes all the running *you* can do, to keep in the same place. If you want to get somewhere else, you must run at least twice as fast as that!"

"I'd rather not try, please!" said Alice. "I'm quite content to stay here – only I AM so hot and thirsty!"

"I know what *you'd* like!" the Queen said good-naturedly, taking a little box out of her pocket. "Have a biscuit?"

Alice thought it would not be civil to say "No," though it wasn't at all what she wanted. So she took it, and ate it as well as she could: and it was *very* dry; and she thought she had never been so nearly choked in all her life.

"While you're refreshing yourself," said the Queen, "I'll just take the measurements." And she took a ribbon out of her pocket, marked in inches, and began measuring the ground, and sticking little pegs in here and there.

"At the end of two yards," she said, putting in a peg to mark the distance, "I shall give you your directions – have another biscuit?"

"No, thank you," said Alice, "one's *quite* enough!"

"Thirst quenched, I hope?" said the Queen.

Alice did not know what to say to this, but luckily the Queen did not wait for an answer, but went on. "At the end of THREE yards I shall repeat them – for fear of your forgetting them. At the end of *four*, I shall say good-bye. And at then end of FIVE, I shall go!"

She had got all the pegs put in by this time, and Alice looked on with great interest as she returned to the tree, and then began slowly walking down the row.

At the two-yard peg she faced round, and said, "A pawn goes two squares in its first move, you know. So you'll go *very* quickly through the Third Square – by railway, I should think – and you'll find yourself in the Fourth Square in no time. Well, *That* square belongs to Tweedledum and Tweedledee – the Fifth is mostly water – the Sixth belongs to Humpty Dumpty – But you make no remark?"

"I – I didn't know I had to make one – just then," Alice faltered out.

"You *should* have said," the Queen went on in a tone of grave reproof, "'It's extremely kind of you to tell me all this' – however, we'll suppose it said – the Seventh Square is all forest – however, one of the Knights will show you the way – and in the Eighth Square we shall be Queens together, and it's all feasting and fun!" Alice got up and curtseyed, and sat down again.

At the next peg the Queen turned again, and this time she said, "Speak in French when you can't think of the English for a thing – turn out your toes as you walk – and remember who you are!" She did not wait for Alice to curtsey this time, but walked on quickly to the next peg, where she turned for a moment to say "Good-bye," and then hurried on to the last.

How it happened, Alice never knew, but exactly as she came to the last peg, she was gone. Whether she vanished into the air, or whether she ran quickly into the wood ("and she can run very fast!" thought Alice), there was no way of guessing, but she was gone, and Alice began to remember that she was a Pawn, and that it would soon be time for her to move.

Chapter 3

Looking-Glass Insects

"I don't REJOICE in insects at all," Alice explained, "because I'm rather afraid of them – at least the large kinds. But I can tell you the names of some of them."

"Of course they answer to their names?" the Gnat remarked carelessly.

"I never knew them do it."

"What's the use of their having names," the Gnat said, "if they won't answer to them?"

"No use to THEM," said Alice; "but it's useful to the people who name them, I suppose. If not, why do things have names at all?"

Of course the first thing to do was to make a grand survey of the country she was going to travel through. "It's something very like learning geography," thought Alice, as she stood on tiptoe in hopes of being able to see a little further. "Principal rivers – there ARE none. Principal mountains – I'm on the only one, but I don't think it's got any name. Principal towns – why, what ARE those creatures, making honey down there? They can't be bees – nobody ever saw bees a mile off, you know – " and for some time she stood silent, watching one of them that was bustling about among the flowers, poking its proboscis into them, "just as if it was a regular bee," thought Alice.

However, this was anything but a regular bee: in fact it was an elephant – as Alice soon found out, though the idea quite took her breath away at first. "And what enormous flowers they must be!" was her next idea. "Something like cottages with the roofs taken off, and stalks put to them – and what quantities of honey they must make! I think I'll go down and – no, I won't JUST yet," she went on, checking herself just as she was beginning to run down the hill, and trying to find some excuse for turning shy so suddenly. "It'll never do to go down among them without a good long branch to brush them away – and what fun it'll be when they ask me how I like my walk. I shall say – 'Oh, I like it well enough – '" (here came the favourite little toss of the head), 'only it was so dusty and hot, and the elephants did tease so!' "I think I'll go down the other way," she said after a pause: "and perhaps I may visit the elephants later on. Besides, I do so want to get into the Third Square!"

So with this excuse she ran down the hill and jumped over the first of the six little brooks.

"Tickets, please!" said the Guard, putting his head in at the window. In a moment everybody was holding out a ticket: they were about the same size as the people, and quite seemed to fill the carriage.

"Now then! Show your ticket, child!" the Guard went on, looking angrily at Alice. And a great many voices all said together ("like the chorus of a song," thought Alice), "Don't keep him waiting, child! Why, his time is worth a thousand pounds a minute!"

"I'm afraid I haven't got one,' Alice said in a frightened tone: "there wasn't a ticket-office where I came from." And again the chorus of voices went on. "There wasn't room for one where she came from. The land there is worth a thousand pounds an inch!"

"Don't make excuses," said the Guard: "you should have bought one from the engine-driver." And once more the chorus of voices went on with "The man that drives the engine. Why, the smoke alone is worth a thousand pounds a puff!"

Alice thought to herself, "Then there's no use in speaking." The voices didn't join in this time, as she hadn't spoken, but to her great surprise, they all *thought* in chorus (I hope you understand what THINKING IN CHORUS means – for *I* must confess that I don't), "Better say nothing at all. Language is worth a thousand pounds a word!"

"I shall dream about a thousand pounds tonight, I know I shall!" thought Alice.

All this time the Guard was looking at her, first through a telescope, then through a microscope, and then through an operaglass. At last he said, "You're travelling the wrong way," and shut up the window and went away.

"So young a child," said the gentleman sitting opposite to her (he was dressed in white paper), "ought to know which way she's going, even if she doesn't know her own name!"

A Goat that was sitting next to the gentleman in white shut his eyes and said in a loud voice, "She ought to know her way to the ticket-office, even if she doesn't know her alphabet!"

There was a Beetle sitting next to the Goat (it was a very queer carriage-full of passengers altogether), and, as the rule seemed to be that they should all speak in turn, HE went on with "She'll have to go back from here as luggage!"

Alice couldn't see who was sitting beyond the Beetle, but a hoarse voice spoke next. "Change engines – " it said, and was obliged to leave off.

"It sounds like a horse," Alice thought to herself. And an extremely small voice, close to her ear, said, "You might make a joke on that – something about 'horse' and 'hoarse', you know."

Then a very gentle voice in the distance said, "She must be labelled 'Lass, with care,' you know – "

And after that other voices went on ("What a number of people there are in the carriage!" thought Alice), saying "She must go by post, as she's got a head on her – " "She must be sent as a message by the telegraph – " "She must draw the train herself the rest of the way –" and so on.

But the gentleman dressed in white paper leaned forwards and whispered in her ear, "Never mind what they all say, my dear, but take a return-ticket every time the train stops."

"Indeed I shan't!" Alice said rather impatiently. "I don't belong to this railway journey at all – I was in a wood just now – and I wish I

could get back there."

"You might make a joke on *that*," said the little voice close to her ear: "something about 'you *would* if you could,' you know."

"Don't tease so," said Alice, looking about in vain to see where the voice came from, "if you're so anxious to have a joke made, why don't you make one yourself?"

The little voice sighed deeply: it was *very* unhappy, evidently, and Alice would have said something pitying to comfort it, "if it would only sigh like other people!" she thought. But this was such a wonderfully small sigh, that she wouldn't have heard it at all, if it hadn't come *quite* close to her ear. The consequence of this was that it tickled her ear very much, and quite took off her thoughts from the unhappiness of the poor little creature.

"I know you are a friend," the little voice went on: "a dear friend, and an old friend. And you won't hurt me, though I AM an insect."

"What kind of insect?" Alice inquired a little anxiously. What she really wanted to know was, whether it could sting or not, but she thought this wouldn't be quite a civil question to ask.

"What, then you don't – " the little voice began, when it was drowned by a shrill scream from the engine, and everybody jumped up in alarm, Alice among the rest.

The Horse, who had put his head out of the window, quietly drew it in and said, "It's only a brook we have to jump over." Everybody seemed satisfied with this, though Alice felt a little nervous at the idea of trains jumping at all. "However, it'll take us into the Fourth Square, that's some comfort!" she said to herself. In another moment she felt the carriage rise straight up into the air, and in her fright she caught at the thing nearest to her hand. which happened to be the Goat's beard.

But the beard seemed to melt away as she touched it, and she found herself sitting quietly under a tree – while the Gnat (for that was the insect she had been talking to) was balancing itself on a twig just over her head, and fanning her with its wings.

It certainly was a *very* large Gnat: about the size of a chicken,' Alice thought. Still, she couldn't feel nervous with it, after they had been talking together so long.

"– then you don't like all insects?" the Gnat went on, as quietly as if nothing had happened.

"I like them when they can talk," Alice said. "None of them ever talk, where *I* come from."

"What sort of insects do you rejoice in, where *you* come from?" the Gnat inquired.

"I don't REJOICE in insects at all," Alice explained, "because I'm rather afraid of them – at least the large kinds. But I can tell you the names of some of them."

"Of course they answer to their names?" the Gnat remarked carelessly.

"I never knew them do it."

"What's the use of their having names," the Gnat said, "if they won't answer to them?"

"No use to THEM," said Alice; "but it's useful to the people who name them, I suppose. If not, why do things have names at all?"

"I can't say," the Gnat replied. "Further on, in the wood down there, they've got no names – however, go on with your list of insects: you're wasting time."

"Well, there's the Horse-fly," Alice began, counting off the names on her fingers.

"All right," said the Gnat: "half way up that bush, you'll see a Rocking-horse-fly, if you look. It's made entirely of wood, and gets about by swinging itself from branch to branch."

"What does it live on?" Alice asked, with great curiosity.

"Sap and sawdust," said the Gnat. "Go on with the list."

Alice looked up at the Rocking-horse-fly with great interest, and made up her mind that it must have been just repainted, it looked so bright and sticky; and then she went on.

"And there's the Dragon-fly."

"Look on the branch above your head," said the Gnat, "and there you'll find a snap-dragon-fly. Its body is made of plum-pudding, its wings of holly-leaves, and its head is a raisin burning in brandy."

"And what does it live on?" Alice asked, as before.

"Frumenty and mince pie,' the Gnat replied; and it makes its nest in a Christmas box."

"And then there's the Butterfly," Alice went on, after she had taken a good look at the insect with its head on fire, and had thought to herself, "I wonder if that's the reason insects are so fond of flying into candles – because they want to turn into Snap-dragon-flies!"

"Crawling at your feet," said the Gnat (Alice drew her feet back in some alarm), "you may observe a Bread-and-Butterfly. Its wings are thin slices of Bread-and-butter, its body is a crust, and its head is a lump of sugar."

"And what does IT live on?"

"Weak tea with cream in it."

A new difficulty came into Alice's head. "Supposing it couldn't find any?" she suggested.

517

"Then it would die, of course."

"But that must happen very often," Alice remarked thoughtfully.

"It always happens," said the Gnat.

After this, Alice was silent for a minute or two, pondering. The Gnat amused itself meanwhile by humming round and round her head: at last it settled again and remarked "I suppose you don't want to lose your name?"

"No, indeed," Alice said, a little anxiously.

"And yet I don't know," the Gnat went on in a careless tone: "only think how convenient it would be if you could manage to go home without it! For instance, if the governess wanted to call you to your lessons, she would call out 'come here – ', and there she would have to leave off, because there wouldn't be any name for her to call, and of course you wouldn't have to go, you know."

"That would never do, I'm sure," said Alice: "the governess would never think of excusing me lessons for that. If she couldn't remember my name, she'd call me 'Miss!' as the servants do."

"Well. if she said 'Miss', and didn't say anything more," the Gnat remarked, "of course you'd miss your lessons. That's a joke. I wish you had made it."

"Why do you wish *I* had made it?" Alice asked. "It's a very bad one."

But the Gnat only sighed deeply, while two large tears came rolling down its cheeks.

"You shouldn't make jokes," Alice said, "if it makes you so unhappy."

Then came another of those melancholy little sighs, and this time the poor Gnat really seemed to have sighed itself away, for, when Alice looked up, there was nothing whatever to be seen on the twig, and, as she was getting quite chilly with sitting still so long, she got up and walked on.

She very soon came to an open field, with a wood on the other side of it: it looked much darker than the last wood, and Alice felt a little timid about going into it. However, on second thoughts, she made up her mind to go on: "for I certainly won't go *back*," she thought to herself, and this was the only way to the Eighth Square.

"This must be the wood," she said thoughtfully to herself, "where things have no names. I wonder what'll become of *my* name when I go in? I shouldn't like to lose it at all – because they'd have to give me another, and it would be almost certain to be an ugly one. But then the fun would be trying to find the creature that had got my old name! That's just like the advertisements, you know, when people lose dogs

– 'ANSWERS TO THE NAME OF "DASH:" *had* ON A BRASS COLLAR' – just fancy calling everything you met 'Alice,' till one of them answered! Only they wouldn't answer at all, if they were wise."

She was rambling on in this way when she reached the wood: it looked very cool and shady. "Well, at any rate it's a great comfort," she said as she stepped under the trees, "after being so hot, to get into the – into *what*?" she went on, rather surprised at not being able to think of the word. "I mean to get under the – under the – under THIS, you know!" putting her hand on the trunk of the tree. "What *does* it call itself, I wonder? I do believe it's got no name – why, to be sure it hasn't!"

She stood silent for a minute, thinking: then she suddenly began again. "Then it really HAS happened, after all! And now, who am I? I WILL remember, if I can! I'm determined to do it!" But being determined didn't help much, and all she could say, after a great deal of puzzling, was "L, I *know* it begins with L!"

Just then a Fawn came wandering by: it looked at Alice with its large gentle eyes, but didn't seem at all frightened. "Here then! Here then!" Alice said, as she held out her hand and tried to stroke it; but it only started back a little, and then stood looking at her again.

"What do you call yourself?" the Fawn said at last. Such a soft sweet voice it had!

"I wish I knew!" thought poor Alice. She answered, rather sadly, "Nothing, just now."

"Think again," it said: "that won't do."

Alice thought, but nothing came of it. "Please, would you tell me what *you* call yourself?" she said timidly. "I think that might help a little."

"I'll tell you, if you'll move a little further on," the Fawn said. "I can't remember here."

So they walked on together though the wood, Alice with her arms clasped lovingly round the soft neck of the Fawn, till they came out into another open field, and here the Fawn gave a sudden bound into the air, and shook itself free from Alice's arms. "I'm a Fawn!" it cried out in a voice of delight. "And, dear me! you're a human child!" A sudden look of alarm came into its beautiful brown eyes, and in another moment it had darted away at full speed.

Alice stood looking after it, almost ready to cry with vexation at having lost her dear little fellow-traveller so suddenly. "However, I know my name now." she said, "that's *some* comfort. Alice – Alice – I won't forget it again. And now, which of these finger-posts ought I to follow, I wonder?"

It was not a very difficult question to answer, as there was only one road through the wood, and the two finger-posts both pointed along it. "I'll settle it," Alice said to herself, "when the road divides and they point different ways."

But this did not seem likely to happen. She went on and on, a long way, but wherever the road divided there were sure to be two finger-posts pointing the same way, one marked

"TO TWEENLEDUM'S HOUSE,"and the other"TO THEHOUSE OF TWEEDLEDEE."

"I do believe," said Alice at last, "that they live in the same house! I wonder I never thought of that before – But I can't stay there long.

I'll just call and say 'how d'you do?' and ask them the way out of the wood. If I could only get to the Eighth Square before it gets dark!" So she wandered on, talking to herself as she went, till, on turning a sharp corner, she came upon two fat little men, so suddenly that she could not help starting back, but in another moment she recovered herself, feeling sure that they must be –

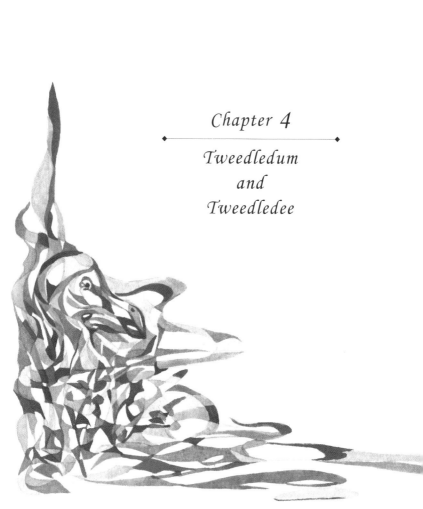

Chapter 4

—————————◆—————————

*Tweedledum
and
Tweedledee*

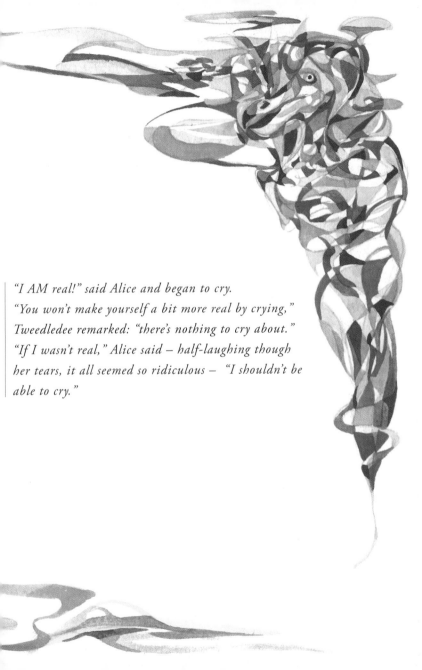

"I AM real!" said Alice and began to cry.
"You won't make yourself a bit more real by crying,"
Tweedledee remarked: "there's nothing to cry about."
"If I wasn't real," Alice said – half-laughing though
her tears, it all seemed so ridiculous – "I shouldn't be
able to cry."

They were standing under a tree, each with an arm round the other's neck, and Alice knew which was which in a moment, because one of them had 'DUM' embroidered on his collar, and the other 'DEE.' "I suppose they've each got 'TWEEDLE' round at the back of the collar," she said to herself.

They stood so still that she quite forgot they were alive, and she was just looking round to see if the word "TWEEDLE" was written at the back of each collar, when she was startled by a voice coming from the one marked 'DUM.'

"If you think we're wax-works," he said, "you ought to pay, you know. Wax-works weren't made to be looked at for nothing, nohow!"

"Contrariwise," added the one marked 'DEE,' "if you think we're alive, you ought to speak."

"I'm sure I'm very sorry," was all Alice could say; for the words of the old song kept ringing through her head like the ticking of a clock, and she could hardly help saying them out loud: –

"Tweedledum and Tweedledee
Agreed to have a battle;
For Tweedledum said Tweedledee
Had spoiled his nice new rattle.
Just then flew down a monstrous crow,
As black as a tar-barrel;
Which frightened both the heroes so,
They quite forgot their quarrel."

"I know what you're thinking about," said Tweedledum: "but it isn't so, nohow."

"Contrariwise," continued Tweedledee, "if it was so, it might be; and if it were so, it would be; but as it isn't, it ain't. That's logic."

"I was thinking," Alice said very politely, "which is the best way out of this wood: it's getting so dark. Would you tell me, please?"

But the little men only looked at each other and grinned.

They looked so exactly like a couple of great schoolboys, that Alice couldn't help pointing her finger at Tweedledum, and saying "First Boy!"

"Nohow!" Tweedledum cried out briskly, and shut his mouth up again with a snap.

"Next Boy!" said Alice, passing on to Tweedledee, though she felt quite certain he would only shout out "Contrariwise!" and so he did.

"You've been wrong!" cried Tweedledum. "The first thing in a visit is to say 'How d'ye do?' and shake hands!" And here the two brothers gave each other a hug, and then they held out the two hands that were free, to shake hands with her.

Alice did not like shaking hands with either of them first, for fear of hurting the other one's feelings; so, as the best way out of the difficulty, she took hold of both hands at once: the next moment they were dancing round in a ring. This seemed quite natural (she remembered afterwards), and she was not even surprised to hear music playing: it seemed to come from the tree under which they were dancing, and it was done (as well as she could make it out) by the branches rubbing one across the other, like fiddles and fiddle-sticks.

"But it certainly WAS funny," (Alice said afterwards, when she was telling her sister the history of all this,) "to find myself singing 'here WE GO ROUND THE MULBERRY BUSH.' I don't know when I began it, but somehow I felt as if I'd been singing it a long long time!"

The other two dancers were fat, and very soon out of breath. "Four times round is enough for one dance," Tweedledum panted out, and they left off dancing as suddenly as they had begun: the music stopped at the same moment.

Then they let go of Alice's hands, and stood looking at her for a minute: there was a rather awkward pause, as Alice didn't know how to begin a conversation with people she had just been dancing with. "It would never do to say 'How d'ye do?' *now*," she said to herself: "we seem to have got beyond that, somehow!"

"I hope you're not much tired?" she said at last.

"Nohow. And thank you *very* much for asking," said Tweedledum.

"So much obliged!" added Tweedledee. "You like poetry?"

"Ye-es, pretty well – *some* poetry," Alice said doubtfully. "Would you tell me which road leads out of the wood?"

"What shall I repeat to her?" said Tweedledee, looking round at Tweedledum with great solemn eyes, and not noticing Alice's question.

"'THE WALRUS AND THE CARPENTER' is the longest," Tweedledum replied, giving his brother an affectionate hug.

Tweedledee began instantly:

"The sun was shining – "

Here Alice ventured to interrupt him. "If it's *very* long," she said, as politely as she could, "would you please tell me first which road – "

Tweedledee smiled gently, and began again:

"The sun was shining on the sea,
Shining with all his might:
He did his very best to make
The billows smooth and bright-
And this was odd, because it was
The middle of the night.

The moon was shining sulkily,
Because she thought the sun
Had got no business to be there
After the day was done-
'It's very rude of him,' she said,
'To come and spoil the fun!'

The sea was wet as wet could be,
The sands were dry as dry.
You could not see a cloud, because
No cloud was in the sky:
No birds were flying over head-
There were no birds to fly.

The Walrus and the Carpenter
Were walking close at hand;
They wept like anything to see
Such quantities of sand:
'If this were only cleared away,'
They said, 'it would be grand!'

'If seven maids with seven mops
Swept it for half a year,
Do you suppose,' the Walrus said,
'That they could get it clear?'
'I doubt it,' said the Carpenter,
And shed a bitter tear.

'O Oysters, come and walk with us!'
The Walrus did beseech.
'A pleasant walk, a pleasant talk,
Along the briny beach:
We cannot do with more than four,
To give a hand to each.'

The eldest Oyster looked at him.
But never a word he said:
The eldest Oyster winked his eye,
And shook his heavy head–
Meaning to say he did not choose
To leave the oyster-bed.

But four young oysters hurried up,
All eager for the treat:
Their coats were brushed, their faces washed,
Their shoes were clean and neat–
And this was odd, because, you know,
They hadn't any feet.

Four other Oysters followed them,
And yet another four;
And thick and fast they came at last,
And more, and more, and more–
All hopping through the frothy waves,
And scrambling to the shore.

The Walrus and the Carpenter
Walked on a mile or so,
And then they rested on a rock
Conveniently low:
And all the little Oysters stood
And waited in a row.

'The time has come,' the Walrus said,
'To talk of many things:
Of shoes – and ships – and sealing-wax–
Of cabbages – and kings–
And why the sea is boiling hot–
And whether pigs have wings.'

'But wait a bit,' the Oysters cried,
'Before we have our chat;
For some of us are out of breath,
And all of us are fat!'
'No hurry!' said the Carpenter.
They thanked him much for that.

'A loaf of bread,' the Walrus said,
'Is what we chiefly need:
Pepper and vinegar besides
Are very good indeed–
Now if you're ready Oysters dear,
We can begin to feed.'

'But not on us!' the Oysters cried,
Turning a little blue.
'After such kindness, that would be
A dismal thing to do!'
'The night is fine,' the Walrus said
'Do you admire the view?'

'It was so kind of you to come!
And you are very nice!'
The Carpenter said nothing but
'Cut us another slice:
I wish you were not quite so deaf–
I've had to ask you twice!'

'It seems a shame,' the Walrus said,
'To play them such a trick,
After we've brought them out so far,
And made them trot so quick!'
The Carpenter said nothing but
'The butter's spread too thick!'
'I weep for you,' the Walrus said:
'I deeply sympathize.'
With sobs and tears he sorted out
Those of the largest size.
Holding his pocket handkerchief
Before his streaming eyes.

534

'O Oysters,' said the Carpenter.
'You've had a pleasant run!
Shall we be trotting home again?'
But answer came there none –
And that was scarcely odd, because
They'd eaten every one."

"I like the Walrus best," said Alice: "because you see he was a *little* sorry for the poor oysters."

"He ate more than the Carpenter, though," said Tweedledee. "You see he held his handkerchief in front, so that the Carpenter couldn't count how many he took: contrariwise."

"That was mean!" Alice said indignantly. "Then I like the Carpenter best – if he didn't eat so many as the Walrus."

"But he ate as many as he could get," said Tweedledum.

This was a puzzler. After a pause, Alice began, "Well! They were BOTH very unpleasant characters–" Here she checked herself in some alarm, at hearing something that sounded to her like the puffing of a large steam-engine in the wood near them, though she feared it was more likely to be a wild beast. "Are there any lions or tigers about here?" she asked timidly.

"It's only the Red King snoring," said Tweedledee.

"Come and look at him!" the brothers cried, and they each took

535

one of Alice's hands, and led her up to where the King was sleeping.

"Isn't he a LOVELY sight?" said Tweedledum.

Alice couldn't say honestly that he was. He had a tall red night-cap on, with a tassel, and he was lying crumpled up into a sort of untidy heap, and snoring loud – "fit to snore his head off!" as Tweedledum remarked.

"I'm afraid he'll catch cold with lying on the damp grass," said Alice, who was a very thoughtful little girl.

"He's dreaming now," said Tweedledee: "and what do you think he's dreaming about?" Alice said "Nobody can guess that."

"Why, about you!" Tweedledee exclaimed, clapping his hands triumphantly. "And if he left off dreaming about you, where do you suppose you'd be?"

"Where I am now, of course," said Alice.

"Not you!" Tweedledee retorted contemptuously. "You'd be nowhere. Why, you're only a sort of thing in his dream!"

"If that there King was to wake," added Tweedledum, "you'd go out – bang! – just like a candle!"

"I shouldn't!" Alice exclaimed indignantly. "Besides, if I'M only a sort of thing in his dream, what are *you*, I should like to know?"

"Ditto" said Tweedledum.

"Ditto, ditto" cried Tweedledee.

He shouted this so loud that Alice couldn't help saying, "Hush! You'll be waking him, I'm afraid, if you make so much noise."

"Well, it no use *your* talking about waking him," said Tweedledum, "when you're only one of the things in his dream. You know very well you're not real."

"I AM real!" said Alice and began to cry.

"You won't make yourself a bit more real by crying," Tweedledee remarked: "there's nothing to cry about."

"If I wasn't real," Alice said – half-laughing though her tears, it all

537

seemed so ridiculous – "I shouldn't be able to cry."

"I hope you don't suppose those are real tears?" Tweedledum interrupted in a tone of great contempt.

"I know they're talking nonsense," Alice thought to herself: "and it's foolish to cry about it." So she brushed away her tears, and went on as cheerfully as she could. "At any rate I'd better be getting out of the wood, for really it's coming on very dark. Do you think it's going to rain?"

Tweedledum spread a large umbrella over himself and his brother, and looked up into it. "No, I don't think it is, he said: at least – not under *here*. Nohow."

"But it may rain OUTSIDE?"

"It may – if it chooses," said Tweedledee: "we've no objection. Contrariwise."

"Selfish things!" thought Alice, and she was just going to say "Good-night" and leave them, when Tweedledum sprang out from under the umbrella and seized her by the wrist.

"Do you see *that*?" he said, in a voice choking with passion, and his eyes grew large and yellow all in a moment, as he pointed with a trembling finger at a small white thing lying under the tree.

"It's only a rattle," Alice said, after a careful examination of the little white thing. "Not a rattle-SNAKE, you know," she added hastily, thinking that he was frightened: "only an old rattle – quite old and broken."

"I knew it was!" cried Tweedledum, beginning to stamp about wildly and tear his hair. "It's spoilt, of course!" Here he looked at Tweedledee, who immediately sat down on the ground, and tried to hide himself under the umbrella.

Alice laid her hand upon his arm, and said in a soothing tone, "You needn't be so angry about an old rattle."

"But it isn't old!" Tweedledum cried, in a greater fury than ever. "It's new, I tell you – I bought it yesterday – my nice *New rattle*!" and his voice rose to a perfect scream.

All this time Tweedledee was trying his best to fold up the umbrella, with himself in it: which was such an extraordinary thing to do, that it quite took off Alice's attention from the angry brother. But he couldn't quite succeed, and it ended in his rolling over, bundled up in the umbrella, with only his head out: and there he lay, opening and shutting his mouth and his large eyes – "looking more like a fish than anything else," Alice thought.

"Of course you agree to have a battle?" Tweedledum said in a calmer tone.

"I suppose so," the other sulkily replied, as he crawled out of the umbrella: "only SHE must help us to dress up, you know." So the two brothers went off hand-in-hand into the wood, and returned in

a minute with their arms full of things – such as bolsters, blankets, hearth-rugs, table-cloths, dish-covers and coal-scuttles. "I hope you're a good hand at pinning and tying strings?" Tweedledum remarked. "Every one of these things has got to go on, somehow or other."

Alice said afterwards she had never seen such a fuss made about anything in all her life – the way those two bustled about-and the quantity of things they put on – and the trouble they gave her in tying strings and fastening buttons – "Really they'll be more like bundles of old clothes that anything else, by the time they're ready!" she said to herself, as she arranged a bolster round the neck of Tweedledee, "to keep his head from being cut off," as he said."You know," he added very gravely, "it's one of the most serious things that can possibly happen to one in a battle – to get one's head cut off."

Alice laughed aloud: but she managed to turn it into a cough, for fear of hurting his feelings.

"Do I look very pale?" said Tweedledum, coming up to have his helmet tied on. (He *called* it a helmet, though it certainly looked much more like a saucepan.)

"Well – yes – a *little,*" Alice replied gently.

"I'm very brave generally," he went on in a low voice: "only to-day I happen to have a headache."

"And *I've* got a toothache!" said Tweedledee, who had overheard the remark. "I'm far worse off than you!"

"Then you'd better not fight to-day," said Alice, thinking it a good opportunity to make peace.

"We *must* have a bit of a fight, but I don't care about going on long," said Tweedledum. "What's the time now?"

Tweedledee looked at his watch, and said "Half-past four."

"Let's fight till six, and then have dinner," said Tweedledum.

"Very well," the other said, rather sadly: "and SHE can watch us – only you'd better not come very close," he added: "I generally hit everything I can see – when I get really excited."

"And *I* hit everything within reach," cried Tweedledum, "whether I can see it or not!'

Alice laughed. "You must hit the TREES pretty often, I should think," she said. Tweedledum looked round him with a satisfied smile.

"I don't suppose," he said, "there'll be a tree left standing, for ever so far round, by the time we've finished!"

"And all about a rattle!" said Alice, still hoping to make them a *little* ashamed of fighting for such a trifle.

"I shouldn't have minded it so much," said Tweedledum, "if it hadn't been a new one."

"I wish the monstrous crow would come!" though Alice.

"There's only one sword, you know," Tweedledum said to his brother: "but you can have the umbrella – it's quite as sharp. Only we must begin quick. It's getting as dark as it can."

"And darker." said Tweedledee.

It was getting dark so suddenly that Alice thought there must be a thunderstorm coming on. "What a thick black cloud that is!" she said. "And how fast it comes! Why, I do believe it's got wings!"

"It's the crow!" Tweedledum cried out in a shrill voice of alarm: and the two brothers took to their heels and were out of sight in a moment.

Alice ran a little way into the wood, and stopped under a large tree. "It can never get at me *here*," she thought: "it's far too large to squeeze itself in among the trees. But I wish it wouldn't flap its wings so – it makes quite a hurricane in the wood-here's somebody's shawl being blown away!"

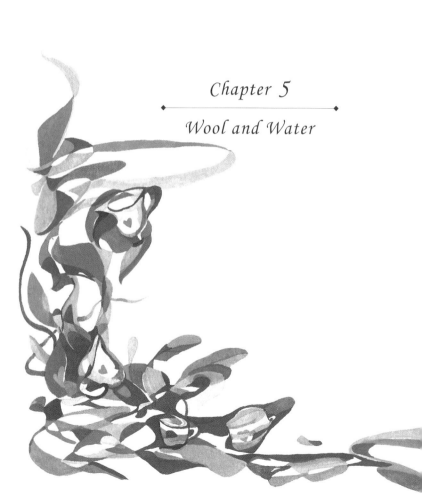

Chapter 5

Wool and Water

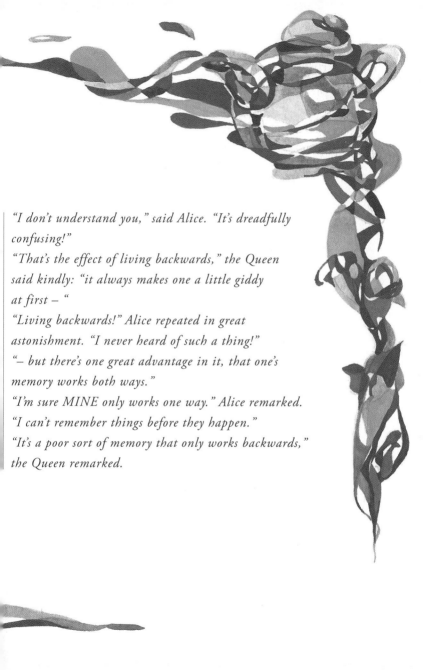

"I don't understand you," said Alice. "It's dreadfully confusing!"

"That's the effect of living backwards," the Queen said kindly: "it always makes one a little giddy at first – "

"Living backwards!" Alice repeated in great astonishment. "I never heard of such a thing!"

"– but there's one great advantage in it, that one's memory works both ways."

"I'm sure MINE only works one way." Alice remarked. "I can't remember things before they happen."

"It's a poor sort of memory that only works backwards," the Queen remarked.

She caught the shawl as she spoke, and looked about for the owner: in another moment the White Queen came running wildly through the wood, with both arms stretched out wide, as if she were flying, and Alice very civilly went to meet her with the shawl.

"I'm very glad I happened to be in the way," Alice said, as she helped her to put on her shawl again.

The White Queen only looked at her in a helpless frightened sort of way, and kept repeating something in a whisper to herself that sounded like "bread-and-butter, bread-and-butter," and Alice felt that if there was to be any conversation at all, she must manage it herself. So she began rather timidly: "Am I addressing the White Queen?"

"Well, yes, if you call that a-dressing," The Queen said. "It isn't *my* notion of the thing, at all."

Alice thought it would never do to have an argument at the very beginning of their conversation, so she smiled and said, "If your Majesty will only tell me the right way to begin, I'll do it as well as I can."

"But I don't want it done at all!" groaned the poor Queen. I've been a-dressing myself for the last two hours.'

It would have been all the better, as it seemed to Alice, if she had got some one else to dress her, she was so dreadfully untidy. "Every single thing's crooked," Alice thought to herself, "and she's all over pins! – may I put your shawl straight for you?" she added aloud.

"I don't know what's the matter with it!" the Queen said, in a melancholy voice. "It's out of temper, I think. I've pinned it here, and I've pinned it there, but there's no pleasing it!"

"It *can't* go straight, you know, if you pin it all on one side," Alice said, as she gently put it right for her; "and, dear me, what a state your hair is in!"

"The brush has got entangled in it!" the Queen said with a sigh. "And I lost the comb yesterday."

Alice carefully released the brush, and did her best to get the hair into order. "Come, you look rather better now!" she said, after altering most of the pins. "But really you should have a lady's maid!"

"I'm sure I'll take you with pleasure! the Queen said. "Two pence a week, and jam every other day."

Alice couldn't help laughing, as she said, "I don't want you to hire ME – and I don't care for jam."

"It's very good jam," said the Queen.

"Well, I don't want any *today,* at any rate."

"You couldn't have it if you *did* want it," the Queen said. "The rule is, jam to-morrow and jam yesterday – but never jam to-day."

"It *must* come sometimes to 'jam today,'" Alice objected.

"No, it can't," said the Queen. "It's jam every *other* day: to-day isn't any *other* day, you know."

"I don't understand you," said Alice. "It's dreadfully confusing!"

"That's the effect of living backwards," the Queen said kindly: "it always makes one a little giddy at first – "

"Living backwards!" Alice repeated in great astonishment. "I never heard of such a thing!"

"– but there's one great advantage in it, that one's memory works both ways."

"I'm sure MINE only works one way." Alice remarked. "I can't remember things before they happen."

"It's a poor sort of memory that only works backwards," the Queen remarked.

"What sort of things do *you* remember best?" Alice ventured to ask.

"Oh, things that happened the week after next," the Queen replied in a careless tone. "For instance, now," she went on, sticking a large piece of plaster on her finger as she spoke, "there's the

King's Messenger. He's in prison now, being punished: and the trial doesn't even begin till next Wednesday: and of course the crime comes last of all."

"Suppose he never commits the crime?" said Alice.

"That would be all the better, wouldn't it?" the Queen said, as she bound the plaster round her finger with a bit of ribbon.

Alice felt there was no denying *that.* "Of course it would be all the better," she said: "but it wouldn't be all the better his being punished."

"You're wrong there, at any rate," said the Queen: "Were *you* ever punished?"

"Only for faults," said Alice.

"And you were all the better for it, I know!" the Queen said triumphantly.

"Yes, but then I *had* done the things I was punished for," said Alice: "that makes all the difference."

"But if you *hadn't* done them," the Queen said, "that would have been better still; better, and better, and better!" Her voice went higher with each 'better', till it got quite to a squeak at last.

Alice was just beginning to say "There's a mistake somewhere – " when the Queen began screaming so loud that she had to leave the sentence unfinished. "Oh, oh, oh!" shouted the Queen, shaking her hand about as if she wanted to shake it off. "My finger's bleeding! Oh, oh, oh, oh!"

Her screams were so exactly like the whistle of a steam-engine, that Alice had to hold both her hands over her ears.

"What IS the matter?" she said, as soon as there was a chance of making herself heard. "Have you pricked your finger?"

"I haven't pricked it *yet,*" the Queen said, but I soon shall–"oh, oh, oh!"

"When do you expect to do it?" Alice asked, feeling very much inclined to laugh.

"When I fasten my shawl again," the poor Queen groaned out: "the brooch will come undone directly. Oh, oh!" As she said the words the brooch flew open, and the Queen clutched wildly at it, and tried to clasp it again.

"Take care!" cried Alice. "You're holding it all crooked!" And she caught at the brooch; but it was too late: the pin had slipped, and the Queen had pricked her finger.

"That accounts for the bleeding, you see," she said to Alice with a smile. "Now you understand the way things happen here."

"But why don't you scream now?" Alice asked, holding her hands ready to put over her ears again.

"Why, I've done all the screaming already," said the Queen. "What would be the good of having it all over again?"

By this time it was getting light. "The crow must have flown away, I think," said Alice: "I'm so glad it's gone. I thought it was the night coming on."

"I wish I could manage to be glad!" the Queen said. "Only I never can remember the rule. You must be very happy, living in this wood, and being glad whenever you like!"

"Only it is so *very* lonely here!" Alice said in a melancholy voice; and at the thought of her loneliness two large tears came rolling down her cheeks.

"Oh, don't go on like that!" cried the poor Queen, wringing her hands in despair. "Consider what a great girl you are. Consider what a long way you've come today. Consider what o'clock it is. Consider anything, only don't cry!"

Alice could not help laughing at this, even in the midst of her tears. "Can *you* keep from crying by considering things?" she asked.

"That's the way it's done," the Queen said with great decision: "nobody can do two things at once, you know. Let's consider your age to begin with – how old are you?"

"I'm seven and a half exactly."

"You needn't say 'exactly,'" the Queen remarked. "I can believe it without that. Now I'll give *you* something to believe. I'm just one hundred and one, five months and a day."

"I can't believe *that!*" said Alice.

"Can't you?" the Queen said in a pitying tone. "Try again: draw a long breath, and shut your eyes."

Alice laughed. "There's no use trying," she said: "one *can't* believe impossible things."

"I dare say you haven't had much practice," said the Queen. "When I was your age, I always did it for half-an-hour a day. Why, sometimes I've believed as many as six impossible things before breakfast. There goes the shawl again!"

The brooch had come undone as she spoke, and a sudden gust of wind blew the Queen's shawl across a little brook. The Queen spread out her arms again, and went flying after it, and this time she succeeded in catching it for herself. "I've got it!" she cried in a triumphant tone. "Now you shall see me pin it on again, all by myself!"

"Then I hope your finger is better now?" Alice said very politely, as she crossed the little brook after the Queen.

"Oh, much better!" cried the Queen, her voice rising to a squeak as she went on. "Much be-etter! Be-etter! Be-e-e-etter! Be-e-ehh!" The last word ended in a long bleat, so like a sheep that Alice quite started.

She looked at the Queen, who seemed to have suddenly wrapped herself up in wool. Alice rubbed her eyes, and looked again. She couldn't make out what had happened at all. Was she in a shop? And was that really – was it really a SHEEP that was sitting on the other side of the counter? Rub as she could, she could make nothing more of it: she was in a little dark shop, leaning with her elbows on the counter, and opposite to her was an old Sheep, sitting in an arm-chair knitting, and every now and then leaving off to look at her through a great pair of spectacles.

"What is it you want to buy?" the Sheep said at last, looking up for a moment from her knitting.

"I don't quite know yet," Alice said, very gently. "I should like to look *all* round me first, if I might."

"You may look in front of you, and on both sides, if you like," said the Sheep, "but you can't look all round you – unless you've got eyes at the back of your head."

But these, as it happened, Alice had not got: so she contented herself with turning round, looking at the shelves as she came to them.

The shop seemed to be full of all manner of curious things-but the oddest part of it all was, that whenever she looked hard at any shelf, to make out exactly what it had on it, that particular shelf was always quite empty: though the others round it were crowded as full as they could hold.

"Things flow about so here!" she said at last in a plaintive tone, after she had spent a minute or so in vainly pursuing a large bright thing, that looked sometimes like a doll and sometimes like a work-box, and was always in the shelf next above the one she was looking at. "And this one is the most provoking of all – but I'll tell you what – " she added, as a sudden thought struck her, "I'll follow it up to the very top shelf of all. It'll puzzle it to go through the ceiling, I expect!"

But even this plan failed: the thing went through the ceiling as quietly as possible, as if it were quite used to it.

"Are you a child or a teetotum?" the Sheep said, as she took up another pair of needles. "You'll make me giddy soon, if you go on turning round like that." She was now working with fourteen pairs at once, and Alice couldn't help looking at her in great astonishment.

"How *can* she knit with so many?" the puzzled child thought to herself. She gets more and more like a porcupine every minute!'

"Can you row?" the Sheep asked, handing her a pair of knitting needles as she spoke.

"Yes, a little – but not on land – and not with needles – " Alice was beginning to say, when suddenly the needles turned into oars in her hands, and she found they were in a little boat, gliding along between banks: so there was nothing for it but to do her best.

"Feather!" cried the Sheep, as she took up another pair of needles.

This didn't sound like a remark that needed any answer, so Alice said nothing, but pulled away. There was something very queer about the water, she thought, as every now and then the oars got fast in it, and would hardly come out again.

"Feather! Feather!" the Sheep cried again, taking more needles. "You'll be catching a crab directly."

"A dear little crab!" thought Alice. "I should like that."

"Didn't you hear me say 'Feather'?" the Sheep cried angrily, taking up quite a bunch of needles.

"Indeed I did," said Alice: "you've said it very often – and very loud. Please, where ARE the crabs?"

"In the water, of course!" said the Sheep, sticking some of the needles into her hair, as her hands were full. "Feather, I say!"

"WHY do you say 'feather' so often?" Alice asked at last, rather vexed. "I'm not a bird!"

"You are," said the Sheep "you're a little goose."

This offended Alice a little, so there was no more conversation for a minute or two, while the boat glided gently on, sometimes among beds of weeds (which made the oars stick fast in the water, worse than ever), and sometimes under trees, but always with the same tall river-banks frowning over their heads.

"Oh, please! There are some scented rushes!" Alice cried in a sudden transport of delight. "There really are – and *such* beauties!"

"You needn't say 'please' to ME about 'em'" the Sheep said, without looking up from her knitting: "I didn't put em there, and I'm not going to take em away."

"No, but *I* meant – please, may we wait and pick some?" Alice pleaded. "If you don't mind stopping the boat for a minute."

"How am I to stop it?" said the Sheep. "If you leave off rowing, it'll stop of itself."

So the boat was left to drift down the stream as it would, till it glided gently in among the waving rushes. And then the little sleeves were carefully rolled up, and the little arms were plunged in elbow-deep to get the rushes a good long way down before breaking them off – and for a while Alice forgot all about the Sheep and the knitting, as she bent over the side of the boat, with just the ends of her tangled hair dipping into the water – while with bright eager eyes she caught at one bunch after another of the darling scented rushes.

"I only hope the boat won't tipple over!" she said to herself. "Oh, *what* a lovely one! Only I couldn't quite reach it." And it certainly *did* seem a little provoking ("almost as if it happened on purpose," she thought) that, though she managed to pick plenty of beautiful rushes as the boat glided by, there was always a more lovely one that she couldn't reach.

"The prettiest are always further!" she said at last, with a sigh at the obstinacy of the rushes in growing so far off, as, with flushed cheeks and dripping hair and hands, she scrambled back into her place, and began to arrange her new-found treasures.

What mattered it to her just than that the rushes had begun to fade, and to lose all their scent and beauty, from the very moment that she picked them? Even real scented rushes, you know, last only a very little while – and these, being dream-rushes, melted away almost like snow, as they lay in heaps at her feet-but Alice hardly noticed this, there were so many other curious things to think about.

They hadn't gone much farther before the blade of one of the oars got fast in the water and *wouldn't* come out again (so Alice explained it afterwards), and the consequence was that the handle of it caught her under the chin, and, in spite of a series of little shrieks of "Oh, oh, oh!" from poor Alice, it swept her straight off the seat, and down among the heap of rushes.

However, she wasn't hurt, and was soon up again: the Sheep went on with her knitting all the while, just as if nothing had happened. "That was a nice crab you caught!" she remarked, as Alice got back into her place, very much relieved to find herself still in the boat.

"Was it? I didn't see it," Said Alice, peeping cautiously over the side of the boat into the dark water. "I wish it hadn't let go – I should so like to see a little crab to take home with me!" But the Sheep only laughed scornfully, and went on with her knitting.

"Are there many crabs here?" said Alice.

"Crabs, and all sorts of things," said the Sheep: "plenty of choice, only make up your mind. Now, what *do* you want to buy?"

"To buy!" Alice echoed in a tone that was half astonished and half frightened – for the oars, and the boat, and the river, had vanished all in a moment, and she was back again in the little dark shop.

"I should like to buy an egg, please," she said timidly. "How do you sell them?"

"Five pence farthing for one – Two pence for two," the Sheep replied.

"Then two are cheaper than one?" Alice said in a surprised tone, taking out her purse.

"Only you *must* eat them both, if you buy two," said the Sheep.

"Then I'll have *one,* please," said Alice, as she put the money down on the counter. For she thought to herself, "They mightn't be at all nice, you know."

The Sheep took the money, and put it away in a box, then she said "I never put things into people's hands – that would never do – you must get it for yourself." And so saying, she went off to the other end of the shop, and set the egg upright on a shelf.

"I wonder WHY it wouldn't do?" thought Alice, as she groped her way among the tables and chairs, for the shop was very dark towards the end. "The egg seems to get further away the more I walk towards

559

it. Let me see, is this a chair? Why, it's got branches, I declare! How very odd to find trees growing here! And actually here's a little brook! Well, this is the very queerest shop I ever saw!"

So she went on, wondering more and more at every step, as everything turned into a tree the moment she came up to it, and she quite expected the egg to do the same.

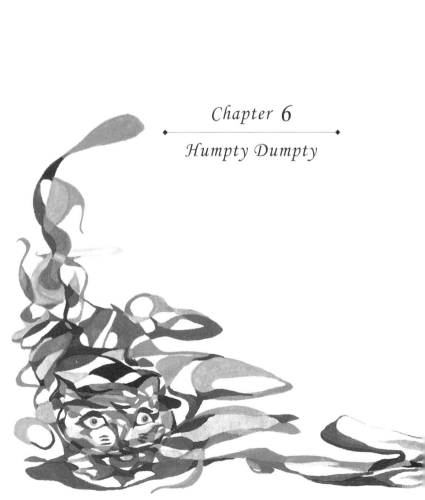

Chapter **6**

Humpty Dumpty

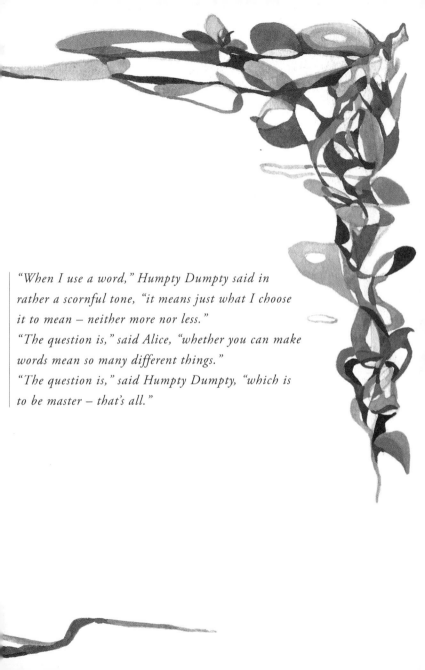

"When I use a word," Humpty Dumpty said in rather a scornful tone, "it means just what I choose it to mean – neither more nor less."

"The question is," said Alice, "whether you can make words mean so many different things."

"The question is," said Humpty Dumpty, "which is to be master – that's all."

However, the egg only got larger and larger, and more and more human: when she had come within a few yards of it, she saw that it had eyes and a nose and mouth; and when she had come close to it, she saw clearly that it was HUMPTY DUMPTY himself. "It can't be anybody else!" she said to herself. "I'm as certain of it, as if his name were written all over his face."

It might have been written a hundred times, easily, on that enormous face. Humpty Dumpty was sitting with his legs crossed, like a Turk, on the top of a high wall – such a narrow one that Alice quite wondered how he could keep his balance – and, as his eyes were steadily fixed in the opposite direction, and he didn't take the least notice of her, she thought he must be a stuffed figure, after all.

"And how exactly like an egg he is!" she said aloud, standing with her hands ready to catch him, for she was every moment expecting him to fall.

"It's very *provoking*," Humpty Dumpty said after a long silence, looking away from Alice as he spoke, "to be called an egg-*very!*"

"I said you LOOKED like an egg, Sir," Alice gently explained. "And some eggs are very pretty, you know" she added, hoping to turn her remark into a sort of a compliment.

"Some people," said Humpty Dumpty, looking away from her as usual, "have no more sense than a baby!"

Alice didn't know what to say to this: it wasn't at all like conversation, she thought, as he never said anything to HER; in fact, his last remark was evidently addressed to a tree – so she stood and softly repeated to herself: –

"Humpty Dumpty sat on a wall:
Humpty Dumpty had a great fall.
All the King's horses and all the King's men
Couldn't put Humpty Dumpty in his place again."

"That last line is much too long for the poetry," she added, almost out loud, forgetting that Humpty Dumpty would hear her.

"Don't stand there chattering to yourself like that," Humpty Dumpty said, looking at her for the first time, "but tell me your name and your business."

"My NAME is Alice, but – "

"It's a stupid enough name!" Humpty Dumpty interrupted impatiently. "What does it mean?"

"*Must* a name mean something?" Alice asked doubtfully.

"Of course it must," Humpty Dumpty said with a short laugh: "*my* name means the shape I am – and a good handsome shape it is, too. With a name like yours, you might be any shape, almost."

"Why do you sit out here all alone?" said Alice, not wishing to begin an argument.

"Why, because there's nobody with me!" cried Humpty Dumpty. "Did you think I didn't know the answer to that? Ask another."

"Don't you think you'd be safer down on the ground?" Alice went on, not with any idea of making another riddle, but simply in her good-natured anxiety for the queer creature. "That wall is so *very* narrow!"

"What tremendously easy riddles you ask!" Humpty Dumpty growled out. "Of course I don't think so! Why, if ever I *did* fall off which there's no chance of – but IF I did – " Here he pursed his lips and looked so solemn and grand that Alice could hardly help laughing. "IF I did fall," he went on, "THE KING HAS PROMISED ME – WITH HIS *very* OWN MOUTH – to – to – "

"To send all his horses and all his men," Alice interrupted, rather unwisely.

"Now I declare that's too bad!" Humpty Dumpty cried, breaking into a sudden passion. "You've been listening at doors – and behind trees-and down chimneys – or you couldn't have known it!"

"I haven't, indeed!" Alice said very gently. "It's in a book."

"Ah, well! They may write such things in a BOOK," Humpty Dumpty said in a calmer tone. "That's what you call a History of England, that is. Now, take a good look at me! I'm one that has spoken to a King, *I* am: mayhap you'll never see such another: and to show you I'm not proud, you may shake hands with me!" And he grinned almost from ear to ear, as he leant forwards (and as nearly as possible fell of the wall in doing so) and offered Alice his hand. She watched him a little anxiously as she took it. "If he smiled much more, the ends of his mouth might meet behind," she thought: "and then I don't know what would happen to his head! I'm afraid it would come off!"

"Yes, all his horses and all his men," Humpty Dumpty went on. "They'd pick me up again in a minute, THEY would! However, this conversation is going on a little too fast: let's go back to the last remark but one."

"I'm afraid I can't quite remember it," Alice said very politely.

"In that case we start fresh," said Humpty Dumpty, "and it's my turn to choose a subject – " ("He talks about it just as if it was a game!" thought Alice.) "So here's a question for you. How old did you say you were?"

Alice made a short calculation, and said "Seven years and six months."

"Wrong!" Humpty Dumpty exclaimed triumphantly. "You never said a word like it!"

"I though you meant 'How old ARE you?'" Alice explained.

"If I'd meant that, I'd have said it," said Humpty Dumpty.

Alice didn't want to begin another argument, so she said nothing.

"Seven years and six months!" Humpty Dumpty repeated

thoughtfully. "An uncomfortable sort of age. Now if you'd asked *my* advice, I'd have said 'Leave off at seven' – but it's too late now."

"I never ask advice about growing," Alice said indignantly.

"Too proud?" the other inquired.

Alice felt even more indignant at this suggestion. "I mean," she said, "that one can't help growing older."

"*One* can't, perhaps," said Humpty Dumpty, "but TWO can. With proper assistance, you might have left off at seven."

"What a beautiful belt you've got on!" Alice suddenly remarked. (They had had quite enough of the subject of age, she thought: and if they really were to take turns in choosing subjects, it was her turn now.) "At least," she corrected herself on second thoughts, "a beautiful cravat, I should have said – no, a belt, I mean – I beg your pardon!" she added in dismay, for Humpty Dumpty looked thoroughly offended, and she began to wish she hadn't chosen that subject. "If I only knew," she thought to herself, "which was neck and which was waist!"

Evidently Humpty Dumpty was very angry, though he said nothing for a minute or two. When he *did* speak again, it was in a deep growl.

"It is a – MOST – PROVOKING – thing," he said at last, "when a person doesn't know a cravat from a belt!"

"I know it's very ignorant of me," Alice said, in so humble a tone that Humpty Dumpty relented.

"It's a cravat, child, and a beautiful one, as you say. It's a present from the White King and Queen. There now!"

"Is it really?" said Alice, quite pleased to find that she *had* chosen a good subject, after all.

"They gave it me," Humpty Dumpty continued thoughtfully, as he crossed one knee over the other and clasped his hands round it, "they gave it me – for an un-birthday present."

"I beg your pardon?" Alice said with a puzzled air.

"I'm not offended," said Humpty Dumpty.

"I mean, what IS an un-birthday present?"

"A present given when it isn't your birthday, of course."

Alice considered a little. "I like birthday presents best," she said at last.

"You don't know what you're talking about!" cried Humpty Dumpty. "How many days are there in a year?"

"Three hundred and sixty-five," said Alice.

"And how many birthdays have you?"

"One."

"And if you take one from three hundred and sixty-five, what remains?"

"Three hundred and sixty-four, of course."

Humpty Dumpty looked doubtful. "I'd rather see that done on paper," he said.

Alice couldn't help smiling as she took out her memorandum book, and worked the sum for him:

$$365$$
$$-1$$
$$\overline{}$$
$$364$$

Humpty Dumpty took the book, and looked at it carefully. "That seems to be done right – "he began.

"You're holding it upside down!" Alice interrupted.

"To be sure I was!" Humpty Dumpty said gaily, as she turned it round for him. "I thought it looked a little queer. As I was saying, that SEEMS to be done right – though I haven't time to look it over thoroughly just now – and that shows that there are three hundred and sixty-four days when you might get un-birthday presents – "

"Certainly," said Alice.

"And only *one* for birthday presents, you know. There's glory for you!"

"I don't know what you mean by 'glory,'" Alice said.

Humpty Dumpty smiled contemptuously. "Of course you don't – till I tell you. I meant 'there's a nice knock-down argument for you!'"

"But 'glory' doesn't mean 'a nice knock-down argument,'" Alice objected.

"When *I* use a word," Humpty Dumpty said in rather a scornful tone, "it means just what I choose it to mean – neither more nor less."

"The question is," said Alice, "whether you *can* make words mean so many different things."

"The question is," said Humpty Dumpty, "which is to be master – that's all."

Alice was too much puzzled to say anything, so after a minute Humpty Dumpty began again. "They've a temper, some of them – particularly verbs, they're the proudest – adjectives you can do anything with, but not verbs – however, I can manage the whole lot of them! Impenetrability! That's what I say!"

"Would you tell me, please," said Alice "what that means?"

"Now you talk like a reasonable child," said Humpty Dumpty, looking very much pleased. "I meant by 'impenetrability' that we've had enough of that subject, and it would be just as well if you'd mention what you mean to do next, as I suppose you don't mean to stop here all the rest of your life."

"That's a great deal to make one word mean," Alice said in a thoughtful tone.

"When I make a word do a lot of work like that," said Humpty Dumpty, "I always pay it extra."

"Oh!" said Alice. She was too much puzzled to make any other remark.

"Ah, you should see 'em come round me of a Saturday night," Humpty Dumpty went on, wagging his head gravely from side to side: "for to get their wages, you know."

(Alice didn't venture to ask what he paid them with; and so you see I can't tell *you.*)

"You seem very clever at explaining words, Sir," said Alice. "Would you kindly tell me the meaning of the poem called 'Jabberwocky'?"

"Let's hear it," said Humpty Dumpty. "I can explain all the poems that were ever invented – and a good many that haven't been invented just yet."

This sounded very hopeful, so Alice repeated the first verse: –

"'Twas brillig, and the slithy toves
Did gyre and gimble in the wabe;
All mimsy were the borogoves,
And the mome raths outgrabe."

"That's enough to begin with," Humpty Dumpty interrupted: "there are plenty of hard words there. 'BRILLIG' means four o'clock in the afternoon – the time when you begin BROILING things for dinner."

"That'll do very well," said Alice: "and 'SLITHY'?"

"Well, 'SLITHY' means 'lithe and slimy.' 'Lithe' is the same as 'active.' You see it's like a portmanteau – there are two meanings packed up into one word."

"I see it now," Alice remarked thoughtfully: "and what are 'TOVES'?"

"Well, 'TOVES' are something like badgers – they're something like lizards – and they're something like corkscrews."

"They must be very curious looking creatures."

"They are that," said Humpty Dumpty: "also they make their nests under sun-dials – also they live on cheese."

"And what's the 'GYRE' and to 'GIMBLE'?"

"To 'GYRE' is to go round and round like a gyroscope. To 'GIM-

BLE' is to make holes like a gimlet."

"And 'THE WABE' is the grass-plot round a sun-dial, I suppose?" said Alice, surprised at her own ingenuity.

"Of course it is. It's called 'WABE,' you know, because it goes a long way before it, and a long way behind it – "

"And a long way beyond it on each side," Alice added.

"Exactly so. Well, then, 'MIMSY' is 'flimsy and miserable' (there's another portmanteau for you). And a 'BOROGOVE' is a thin shabby-looking bird with its feathers sticking out all round-something like a live mop."

"And then 'MOME RATHS'?" said Alice. "I'm afraid I'm giving you a great deal of trouble."

"Well, a 'RATH' is a sort of green pig: but 'MOME' I'm not certain about. I think it's short for 'from home' – meaning that they'd lost their way, you know."

"And what does 'OUTGRABE' mean?"

"Well, 'OUTGRABING' is something between bellowing and whistling, with a kind of sneeze in the middle: however, you'll hear it done, maybe – down in the wood yonder – and when you've once heard it you'll be *quite* content. Who's been repeating all that hard stuff to you?"

"I read it in a book," said Alice. "But I had some poetry repeated to me, much easier than that, by – Tweedledee, I think it was."

"As to poetry, you know," said Humpty Dumpty, stretching out one of his great hands," *I* can repeat poetry as well as other folk, if it comes to that – "

"Oh, it needn't come to that!" Alice hastily said, hoping to keep him from beginning.

"The piece I'm going to repeat," he went on without noticing her remark, "was written entirely for your amusement."

Alice felt that in that case she really *ought* to listen to it, so she sat down, and said "Thank you" rather sadly.

"In winter, when the fields are white,
I sing this song for your delight–

575

only I don't sing it," he added, as an explanation.

"I see you don't," said Alice.

"If you can SEE whether I'm singing or not, you've sharper eyes than most." Humpty Dumpty remarked severely. Alice was silent.

"In spring, when woods are getting green,
I'll try and tell you what I mean."

"Thank you very much," said Alice.

"In summer, when the days are long,
Perhaps you'll understand the song:
In autumn, when the leaves are brown,
Take pen and ink, and write it down."

"I will, if I can remember it so long," said Alice.

"You needn't go on making remarks like that," Humpty Dumpty said: "they're not sensible, and they put me out."

"I sent a message to the fish:
I told them 'This is what I wish.'
The little fishes of the sea,
They sent an answer back to me.

The little fishes' answer was
'We cannot do it, Sir, because –'"

"I'm afraid I don't quite understand," said Alice.

"It gets easier further on," Humpty Dumpty replied.

I sent to them again to say
'It will be better to obey.'

The fishes answered with a grin,
'Why, what a temper you are in!'

I told them once, I told them twice:
They would not listen to advice.

I took a kettle large and new,
Fit for the deed I had to do.

My heart went hop, my heart went thump;
I filled the kettle at the pump.

Then some one came to me and said,
'The little fishes are in bed.'

I said to him, I said it plain,
'Then you must wake them up again.'

I said it very loud and clear:
I went and shouted in his ear."

Humpty Dumpty raised his voice almost to a scream as he repeated this verse, and Alice thought with a shudder, "I wouldn't have been the messenger for *anything!*"

"But he was very stiff and proud;
He said 'You needn't shout so loud!'

And he was very proud and stiff;
He said 'I'd go and wake them, if – '

I took a corkscrew from the shelf:
I went to wake them up myself.

And when I found the door was locked,
I pulled and pushed and kicked and knocked.

And when I found the door was shut,
I tried to turn the handle, but – "

There was a long pause.

"Is that all?" Alice timidly asked.

"That's all," said Humpty Dumpty. "Good-bye."

This was rather sudden, Alice thought. but, after such a *very* strong hint that she ought to be going, she felt that it would hardly be civil to stay. So she got up, and held out her hand. "Good-bye, till we meet again!" she said as cheerfully as she could.

"I shouldn't know you again if we *did* meet," Humpty Dumpty replied in a discontented tone, giving her one of his fingers to shake; "you're so exactly like other people."

"The face is what one goes by, generally," Alice remarked in a thoughtful tone.

"That's just what I complain of," said Humpty Dumpty. "Your face is the same as everybody has – the two eyes, so – " (marking their places in the air with his thumb) "nose in the middle, mouth under. It's always the same. Now if you had the two eyes on the same side of the nose, for instance – or the mouth at the top – that would be some help."

"It wouldn't look nice, Alice objected. But Humpty Dumpty only shut his eyes and said Wait till you've tried."

Alice waited a minute to see if he would speak again, but as he never opened his eyes or took any further notice of her, she said "Good-bye!" once more, and, getting no answer to this, she quietly walked away: but she couldn't help saying to herself as she went, "Of all the unsatisfactory – " (she repeated this aloud, as it was a great comfort to have such a long word to say) "of all the unsatisfactory people I EVER met – " She never finished the sentence, for at this moment a heavy crash shook the forest from end to end.

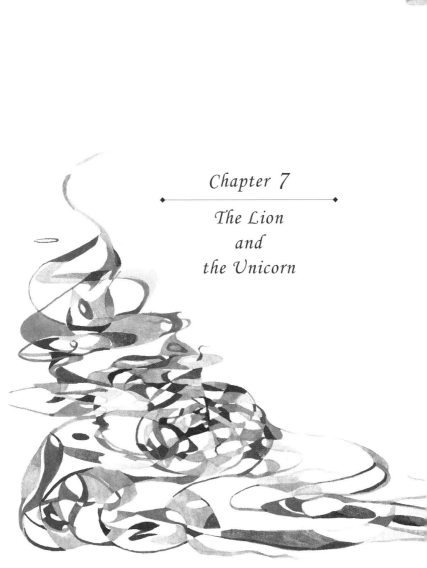

Chapter 7

◆ ━━━━━━━━━━━━ ◆

*The Lion
and
the Unicorn*

"I always thought they were fabulous monsters!"
said the Unicorn. "Is it alive?"
Alice could not help her lips curling up into a smile
as she began: "Do you know, I always thought
Unicorns were fabulous monsters, too! I never saw
one alive before!"
"Well, now that we HAVE seen each other," said the
Unicorn, "if you'll believe in me, I'll believe in you.
Is that a bargain?"

The next moment soldiers came running through the wood, at first in twos and threes, then ten or twenty together, and at last in such crowds that they seemed to fill the whole forest. Alice got behind a tree, for fear of being run over, and watched them go by.

She thought that in all her life she had never seen soldiers so uncertain on their feet: they were always tripping over something or other, and whenever one went down, several more always fell over him, so that the ground was soon covered with little heaps of men.

Then came the horses. Having four feet, these managed rather better than the foot-soldiers; but even THEY stumbled now and then; and it seemed to be a regular rule that, whenever a horse stumbled the rider fell off instantly. The confusion got worse every moment, and Alice was very glad to get out of the wood into an open place, where she found the White King seated on the ground, busily writing in his memorandum-book.

"I've sent them all!" the King cried in a tone of delight, on seeing Alice. "Did you happen to meet any soldiers, my dear, as you came through the wood?"

"Yes, I did," said Alice: "several thousand, I should think."

"Four thousand two hundred and seven, that's the exact number," the King said, referring to his book. "I couldn't send all the horses, you know, because two of them are wanted in the game. And I haven't sent the two Messengers, either. They're both gone to the town. Just look along the road, and tell me if you can see either of them."

"I see nobody on the road," said Alice.

"I only wish *I* had such eyes," the King remarked in a fretful tone. "To be able to see Nobody! And at that distance, too! Why, it's as much as I can do to see real people, by this light!"

All this was lost on Alice, who was still looking intently along the road, shading her eyes with one hand. "I see somebody now!" she exclaimed at last. "But he's coming very slowly – and what curious attitudes he goes into!" (For the messenger kept skipping up and down, and wriggling like an eel, as he came along, with his great hands spread out like fans on each side.)

"Not at all," said the King. He's an Anglo-Saxon Messenger-and those are Anglo-Saxon attitudes. "He only does them when he's happy. His name is Haigha." (He pronounced it so as to rhyme with 'mayor.')

"I love my love with an H," Alice couldn't help beginning, "because he is Happy. I hate him with an H, because he is Hideous. I fed him with – with – with Ham-sandwiches and Hay. His name is Haigha, and he lives – "

"He lives on the Hill," the King remarked simply, without the least idea that he was joining in the game, while Alice was still hesitating for the name of a town beginning with H. "The other Messenger's called Hatta. I must have TWO, you know – to come and go. One to come, and one to go."

"I beg your pardon?" said Alice.

"It isn't respectable to beg," said the King.

"I only meant that I didn't understand," said Alice. "Why one to come and one to go?"

"Didn't I tell you?" the King repeated impatiently. "I must have Two – to fetch and carry. One to fetch, and one to carry."

At this moment the Messenger arrived: he was far too much out of breath to say a word, and could only wave his hands about, and make the most fearful faces at the poor King.

"This young lady loves you with an H," the King said, introducing Alice in the hope of turning off the Messenger's attention from himself – but it was no use – the Anglo-Saxon attitudes only got more extraordinary every moment, while the great eyes rolled wildly from side to side.

"You alarm me!" said the King. "I feel faint – Give me a ham sandwich!"

On which the Messenger, to Alice's great amusement, opened a bag that hung round his neck, and handed a sandwich to the King, who devoured it greedily.

"Another sandwich!" said the King.

"There's nothing but hay left now," the Messenger said, peeping into the bag.

"Hay, then," the King murmured in a faint whisper.

Alice was glad to see that it revived him a good deal. "There's nothing like eating hay when you're faint," he remarked to her, as he munched away.

"I should think throwing cold water over you would be better," Alice suggested: "or some sal-volatile."

"I didn't say there was nothing BETTER," the King replied. "I said there was nothing LIKE it." Which Alice did not venture to deny.

"Who did you pass on the road?" the King went on, holding out his hand to the Messenger for some more hay.

"Nobody," said the Messenger.

"Quite right," said the King: "this young lady saw him too. So of course Nobody walks slower than you."

"I do my best," the Messenger said in a sulky tone. "I'm sure nobody walks much faster than I do!"

"He can't do that," said the King, "or else he'd have been here first. However, now you've got your breath, you may tell us what's happened in the town."

"I'll whisper it," said the Messenger, putting his hands to his mouth in the shape of a trumpet, and stooping so as to get close to the King's ear. Alice was sorry for this, as she wanted to hear the news too. However, instead of whispering, he simply shouted at the top of his voice, "They're at it again!"

"Do you call *that* a whisper?" cried the poor King, jumping up and shaking himself. "If you do such a thing again, I'll have you buttered! It went through and through my head like an earthquake!"

"It would have to be a very tiny earthquake!" thought Alice. "Who are at it again?" she ventured to ask.

"Why, the Lion and the Unicorn, of course," said the King.

"Fighting for the crown?"

"Yes, to be sure," said the King: "and the best of the joke is, that it's *my* crown all the while! Let's run and see them." And they trotted off, Alice repeating to herself, as she ran, the words of the old song:

> *"The Lion and the Unicorn were fighting for the crown:*
> *The Lion beat the Unicorn all round the town.*
> *Some gave them white bread, some gave them brown;*
> *Some gave them plum-cake and drummed them out of town."*

"Does – the one – that wins – get the crown?" she asked, as well as she could, for the run was putting her quite out of breath.

"Dear me, no!" said the King. "What an idea!"

"Would you – be good enough," Alice panted out, after running a little further, "to stop a minute – just to get – one's breath again?"

"I'm GOOD enough," the King said, "only I'm not STRONG enough. You see, a minute goes by so fearfully quick. You might as well try to stop a Bandersnatch!"

Alice had no more breath for talking, so they trotted on in silence, till they came in sight of a great crowd, in the middle of which the Lion and Unicorn were fighting. They were in such a cloud of dust, that at first Alice could not make out which was which: but she soon managed to distinguish the Unicorn by his horn.

They placed themselves close to where Hatta, the other messenger, was standing watching the fight, with a cup of tea in one hand and a piece of bread-and-butter in the other.

"He's only just out of prison, and he hadn't finished his tea when he was sent in," Haigha whispered to Alice: "and they only give them oyster-shells in there – so you see he's very hungry and thirsty. How are you, dear child?" he went on, putting his arm affectionately round Hatta's neck.

Hatta looked round and nodded, and went on with his bread and butter.

"Were you happy in prison, dear child?" said Haigha.

Hatta looked round once more, and this time a tear or two trickled down his cheek; but not a word he would say.

"Speak, can't you!" Haigha cried impatiently. But Hatta only munched away, and drank some more tea.

"Speak, won't you!" cried the King. "How are they getting on with

the fight?"

Hatta made a desperate effort, and swallowed a large piece of bread-and-butter. "They're getting on very well," he said in a choking voice: "each of them has been down about eighty-seven times."

"Then I suppose they'll soon bring the white bread and the brown?" Alice ventured to remark.

"It's waiting for em now," said Hatta: "this is a bit of it as I'm eating."

There was a pause in the fight just then, and the Lion and the Unicorn sat down, panting, while the King called out "Ten minutes allowed for refreshments!" Haigha and Hatta set to work at once, carrying rough trays of white and brown bread. Alice took a piece to taste, but it was *very* dry.

"I don't think they'll fight any more today," the King said to Hatta: "go and order the drums to begin." And Hatta went bounding away like a grasshopper.

For a minute or two Alice stood silent, watching him. Suddenly she brightened up. "Look, look!" she cried, pointing eagerly. "There's the White Queen running across the country! She came flying out of the wood over yonder – How fast those Queens *can* run!"

"There's some enemy after her, no doubt," the King said, without even looking round. "That wood's full of them."

"But aren't you going to run and help her?" Alice asked, very much surprised at his taking it so quietly.

"No use, no use!" said the King. "She runs so fearfully quick. You might as well try to catch a Bandersnatch! But I'll make a memorandum about her, if you like – She's a dear good creature," he repeated softly to himself, as he opened his memorandum-book. "Do you spell 'creature' with a double 'e'?"

At this moment the Unicorn sauntered by them, with his hands in his pockets. "I had the best of it this time?" he said to the King, just glancing at him as he passed.

"A little – a little," the King replied, rather nervously. "You shouldn't have run him through with your horn, you know."

"It didn't hurt him," the Unicorn said carelessly, and he was going on, when his eye happened to fall upon Alice: he turned round rather instantly, and stood for some time looking at her with an air of the deepest disgust.

"What – is – this?" he said at last.

"This is a child!" Haigha replied eagerly, coming in front of Alice to introduce her, and spreading out both his hands towards her in an Anglo-Saxon attitude. "We only found it to-day. It's as large as life, and twice as natural!"

"I always thought they were fabulous monsters!" said the Unicorn. "Is it alive?"

"It can talk," said Haigha, solemnly.

The Unicorn looked dreamily at Alice, and said "Talk, child."

Alice could not help her lips curling up into a smile as she began: "Do you know, I always thought Unicorns were fabulous monsters, too! I never saw one alive before!"

"Well, now that we HAVE seen each other," said the Unicorn, "if you'll believe in me, I'll believe in you. Is that a bargain?"

"Yes, if you like," said Alice.

"Come, fetch out the plum-cake, old man!" the Unicorn went on, turning from her to the King. "None of your brown bread for me!"

"Certainly – certainly!" the King muttered, and beckoned to Haigha. "Open the bag!" he whispered. "Quick! Not that one-that's full of hay!"

Haigha took a large cake out of the bag, and gave it to Alice to hold, while he got out a dish and carving-knife. How they all came out of it Alice couldn't guess. It was just like a conjuring-trick, she thought.

The Lion had joined them while this was going on: he looked very tired and sleepy, and his eyes were half shut. "What's this!" he said, blinking lazily at Alice, and speaking in a deep hollow tone that sounded like the tolling of a great bell.

"Ah, what IS it, now?" the Unicorn cried eagerly. "You'll never guess! I couldn't."

The Lion looked at Alice wearily. "Are you animal – vegetable – or mineral?" he said, yawning at every other word.

"It's a fabulous monster!" the Unicorn cried out, before Alice could reply.

"Then hand round the plum-cake, Monster," the Lion said, lying down and putting his chin on this paws. "And sit down, both of you," (to the King and the Unicorn): "fair play with the cake, you know!"

The King was evidently very uncomfortable at having to sit down between the two great creatures; but there was no other place for him.

"What a fight we might have for the crown, *now*!" the Unicorn said, looking slyly up at the crown, which the poor King was nearly shaking off his head, he trembled so much.

"I should win easy," said the Lion.

"I'm not so sure of that," said the Unicorn.

"Why, I beat you all round the town, you chicken!" the Lion replied angrily, half getting up as he spoke.

Here the King interrupted, to prevent the quarrel going on: he was very nervous, and his voice quite quivered. "All round the town?" he said. "That's a good long way. Did you go by the old bridge, or the market-place? You get the best view by the old bridge."

"I'm sure I don't know," the Lion growled out as he lay down again. "There was too much dust to see anything. What a time the

Monster is, cutting up that cake!"

Alice had seated herself on the bank of a little brook, with the great dish on her knees, and was sawing away diligently with the knife. "It's very provoking!" she said, in reply to the Lion (she was getting quite used to being called the 'Monster'). "I've cut several slices already, but they always join on again!"

"You don't know how to manage Looking-glass cakes," the Unicorn remarked. "Hand it round first, and cut it afterwards."

This sounded nonsense, but Alice very obediently got up, and carried the dish round, and the cake divided itself into three pieces as she did so. "*now* cut it up,' said the Lion, as she returned to her place with the empty dish."

"I say, this isn't fair!" cried the Unicorn, as Alice sat with the knife in her hand, very much puzzled how to begin. "The Monster has given the Lion twice as much as me!"

"She's kept none for herself, anyhow," said the Lion. "Do you like plum-cake, Monster?"

But before Alice could answer him, the drums began.

Where the noise came from, she couldn't make out: the air seemed full of it, and it rang through and through her head till she felt quite deafened. She started to her feet and sprang across the little brook in her terror, and had just time to see the Lion and the Unicorn rise to their feet, with angry looks at being interrupted in their feast, before she dropped to her knees, and put her hands over her ears, vainly trying to shut out the dreadful uproar.

"If that doesn't 'drum them out of town'," she thought to herself, "nothing ever will!"

Chapter 8

"It's My Own Invention"

"So I wasn't dreaming, after all," she said to herself, "unless – unless we're all part of the same dream. Only I do hope it's *my* dream, and not the Red King's! I don't like belonging to another person's dream," she went on in a rather complaining tone: "I've a great mind to go and wake him, and see what happens!"

After a while the noise seemed gradually to die away, till all was dead silence, and Alice lifted up her head in some alarm. There was no one to be seen, and her first thought was that she must have been dreaming about the Lion and the Unicorn and those still lying at her feet, on which she had tried to cut the plumcake, "So I wasn't dreaming, after all," she said to herself, "unless – unless we're all part of the same dream. Only I do hope it's *my* dream, and not the Red King's! I don't like belonging to another person's dream," she went on in a rather complaining tone: "I've a great mind to go and wake him, and see what happens!"

At this moment her thoughts were interrupted by a loud shouting of "Ahoy! Ahoy! Check!" and a Knight dressed in crimson armour came galloping down upon her, brandishing a great club. Just as he reached her, the horse stopped suddenly: "You're my prisoner!" the Knight cried, as he tumbled off his horse.

Startled as she was, Alice was more frightened for him than for herself at the moment, and watched him with some anxiety as he mounted again. As soon as he was comfortably in the saddle, he began once more "You're my – "but here another voice broke in "Ahoy! Ahoy! Check!" and Alice looked round in some surprise for the new enemy.

This time it was a White Knight. He drew up at Alice's side, and tumbled off his horse just as the Red Knight had done; then he got on again, and the two Knights sat and looked at each other for some time without speaking. Alice looked from one to the other in some bewilderment.

"She's *my* prisoner, you know!" the Red Knight said at last.

"Yes, but then *I* came and rescued her!" the White Knight replied.

"Well, we must fight for her, then," said the Red Knight, as he took up his helmet (which hung from the saddle, and was something the shape of a horse's head), and put it on.

"You will observe the Rules of Battle, of course?" the White Knight remarked, putting on his helmet too.

"I always do," said the Red Knight, and they began banging away at each other with such fury that Alice got behind a tree to be out of the way of the blows.

601

"I wonder, now, what the Rules of Battle are," she said to herself, as she watched the fight, timidly peeping out from her hiding-place: One Rule seems to be, that if one Knight hits the other, he knocks him off his horse, and if he misses, he tumbles off himself – and another Rule seems to be that they hold their clubs with their arms, as if they were Punch and Judy – What a noise they make when they tumble! Just like a whole set of fire irons falling into the fender! And how quiet the horses are! They let them get on and off them just as if they were tables!'

Another Rule of Battle, that Alice had not noticed, seemed to be that they always fell on their heads, and the battle ended with their both falling off in this way, side by side: when they got up again, they shook hands, and then the Red Knight mounted and galloped off.

"It was a glorious victory, wasn't it?" said the White Knight, as he came up panting.

"I don't know," Alice said doubtfully. "I don't want to be anybody's prisoner. I want to be a Queen."

"So you will, when you've crossed the next brook," said the White Knight. "I'll see you safe to the end of the wood – and then I must go back, you know. That's the end of my move."

"Thank you very much," said Alice. "May I help you off with your helmet?" It was evidently more than he could manage by himself; however, she managed to shake him out of it at last.

"Now one can breathe more easily," said the Knight, putting back his shaggy hair with both hands, and turning his gentle face and large mild eyes to Alice. She thought she had never seen such a strange-looking soldier in all her life.

He was dressed in tin armour, which seemed to fit him very badly, and he had a queer-shaped little deal box fastened across his shoulder, upside-down, and with the lid hanging open. Alice looked at it with great curiosity.

"I see you're admiring my little box." the Knight said in a friendly tone. "It's my own invention – to keep clothes and sandwiches in. You see I carry it upside-down, so that the rain can't get in."

"But the things can get OUT," Alice gently remarked. "Do you know the lid's open?"

"I didn't know it," the Knight said, a shade of vexation passing over his face. "Then all the things much have fallen out! And the box is no use without them." He unfastened it as he spoke, and was just going to throw it into the bushes, when a sudden thought seemed to strike him, and he hung it carefully on a tree. "Can you guess why I did that?" he said to Alice.

Alice shook her head.

"In hopes some bees may make a nest in it – then I should get the honey."

"But you've got a bee-hive – or something like one – fastened to the saddle," said Alice.

"Yes, it's a very good bee-hive," the Knight said in a discontented tone, "one of the best kind. But not a single bee has come near it yet. And the other thing is a mouse-trap. I suppose the mice keep the bees out – or the bees keep the mice out, I don't know which."

"I was wondering what the mouse-trap was for," said Alice. "It isn't very likely there would be any mice on the horse's back."

"Not very likely, perhaps," said the Knight: "but if they *do* come, I don't choose to have them running all about."

"You see," he went on after a pause, "it's as well to be provided for *everything*. That's the reason the horse has all those anklets round his feet."

"But what are they for?" Alice asked in a tone of great curiosity.

"To guard against the bites of sharks," the Knight replied. "It's an invention of my own. And now help me on. I'll go with you to the end of the wood – What's the dish for?"

"It's meant for plum-cake," said Alice.

"We'd better take it with us," the Knight said. "It'll come in handy if we find any plum-cake. Help me to get it into this bag."

This took a very long time to manage, though Alice held the bag open very carefully, because the Knight was so *very* awkward in putting in the dish: the first two or three times that he tried he fell in himself instead. "It's rather a tight fit, you see," he said, as they got it in at last; "there are so many candlesticks in the bag." And he hung it to the saddle, which was already loaded with bunches of carrots, and fire-irons, and many other things.

"I hope you've got your hair well fastened on?" he continued, as they set off.

"Only in the usual way," Alice said, smiling.

"That's hardly enough," he said, anxiously. "You see the wind is so *very* strong here. It's as strong as soup."

"Have you invented a plan for keeping the hair from being blown off?" Alice enquired.

"Not yet," said the Knight. "But I've got a plan for keeping it from *falling* off."

"I should like to hear it, very much."

"First you take an upright stick," said the Knight. "Then you make your hair creep up it, like a fruit-tree. Now the reason hair falls off is because it hangs down – things never fall UPWARDS, you know. It's a plan of my own invention. You may try it if you like."

It didn't sound a comfortable plan, Alice thought, and for a few minutes she walked on in silence, puzzling over the idea, and every now and then stopping to help the poor Knight, who certainly was *not* a good rider.

Whenever the horse stopped (which it did very often), he fell off in front; and whenever it went on again (which it generally did rather suddenly), he fell off behind. Otherwise he kept on pretty well, except that he had a habit of now and then falling off sideways; and as he generally did this on the side on which Alice was walking, she soon found that it was the best plan not to walk *quite* close to the horse.

"I'm afraid you've not had much practice in riding," she ventured to say, as she was helping him up from his fifth tumble.

The Knight looked very much surprised, and a little offended at the remark. "What makes you say that?" he asked, as he scrambled back into the saddle, keeping hold of Alice's hair with one hand, to save himself from falling over on the other side.

"Because people don't fall off quite so often, when they've had much practice."

"I've had plenty of practice," the Knight said very gravely: "plenty of practice!"

Alice could think of nothing better to say than "Indeed?" but she said it as heartily as she could. They went on a little way in silence after this, the Knight with his eyes shut, muttering to himself, and Alice watching anxiously for the next tumble.

"The great art of riding," the Knight suddenly began in a loud voice, waving his right arm as he spoke, "is to keep – "Here the sentence ended as suddenly as it had begun, as the Knight fell heavily on the top of his head exactly in the path where Alice was walking. She was quite frightened this time, and said in an anxious tone, as she picked him up, "I hope no bones are broken?"

"None to speak of," the Knight said, as if he didn't mind breaking two or three of them. "The great art of riding, as I was saying, is – to keep your balance properly. Like this, you know – "

He let go the bridle, and stretched out both his arms to show Alice what he meant, and this time he fell flat on his back, right under the horse's feet.

"Plenty of practice!" he went on repeating, all the time that Alice was getting him on his feet again. "Plenty of practice!"

"It's too ridiculous!" cried Alice, losing all her patience this time. "You ought to have a wooden horse on wheels, that you ought!"

"Does that kind go smoothly?" the Knight asked in a tone of great interest, clasping his arms round the horse's neck as he spoke, just in time to save himself from tumbling off again.

"Much more smoothly than a live horse,"Alice said, with a little scream of laughter, in spite of all she could do to prevent it.

"I'll get one," the Knight said thoughtfully to himself. "One or two – several."

There was a short silence after this, and then the Knight went on again. "I'm a great hand at inventing things. Now, I dare say you noticed, that last time you picked me up, that I was looking rather thoughtful?"

"You WERE a little grave," said Alice.

"Well, just then I was inventing a new way of getting over a gate – would you like to hear it?"

"Very much indeed," Alice said politely.

"I'll tell you how I came to think of it," said the Knight. "You see, I said to myself, 'The only difficulty is with the feet: the HEAD is high enough already.' Now, first I put my head on the top of the gate – then I stand on my head – then the feet are high enough, you see – then I'm over, you see."

"Yes, I suppose you'd be over when that was done," Alice said thoughtfully: "but don't you think it would be rather hard?"

"I haven't tried it yet," the Knight said, gravely; "so I can't tell for certain – but I'm afraid it *would* be a little hard."

He looked so vexed at the idea, that Alice changed the subject hastily. "What a curious helmet you've got!" she said cheerfully. "Is that your invention too?"

The Knight looked down proudly at his helmet, which hung from the saddle. "Yes," he said, "but I've invented a better one than that – like a sugar loaf. When I used to wear it, if I fell off the horse, it always touched the ground  directly. So I had a *very* little way to fall, you see – But there WAS the danger of falling INTO it, to be sure. That happened to me once – and the worst of it was, before I could get out again, the other White Knight came and put it on. He thought it was his own helmet."

The knight looked so solemn about it that Alice did not dare to laugh. "I'm afraid you must have hurt him," she said in a trembling voice, "being on the top of his head."

"I had to kick him, of course," the Knight said, very seriously. "And then he took the helmet off again – but it took hours and hours to get me out. I was as fast as – as lightning, you know."

"But that's a different kind of fastness," Alice objected.

The Knight shook his head. "It was all kinds of fastness with me, I can assure you!" he said. He raised his hands in some excitement as he said this, and instantly rolled out of the saddle, and fell headlong into a deep ditch.

Alice ran to the side of the ditch to look for him. She was rather startled by the fall, as for some time he had kept on very well, and she was afraid that he really WAS hurt this time. However, though she could see nothing but the soles of his feet, she was much relieved to hear that he was talking on in his usual tone. "All kinds of fastness," he repeated: "but it was careless of him to put another man's helmet on – with the man in it, too."

"How *can* you go on talking so quietly, head downwards?" Alice asked, as she dragged him out by the feet, and laid him in a heap on the bank.

The Knight looked surprised at the question. "What does it matter where my body happens to be?" he said. "My mind goes on working all the same. In fact, the more head downwards I am, the more I keep inventing new things."

"Now the cleverest thing of the sort that I ever did," he went on after a pause, "was inventing a new pudding during the meat course."

"In time to have it cooked for the next course?" said Alice. "Well, not the next course," the Knight said in a slow thoughtful tone: "no, certainly not the next *course*."

"Then it would have to be the next day. I suppose you wouldn't have two pudding-courses in one dinner?"

"Well, not the *next* day," the Knight repeated as before: "not the next *day*. In fact," he went on, holding his head down, and his voice getting lower and lower, "I don't believe that pudding ever WAS cooked! In fact, I don't believe that pudding ever WILL be cooked! And yet it was a very clever pudding to invent."

"What did you mean it to be made of?" Alice asked, hoping to cheer him up, for the poor Knight seemed quite low-spirited about it.

"It began with blotting paper," the Knight answered with a groan.

"That wouldn't be very nice, I'm afraid – "

"Not very nice *alone*," he interrupted, quite eagerly: "but you've no idea what a difference it makes mixing it with other things – such as gunpowder and sealing-wax. And here I must leave you." They had just come to the end of the wood.

Alice could only look puzzled: she was thinking of the pudding.

"You are sad," the Knight said in an anxious tone: "let me sing you a song to comfort you."

"Is it very long?" Alice asked, for she had heard a good deal of poetry that day.

"It's long," said the Knight, "but very, *very* beautiful. Everybody that hears me sing it – either it brings the TEARS into their eyes, or else – "

"Or else what?" said Alice, for the Knight had made a sudden pause.

"Or else it doesn't, you know. The name of the song is called 'HADDOCKS' EYES.'"

"Oh, that's the name of the song, is it?" Alice said, trying to feel interested.

"No, you don't understand," the Knight said, looking a little vexed. "That's what the name is *called*. The name really IS 'THE AGED AGED MAN.'"

"Then I ought to have said 'That's what the song is called'?" Alice corrected herself.

No, you oughtn't: that's quite another thing! The song is called

'WAYS AND MEANS'; but that's only what it's *called,* you know!"

"Well, what IS the song, then?" said Alice, who was by this time completely bewildered.

"I was coming to that," the Knight said. "The song really *is* 'A-SITTING ON A GATE': and the tune's my own invention."

So saying, he stopped his horse and let the reins fall on its neck: then, slowly beating time with one hand, and with a faint smile lighting up his gentle foolish face, as if he enjoyed the music of his song, he began.

Of all the strange things that Alice saw in her journey Through The Looking-Glass, this was the one that she always remembered most clearly. Years afterwards she could bring the whole scene back again, as if it had been only yesterday – the mild blue eyes and kindly smile of the Knight – the setting sun gleaming through his hair, and shining on his armour in a blaze of light that quite dazzled her – the horse quietly moving about, with the reins hanging loose on his neck, cropping the grass at her feet – and the black shadows of the forest behind – all this she took in like a picture, as, with one hand shading her eyes, she leant against a tree, watching the strange pair, and listening, in a half dream, to the melancholy music of the song.

"But the tune ISN'T his own invention," she said to herself: "it's 'I give thee all, I can no more.'" She stood and listened very attentively, but no tears came into her eyes.

"I'll tell thee everything I can;
There's little to relate.
I saw an aged aged man,
A-sitting on a gate.
'Who are you, aged man?' I said,
'and how is it you live?'
And his answer trickled through my head
Like water through a sieve.

He said 'I look for butterflies
That sleep among the wheat:
I make them into mutton-pies,
And sell them in the street.
I sell them unto men,' he said,
'Who sail on stormy seas;
And that's the way I get my bread–
A trifle, if you please.'

But I was thinking of a plan
To dye one's whiskers green,
And always use so large a fan
That they could not be seen.
So, having no reply to give
To what the old man said,
I cried, 'Come, tell me how you live!'
And thumped him on the head.

His accents mild took up the tale:

He said 'I go my ways,
And when I find a mountain-rill,
I set it in a blaze;
And thence they make a stuff they call
Rolands' Macassar Oil –
Yet two pence-halfpenny is all
They give me for my toil.'

But I was thinking of a way
To feed oneself on batter,
And so go on from day to day
Getting a little fatter.
I shook him well from side to side,
Until his face was blue:
'Come, tell me how you live,' I cried,
'And what it is you do!'

He said 'I hunt for haddocks' eyes
Among the heather bright,
And work them into waistcoat-buttons
In the silent night.
And these I do not sell for gold
Or coin of silvery shine
But for a copper halfpenny,
And that will purchase nine.'

'I sometimes dig for buttered rolls,
Or set limed twigs for crabs;

615

I sometimes search the grassy knolls
For wheels of Hansom-cabs.
And that's the way (he gave a wink)
By which I get my wealth –
And very gladly will I drink
Your Honour's noble health.'

I heard him then, for I had just
Completed my design
To keep the Menai bridge from rust
By boiling it in wine.
I thanked much for telling me
The way he got his wealth,
But chiefly for his wish that he
Might drink my noble health.

And now, if e'er by chance I put
My fingers into glue
Or madly squeeze a right-hand foot
Into a left-hand shoe,
Or if I drop upon my toe
A very heavy weight,
I weep, for it reminds me so,
Of that old man I used to know –
Whose look was mild,
whose speech was slow,
Whose hair was whiter than the snow,
Whose face was very like a crow,

> *With eyes, like cinders, all aglow,*
> *Who seemed distracted with his woe,*
> *Who rocked his body to and fro,*
> *And muttered mumblingly and low,*
> *As if his mouth were full of dough,*
> *Who snorted like a buffalo –*
> *That summer evening, long ago,*
> *A-sitting on a gate."*

As the Knight sang the last words of the ballad, he gathered up the reins, and turned his horse's head along the road by which they had come. "You've only a few yards to go," he said, "down the hill and over that little brook, and then you'll be a Queen–But you'll stay and see me off first?" he added as Alice turned with an eager look in the direction to which he pointed. "I shan't be long. You'll wait and wave your handkerchief when I get to that turn in the road? I think it'll encourage me, you see."

"Of course I'll wait," said Alice: "and thank you very much for coming so far – and for the song – I liked it very much."

"I hope so," the Knight said doubtfully: "but you didn't cry so much as I thought you would."

So they shook hands, and then the Knight rode slowly away into the forest. "It won't take long to see him *off,* I expect," Alice said to herself, as she stood watching him. "There he goes! Right on his head as usual! However, he gets on again pretty easily – that comes of having so many things hung round the horse – " So she went on talking to herself, as she watched the horse walking leisurely along the road, and the Knight tumbling off, first on one side and then on the other. After the fourth or fifth tumble he reached the turn, and then she waved her handkerchief to him, and waited till he was out of sight.

"I hope it encouraged him," she said, as she turned to run down the hill: "and now for the last brook, and to be a Queen! How grand it sounds!" A very few steps brought her to the edge of the brook. "The Eighth Square at last!" she cried as she bounded across, and threw herself down to rest on a lawn as soft as moss, with little flower-beds dotted about it here and there. "Oh, how glad I am to get here! And what IS this on my head?" she exclaimed in a tone of dismay, as she put her hands up to something very heavy, and fitted tight all round her head.

"But how *can* it have got there without my knowing it?" she said to herself, as she lifted it off, and set it on her lap to make out what it could possibly be.

It was a golden crown.

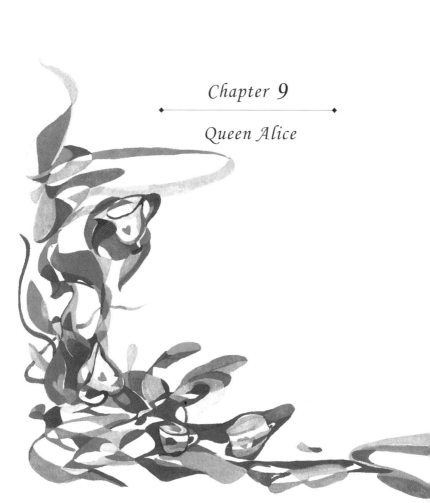

Chapter **9**

Queen Alice

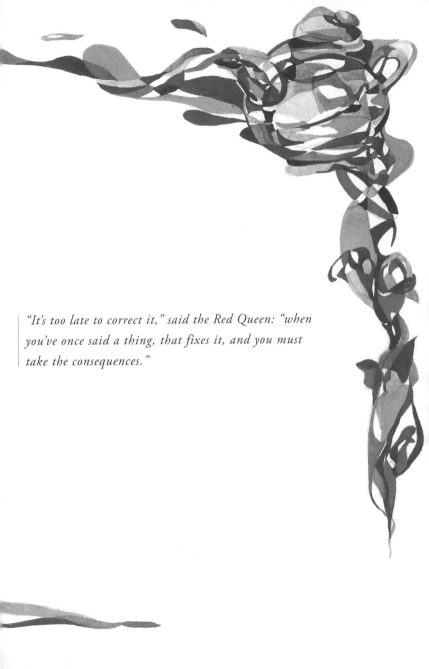

"It's too late to correct it," said the Red Queen: "when you've once said a thing, that fixes it, and you must take the consequences."

"Well, this IS grand!" said Alice. "I never expected I should be a Queen so soon – and I'll tell you what it is, your majesty," she went on in a severe tone (she was always rather fond of scolding herself), "it'll never do for you to be lolling about on the grass like that! Queens have to be dignified, you know!"

So she got up and walked about – rather stiffly just at first, as she was afraid that the crown might come off: but she comforted herself with the thought that there was nobody to see her, "and if I really am a Queen," she said as she sat down again, "I shall be able to manage it quite well in time."

Everything was happening so oddly that she didn't feel a bit surprised at finding the Red Queen and the White Queen sitting close to her, one on each side: she would have liked very much to ask them how they came there, but she feared it would not be quite civil.

However, there would be no harm, she thought, in asking if the game was over. "Please, would you tell me – " she began, looking timidly at the Red Queen.

"Speak when you're spoken to!" The Queen sharply interrupted her.

"But if everybody obeyed that rule," said Alice, who was always ready for a little argument, "and if you only spoke when you were spoken to, and the other person always waited for *you* to begin, you see nobody would ever say anything, so that – "

"Ridiculous!" cried the Queen. "Why, don't you see, child – " here she broke off with a frown, and, after thinking for a minute, suddenly changed the subject of the conversation. "What do you mean by 'If you really are a Queen?' What right have you to call yourself so? You can't be a Queen, you know, till you've passed the proper examination. And the sooner we begin it, the better."

"I only said 'if'!" poor Alice pleaded in a piteous tone.

The two Queens looked at each other, and the Red Queen remarked, with a little shudder, "She SAYS she only said 'if'"

"But she said a great deal more than that!" the White Queen moaned, wringing her hands. "Oh, ever so much more than that!"

"So you did, you know," the Red Queen said to Alice. "Always speak the truth – think before you speak – and write it down afterwards."

623

"I'm sure I didn't mean – " Alice was beginning, but the Red Queen interrupted her impatiently.

"That's just what I complain of! You *should* have meant! What do you suppose is the use of child without any meaning? Even a joke should have some meaning – and a child's more important than a joke, I hope. You couldn't deny that, even if you tried with both hands."

"I don't deny things with my *hands*," Alice objected.

"Nobody said you did," said the Red Queen. "I said you couldn't if you tried."

"She's in that state of mind," said the White Queen, that she wants to deny *something* – only she doesn't know what to deny!"

"A nasty, vicious temper," the Red Queen remarked; and then there was an uncomfortable silence for a minute or two.

The Red Queen broke the silence by saying to the White Queen, "I invite you to Alice's dinner-party this afternoon."

The White Queen smiled feebly, and said "And I invite *you*."

"I didn't know I was to have a party at all," said Alice; "but if there is to be one, I think *I* ought to invite the guests."

"We gave you the opportunity of doing it," the Red Queen remarked: "but I daresay you've not had many lessons in manners yet?"

"Manners are not taught in lessons," said Alice. "Lessons teach you to do sums, and things of that sort."

"Can you do Addition?" the White Queen asked. "What's one and one and one and one and one and one and one and one and one and one?"

"I don't know," said Alice. "I lost count."

"She can't do Addition," the Red Queen interrupted. "Can you do Subtraction? Take nine from eight."

"Nine from eight I can't, you know," Alice replied very readily: "but – "

"She can't do Subtraction," said the White Queen. "Can you do Division? Divide a loaf by a knife – what's the answer to that?"

"I suppose – " Alice was beginning, but the Red Queen answered for her. "Bread-and-butter, of course. Try another Subtraction sum. Take a bone from a dog: what remains?"

Alice considered. "The bone wouldn't remain, of course, if I took it – and the dog wouldn't remain; it would come to bite me – and I'm sure I shouldn't remain!"

"Then you think nothing would remain?" said the Red Queen.

"I think that's the answer."

"Wrong, as usual," said the Red Queen: "the dog's temper would remain."

"But I don't see how – "

"Why, look here!" the Red Queen cried. "The dog would lose its temper, wouldn't it?"

"Perhaps it would," Alice replied cautiously.

"Then if the dog went away, its temper would remain!" the Queen exclaimed triumphantly.

Alice said, as gravely as she could, "They might go different ways." But she couldn't help thinking to herself, "What dreadful nonsense we ARE talking!"

"She can't do sums a BIT!" the Queens said together, with great emphasis.

"Can *you* do sums?" Alice said, turning suddenly on the White Queen, for she didn't like being found fault with so much.

The Queen gasped and shut her eyes. "I can do Addition," she said, "if you give me time – but I can't do Subtraction, under ANY circumstances!"

"Of course you know your A B C?" said the Red Queen.

"To be sure I do." said Alice.

"So do I," the White Queen whispered: "we'll often say it over together, dear. And I'll tell you a secret – I can read words of one letter! Isn't *that* grand! However, don't be discouraged. You'll come to it in time."

Here the Red Queen began again. "Can you answer useful questions?' she said. How is bread made?"

"I know *that*!" Alice cried eagerly. "You take some flour – "

"Where do you pick the flower?" the White Queen asked. "In a garden, or in the hedges?"

"Well, it isn't *picked* at all," Alice explained: "it's *ground* – "

"How many acres of ground?" said the White Queen. "You mustn't leave out so many things."

"Fan her head!" the Red Queen anxiously interrupted. "She'll be feverish after so much thinking." So they set to work and fanned her with bunches of leaves, till she had to beg them to leave off, it blew her hair about so.

"She's all right again now," said the Red Queen. "Do you know Languages? What's the French for fiddle-de-dee?"

"Fiddle-de-dee's not English," Alice replied gravely.

"Who ever said it was?" said the Red Queen.

Alice thought she saw a way out of the difficulty this time. "If you'll tell me what language 'fiddle-de-dee' is, I'll tell you the French for it!" she exclaimed triumphantly.

But the Red Queen drew herself up rather stiffly, and said "Queens never make bargains."

"I wish Queens never asked questions," Alice thought to herself.

"Don't let us quarrel," the White Queen said in an anxious tone. "What is the cause of lightning?"

"The cause of lightning," Alice said very decidedly, for she felt quite certain about this, "is the thunder – no, no!" she hastily corrected herself. "I meant the other way."

"It's too late to correct it," said the Red Queen: "when you've once said a thing, that fixes it, and you must take the consequences."

"Which reminds me – " the White Queen said, looking down and nervously clasping and unclasping her hands, "we had *such* a thunderstorm last Tuesday – I mean one of the last set of Tuesdays, you know."

Alice was puzzled. "In *our* country," she remarked, "there's only one day at a time."

The Red Queen said, "That's a poor thin way of doing things. Now *here*, we mostly have days and nights two or three at a time, and sometimes in the winter we take as many as five nights together – for warmth, you know."

"Are five nights warmer than one night, then?" Alice ventured to ask.

"Five times as warm, of course."

"But they should be five times as *cold,* by the same rule – "

"Just so!" cried the Red Queen. "Five times as warm, *and* five times as cold – just as I'm five times as rich as you are, *and* five times as clever!"

Alice sighed and gave it up. "It's exactly like a riddle with no answer!" she thought.

"Humpty Dumpty saw it too," the White Queen went on in a low voice, more as if she were talking to herself. "He came to the door with a corkscrew in his hand – "

"What did he want?" said the Red Queen.

"He said he *would* come in," the White Queen went on, "because he was looking for a hippopotamus. Now, as it happened, there wasn't such a thing in the house, that morning."

"Is there generally?" Alice asked in an astonished tone.

"Well, only on Thursdays," said the Queen.

"I know what he came for," said Alice: "he wanted to punish the fish, because – "

Here the White Queen began again. "It was such a thunderstorm, you can't think!" ("She *never* could, you know," said the Red Queen.)

"And part of the roof came off, and ever so much thunder got in – and it went rolling round the room in great lumps-and knocking over the tables and things – till I was so frightened, I couldn't remember my own name!"

Alice thought to herself, "I never should TRY to remember my name in the middle of an accident! Where would be the use of it?" but she did not say this aloud, for fear of hurting the poor Queen's feeling.

"Your Majesty must excuse her," the Red Queen said to Alice, taking one of the White Queen's hands in her own, and gently stroking it: "she means well, but she can't help saying foolish things, as a general rule."

The White Queen looked timidly at Alice, who felt she ought to say something kind, but really couldn't think of anything at the moment.

"She never was really well brought up," the Red Queen went on: "but it's amazing how good-tempered she is! Pat her on the head, and see how pleased she'll be!" But this was more than Alice had courage to do.

"A little kindness – and putting her hair in papers – would do wonders with her – "

The White Queen gave a deep sigh, and laid her head on Alice's shoulder. "I *am* so sleepy?" she moaned.

"She's tired, poor thing!" said the Red Queen. "Smooth her hair – lend her your nightcap – and sing her a soothing lullaby."

"I haven't got a nightcap with me," said Alice, as she tried to obey the first direction: "and I don't know any soothing lullabies."

"I must do it myself, then," said the Red Queen, and she began:

"Hush-a-by lady, in Alice's lap!
Till the feast's ready, we've time for a nap:
When the feast's over, we'll go to the ball—
Red Queen, and White Queen, and Alice, and all!"

"And now you know the words," she added, as she put her head down on Alice's other shoulder, "just sing it through to ME. I'm getting sleepy, too." In another moment both Queens were fast asleep, and snoring loud.

"What AM I to do?" exclaimed Alice, looking about in great perplexity, as first one round head, and then the other, rolled down from her shoulder, and lay like a heavy lump in her lap. "I don't think it EVER happened before, that any one had to take care of two Queens asleep at once! No, not in all the History of England – it couldn't, you know, because there never was more than one Queen at a time. Do wake up, you heavy things!" she went on in an impatient tone; but

there was no answer but a gentle snoring.

The snoring got more distinct every minute, and sounded more like a tune: at last she could even make out the words, and she listened so eagerly that, when the two great heads vanished from her lap, she hardly missed them.

She was standing before an arched doorway over which were the words "QUEEN ALICE" in large letters, and on each side of the arch there was a bell-handle; one was marked "Visitors' Bell," and the other "Servants' Bell."

"I'll wait till the song's over," thought Alice, "and then I'll ring – the – *Which* bell must I ring?" she went on, very much puzzled by the names. "I'm not a visitor, and I'm not a servant. There *ought* to be one marked 'Queen,' you know – "

Just then the door opened a little way, and a creature with a long beak put its head out for a moment and said "No admittance till the week after next!" and shut the door again with a bang.

Alice knocked and rang in vain for a long time; but at last, a very old Frog, who was sitting under a tree, got up and hobbled slowly towards her: he was dressed in bright yellow, and had enormous boots on.

"What is it, now?" the Frog said in a deep hoarse whisper.

Alice turned round, ready to find fault with anybody. "Where's the servant whose business it is to answer the door?" she began angrily.

"Which door?" said the Frog.

Alice almost stamped with irritation at the slow drawl in which he spoke. "THIS door, of course!"

The Frog looked at the door with his large dull eyes for a minute: then he went nearer and rubbed it with his thumb, as if he were trying whether the paint would come off; then he looked at Alice.

"To answer the door?" he said. "What's it been asking of?" He was so hoarse that Alice could scarcely hear him.

"I don't know what you mean," she said.

"I talks English, doesn't I?" the Frog went on. "Or are you deaf? What did it ask you?"

"Nothing!" Alice said impatiently. "I've been knocking at it!"

"Shouldn't do that – shouldn't do that – " the Frog muttered. "Vexes it, you know." Then he went up and gave the door a kick with one of his great feet. "You let IT alone," he panted out, as he hobbled back to his tree, "and it'll let *you* alone, you know."

At this moment the door was flung open, and a shrill voice was heard singing: –

"To the Looking-Glass world it was Alice that said,
'I've a sceptre in hand, I've a crown on my head;
Let the Looking-Glass creatures, whatever they be,
Come and dine with the Red Queen, the White Queen, and me.' "

And hundreds of voices joined in the chorus: –

"Then fill up the glasses as quick as you can,
And sprinkle the table with buttons and bran:
Put cats in the coffee, and mice in the tea–
And welcome Queen Alice with thirty-times-three!'

Then followed a confused noise of cheering, and Alice thought to herself, "Thirty times three makes ninety. I wonder if any one's counting?" In a minute there was silence again, and the same shrill voice sang another verse: –

"'O Looking-Glass creatures,' quote Alice, 'draw near!
'Tis an honour to see me, a favour to hear:
'Tis a privilege high to have dinner and tea
Along with the Red Queen, the White Queen, and me!'"
Then came the chorus again: –

"Then fill up the glasses with treacle and ink,
Or anything else that is pleasant to drink:
Mix sand with the cider, and wool with the wine–

And welcome Queen Alice with ninety-times-nine!"

"Ninety times nine!" Alice repeated in despair, "Oh, that'll never be done! I'd better go in at once – " and there was a dead silence the moment she appeared.

Alice glanced nervously along the table, as she walked up the large hall, and noticed that there were about fifty guests, of all kinds: some were animals, some birds, and there were even a few flowers among them. "I'm glad they've come without waiting to be asked," she thought: "I should never have known who were the right people to invite!"

There were three chairs at the head of the table; the Red and White Queens had already taken two of them, but the middle one was empty. Alice sat down in it, rather uncomfortable in the silence, and longing for some one to speak.

At last the Red Queen began. "You've missed the soup and fish," she said. "Put on the joint!" And the waiters set a leg of mutton before Alice, who looked at it rather anxiously, as she had never had to carve a joint before.

"You look a little shy; let me introduce you to that leg of mutton," said the Red Queen. "Alice – Mutton; Mutton – Alice." The leg of mutton got up in the dish and made a little bow to Alice; and Alice returned the bow, not knowing whether to be frightened or amused.

"May I give you a slice?" she said, taking up the knife and fork, and looking from one Queen to the other.

"Certainly not," the Red Queen said, very decidedly: "it isn't etiquette to cut any one you've been introduced to. Remove the joint!"

And the waiters carried it off, and brought a large plum-pudding in its place.

"I won't be introduced to the pudding, please," Alice said rather hastily, "or we shall get no dinner at all. May I give you some?"

But the Red Queen looked sulky, and growled "Pudding – Alice ; Alice – Pudding. Remove the pudding!" and the waiters took it away so quickly that Alice couldn't return its bow.

However, she didn't see why the Red Queen should be the only one to give orders, so, as an experiment, she called out "Waiter! Bring back the pudding!" and there it was again in a moment like a conjuring-trick. It was so large that she couldn't help feeling a *little* shy with it, as she had been with the mutton; however, she conquered her shyness by a great effort and cut a slice and handed it to the Red Queen.

"What impertinence!" said the Pudding. "I wonder how you'd like it, if I were to cut a slice out of *you,* you creature!"

It spoke in a thick, suety sort of voice, and Alice hadn't a word to say in reply: she could only sit and look at it and gasp.

"Make a remark," said the Red Queen: "it's ridiculous to leave all the conversation to the pudding!"

"Do you know, I've had such a quantity of poetry repeated to me today," Alice began, a little frightened at finding that, the moment she opened her lips, there was dead silence, "and all eyes were fixed upon her; "and it's a very curious thing, I think-every poem was about fishes in some way. Do you know why they're so fond of fishes, all about here?"

She spoke to the Red Queen, whose answer was a little wide of the mark. "As to fishes," she said, very slowly and solemnly, putting her mouth close to Alice's ear, "her White Majesty knows a lovely riddle – all in poetry – all about fishes. Shall she repeat it?"

"Her Red Majesty's very kind to mention it," the White Queen murmured into Alice's other ear, in a voice like the cooing of a pigeon. "It would be *such* a treat! May I?" "Please do," Alice said very politely.

The White Queen laughed with delight, and stroked Alice's cheek. Then she began:

"First, the fish must be caught."
That is easy: a baby, I think, could have caught it.
"Next, the fish must be bought."
That is easy: a penny, I think, would have bought it.

"Now cook me the fish!"
That is easy, and will not take more than a minute.
"Let it lie in a dish!"
That is easy, because it already is in it.

"Bring it here! Let me sup!"
It is easy to set such a dish on the table.
"Take the dish-cover up!"
Ah, that is so hard that I fear I'm unable!
For it holds it like glue –
Holds the lid to the dish, while it lies in the middle:
Which is easiest to do,
Un-dish-cover the fish, or dishcover the riddle?'

"Take a minute to think about it, and then guess," said the Red Queen. "Meanwhile, we'll drink your health – Queen Alice's health!" she screamed at the top of her voice, and all the guests began drinking it directly, and very queerly they managed it: some of them put their glasses upon their heads like extinguishers, and drank all that trickled down their faces – others upset the decanters, and drank the wine as it ran off the edges of the table – and three of them (who looked like kangaroos) scrambled into the dish of roast mutton, and began eagerly lapping up the gravy, "just like pigs in a trough!" thought Alice.

"You ought to return thanks in a neat speech," the Red Queen said, frowning at Alice as she spoke.

"We must support you, you know," the White Queen whispered, as

Alice got up to do it, very obediently, but a little frightened.

"Thank you very much," she whispered in reply, "but I can do quite well without."

"That wouldn't be at all the thing," the Red Queen said very decidedly: so Alice tried to submit to it with a good grace.

("And they *did* push so!" she said afterwards, when she was telling her sister the history of the feast. "You would have thought they wanted to squeeze me flat!")

In fact it was rather difficult for her to keep in her place while she made her speech: the two Queens pushed her so, one on each side, that they nearly lifted her up into the air: "I rise to return thanks – " Alice began: and she really *did* rise as she spoke, several inches; but she got hold of the edge of the table, and managed to pull herself down again.

"Take care of yourself!" screamed the White Queen, seizing Alice's hair with both her hands. "Something's going to happen!"

And then (as Alice afterwards described it) all sorts of thing happened in a moment. The candles all grew up to the ceiling, looking something like a bed of rushes with fireworks at the top. As to the bottles, they each took a pair of plates, which they hastily fitted on as wings, and so, with forks for legs, went fluttering about in all directions: "and very like birds they look," Alice thought to herself, as well as she could in the dreadful confusion that was beginning.

At this moment she heard a hoarse laugh at her side, and turned to see what was the matter with the White Queen; but, instead of the Queen, there was the leg of mutton sitting in the chair. "Here I am!" cried a voice from the soup tureen, and Alice turned again, just in time to see the Queen's broad good-natured face grinning at her for a moment over the edge of the tureen, before she disappeared into the soup.

There was not a moment to be lost. Already several of the guests were lying down in the dishes, and the soup ladle was walking up the table towards Alice's chair, and beckoning to her impatiently to get out of its way.

"I can't stand this any longer!" she cried as she jumped up and seized the table-cloth with both hands: one good pull, and plates, dishes, guests, and candles came crashing down together in a heap on the floor.

"And as for *you*," she went on, turning fiercely upon the Red Queen, whom she considered as the cause of all the mischief – but the Queen was no longer at her side – she had suddenly dwindled down to the size of a little doll, and was now on the table, merrily running round and round after her own shawl, which was trailing behind her.

At any other time, Alice would have felt surprised at this, but she was far too much excited to be surprised at anything now. "As for you," she repeated, catching hold of the little creature in the very act of jumping over a bottle which had just lighted upon the table, "I'll shake you into a kitten, that I will!"

Chapter 10

———————

Shaking

"As for you," she repeated, catching hold of the little creature in the very act of jumping over a bottle which had just lighted upon the table, "I'll shake you into a kitten, that I will!"

She took her off the table as she spoke, and shook her backwards and forwards with all her might.

The Red Queen made no resistance whatever; only her face grew very small, and her eyes got large and green: and still, as Alice went on shaking her, she kept on growing shorter – and fatter – and softer – and rounder – and –

Chapter 11

◆————————————————◆

Waking

...she kept on growing shorter – and fatter – and softer – and rounder – and –

And it really WAS a kitten, after all.

Chapter 12

Which Dreamed it?

"Now, Kitty, let's consider who it was that dreamed it all. This is a serious question, my dear, and you should not go on licking your paw like that — as if Dinah hadn't washed you this morning! You see, Kitty, it must have been either me or the Red King. He was part of my dream, of course — but then I was part of his dream, too! WAS it the Red King, Kitty?

"**Y**our majesty shouldn't purr so loud," Alice said, rubbing her eyes, and addressing the kitten, respectfully, yet with some severity. "You woke me out of oh! such a nice dream! And you've been along with me, Kitty – all through the Looking-Glass world. Did you know it, dear?"

It is a very inconvenient habit of kittens (Alice had once made the remark) that, whatever you say to them, they *always* purr. "If them would only purr for 'yes' and mew for 'no', or any rule of that sort, " she had said, "so that one could keep up a conversation! But how *can* you talk with a person if they always say the same thing? "

On this occasion the kitten only purred: and it was impossible to guess whether it meant 'yes' or 'no'. So Alice hunted among the chessmen on the table till she had found the Red Queen: then she went down on her knees on the hearth-rug, and put the kitten and the Queen to look at each other. "Now, Kitty!" she cried, clapping her hands triumphantly. "Confess that was what you turned into!"

("But it wouldn't look at it," she said, when she was explaining the thing afterwards to her sister: "it turned away its head, and pretended not to see it: but it looked a *little* ashamed of itself, so I think it must have been the Red Queen.")

"Sit up a little more stiffly, dear!" Alice cried with a merry laugh. "And curtsey while you're thinking what to – what to purr. It saves time, remember!" And she caught it up and gave it one little kiss, "just in honour of having been a Red Queen."

"Snowdrop, my pet!" she went on, looking over her shoulder at the White Kitten, which was still patiently undergoing its toilet, "when WILL Dinah have finished with your White Majesty, I wonder? That must be the reason you were so untidy in my dream-Dinah! Do you know that you're scrubbing a White Queen? Really, it's most disrespectful of you!"

"And what did *Dinah* turn to, I wonder?" she prattled on, as she settled comfortably down, with one elbow in the rug, and her chin in her hand, to watch the kittens. Tell me, Dinah, did you turn to Humpty Dumpty? I *think* you did – however, you'd better not mention it to your friends just yet, for I'm not sure.

653

"By the way, Kitty, if only you'd been really with me in my dream, there was one thing you *would* have enjoyed – I had such a quantity of poetry said to me, all about fishes! Tomorrow morning you shall have a real treat. All the time you're eating your breakfast, I'll repeat "The Walrus and the Carpenter" to you; and then you can make believe it's oysters, dear!

"Now, Kitty, let's consider who it was that dreamed it all. This is a serious question, my dear, and you should *not* go on licking your paw like that – as if Dinah hadn't washed you this morning! You see, Kitty, it *must* have been either me or the Red King. He was part of my dream, of course – but then I was part of his dream, too! WAS it the Red King, Kitty? You were his wife, my dear, so you ought to know – Oh, Kitty, *Do* help to settle it! I'm sure your paw can wait!" But the provoking kitten only began on the other paw, and pretended it hadn't heard the question.

Which do you think it was?

A boat beneath a sunny sky,
Lingering onward dreamily
In an evening of July –

Children three that nestle near,
Eager eye and willing ear,
Pleased a simple tale to hear –

Long has paled that sunny sky:
Echoes fade and memories die.
Autumn frosts have slain July.

Still she haunts me, phantomwise,
Alice moving under skies
Never seen by waking eyes.

Children yet, the tale to hear,
Eager eye and willing ear,
Lovingly shall nestle near.

In a Wonderland they lie,
Dreaming as the days go by,
Dreaming as the summers die:

Ever drifting down the stream-
Lingering in the golden gleam-
Life, what is it but a dream?

愛麗絲夢遊仙境與鏡中奇遇 /路易斯·卡洛爾(Lewis Carroll)著；
盛世教育西方名著翻譯委員會譯；約翰·坦尼爾(Sir John Tenniel)插圖
-- 三版. -- 臺北市：笛藤, 2022.06
面；　公分 奇幻夢境版 中英對照

譯自：Alice's adventures in wonderland & through the looking-glass
ISBN 978-957-710-857-9（精裝）

873.57　　　　　　111007233

中英對照奇幻夢境版

**愛麗絲
夢遊仙境 & 鏡中奇**

附
~ 音檔連結 ~

總長13.2小時
情境配樂
中英雙語朗讀

2022年6月24日　三版第1刷　定價420元

作者	路易斯·卡洛爾 Lewis Carroll
插圖	約翰·坦尼爾 Sir John Tenniel
章節頁插圖	Vivian Wang
翻譯	盛世教育西方名著翻譯委員會
配音員	陳進益、謝佼娟、
	James Baron、Clare Lear、Stephanie Buckley
封面設計	王舒玗
內頁設計	碼非創意
總編輯	賴巧凌
編輯	林子鈺、江品萱
發行所	笛藤出版圖書有限公司
發行人	林建仲
地址	台北市中山區長安東路二段171號3樓3室
電話	(02) 2777-3682
傳真	(02) 2777-3672
總經銷	聯合發行股份有限公司
地址	新北市新店區寶橋路235巷6弄6號2樓
電話	(02)2917-8022 · (02)2917-8042
製版廠	造極彩色印刷製版股份有限公司
地址	新北市中和區中山路2段340巷36號
電話	(02)2240-0333 · (02)2248-3904
郵撥帳戶	八方出版股份有限公司
郵撥帳號	19809050